MW01488910

RUTH

Woman of Valor

A VIRTUOUS WOMAN IN AN IMMORAL LAND

RUTH

Woman of Valor

A VIRTUOUS WOMAN IN AN IMMORAL LAND

❖ JIM BAUMGARDNER ❖

Published by Baumgardner Press
14411 Maple / Wichita, Ks. 67235 USA

ISBN: 978-0-98841-075-6
EBOOK ISBN: 978-1-68222-202-7

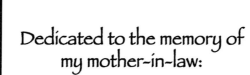

Dedicated to the memory of
my mother-in-law:

Lucinda Elouise Lundry

A woman meek in spirit and
mild in manner, she gained my
admiration for the loving care
she gave to her family.
Rest in peace Mom Lundry

Introduction

Writing historical fiction requires imagination. Envisioning what if and what was. I ask the questions of what if the character said this or acted like this. On the other hand, it requires questions about what forces in the past brought the character to his or her way of thinking and acting.

I approach Biblical fiction much the same as any historical fiction author, except the story has been written, and my job is to fill in the gaps.

I believe the Bible is the inerrant word of God. Therefore, from the standpoint of history, it is all true. The Bible has been written to spotlight God's working among men and women from the first days in the Garden of Eden to the establishment of the church and the first years of its growth.

The Bible disregards more days in the lives of its characters than it includes. As an author of Bible fiction, I take what is known from Scripture, add to it my best reasoning and imagination as to what important things happened on the days the Bible does not mention, and write a plausible story filling in the gaps.

I seek to keep the story as close to the Biblical narrative as possible. This is done by asking the questions mentioned above, and including manners and customs of ancient times, with explanations when essential. All of the strange rites of the foreign gods, priests, healers and sorcerers mentioned in the story have been recorded in ancient documents.

An additional note is necessary. In the Old Testament Hebrew text, YHWH is used for God's name. In English versions, it is translated as LORD, Jehovah or Yahweh. The <u>Orthodox Jewish Bible</u> translates it, Hashem. I use Yahweh in this book. For a more detailed explanation see the introduction to my book: <u>Esther Queen of Persia, A Courageous Woman for a Dangerous Time</u>.

Who can find a woman of valor?
For her worth is far above
rubies.

Proverbs 31:10

(OJB)

In the Country of Moab

And a certain man of Bethlehem, Judah, went to dwell in the country of Moab, he and his wife, and his two sons.

–Ruth 1:1

Chapter 1

"Your friend has earned the privilege of dying, surely you can understand her happiness."

Ruth's full, perfectly sculptured lips, curved down, her jaw clenched. Turning her head, she glared at her mother with cold, careful eyes, eyes that held misery. Figat's fierce look, etched into a face of stone, held on the young Moabitess. Finally, Ruth lowered her head and watched her sandaled feet kicking up tiny dust clouds.

Muttering words best unheard, the woman slanted narrow eyes toward Ruth's father, Paebel. Figat's lip curled into an ugly sneer.

"How much longer will I attempt reasoning with this rebellious daughter? She is 15 years old and still has no understanding of Moab's gods. Why do we waste words on this obstinate girl?"

Paebel ignored her and kept walking.

I am her mother; Figat said to herself. *I demand obedience and accept no arguments. Ruth will pay dearly if she continues her stubborn attitude.*

The sun rose like a ball of fire, blinding yellow, and unbearably hot. It was midday when the family passed through the main gates of Ar, the chief city in Northern Moab. A sea of frenzied worshippers pushed and shoved them along toward the gigantic idol that sat in the middle of town. Thousands of Moabites joined in the cries of devotion to their fiery god.

"Great is Chemosh, god of the Moabites! Great is Chemosh, god of the Moabites!" A myriad of worshippers shrieked the god-loving words in mindless repetition, and those praises to their fire-breathing deity banged around the inside of Ruth's head like a hammer on an anvil.

The blazing sun triggered sweat, which ran profusely down her spine. Choking smoke filled her nostrils, and the loud, never-ceasing praise of Chemosh had her on the brink of vomiting as the gut-wrenching events of this abominable, debauched, worship service drew nigh.

Figat, a tall, straight woman with small, brutish eyes held the Moabite gods in high esteem and had little use for anyone who did not. Her daughter did not have the same enthusiasm for the gods, and beating Ruth with a rod probably would not change her attitude.

"Today, you will see our great Chemosh, the supreme god of all our gods, given the ultimate sacrificial offering, a human life. Offering Donatiya will appease his fury and beseech his blessings upon our people."

"Must she be sacrificed?" Ruth's voice cracked. "I—I know her. All my life I have known her."

"It is our god's will." Figat breathed a loud sigh to make her point. "You know that! He requires a child."

"She is not a child." Ruth moaned softly, wrapping her arms across her chest. "She is thirteen. It, it is not just."

"Thirteen *is* a child," Figat said with a pinched expression, "and Chemosh decides what is just. Donatiya will join all the other privileged ones who have gone before her into the next world. Sanctification awaits her in the next life. She willingly climbs the steps. She wants this. Would you deny her?"

Ruth's jaw fixed tight, her nostrils flared. "Would you be so quick to defend Chemosh if it were me?"

Figat's hard eyes turned a bit firmer. Her lips pinched tight, and her fists even tighter.

Opening her mouth to answer her daughter, she reconsidered and stifled her rebuke.

We will handle this rebellious attitude later. Beating her back with a rod appears to be the only thing left to do. I will not tolerate insolence directed at Chemosh.

Reading her mother's expression of utter contempt, Ruth said no more. The blackest of nightmares, an idolatrous worship spawned in the pit of hell, would start soon, and she could only stand by helpless.

Her parents had forced her to attend, but she would not look. She would refuse. If they beat her—well, it would be worth it. Compelled to watch her beautiful friend being cast into the fires of Chemosh would rip her heart out.

How could this human sacrifice possibly be acceptable? Yet, he *was* the god of Moab. All Moabites understood their god had blessed them more than Yahweh, the Israelite God.

The Israelites dwelt a few miles away on the west side of the Salt Sea. The rain fell in Moab, yet it stopped at the sea. Why that continued month after month was a mystery. The only reasonable answer most Moabites could give was Israel's God had forsaken his people. Ruth believed it.

For as long as Ruth could remember, Israel had produced meager crops from their parched land while the fields of Moab flourished. Over the years, she had gazed at the dearth of Israel's crops from her family's lush fields located in the highlands of Moab a short twenty-five miles across the waters. On clear days, the ugly, dirty-brown earth of Judah was shockingly visible across the narrow sea.

How could her country be so blessed with green, abundant fields and enormous crops while within sight of her family's property Israel suffered scorched earth? The answer had to be Chemosh and the Baals. Her gods made all the difference for the Moabites.

Year after year, they proved their dominance with unimaginable blessings bestowed upon Moabite worshippers while Yahweh would not, and probably could not provide for his people. The Israelites served an impotent God. The allegation had been stated many times by her friends, including Donatiya. That explanation satisfied everyone.

Ruth raised her hands and cried out, "Great is Chemosh, god of the Moabites!" She meant the words, had faith in her god, yet questioned the horrifying practice of sacrificing children to Chemosh.

The idol, which loomed far above the surrounding city streets, would soon gather into his enormous, gaping mouth, Donatiya, Ruth's lifelong friend.

Huge flames stretched out fiery fingers from the vast cavern that served as the mouth and throat of Chemosh. Those fires produced horrendous heat belching from the inferno and compelled the king's eunuchs to remain a far distance from that fiery cavity.

Soon the time would arrive to cast Donatiya into the flames. Then, the eunuchs would pick her up by her arms and legs, and with immense strength, launch her up and into the yawning, sizzling mouth of Moab's chief god.

Ruth's tear-stained face laid bare her feelings at this spectacle of the violent, monstrous worship of her god. She understood completely why the multitude soon would scream praises to Chemosh. Those deafening shrieks served to drown out the horrifying cries of agony as her friend inhaled the super-heated air. Death would come instantly. Then her skin would melt as her body roasted in the flames, leaving Donatiya a charred mass. What remained would never leave the idol. She would never receive a proper burial in a tomb or the ground. Chemosh was the tomb.

Ruth's stomach churned as smoke from the blazing fire leaping inside the idol's mouth drifted across the city, assaulting her eyes and nose. Retching had become a genuine possibility. Surely a more humane way to worship and appease Chemosh could be instituted. Why this? It made no sense that her god, in whom she believed with all her heart, would require such heart-wrenching sacrifice. Nevertheless, the Baal gods and Moloch, gods of the Canaanites, demanded human sacrifices, also.

All gods require a human sacrifice, Ruth told herself, *except Yahweh, the Israelite God. Why? I must know.*

So sudden did the crowd fall silent that it jarred Ruth. The eerie calm hurt her ears. Reluctantly she raised her eyes and then bit her lip. She tasted blood. Donatiya, her dear friend, had started to climb the temple steps. Soon she would be torn from this life and sent on to the next.

Recoiling from the appalling sight, the teenager burst into tears. Refusing to watch the scene unfold, she buried her face into her mother's shoulder. Figat shrugged her off. Ruth refused to lift her eyes.

Although Ruth did not witness Donatiya raise her hands to Chemosh, nor hear her speak words drowned out by the roar of the crowd, the ritual of this ceremony she had observed on other occasions.

Drums began to pound, and Ruth dug her fingernails deep into her palms. Screeches bellowing from the mouths of the worshipers filled the air. Minutes passed, and with each drum beat, the horrid yells grew louder. "Great is Chemosh, god of the Moabites!" The frenzied crowd droned the same monotonous words countless times.

Ruth peeked through swollen eyelids. Donatiya had reached the top step and the king's eunuchs, chosen for their gigantic size and strength, approached the delicate and beautiful girl. Within seconds, they would sling her into eternity.

Ruth dried her tears with her sleeve. Screaming her words over the din, she asked, "Should we not worship a god who wants us to be happy? Why cannot Donatiya live and continue to worship Chemosh, not die and leave friends to be sad and mourn her? Answer me, Mother, please! I do not understand our god!"

"We cannot know all of the ways of a god!" Figat shouted back making her voice heard over the roar of the people. "It is especially true of our chief god." Figat grabbed Ruth's shoulders.

"Be careful my daughter, do not blaspheme the one who blesses our people and our fields."

"Ruth! You have said enough!" Her father's gravel voice shook her to the core.

Paebel, a man who never seemed to smile, had a cold manner about him—watchful, glaring from coal-black eyes that never appeared to move or warm regardless of who might be standing before him. Ruth had experienced his fierce anger on other occasions, and many times it had escalated into viciousness. A streak of poison ran through the man, and Ruth had no desire to aggravate him further.

"The Baals are our gods and Chemosh our chief god. You will say no more words against them, or I shall beat you with the bamboo stick as I do your brothers." His face turned ugly and dark with rage. "Will it come to that, daughter? Shall I lay stripes on your back as punishment?"

Ruth slowly shook her head. "No, father."

"Now, join with the rest of your fellow citizens and praise your god. Great is Chemosh, god of the Moabites!"

Ruth stood stoop-shouldered, staring blankly at her hollow-eyed god. "Great is Chemosh, god of the Moabites!" Ruth mouthed the words in a monotone with no energy. "Great is Chemosh, god of the Moabites!"

Paebel put his arm around her shoulders, and Figat held her hand. Together, they shouted praises upward to the raging, fire-breathing mouth of Chemosh. The climax of this rite, the sacrifice of a young virgin to the fires, would propitiate their god. The time had come. The eunuchs grasped Donatiya and held her suspended between them. The short train of her pure white gown sagged to the stone pavement of the top step. The girl's lips moved in prayer to her god. The frenzied worshippers eagerly anticipated the eunuchs flinging the girl into the hungry slack-jawed mouth.

"Great is Chemosh, god of the Moabites! Great is Chemosh, god of the Moabites. Great is Chemosh, god of the Moabites!" Their screeches of approbation for Ruth's blood-thirsty god grew louder. The drumbeat quickened. Within moments, the worshipers' screams, praising their god, became deafening.

Finally, the eunuchs, with one powerful heave, hurled Donatiya up and into the roaring fires of the Moabite god. The scream—an indecent, terrifying, mortifying scream—one among thousands chilled Ruth to the bone. Her dear friend's terrifying shriek of inconceivable pain, heard above the shrieking praises of the crowd, angered and sickened her.

How is it possible? The ear-splitting chants drowned out her final moments. Ruth violently shook her head. *It does not matter whether it was her or not. I know her fate.*

She wept.

After returning home, Ruth moped about the house, brooding over the death of her friend. Though her mother tried several times to converse, Ruth completed her chores in silence.

The appeasement of Chemosh through the sacrifice of Donatiya had flayed her heart, devastating her like nothing before. True, she had participated in sacrificial worship on other occasions. However, those sacrifices had been animals or in the case of a human, a baby or small child, always a stranger, someone unknown. This time she did know the person, Donatiya, her friend and frequent companion, one she favored.

Watching her friend ascend those steps had opened her eyes to the ugliness and futility of human sacrifice.

She recalled the others. Should she not have been upset by them? Each had been some parent's son or daughter. Grandparents undoubtedly grieved over the loss of their grandchildren.

Ruth's throat, tight with emotion, caused her to choke on her words. "Mother, I wou-I-I would like to be alone. May I," her voice quavered, "May I go to the woods?"

Figat, still comely of face, which gave evidence that she had been a lovely young woman at one time, at least physically, shouted, "Go! You have been worthless company for me today. Yes, go think about how you have treated me and your father."

Ruth swallowed hard. Her throat hurt, yet her mother's words hurt even more.

The deep meadow glen, wild, lonely, surrounded by ancient trees, and darkened from the lack of the sun's rays, made a peaceful place for meditation. The clear water chuckling over a rock-strewn brook permitted Ruth blissful relief from her family. No one had discovered her secret place.

Silently and on nimble feet, she moved through the woods like a ghost. Arriving at the unique dell, Ruth took up a long stick and beat the grass. She had no desire to share her spot with a snake. Then, lying on her back in the lush grass, gazing at the passing clouds through openings in the trees, she reflected on events of the day, and her contemplations were many and varied. Ruth had questions that seemed unanswerable.

Her gods had been faithful to Moab. The land flourished with crops, and the people laughed and danced with glee. Israel's God had withdrawn his blessings from their land. Another possible explanation put forward by many Moabites was the Canaanites had asked their grain and fish god, Dagon, to curse Israel.

It was well-known that the Israelites went to war against the Canaanites and the Israelites drove many out of the land of Canaan and killed many others. So, the Canaanite god had cursed Israel, and Yahweh could not overcome the curse.

Regardless of the explanation, Moabites believed Chemosh as the superior god, and they pointed to the prosperity of Moab and the destitution of Israel. However, Ruth had doubts. Why?

She chewed on a blade of grass as she sorted through recent events. One kept returning to her mind, the recently arrived Israelite family living on her father's land. That family was not the first. Since Moab and Israel were at peace, the intermingling of the two countries was commonplace. She had met none of the Israelites, but almost anyone in Moab could provide second-hand information about their religion. It intrigued her, and she desired to learn more.

After much reflection, she dozed. The sleep, though only a few minutes, refreshed her mind and body. Awakened by the sound of an animal rustling the leaves under a nearby bush, Ruth got to her feet.

Then, leaving that spot, she strolled along the swift downhill rush of the brook until it slowed and climbed a gentle slope. Suddenly, Ruth stopped and cocked an ear to listen. Somewhere ahead a woodpecker tapped a tree searching for insects. She smiled, loving the sights and sounds of nature. Dropping to her knees, she cupped the cold water in her hands and drank.

Walking on, she came to a familiar pool carved out by the rushing water. A tree branch hung out over a small section of the pool, supplying shade for the fish. Here, the quiet water afforded her a reflection, one much clearer than the bronze looking glass her mother owned.

Ruth removed her head covering and stared at the young woman in the water. Unmarried women and widows did not wear a veil at that time. Only a married woman would veil herself when in public.

I am not an ugly girl, at least I do not believe I am. I give diligence to being pleasant. Why do I remain a virgin?

Confused, she studied the face in the water. Long eyelashes floated over large, coal-black eyes that flashed from a perfectly formed, cinnamon-shaded face. She had spent many hours toiling under the hot Moab sun, which over time had darkened by several shades her deep tan. The men of the village, both single and married, mesmerized by her breathtaking beauty, frequently speculated aloud which man would claim the virgin as his bride. Ruth, a chaste and proper young woman, would have been mortified if she had overheard the chatter.

The custom in many cultures was for a man to place a veil over a woman and declare that she was his wife. This practice indicated she belonged to a husband.

Ruth, being fifteen, should have been claimed. Without any offers, from the men of the village, she lived with the embarrassment of being passed over. Why? How long would this rejection continue?

Men married much later, the average age about thirty. Ar and the surrounding villages had plenty of men in that age group, yet none of them had shown any interest in her. They had talked about her, praised her beauty and graciousness, yet not one man had stepped forward asking for her in marriage.

The situation baffled Ruth, but she was too ashamed to ask her parents about it.

Eyeing her image, she stood straight, shoulders back and head level. A lovely smile crossed her face. She recalled her lessons from childhood. Figat taught Ruth to walk with her shoulders back and chin level while carrying an empty basket on her head. When Ruth became proficient with the empty basket, her mother gradually added over a period of weeks small amounts of grain. Soon she could carry heavy burdens and not break stride.

Now, her mane of silky-smooth, raven-black hair fell past those shoulders and sparkled in the blistering sunlight. In face and form, she had been described as perfect. Ruth was like the men of Ar had discussed with one another—gorgeous though her modest and unassuming disposition did not realize it.

She replaced her head covering, bowed her head and talked to the vision of womanhood in the water.

"Yahweh requires sacrifice, yet only grains and animals, not humans. If only the God of Israel had the power of Chemosh, he would be worthy of worship."

Suddenly, she caught herself talking, and no one around to hear. She chuckled.

All of the other gods of whom she was familiar required human sacrifice. It seemed odd that this Israelite God did not. Did that make a difference in being strong or weak?

She must learn more, and that meant speaking to one of those foreigners. All it would take would be to ask a question or two of her brother about the family. He worked with the men and had become friendly with them.

If her brother refused help, she could pursue it herself. Ruth had not been forbidden to approach an Israelite.

Chapter 2

Under a broiling, unforgiving sun, Elimelech and his wife, Naomi, walked the family's parched wheat fields baked dry by the torrid heat.

"Look at these heads." Stooping, the man picked a few and handed them to the woman. "No moisture. Stunted. Dry as sun-baked leather! This field will barely feed our family."

Raising an eyebrow, Naomi replied with a pleasant voice, "Yes, my husband, but we *will* have food."

"Another year or two like this and we will starve," he snapped. "I will not allow that to happen. Barely eking out a meal is not enough. We shall remove ourselves from this country. I have made my decision and will not waver."

"We have the sheep and cattle." Naomi smiled. "I am not too old to spin." She held up her hands flexing her fingers. "Our family will be clothed. Let us thank the Almighty for these things."

Cocking his head to one side, Elimelech gave her a hard as granite look. "Naomi, you speak as the silly women of this town. You do not understand business. I have made my decision, and it is absolute."

Her limp hands hung quietly. Staring at the ground, she remained silent for a few moments. "I do not question your authority," she said in a voice barely above a whisper. "You have control over me as did my parents when I was a child. However, they also taught me to respect our God and obey him, too. I do not, um, I—."

"Why do you stutter? What do want to say?" His eyes narrowed to a squint. "Will you lecture your lord—your husband of so many years?"

Naomi walked on, leaving Elimelech standing. How to explain that her husband had made a terrible decision disturbed and baffled her. He was determined to move the family to Moab, a country on the other side of the Salt Sea. It was not far, yet it might as well be thousands of miles. Moab, an idol worshipping nation, would have nothing to offer her sons except foreign women and the heartache that would attend them.

Elimelech hurried and caught his wife by the arm. He mopped his brow of sweat with the sleeve of his garment.

"Do not walk away." A scowl lined his face. "You do not agree with me. Why? Can you not comprehend I do what is best for you and our sons?"

Tilting her head to the sky, she let out a heavy sigh. "Will you persist? It is not agreeable to remove our sons to Moab. They belong in Israel. Soon they will choose to marry, and I want Hebrew wives for them. Several young women in Bethlehem are of age and would make excellent wives and mothers. Moabite women are idol worshipers, bowing their knees to Chemosh and the Baals."

"Naomi, it is best for them and us. Mahlon and Chilion are my sons, also. We will sojourn there, not put down roots. This," he waved a hand, "is our land, but at this moment, this soil does not produce what we need. I want more, and we can have it in Moab. Come," he reached for her hand, "we shall take the path to the top."

Hand in hand, Elimelech and Naomi climbed the gradually sloping zigzag path up the hillside until they reached the summit. Bethlehem sat on a ridge some five miles south of Jebus, a town also known as Jerusalem and home of the Jebusites. Elimelech's property encompassed many pastures where his sheep and cattle grazed. His extensive fields of wheat and barley, adjacent to that grazing land, now withered away from lack of moisture.

At the top of the ridge, the pasture butted up to the threshing floor where the family winnowed grain from the wheat and barley heads. At that place, his property ended.

Both stood quietly gazing across the bronze countryside. After a few moments, Elimelech glanced up at the blinding sun. That searing ball of fire had decimated his crops and threatened to kill his animals. The streams, which previously ran full with clear, cold water, now trickled.

Closing his eyes, he tried to remember the scent and feel of a sweet rain. Oh, how much he longed to see the dark clouds, laden with rain, blotting out the blistering sun. If he could feel the cool, refreshing wetness striking his face, and the sweet taste of rainwater on his lips, those things would certainly keep him home.

Why did Yahweh punish him for the misdeeds of others? God could make it rain on his land and not on the sinners. He had the power. Why not use it?

Elimelech's face flushed with rage, and it coursed throughout him. His body trembled. Until this day, he had curbed the mounting anger. But for how long? He believed he must leave before that anger became uncontrollable.

Pointing east, Elimelech began to make his case for removing his family from the Promised Land. On this bright day, which most were, one could see vast distances from this spot in the hills. The Sea of Chinnereth, later known as the Sea of Galilee could be seen clearly in the north. His eyes followed the Jordan River as it snaked its way to the point where in emptied into the Salt Sea.

"See the land. The difference is obvious enough."

The boundaries of Moab began on the east side of the Salt Sea, some twenty–five miles across the waters and ended about thirty miles inland at the desert. No one had clearly defined the eastern border. The Arnon River marked the northern border and Moab ended somewhere forty miles south; Elimelech was unsure of where.

"Can you see the difference?" Elimelech pushed Naomi for an answer. He wanted her to admit that Judah, brown with famine, could not compare to Moab with its lush green fields.

Agreeing reluctantly, Naomi nodded, her unhappy eyes admitted the truth. Leading her up the hill had not been necessary. For months, she had been quite aware of the difference.

"We live in God's Promised Land," she softly breathed out the words. "Can we so easily forsake it for Moab?"

Elimelech's jaw locked hard, his eyes tightened. "I have told you it is vital to our family's welfare. What will it take for you to appreciate our situation? Do not question my judgment."

"Oh, my husband!" She clasped her hands as if begging. "We have enough, more land than most."

"We will not if this famine continues. I will have to sell my holdings so we can buy food for our table. After the land and silver is gone, then what shall we do? No, I sell now and receive a fair price. When I return, I will redeem my land, and we will live well."

"Yahweh will provide. He always has."

"Our God expects us to work, also. He will not give us bread in our baskets as he gave our forefathers manna. Shall I squander my goods now, and have nothing after the famine?"

Tears formed in Naomi's eyes. "You think of bread—do you consider our sons? They already speak of marriage. Shall they marry Moabites?"

Elimelech's mouth grew tight. His teeth were visible behind angry lips. "They will not marry *any* woman if they do not have food to eat. They will be dead!" He turned away and stared at the land of Moab across the waters of the sea. "Do you remember the writings of Moses? He told of Jacob taking his family to sojourn in Egypt. They went there to survive the famine."

"Yes, but our God told them to go. Has the Almighty spoken to you?"

"No!" He said it quick and did not like the insinuation.

Naomi gently clasped his arm and also looked at the land to the east. "At that time, our people had been promised the land we now stand upon, but they had yet to inherit it."

Naomi moved in front of her husband. "Look at me," she said softly. "It has been but a few years since Rahab hid the spies, and our people entered from across the Jordan taking this land. Shall we now give up our inheritance so easily?"

Elimelech refused to look at his wife. He did not want to gaze into her knowing eyes. Naomi knew the truth. He refused to accept it. Deep within his being he silently acknowledged he should remain.

Salmon, his brother, Boaz, his nephew, and many of his kinsmen, along with most of his friends had no plans to turn their backs on the Promised Land. However, Naomi's husband had a taste for adventure, and she could not dissuade him from embarking on this journey.

"We will sojourn for a time," he said gently, "not long."

Next morning, Elimelech visited Salmon his older brother and Rahab his sister-in-law, in the courtyard of their home. The time had come to break the news that he and his family would depart for Moab. He dreaded the visit for he anticipated Salmon would not be receptive to his decision.

Entering the courtyard, Elimelech groaned within himself. He would have turned to leave, but Salmon waved. Under a large sycamore tree, several benches invited family and guests to relax. Today, Rahab, Salmon and his son Boaz sat, visiting.

Passing a large, round pit, which served as a cistern, and many courtyards were equipped with one similar to Salmon's, Elimelech glanced down. The dry cistern emboldened his resolve to depart before all of the streams and rivers stopped flowing.

"Elimelech, my brother, come and rest. It has been days since we have talked."

He took a seat on a bench facing Salmon and Rahab. Boaz sat to the side. "It is going to be a warm day."

Salmon chuckled. "It is always warm. The weather is the message you bring me?" He leaned forward. "I think not. You never visit in the morning—morning is when you work the vineyard and fields. You have come this morning to deliver news. Your eyes and face speak this truth. So, what is it my younger brother?"

Elimelech glanced at Rahab. Several years had intervened from the destruction of Jericho, yet she remained an attractive woman. Always a heroine in the eyes of those who were there to see the walls of Jericho collapse, her story of favor to Israel's spies had been told and retold ever since.

Rahab, a former harlot of Jericho, hid spies sent out from the Israelites to spy out the land. A pagan woman bartered for her life and the lives of her family. The spies made a commitment to protect her when God's people destroyed the city. So, she hid the spies, and they kept their promise and saved her.

Since that day, she had given up her pagan gods and embraced Yahweh, the God of the Hebrews.

"I see fear in his eyes," Rahab said, glancing over at Salmon. "What do you fear, Elimelech?"

He had listened to Naomi whine about leaving, now Rahab accused him of fear. How dare she? He had the courage to sell out and journey to an unknown country. He would be a stranger in a foreign land. The Moabites did not speak Hebrew though their language was related. So it would be difficult to communicate and, in addition, he must find employment. He was the courageous one, and she should understand it. Her comment infuriated him, and words exploded from his mouth.

"I shall lose all if I do not leave this God-forsaken country!"

Salmon's eyes grew wide, and he started to rise to his feet. Rahab grabbed his arm, and he sat down.

"The Almighty has not abandoned this country. This is our promised land," Salmon said in a tone of rebuke. "Most of my Israelite brothers *have* forsaken our God. They worship lifeless Canaanite idols in the high places. They not only sin but are foolish. It is because of *them* we suffer from famine."

"You are right. God has not forsaken us, but he punishes all of us for the sins of many. I am leaving."

"I have seen this coming, my brother. I do not like it, and neither does Rahab. Our inheritance is this land, given to us by our blessed Lord God."

Elimelech's face slowly tightened like wet leather drying over a barrel in the summer sun.

Rahab leaned forward and reached out a hand. "Will you forsake your land, which our people bought with blood by fighting the heathen?"

"I must think of my family," he said with measured words, desperately trying to control the unwarranted rage welling up in him. "It will be for a short time."

Salmon squinted wary eyes at him. "Do you journey to the Northern tribes? It is well-known they are spared from drought since they continue to worship Yahweh."

Elimelech averted the gaze of his brother and stared at the ground. "I will sojourn in Moab."

"Moab!" Salmon's eyes bugged out. Rahab clutched her husband's arm.

"I will only sojourn. I will come home immediately when the famine is over."

"Do not do this! Do not sin against our God by dwelling in that heathen nation. They worship that hideous god, Chemosh, and the Baals." Getting to his feet, Salmon walked out of the courtyard.

"It will be for a short time," Elimelech called after his brother. Salmon kept walking.

Glancing at Rahab, hoping for a kind word, he received a cold look as she turned away. "You turn your back on me?" His tone came across harsh, more severe than intended. "Surely you appreciate the trials of living among foreigners. You have been doing it for years."

Rahab jerked her head around, eyes blazing. He cringed at the sight of his sister-in-law's angry eyes. Those fiery orbs made Elimelech sweat from the heat. "I reside among *my* people! My old life with the Canaanites, I gave up many years ago. It seems like a lifetime. I worship Yahweh; he is my God. You know that." She stood. "Do not ever suggest I live among foreigners. Judah is my home, and the Hebrews are my people."

"I only…." He stopped. Rahab had gone after Salmon leaving him to watch her disappear through the courtyard entryway.

His eyes moved over to Boaz. They gazed at one another for a moment. Boaz remained silent.

Elimelech stood, shook his head and slowly trudged home.

Naomi stared while her husband and sons made ready all things necessary for the journey to Moab. A bitter taste in her mouth caused her to swallow—she choked. Elimelech had sold most of his tools, his grain, and many household items, which he could not take with him. He counted on using the funds received from the sales, to purchase items he would need to start over in his new surroundings. He had found a buyer for his land, also. The Law of Moses gave him the right to redeem it when he returned, which he intended to do.

"Father, what occupation will we follow in Moab?" asked Chilion. "Will our flocks follow us?"

Elimelech ignored him.

"Will the Moabites employ us in the fields?"

Silence.

"Where will we settle? Is there a city nearby? You have told us nothing."

"My son! Stop the questions," he yelled. "You will see and understand all of this soon. At this moment, I am overwhelmed. There are many duties to complete before our journey."

"But, father, I—."

"We shall discuss it later!" He cut him off. "Do you insist on contending with me about it?"

Twenty-eight-year-old Chilion, the youngest son, gazed at the ground, his face flushed with humiliation. A sickly man with pallid complexion, he cowered before his father's domineering presence. "No, I shall wait."

"My uncle," the familiar voice caught Elimelech's attention. "I want to discuss this situation."

Boaz stood at the courtyard gate. A strikingly good-looking man, Boaz had been a warrior, commander, one known as a mighty man of God. He carried himself and spoke with such authority that men and women willingly respected him.

Boaz was a man of action. Whether on the battlefield or the grain field, things happened. When he spoke, people listened. Some men speak a lot and say little if anything meaningful. Boaz spoke little, yet it was enough. Whether warrior or field worker, a man always understood Boaz.

Elimelech waved his nephew over to his bench in the spacious courtyard. "Sit and talk. The situation I assume you would like to discuss is our move to Moab? Do you intend to tell me how wrong I am as your father believes and has said?"

"My father grieves over your decision. Do you not know that he was one of the valiant men who helped to conquer this Promised Land? You were too young to fight; nevertheless he fought for you and all Israelites."

"Yes, and I have thanked Salmon for his loyalty to Yahweh and Israel. Shall I bear the burden of always having to acknowledge his service to our nation? If I could have fought, I would have carried a sword and swung it." Elimelech crossed his arms on his chest. "Am I rubbish because I did not?"

"Elimelech, why cast yourself as one we must pity? No one asks you to thank your brother regularly for his service to our country. I was not even born and feel no obligation to thank him continually."

"What is it you have come to say?" He asked with a face and voice full of irritation. "I am to meet a man about business this day."

Boaz's face fell. Talking to his uncle would be like talking to a deaf man. Elimelech would not seriously consider his words. They would be only so much indiscernible noise.

Regardless, Boaz must have his say, and not mince words. Others had tried the soft-spoken pleas, all without success. Now, his time had come, and he would clear his conscience and return home to face his father telling him that he tried.

"You desire the easy way over the way of righteousness," Boaz began. The words hit Elimelech hard. He flinched. "Judah has its evil, yet not as Moab. Will you give up family, friends, and our God for the Baals and that worthless god, Chemosh?"

"Do you dare speak to your uncle in that tone?" Elimelech's eyes popped in their sockets; much more, and he would have had to pick them off the ground. "You know nothing of what I will do. Nonetheless, to put your mind at rest, I have no intention of residing in the cities where the idol worshippers and debauchery that attends that corrupt worship is in abundance. I give up nothing, and especially our God. Keep your accusations to yourself!"

"Where in Moab will you settle?"

"In the north, near the chief city of Ar. I should not have a problem finding work in that area. It is only five miles south of the Arnon River, barely within the border of Moab. When the rains again come to Judah, I shall return. The entire distance is only eighty miles, a three-day journey from here to there."

"It might as well be a thousand-day journey to that distant land. The time is not important. Leaving is. We have a shortage, yet we do not starve. Israel is our land, given to all of us by the Almighty. Please, do not abandon it."

"Boaz, you speak as if you do not know me—your uncle. I am an Ephrathite. Bethlehem is my home. I come from noble people. My ancestry is ancient, and we are not reprobates!

"Have you not seen the herds, flocks, and crops on my land? I am a man of means, and I do not want to lose it. And, as far as Moab being a distant land—it is not! *Egypt* is a distant land. We can see Moab from Bethlehem, a few, short miles across the Salt Sea. It is not a journey of any significance.

"Besides, I only go to sojourn, work in the fields of a Moabite property owner, and then return. I have no intention of living in tents the rest of my life. My sheep can graze the abundant pastures of Moab where there are grass and water aplenty. When the drought breaks, I will return. Hopefully," he raised a pleading hand toward heaven, "that will not be long."

"We do not know how long. It might last several years."

Elimelech regarded them all a pack of fools for questioning his wisdom. "I tire of repeating my words to you and the rest of my kinsmen. If God is good, which you claim, then I will be home soon. That—my nephew—is the end of it."

"*If* he is good!" His voice rose. "Do you mock God?"

"I do the smart thing—I go where there is water."

Boaz believed he was making a ghastly mistake so gave one last reproof. He had nothing left. "Elimelech, if we all did as you and forsook our land, Judah would be empty of Israelites and the fields desolate."

Chapter 3

"Step over here." The voice prickled the hair on the back of Ruth's neck.

She looked sideways. A fierce-faced, middle-aged man, with a crinkled, bulbous nose, bent to the left, gazed at her with cold, taunting eyes, sending a chill through her. Making it worse, he grinned through broken teeth, likely made so by some man's fist.

He walked over and stood close. "I have many bolts of exquisite cloth from which to choose." His flint hard, ice-cold, rasping voice seized Ruth's insides like red-hot tongs pin metal to an anvil. He smelled of stale sweat.

From under thick black eyebrows, his roving, lust-filled eyes examined her from head to foot. Slowly he took in her fresh loveliness. Then, attempting to cover his lewd gaze, he held out the cloth with a thumb and forefinger—the other three fingers were missing.

Her cheeks burned. Shamed by his nauseating look of desire, Ruth shuddered and moved on. He lunged, grasping her arm. She jerked free and rushed away.

His horrid face flushed dark with rage, yet he kept the quick anger from his voice. "Please, come back, my beauty. I shall wrap you with this." He fluttered the cloth. "Men will think you a goddess, a temple goddess!"

Ruth took a long breath, a settling breath. She never looked back. Shopping for the family's needs had become an increasing burden ever since she had fully developed as a woman. Ruth's pretty face and graceful manner always attracted the men in the marketplace. On several occasions, men had approached her, and not for good reasons. The unwanted attention always happened when unaccompanied by her mother or brothers.

Ruth lived in a valley, four miles outside the city of Ar near a small village. There she enjoyed a sanctuary, away from the vice of the big city. The village had no wall about it and depended on Ar for safety in time of war.

The massive wooden gates of Ar, armored with metal for strength and fortification, never ceased to impress Ruth. She admired them each time passing through, whether coming into or leaving the city.

The gateway served several purposes. Above the gates, one of the many watchtowers had been built. Watchmen, stationed all along the top of the walls and in the towers kept vigil over the countryside. With careful eyes, constantly roving the horizon, they would take notice of any dust cloud, regardless of how tiny. Identifying whether the soil had been disturbed by the wind or by a human was essential. If human-made, the guards' sharp eyes sought to determine if an enemy advanced on the city.

The area around the gates had developed into a hub in which the citizens gathered for various events, including speeches by those in authority. The rulers of Ar would stand on a platform and give announcements, proclaim edicts to the citizens, and conduct official business of the city.

Also, the city elders came daily to the gates, sat on stone seats provided them, and judged disputes that must be settled by arbitration.

Gossipers gained much information at the gates. Whether the information of settled disputes or news from travelers entering Ar, the talebearers passed it along throughout the city.

On this day, Ruth entered the gates with instructions from her father to buy a water pot. In a town the size of Ar many potters conducted business. However, her father gave all of his business to one in particular.

Strolling along the street toward the potter's shop, the sight of a heavy-laden porter caught her eye. She winced. Porters, usually the poorest of citizens, carried heavy bundles, which held merchandise for sale in the markets. Some cities did not allow beasts of burden into the market area because of the dung that the animals dropped. So porters were employed to transport goods from the area designated to corral donkeys, camels or other beasts of burden.

The porter, wearing a ragged, threadbare tunic, and bent cruelly forward from the heavy load bound onto his back, slowly shuffled along. If he stumbled, the weight would drive him to the stone pavement.

Ruth's generous nature urged her to offer him help—lighten his load. She had offered on other occasions and had been turned down. The porters, though poor, were proud men and had no inclination to allow a woman to help.

"Hello, Ruth." She recognized the sweet voice. Orpah stood next to the cart of a pottery merchant. "Do you shop for the family today?"

Ruth produced a forced smile and then hugged her longtime friend. "Yes, today I must bring home a water pot."

Orpah held Ruth's shoulders at arm's length and studied her face. "What is the trouble?"

"A man!" Ruth had come too far to remain in eyesight of the fellow but, without thinking, she glanced over her shoulder.

"Where?"

"Down the street, he cannot be seen from here."

"Did he touch you?"

"He grabbed my arm, and his look told me what he wanted," she said with a quivering voice. "I kept moving."

"I am sorry. I have had the same treatment, also. Not like you, your loveliness far surpasses most."

Ruth ducked her head. "Please do not say such things. I am only a girl," she stammered.

Orpah laughed. "A girl in a woman's body."

"I must be going."

"You shop for a water pot? This potter has several."

Ruth glanced over at the man as he bargained with a buyer. "My father gives all his business to one man, a friend."

"You were at the sacrifice worship to Chemosh. Why did you look so sad? It was a great day for Donatiya, was it not?"

Ruth cringed at the comment. It had been a week since the sacrificial offering to the fire-breathing god. Her suffering heart remained broken, and Orpah unknowingly opened the fresh wound that scarcely had scabbed over.

Ruth stepped back. "I must go. We will talk another time." She turned and disappeared into the crowd.

As she pushed her way through the throng, dark eyes gleaming with tears, Ruth gritted her teeth in anguish. Donatiya—dead! How would she ever cope with her friend being sacrificed to Chemosh? A life had been wasted. The words ran over and over in her head.

After several minutes had passed, she rounded a curve in the street and entered the pottery shop. Instinctively brushing the last tears from her cheeks, she put on her best face.

The owner, Joel of Kir-hareseth, greeted her. This man of forty years, thick about the middle, slightly stoop-shouldered, with an unkempt beard sprawling across his wide face, laughed at her. Ruth's inadequate attempt to hide her emotions did not fool him.

"Ruth, what have you broken today?" The comment jarred her from the memories of Donatiya. "Your eyes are red. Do you cry over broken pottery?"

"You believe I have broken something?" She asked with a soft, innocent voice, ignoring his comment about her eyes.

"You have been known to drop a pot or pitcher from time to time."

Her lips strained to curve into a smile. "I have broken nothing. My mother is guilty this time."

"Figat? I cannot remember the last time she broke anything. So, a pitcher or pot, which do you replace today?"

"A water pot. Mother set the pot down on the stones at the well, but too hard. It cracked."

He chuckled. "Tell her she grows old and weak. Carrying heavy water pots is for the young."

Ruth ignored his words. There was no way she would repeat anything of the like to her short-tempered mother. She found a water pot, checking it for cracks. "I will take this one. How much?"

He peered over at the young woman. She had ignored his suggestion and Joel understood. He had known Figat for years.

"Joel, how much?" Ruth asked in a tone with an edge to it. "I must be on my way. My father expects me to help in the field after the midday meal."

The man's eyebrows raised in surprise at her tone. "Two ephahs of wheat."

Ruth shook her head. "I will tell my father, but I know his answer now."

He crossed his arms over his chest. "And, what will be his answer?"

Ruth widened her eyes and dipped her head ever so slightly. "Two ephahs he will accept, but of barley, not wheat."

"This is a fine water pot. The workmanship is top quality. No, it is worth the better grain. Wheat! Tell Paebel, if he balks at my price, not to be so stingy."

Ruth's stomach rolled; a tingle went through her chest. "You will say it, not me," she said in a curt tone. "My father does not smile much and laughs less. If he does not accept the price, I will return the pot tomorrow. If he does, I shall go to the storehouse and bring two ephahs of wheat."

"May the gods bless you, Ruth. You are a woman of virtue."

'*You are a woman of virtue.*' Joel's words stunned her. As she made her way along the crowded street, the man's words kept coming to her. Nobody had ever called her a woman, at least she could not recall it. Called virtuous did not impress her but a woman? A wide smile crossed her face.

Her parents continually treated her as a child, one incapable of thinking for herself. She had accepted that judgment. Now, the woman Ruth had begun to doubt.

At age fifteen, many girls had already been claimed in marriage. Ruth had come into her full womanhood early, age twelve; yet, this young woman continued to await an offer. She supposed no man had ever approached her father. She had no idea that her supposition was far from the truth.

Actually, more than one fellow had asked for her hand in marriage. Paebel had sent all of them away. Ruth was to remain unmarried, at least for another year or two. Her parents' motive for this ban on a husband was unknown to her.

A cart filled with many trinkets caught Ruth's eye. She walked over. One item stood out, a bronze looking glass. She carefully set the water pot on the ground and picked up the mirror. Moving it from right to left and up and down, the reflection of a woman smiled back. However, that woman had not fully matured in her logic and emotions.

She recalled Orpah's words. '*A girl in a woman's body.*' *There are others prettier than me, yet I do not appear to be ugly. Why have I not been betrothed to someone? Surely the gods do not favor me like other girls. Chemosh is angry with me. He knows I question the human sacrifices.*

She had trusted the gods to bless her, a belief she had embraced all of her life. Now it appeared they had a charge against her and had withheld the blessing of a man from her.

A big tear formed in the corner of one eye. It trickled down her cheek. Not bothering to brush it aside, she picked up the pot and ambled on.

At the gates, intending to rest a moment before taking the path from the city to her house, Ruth gently placed the water pot on the stone pavement.

"May I help you with that?"

Ruth looked up into the dark, intense eyes of a quite handsome, broad-shouldered young man. His kind face caught her off guard. "I—I do not know you. Thank you, but no, I can manage it alone."

The man gave her his best smile. "I am sure you can, but I am going your way. My parents till a portion of the ground that your father owns. Our tents are down the road from your dwelling."

A feather would have knocked Ruth to the ground at that moment. Her hands hung limp, and a lump, large as a grapefruit, stuck in her throat. This man was one of *them*—an Israelite. Finally, her opportunity to meet a Hebrew.

Ruth lowered her eyes. "I did not mean to offend, but I shy away from strangers. There have been a few who have tried to, uh, well—."

"I understand," he said, cutting her off and rescuing her from having to explain what she did not want to say.

"Thank you." She lifted her eyes to his. "My name is Ruth."

"I am Zaylin."

"How do you know me? We have never spoken."

"No, but one so lovely is noticed, even by the lowly field workers. We ask questions, and there are people with answers."

"You are an Israelite," she blurted and regretted it.

He nodded. "From the tribe of Simeon. We sojourn here to escape the famine in our land. Our home is in Beersheba."

"I do not know the place."

"It is west, across the Salt Sea. Judah surrounds the area of Simeon. Beersheba lies southwest of Hebron."

Ruth chuckled. "I do not know the place."

Zaylin burst out laughing. "It is not important, except for Israelites."

Ruth lifted the water pot and set it on her head. "I must be going."

Reaching over, Zaylin relieved her of the burden. "Please, allow me to carry it. Your head is much too pretty for such a load."

Her face flushed and spread to her neck. "I am not sure—."

"I am! Do not dispute me, it is much to pretty."

She let out an embarrassed giggle. "Thank you."

The monotonous four-mile walk, which Ruth made quite often, this day, cheered her from her dejection over Donatiya. The young man beside her conversed in a pleasant, not overbearing tone.

They talked about things of no significance. Bringing up the subject of his God kept crossing her mind. The price of the water pot, grain, and the size of her father's flocks meant nothing compared knowing more about Yahweh the Israelite God.

At the spot where the path forked to the right and her home; and toward the left and his tents, he gently placed the pot on the grass. "I would be happy to tote this all the way," Zaylin offered.

"Thank you, but you have been kind enough to bring it this far. The distance to my house," she motioned toward a stand of trees, "is but 2000 cubits, not far."

"A Sabbath Day's journey."

Ruth gave him a quizzical look.

"It is the distance we are allowed to walk on the Sabbath."

"Your father forbids traveling more than 2000 cubits on the seventh day of the week?"

"Our God requires it. We must rest on the seventh day and remember that Yahweh created the world in six days and rested on the seventh."

At the mention of Yahweh, Ruth's heart jumped. Now she could speak of his God and not raise questions of her intent. Zaylin would not think her too forward. "This is why my father grumbles every seventh day! You do not work, and he says it is your custom, a custom he does not like."

"It is more than a custom; it is a commandment from the mouth of our God."

"I must go before my father sends one of my brothers to find me. He would not wish to hear I am standing here speaking to you. I am sorry. I should like to hear more of your strange God."

Zaylin peered through cool, dark, condescending eyes.

Embarrassment flushed Ruth's cheeks. She felt the unwanted heat. "Forgive me, I did not mean to offend. I sought to express that he is a different God from what I know."

A quick smile returned to Zaylin's lips. "When can we talk?"

Ruth raised the water pot securing it on her head. She turned and walked away. "I do not know when, but soon," she called over her shoulder.

Chapter 4

Departure day arrived with a blazing glare of yellow streaming over the horizon, a grim foretaste of the stifling, fiery heat which daily toasted the brown fields of Judah.

The previous evening, all of the goodbyes had been said, hugs given, and tears shed. Both sides laid aside all of the reasoning, bickering, and hard feelings and recited only noble blessings over those leaving and those remaining.

The sun had scarcely cleared the horizon when Elimelech and his sons had the sheep ready to move out. The journey to Moab would be eighty miles to the Arnon River, which divided the land of Reuben from Moab. The city of Ar sat five miles south of the river and Elimelech counted on that area as an excellent place to find work from a Moabite landowner.

Danger was a way of life on the narrow roads of the land. They faced threats from dangerous animals, dangerous criminals, and dangerous weather. A man either met it head on or cowered. Elimelech would face it—he had no choice if he wanted a life in Moab.

Elimelech warned Naomi and their sons that the journey would be slow and often hazardous. "There is a risk connected with everything worth doing," he said. "Keeping a flock of sheep together will present problems, and being alert for robbers and wild animals concerns me even more. Nonetheless, I believe the Almighty will guide and keep us safe."

Naomi led an ox, which pulled a large cart filled with personal belongings. A goat tied to the rear of the cart led the flock. Sheep naturally follow a goat, and shepherds often use goats to lead their flocks into the sheepfold at sundown.

Mahlon and Chilion, along with their dogs, walked on either side of the flock, keeping the sheep from straying. Elimelech kept the back of the flock together by goading the stragglers.

Each member of the family wore new sandals, and they loaded another new pair onto the cart. At journey's end, their sandals would be worn out, and the new ones would be at hand.

Elimelech had studied all of the pitfalls that might bedevil them along the way. Hoping to ease Naomi's fears, he had explained to her several times everything that possibly could go wrong. "I have considered everything."

He was well aware of situations he had not considered that could delay the journey. Nevertheless, the man had determined nothing would cause him to turn back. All difficulties and delays would be met and overcome.

The first town, Jebus, sat on the east side of a mountain range, some five miles up the road. Skirting the city, they went around a large grove of olive trees on the east side, outside the wall. From there, the road began a twisting descent into the Jordan River valley until it reached the water, a distance of about twenty miles.

Known by many as the Jericho Road, it was a long, lonely stretch with dangers lurking everywhere. Thieves, awaiting an opportunity to strike, holed up in caves and rocky areas. Typically, groups of Israelites traveled together along such hazardous areas. Elimelech hoped to do the same.

An immense caravan of Egyptian traders happened upon the family as they left the environs of Jebus. The impressive convoy included 1000 camels, numerous donkeys, and the merchants.

The camels followed one after the other in a straight line, with each camel secured to the one in front with a rope. The first camel was tied to a donkey that led the way. A trader walked alongside this lead donkey holding a rope attached to the donkey's harness.

Elimelech, unable to speak the Egyptian language, hiked back to greet the caravan leader with the hope he spoke Hebrew. Enormous groups, like this one, would always employ several men who could communicate in many languages. A successful sale of goods required people with language skills.

"Peace to you, my friend," said Elimelech, holding up a hand. "Do you speak the Hebrew language?"

The Egyptian grinned, showing a mouth full of gaps where teeth once resided. "I do. I speak many tongues. From where do you journey?"

"Bethlehem Ephrath. I am an Ephrathite from Judah."

"What is your name?"

"Elimelech. My wife, Naomi, travels with me, so also my sons, Mahlon, and Chilion."

"Do you have other children?"

"No, only these."

"You dwell in Judah; you must be from that tribe."

"Yes, we are of the tribe of Judah."

The greetings and salutations continued, and the length and mind-numbing nature of such greetings were typical. Finally, after all of the salutes and gestures of good will, the Egyptians agreed to follow the family.

Elimelech clasped hands with the Egyptian. "My wife will rest easy tonight knowing you are close by."

Although the caravan followed, Elimelech and his sons warily descended the road from Jebus to Jericho. The fact that robbers were thick in the rocks never left their minds.

A long day's journey would have meant reaching the Jordan the first day, but the sheep slowed the pace. So, they arrived at a spot south of the ruins of Jericho as the sun fell below the horizon. The road forked, and to the left would have taken them into the city. They remained on the road that led to the river and made camp east of the fork in the road. A small party of merchants from the caravan traveled the short distance to where Jericho once stood. Their mission was to investigate if anyone had begun to rebuild the city.

Elimelech and his sons bedded the sheep on a piece of ground with scant grass and a trickle of water, which at one time by the look of the deeply cut streamed flowed rapidly toward the Jordan.

The merchants, Elimelech, and his sons sat around the campfire discussing news from Egypt.

One of the spokesmen for the traders, Habeed, a short, heavy and somewhat stooped man, with a hard, round face and cruel eyes, led the conversation. "The curse of your God is known in Egypt." He smiled, showing a mouth full of broken teeth.

Elimelech glanced sideways. "Curse?" He snorted. "I know of no curse."

"Your land has famine," he slowly shook his head, "that is always a judgment from the gods."

"If it is true Yahweh has cursed the Israelites with drought, then I shall escape his judgment in Moab. My God has no reason to bring evil upon me. I sacrifice to him as he has commanded."

"It is good to hear you are faithful to the Hebrews' one and only God."

Elimelech nodded. "Only one, we believe there is *only* one."

The Egyptian laughed loud, slapping his knee. "Only one!" The other Egyptians joined in the laughter. "We have many," the man gestured toward his fellow merchants, "and so do the Canaanites and Moabites. A nation should have several gods to bless it. One is not enough."

"One is all we need," said Elimelech and his sons nodded in agreement.

In the gray of dawn, before the first rays of yellow peeked over the horizon, Naomi had prepared a breakfast of dried fruit, cheese and bread for the family. The dogs, natural scavengers, ate pieces of cheese and bread, plus what they could beg from the Egyptians.

As Elimelech finished loading his cart the men who had been sent to the city returned.

"Only a few tent-dwellers have put down stakes. The city lies in ruins. The shepherds say men will one day rebuild, but no one has moved a stone. They have no ambition to start."

Elimelech eyed Naomi. "I shall tell Salmon and Rahab when we return to Bethlehem. It will be a big undertaking to rebuild a city so utterly destroyed by Yahweh."

An hour into the day's journey, Mahlon pointed to the sky. Off to the right buzzards circled low over a dry creek bed. A thing, whether man or beast, dead or dying, lie in the ravine behind some half-dead bushes.

"Naomi, stop the cart. I will go look," said Elimelech.

"No, my husband, it is too dangerous."

"Do we leave a man while the birds bide their time to feast on his body? He may still live. My sons, you shall remain here with your mother. I will have a look."

Elimelech disappeared into the ravine, and then climbed a low rise, which on the other side took him down to the creek bed. Behind the bushes, the man lay dying. Elimelech did not go near.

With her husband out of sight, Naomi held tight to Mahlon's arm, fearing the worse.

Elimelech returned, his dark eyes contained a haunting look. His face turned grim in resignation. "The man is near death."

Chilion started for the ravine. "Mahlon, let us go and carry him up."

"No!"

"Father, you leave a man to die?" asked Chilion.

"It is too late. He is beyond help. He will die shortly."

"You cannot know that."

"Chilion! Do not dispute me. I do know it."

"Then, we can bury him, not leave the body for buzzards and coyotes."

"It is too risky, my son. I stood at a distance, yet close enough to see. I know what crawls over this land. Snakes, with heads full of poison, are on him and about him. His chest moves with breath, but it will not be long."

"Wife." He motioned for her to move on.

Naomi stared at the heat waves and plodded forward.

At the Jordan, the family found the water running low. So low that men were crossing without the aid of a ferry. Elimelech understood the situation. Mount Herman in the north had a dearth of snow on its slopes. Since the creation of time, melting snow had fed Lake Chinnereth, which in turn emptied into the Jordan River, and that crooked stream, which meandered through the valley, finally flowed into the Salt Sea.

Elimelech shook his head in disgust. "The Almighty, not only withholds the rains from my crops, but the snows no longer blanket the mountains."

Moving the animals across the river became a slow slog. The ox stopped to drink, and so also the goat, the sheep, and the dogs. "Keep going once you are across," said Elimelech.

Naomi, weary from walking, gazed at her husband through tired eyes. The heat had taken a toll on her, and she fought to think clearly. A raw and lonely land, the Jordan River valley shimmered with heat waves. She mopped the sweat from her forehead and neck.

Elimelech recognized his wife's distress and softened his tone. "The camel train will only stop briefly for the donkeys to drink. The camels drank at the springs near Jericho and will drink again when the Egyptians reach the Arnon River."

The summer heat had scorched everything in Reuben as in Judah. Later that day when the family reached the road going south from Heshbon to Moab the helpless sheep were hotly bleating their hunger and thirst. Dancing heat waves wiggled from the ground, and Naomi's tongue had become like a dry stick in her mouth. Her lips had dried, cracked, and bled. A rivulet of dried blood marked her chin.

Lack of rain had turned refreshing ponds into sand-blown, cracked, encrusted pits. Since leaving Bethlehem, they had seen more cracked mud at the bottom of mud holes than water holes full of fresh water.

Swirling winds stirred the hot dust. With each breath, Naomi's nose packed in a little more of that dust. Every so often she put a finger in and dug it out. She hated the heat, the never-ending thirst, the whole journey. She longed for home.

Toward the end of day, Naomi brought a hot, trembling hand to her grimy face, brushing away the tears. Sweat wiggled down her neck and back, and she itched from the dust. A fly buzzed her face; she swatted at it, missed, and it buzzed her again.

She gestured with her hand. The land lay dry and desolate, patches of grass showed here and there, not enough to keep a small flock alive for a month. "This is not good, my husband. Please, turn back," she pleaded. "I do not believe Yahweh blesses us on this journey. At least in Judah the animals had little, here they have nothing."

His eyes narrowed, his teeth clenched, and his patience with Naomi had met its end. "I will hear no more from you, wife. The Egyptians have told me it is only another day or two until we enter Moab. The animals will not die of thirst, nor shall we, before we cross over."

"They cry out!"

Noting the hurt look on her face, he softened his tone. "Yes, and it will continue until we reach the green fields of Moab. There, God will bless us with food and shelter until the famine ends in Israel. Wait and see, all will be well."

Naomi threw him a sharp look and held her words. Mahlon and Chilion, wanting to believe their father, were torn between the common sense of their mother and devotion to their father. Both sons, weak in body because of poor heath, longed for better pastures and a plentiful food supply.

After supper, when Elimelech went to the fire of the Egyptians, Mahlon asked, "Mother, why is your attitude toward Moab so harsh? We know of Moab's origination, yet the good people there had nothing to do with it."

The question caught Naomi by surprise.

Now her mouth dried up, her heart pounded in her ears. She had no desire to speak of sexual sins. However, she found herself being forced to defend her stance against Moab and its vile origin of father and daughter incest. She could overlook it if it were not for their blatant, deviant, sex worship of Chemosh and the Baals, which compelled her to condemn them and those who participated.

She took a place on a goatskin and beckoned her sons to sit facing her. "Since you know about Moab's beginning why is it hard to understand my feelings. Remember the Hebrews beginnings? I know you do.

"Hundreds of years ago our father Abraham traveled from Ur in the Chaldees to this new land that our God showed him. After sojourning in Canaan for a time, Abraham's nephew, Lot, accompanied his uncle to Egypt. They went because of a famine in the land and had the intention of residing there a short while."

"As we do now going to Moab," said Chilion. "It is—."

"No!" Naomi snapped, cutting him off. "It is not the same. Abraham only sojourned here; he did not own the land at that time. It is we who have been given the Land of Promise, and after conquering the inhabitants, possess it. We should not be forsaking it. The land belongs to us—the Hebrews."

The men glanced at each other wide-eyed. Chilion spoke up.

"Mother, we know the story of Lot and his daughters. You could tell us nothing new if you chose to repeat the history of Moab."

"We understand Israelites hate Moabites because of Lot and his daughters," said Mahlon. "Is it not time to lay aside such feelings? Do you condemn these people," he pointed toward Moab, "for something they did not do?"

"Yes!" Naomi blurted through trembling lips. She touched her damp neck. "They are people of incest and our God condemns that vile sin."

"But Mother, Lot, and his daughters committed the sins, not their descendants."

"Chilion, the sons, and daughters inherit their fathers' sins. We should have nothing to do with Moabites."

"I must think on it. It does not seem right."

"My son, listen to me. They worship heathen gods. Those gods require human blood. They pass their young through the fire, which our God condemns. So too, they commit sexual perversion with harlots in their temples.

"This pagan nation claims that a man should have relations with the shrine prostitutes for in doing so that act causes their fertility gods to do the same. So, as a result of these heathens worshiping in the temple with the harlots, the fertility gods will bless and fertilize the crops, which will bring about a great harvest. They should be condemned, and I do condemn them.

"Our God will bring destruction upon those Moabites, along with the Canaanites, a people who practice much the same in their religion."

In a voice barely above a whisper, Mahlon said, "do you condemn people you do not know? They are ignorant of the true God."

Naomi forced a smile. A compassionate person by nature, she had grown angrier with each step that took her further away from Bethlehem. Now, she manifested that anger in her tone and condemnation. "My son," she said tenderly, "it is Yahweh who judges all people. You are correct. It is not my place to condemn anyone. Nevertheless, my feelings cannot change."

Two days later, toward the end of day, the ox quickened his pace, and the goat kept close behind. The animals smelled water.

Within minutes, the road began a gentle downhill slope toward the River Arnon not more than a mile away.

Naomi ran out of her sandals trying to keep up with the animals. Finally, she let go of the rope and watched them race to the river.

"It is all right," Elimelech said, a smile played on his lips. "We shall gather them at the water's edge."

"My husband, do you notice something of which we have not seen in months?"

Elimelech chuckled. "Yes, I have watched them gather." He pointed toward the southwestern sky. "Storm clouds! Dark clouds that hide the going down of the sun. God is blessing our arrival in Moab. I promised you that the Almighty's grace would be upon us. Is this not proof?"

Naomi smiled yet withheld comment. In her heart, she did not believe it. However, she only wanted happiness for her husband.

"Mother, Father, I smell it!" Chilion exclaimed. "Not the river—the rain! How long has it been?"

Elimelech shrugged. "Too long. I cannot remember the last time, but I promise this, there will be many more days like today."

At the river, the family gathered the sheep with the help of the goat and dogs. "Tomorrow we will hire the ferry to move us across the river. It runs deep, not like the Jordan. Yes, we begin our sojourn in this new land to which Yahweh has brought us.

"Now, my sons, let us help your mother raise our tent so we may remain dry when the rains come."

"I do not wish to remain dry," Mahlon shouted, his hand raised to the sky. "I will stand and allow the rain to wash me clean of this barren wilderness. I will enter Moab fresh, ready for my new life."

Naomi stifled a cry and turned away. She could not quell her tears. They gushed, enough to wash her cheeks. Like a hand slap to the face, the truth hit her. If the rains continued, Mahlon and Chilion would be delighted to remain in Moab. She also foresaw the longer they sojourned, the easier it would be to give up the Promised Land and settle permanently with those heathens. She hated that fact, yet, being a woman she had absolutely no authority to make her husband or sons go home.

Later, the evening meal had long since been consumed, and still the rain did not fall. The boys could hear it, yet the refreshing wetness remained distant. Why? So close, it had come so very close, yet had not crossed the river.

At dawn, a pink glow stained the eastern sky. Mahlon and Chilion, along with their father, stood on the river bank gazing over into Moab. The green could not be hidden. The trees dripped, and the Arnon flowed swiftly toward the sea.

Elimelech kicked the ground and dust flew. "Do you now understand why I have insisted on departing this land? Our God *has* cursed it. He does not even allow the rain to cross the river.

"Our people have sinned. They have built high places to worship foreign gods and have brought the Almighty's wrath upon all of us. It is not right that God should punish us for another's sins.

"Our judges claim, 'Everyone does what is right in his own eyes.' No! They are wrong. They have no business including me in that pronouncement. *I* do what is right in Yahweh's eyes. I worship him, bow down to him in prayer, and offer the sacrifices he has commanded. What more can I do?"

Mahlon and Chilion looked steadily at their father. They had neither advice nor wisdom to impart. Afraid of saying something wrong, they said nothing.

"We go to Moab today. I will not return to Judah until the famine is over. It should not be long my sons. It has lasted much too long as it is."

Mahlon gave a guarded reply, words Elimelech readily accepted. "We will follow you, father."

"That is good, my son. Now, let us pull the stakes. We should have slept under the stars last night like all of the other nights."

Chapter 5

Ruth answered the door. Zaylin stood next to an older man both had serious looks. Her breath quickened. A sense of concern that she had caused the young man trouble coursed through her. Then came the knot in the belly. Her mind raced. This man, who must be Zaylin's father, wanted to complain to her parents about the previous day. The young man had escorted her home, and the Israelite did not like his son associating with her.

"Hello."

"Ruth, this is my father, Chasdiel. He has come to speak with your father. Is he here?"

"Yes," she said haltingly, a twinge of guilt hit her. She *had* brought trouble to Zaylin and now upon herself. "Please, sit on the benches and refresh yourselves. The goatskin has water and cups are on the table. I shall tell my father you are here."

In the fieldstone courtyard, which spread across the front of her home and extended to a small road one hundred feet away, were several tables and benches, plus basins for foot washing. In the center, a cistern had been built to catch rainwater. Zaylin walked about looking at various items on the tables. Stopping at the low wall made of hewn stone, which surrounded the court-yard, he gazed upon the lush, green countryside.

His father had come to tell Paebel that he would be returning to Beersheba. Zaylin believed it foolish, but his father's word was law. Chasdiel and Zaylin's mother longed to be with family and regretted leaving Israel.

Ruth's delicate footsteps turned the young man around. Oh, he would miss her. She exhibited quality. Regardless of the fact that she worshiped the pagan gods and had probably participated in their debauchery, Zaylin almost did not care. He had been so mesmerized by her good looks and gentle manner that it took all of his willpower to resist falling hopelessly in love with this young woman. He shook his head in disbelief, refusing to believe one so sweet would worship Chemosh.

"Good day, Chasdiel."

"A very good day to you, Paebel."

"This is an unexpected visit. Is there trouble in the field today? I do not recall you ever coming to my home. We have always met at your tent or in the fields."

"Yes, it is so. I do not wish to disturb your peace, but the matter is important." Nervous, he shuffled his feet and cleared throat. "I will be returning to Beersheba. We should never have left our land."

A cold look shot from Paebel's eyes. "The grapes ripen soon and then the gathering. I did not plan to look for other workers."

Chasdiel licked his lips, eyes darting from Ruth back to Paebel. "We do not wish to inconvenience you," he said with an even tone. "We shall stay until you find replacements."

Paebel's face showed only contempt. "No! You wish to depart and leave me short-handed—then go. I am sure your work will be better received in your land than on my land. I took you in with your promise to work hard and give me no trouble."

Chasdiel's eyes drifted over to Ruth. Her face flushed at her father's embarrassing rebuke. Harsh and unnecessary, yet his words came as no surprise to her.

Wincing at the rebuke, Chasdiel spoke in a weak voice. "Paebel, I beg your forgiveness for causing you trouble. I will remain on until you find good workers to replace my son and me. We shall not leave you short-handed."

Paebel, a bull-headed man, nodded toward the vine-covered archway and gate, which opened into the courtyard. "You *will* leave me short-handed, *and* leave my property today. Pull your stakes, gather your belongings, and remove your family from my property. I shall send Ruth to your tent within the hour with the pay due you. I cannot spare a son to bring it. They will be taking on your share of the work."

"Sir," he held his hands out, palms up, "please allow us to remain. We do not—."

"You will *not* remain." Paebel, a bitter, savage man, was not a person to stir up. He stepped forward. Now at arm's length and eye to eye, he elevated his tone. "Go now! I will not have shirkers on my land." He wheeled about and walked away.

A cold sweat broke out on Ruth's forehead. She clutched her stomach in complete mortification. Why did her father choose to act in such a manner? 'A hard man,' he had been called by more than one person.

Zaylin's eyes told Ruth he wanted to be anywhere but standing in front of her.

Chasdiel turned to Ruth. "Good day to you. Peace be upon your home."

Ruth's face had turned pallid. She nodded, unable to speak.

Elimelech, Naomi, and their sons spent most of the morning transporting their cart, flock, and other animals by ferry across the swollen river. The Moabite with the log raft charged plenty. Elimelech grumbled but had no choice, except to wait days for the river to drop, so they might cross in shallow water. The Moabite told him it would be weeks, maybe never as the rains frequently fell. Elimelech slapped silver into the man's hand and walked away grumbling to himself.

Spotting a man leading his donkey toward the river, Elimelech groused, "How far to Ar?"

The stranger peered through hard eyes at the grimy family, made so by days on the dusty roads of Judah and Reuben. "You Israelites?"

"From Judah," Mahlon said. "We are here to sojourn until the famine ends in our country."

Naomi placed a hand on her son's shoulder. He glanced at her unsmiling face. She shook her head. The father of the family should answer, and she had warned him on other occasions, not to speak out of turn.

"Sorry," he said, looking at the man. "My father speaks for our family."

"A fourth-day." The stranger waved a dismissing hand. "Been a fourth-day journey for years." He moved on.

"Thank you, sir."

The stranger looked back at Elimelech. "You want some advice?" He smirked.

"We are visitors here. Yes, I am sure it would be helpful."

The man's eyes moved over to Naomi as she stood near the flock, and then on to the boys at their positions on either side of the sheep. "Keep that flock out of Ar," he said with a bite to his tone. "By the time you leave the city you will be a few sheep short of a full flock."

Naomi's eyes grew to the size of her drinking cup. She wanted to ask about thieves but, since she had given warning that the patriarch of the family spoke for all, she remained quiet.

"Do you refer to thieves?" Unknown to Elimelech, he asked the question for her.

The man gave out an arrogant laugh. "Thieves, robbers, call them what you will, they are everywhere in the city. You will be distracted by one man, and another will snatch a lamb and be gone. There is a place for travelers, a lodging-place, near the city, on this side. It is an open field. This road passes by it on the east. Pitch your tent there, and keep the animals in the center area. A low, stone wall surrounds this area. If you must go into the city, enter alone and leave the animals and cart with your wife and sons." Finally, he forced a smile. "May the gods look upon you kindly." He walked on.

"Thank you again," Elimelech shouted. He stared at Naomi, and she gave him the 'we should have remained in Judah' look. "You shall remain quiet, woman. I have no intention of residing in the city, which you very well know."

Naomi tugged the rope, and the ox began the walk toward Ar. The animal pulled the cart with hardly an effort. However, because of the rain-soaked road, it became a slow trek as the flock, bit by bit, squished through the mud.

The fourth-day journey took a half-day. Exhausted, the family entered the gates of the lodging-place in the late afternoon. Elimelech open the gate to the sheepfold and the goat led the sheep into the large area for animals. Mahlon and Chilion unhooked the ox from the cart and staked him out on a patch of tall grass that gave further evidence of an abundance of rain.

"Our sons are much too exhausted to raise the tent," said Elimelech. "You and they can rest. At sundown, we shall drive the stakes."

Naomi smiled. Her husband, a proud man, would not admit he too needed rest. "Come," she held out her hand, "we can all spread our mats and rest. You too, my husband."

He did not argue. It would take too much effort.

As Ruth approached the tents of Chasdiel, her cotton mouth dried further. To swallow meant pain. How could she face Zaylin again?

She wanted to toss the bag of silver at the tent door and run. Unfortunately, she arrived late, and her heart sank at the sight— no tent door. Chasdiel and Zaylin had pulled stakes, dropped the tents, and were on their knees in the process of folding them when Ruth arrived.

She watched from the edge of a stand of trees, her mind racing with various things to say. However, nothing seemed appropriate. Paebel's reaction ruined her day and her hope of learning about the Israelite God. She wanted to become friends with Zaylin, so not to appear too forward. Her overbearing father succeeded in dashing that idea.

I will ask him about Yahweh. I must. How soon will I meet another Israelite? Maybe—never! Ruth strolled quietly forward. Zaylin straightened up to rest his sore back. "Ruth!"

"Hello! I am sorry for the treatment you received from my father."

Chasdiel got to his feet. Bowing to the young woman, he said, "Thank you! We do not hold his words against you. My son told me he escorted you home from the city a few days ago. He told me many favorable things about you."

Ruth lowered her eyes, blushing. She had never had such gracious treatment from anyone, except the potter, Joel of Kirhareseth. These kind words from Chasdiel meant more to her than he could have imagined.

"Thank you, I—I do not, uh…." She mumbled the last few words.

"Do you come to say goodbye?" Zaylin asked.

Ruth held out the bag of silver. "From my father." She drew back, glancing from Zaylin to his father with uneasy eyes.

Chasdiel took the wages and placed it in his scrip.

"I must hurry home." Ruth turned to leave.

Zaylin eyed his father. Chasdiel nodded.

"Ruth, I shall walk with you." His eyes danced with anticipation. "I have not had the opportunity to tell you about my 'strange God.' What do you wish to hear?"

Her eyes went to his. Zaylin smiled, which brought a giggle from Ruth. "I should like to hear something new. A bit of information of which I am not aware."

They started for her house, neither in any hurry.

"What do you wish to know about Yahweh?"

"We have household gods who protect us. We keep them on a special table and pray to them every morning and evening. Do you keep your God in a prominent place in your home?"

"Our God gave us ten commandments, written on tables of stone, which Moses brought down from the mountain. The first two commandments tell us to worship only him and not to make any idols."

Ruth looked over with curious eyes. "A religion without idols? It is not done." She sucked a quick breath. "Such beliefs are strange to me. What are these commandments? Can you tell me?"

"Tell you?" He grinned. "Hebrew children recite them daily when very young, even before we can read. They are all in my memory and my heart."

Her bright eyes slanted over. "Tell me those first two about your God."

"They are found in the scroll of Exodus. It reads: 'I am Yahweh your God, who brought you out of the land of Egypt, out of the house of bondage.

"'You shall have no other gods before me.'" He held up one finger. She chuckled.

"'You shall not make for yourself a carved image—any likeness of anything that is in heaven above, or that is in the earth beneath, or that is in the water under the earth; you shall not bow down to them nor serve them. For I, Yahweh your God, am a jealous God.'" A second finger went up.

This time Ruth remained quiet, thinking about the words. Suddenly she stopped and turned toward him. "You have never seen your God!" She stared, mouth open. Then, cocking her head to the side, she said, "I think it strange, not to know him."

"We know him. He is Yahweh, the only true God."

"Only?" Ruth kept her head still while shooting him a sideglance. "There are many gods. We worship Chemosh and the Baals. The Canaanites worship Dagon and many other gods."

She strolled on. She did not care for how Zaylin presented his God as the only one. A slight quiver moved her stomach.

"I know little of the Baals. Tell me."

Ruth rarely showed annoyance and strove hard not to show it to Zaylin, yet he spoke as though his God was the only one worth having. She did not like the child sacrifices but, Chemosh blessed the Moabites, more so than Yahweh did the Israelites. "Baal-peor is the god of the Moabite mountains." Her chin jutted out giving Ruth, a proud look. "Surely you are aware of Mount Peor?"

Zaylin noted her haughty look. It struck him as entirely out of place on her face. Nevertheless, he being in the right, would push his opinion. "My people know of the time when Israel camped at Shittim. The Israelite men began whoring with the women of Moab."

Ruth peeked sideways catching Zaylin's eye. "Whoring?" she exclaimed. A nervous chuckle escaped her lips. She had *never* discussed such things with a man. "What do you mean by calling Moabite women—whores?"

Zaylin touched her arm to stop her. Ruth recoiled. "Ruth, please—pardon my touch. Let us sit here for a moment." He motioned toward a fallen log.

Watching him with wary eyes, she shook her head. "I can hear your words here, standing."

He shrugged. "The Moabite women invited my people to the worship sacrifices of your gods. In total disregard of Yahweh's commandments, the Hebrews ate and bowed down to idols. My ancestors sexually joined themselves to Moabite whores in idol worship of Baal of Peor and other Baal gods. They offered sacrifices to the Moabite gods that brought about Yahweh's white-hot anger at his people. Then—."

"Those women were not whores," Ruth cut him off. They offered their bodies for worship to our fertility gods. Part of Baal worship and also Chemosh worship is to copulate with the high priests and the holy women."

Zaylin laughed. Ruth's hands clenched into fists, her knuckles turned white. Irritated and insulted by his behavior, she hurried on.

"Ruth, Ruth, please wait! I did not mean to anger you." He caught up and walked beside her. "It is the titles you give those promiscuous women that I find humorous.

"My God hated what happened that day. He told Moses, 'Take all the chiefs of the people and hang them facing the sun before Yahweh so that the raging fury of Yahweh will turn away from Israel.'

"Moses obeyed the Lord's command. He had every Israelite killed who had joined themselves to Baal-peor by whoring with the Moabites."

Ruth shook her head in disbelief. "Your God judges my gods unworthy, and then takes his anger out on his people by having them killed. Do you seriously believe Yahweh is a good God? He commands leaders of his people to kill his followers. Surely that is wrong. He also withholds rain from your land to punish you."

Her mind raced, asking questions, but the truth she sought remained elusive. Zaylin conceitedly accused her gods of being imperfect while his God seemed no better.

Ruth wanted to believe Yahweh treated his worshippers differently than Chemosh, yet the evidence said otherwise. She closed her mind; the conversation had ended.

Suddenly she picked up the pace. He walked faster to keep up. "Please, go to your father and finish your packing." She waved him off. "I must help my family in the fields."

Sudden anger slowed him, and he watched her walk down the pathway. "Does not Chemosh kill children by having his Moabite simpletons throw innocent victims into the fire?" He shouted. "Yahweh condemns such worship."

Ruth tensed. His words hit hard, and her shoulders bunched. Zaylin, of course, spoke the truth. Her god demanded child sacrifices, innocent children and babies killed in worship of Chemosh.

"Why?" she screamed. "Why? Why are the gods killing us? I cannot understand!"

Ruth dropped to her knees. "Help me, Lord Chemosh! It is too mysterious for me." She breathed out softly. "Please, help me to comprehend your ways."

Chapter 6

Mahlon and Chilion watched as a man, his wife, and son coaxed an ill-tempered donkey into the center area. The son staked the animal onto a patch of grass and then unhitched their cart.

"Peace to you," Elimelech called out.

Chasdiel replied, "And to you." He waved a hand.

"Have you come far today?"

"About four miles," the new arrival said with a sheepish grin barely noticeable under his bushy beard.

Naomi gave a quick questioning glance at her husband.

"Four miles? You must have come from the river," said Elimelech, motioning toward the Arnon.

Chasdiel shook his head. "No, from west of Ar. We started late."

"Quite late to come only four miles." Elimelech swallowed his laugh. "Perhaps you should have remained at home until tomorrow morning."

Having no desire to reference the trouble with Paebel, Chasdiel gave a quick nod and went to work with the help of Zaylin to put up his tent.

"Father," he threw up his hands, annoyed. "You avoided mentioning why we started so late."

Chasdiel walked over. "It is our affair!" He tapped his son on the chest. "We do not drag others into it."

Zaylin's jaw set hard. "Yes, but we should warn others of that man."

"Lower your voice," Chasdiel whispered.

"I overheard the young man though I did not do it intentionally," Elimelech said. "We came over to help. Be happy to listen to any warnings. We have newly arrived in Moab."

Chasdiel, not happy, stared daggers at his son. "Thank you for offering. It would be nice to have the tent up before dark."

"I am Elimelech and these are my sons Mahlon and Chilion. Naomi, my wife, is resting in our tent. We crossed the Arnon River today. Our home is Bethlehem in Judah."

A broad smile opened up Chasdiel's face. "We too are Israelites from Beersheba, and we are returning to our land."

"Peace to you my brother," said Elimelech. "Surely you know the famine remains. It is not an opportune time to return."

Chasdiel stood tall, shoulders back and chest out. "We long for our home in the Promised Land." He looked Elimelech straight in the eyes. "We shall endure. Others have chosen to stay, and we shall join them. Yahweh will provide as he did for Father Abraham when he raised the knife to slay his son."

Elimelech drove the final stake. Getting to his feet, he handed the mallet back to Chasdiel. "I fear you will starve. We have escaped the famine and will remain here until Yahweh visits the land with rain." He rocked back on his heels; a smug look shadowed his face. "It should not be long."

The man put an arm around Zaylin's shoulders. "We may starve, but we shall starve on our land."

Elimelech shrugged his shoulders and returned to his tent. Mahlon and Chilion lingered. "We shall be along shortly," Mahlon called to his father.

Selecting several sticks from a pile of kindling, Zaylin said, "I will light a fire."

"There are fallen trees in the woods. We gathered firewood in there for our fire. I will bring the fuel." Chilion rushed away.

Zaylin stacked the kindling and Mahlon brought hot coals from his fire. The fire-pits of others in the camp area kept the fires burning day and night as new travelers arrived and added new sticks to the fires.

The wood smoked and quickly flamed up. Zaylin spread a goatskin for his new acquaintances. "Please sit."

Mahlon took a spot at the corner of the skin while Chasdiel and Zaylin sat across the fire. Like Naomi, Zaylin's mother had retired to her tent.

Mahlon, curious and always the one to speak first, asked, "You departed so late in the day. Why not wait until morning?"

Zaylin wanted to tell him but deferred to his father. Chasdiel, not willing to make a fuss, avoided answering, but also understood his son had a point. Maybe these brothers should be warned of Paebel. Tomorrow, if they go to find work, someone will surely direct them to the area where the day-workers congregate. Paebel would likely be there hiring for the day, looking to find permanent workers.

"My son will tell you the story." Chasdiel got to his feet. "I am weary and wish to rest."

With curious eyes, Mahlon watched the man enter his tent. At that moment, Chilion returned. Dumping the firewood he took a place beside his brother.

"My father does not like to speak of difficulties. I have no problem with it."

"So, you are not leaving here on good terms," Mahlon said.

Zaylin shook his head. "Only one person has given us problems, and he is a hard man. How Ruth is that man's issue, well it cannot be explained. She is sweet. He is sour."

Chilion leaned forward. "What happened?"

Mahlon's eyes lit up. "Ruth must be his daughter."

Zaylin gave him a sly grin. "Yes, and pretty. Not only in face and form, but she has a lovely spirit. I have never met her mother, but she is not much better than Paebel."

"That must be gossip," Mahlon said. "If Ruth is as good as you say, would not that trait come from her mother?"

Zaylin shook his head. "My father told me. He has spoken to her once or twice—not a friendly woman."

"I should like to meet this Ruth." Mahlon winked at his brother. "I *am* a good judge of character."

Chilion laughed loud falling against Mahlon's shoulder. Looking at Zaylin, he said, "I do not think it is her character he would like to judge. You said she is pretty—now that he would like to see. Judging her character comes later." He gave Mahlon a playful shove.

Zaylin spoke from frowning lips. "She is all I said, and I wanted to know her better. But—."

"Your parents wanted to go home," Chilion finished his statement.

"Yes!" he whispered convincingly. He stared at the brothers through hard eyes.

"You *are* angry. Why?" asked Mahlon.

"I am persuaded that sojourning here is best. We do not have to worry about our next meal. In Judah—what are my father and mother thinking? They are sentimental, believing everything will be all right as long as they are home and among family. To me, that makes no sense.

"The Almighty has given us minds to reason things out, and I believe hard times are ahead." He shook his head in disgust. "And, there is Ruth. I think she likes me." He smiled.

Chilion laughed. "Is Ruth an afterthought? I think not." He gave Mahlon a knowing look.

Zaylin nodded. "You are very perceptive."

The three fell silent for a few moments. As they gazed around the camping area, the sun dropped below the jagged horizon. Zaylin tossed another log on the fire, and sparks flew toward the evening sky.

"It would not have worked out anyway."

Mahlon's brow furrowed, his eyes questioning the remark.

Zaylin glared back, his thoughts sorting through the last moments with Ruth. "I see your curious look, and yes, it is Ruth. We had a big disagreement when we parted."

"Is she a Moabite?" asked Chilion.

"Do you read minds?" He did not answer directly, but his sad eyes told Chilion he had hit a nerve.

Mahlon peered into the fire. The flames danced and sizzled, licking at the rain-soaked sticks. "I still should like to meet her. Foreigners have been known to embrace our God. That is it, is it not? She will not accept our God. But, she might be one who would listen to the truth about Yahweh."

Zaylin slowly shook his head. "I tried. She believes in Chemosh and her Baal gods. I told her of how the Moabite women seduced Israelite men at Shittim. She became furious, said they were holy women, and it was worship."

"Worship!" Mahlon exclaimed.

"Ruth is young. She knows nothing." He gently bit his lip. "I had hoped to be the man to bring her around."

"Man? You?" Chilion laughed. "You are barely twenty years old with a scraggly beard. You remain a boy."

Zaylin crossed his arms on his chest. "You speak to me with that tone and words? You do not know me. The light has grown dim now, but I have plenty of whiskers. In better light, you would see them. They are quite visible."

Mahlon smirked at the young man's attempt to prove his manhood. He might have a start to a beard, but he was still too young to have a woman. He held back a laugh, not wishing to insult him further. "Where is Ruth's home from here?"

Zaylin pointed. "Take the road about four miles. Paebel's house is down a path. You cannot pass by without seeing it."

Mahlon tossed another stick on the fire. It smoked for a time, the heat drying the bark, and then it blazed up allowing the men to see clearly each other for a few moments. "I believe you are correct. Ruth needs a man." He pulled at his beard. "As you can plainly see, *I* have a beard, and I am of marrying age. If the Almighty blesses me with the opportunity to speak with her, she *will* listen to me."

Elimelech rose to his feet, slipped into his sandals and wrapped his cloak about his shoulders. The feeling of dampness had awakened him.

"Mahlon," he whispered. No response, so he nudged him with a foot. "Mahlon!"

Thunder rumbled in the distance.

The young man stirred, turned over and slept.

Elimelech stepped outside. The sky lit up with jagged bolts of lightning. A drop of rain hit him, and he lifted his face to the heavens. Soon the sprinkling had wet his face, and it ran down his beard.

A flash and a streak of lightning shot to the ground. It came close. Then the flashes increased, flaring over and over from cloud to ground with the thunder following within seconds.

Elimelech ducked back into the tent. Mahlon was awake and sitting up. Loud bleating of the panicked flock had become a nerve-wracking uproar.

Chilion rolled out of his bed. "I will go and calm them."

"You will do no such thing. Lightning is striking all around. Going out there and you will soon be dead."

"It can strike the tent, too."

"Maybe, and if it does we shall die together, but you shall not go out there and die alone."

Chilion dropped back into his bed. A few more seconds and the storm hit with giant sheets of rain slamming the ground.

Mahlon shook his head. "No one will be hiring today."

"You know that, do you?" Naomi's voice came from the other side of the curtain that divided the tent.

"Forgive me, Mother. I did not mean to wake you."

Naomi drew back the partition. "Son, do you think I could sleep through all of this commotion?"

Mahlon grinned. "No."

"Go to the city as planned. You know full well the merchants will be there on the rainy days, too. No one may hire you today, but you can ask questions about who does and what type of work is available when the sun shines."

He got to his feet and readied himself for the day. Remembering the girl named Ruth changed his attitude. He might meet her father since the man would be there looking to hire laborers.

A half-hour later, dawn came with a slow drizzle pelting the tent. After eating bread, cheese, and raisin cake, Elimelech and Mahlon readied themselves to walk the road into Ar.

"Chilion, I shall take you next time, and your brother will remain here."

"Yes, father."

"It is not far to the city. We shall return this morning if no one hires us. You care for the animals."

The city of Ar, only a mile down the road, had opened its gates before Elimelech and Mahlon arrived. The huge, iron gates impressed the men as they did Ruth.

The drizzle had stopped. However, the road had done its work on father and son's feet. Mud covered their sandals and oozed from between their toes.

"Where do the day-laborers gather?" Elimelech asked an old man sitting on a stone seat.

"On that side of the square," he pointed to a spot, not over a hundred yards away. Several men stood about talking, some laughing, and all munched on fresh bread and drank from cups.

"And the bakers?" Mahlon caught his father's eye. "That bread, cheese, and cake was not enough. I am still hungry."

The man chuckled and gestured toward a narrow street opening onto the square. "Bakers' street. You have a cup?"

"Yes." Mahlon produced a cup from under his cloak.

"Fresh bread and warm milk." He waved a careless hand. "All you want."

Elimelech and Mahlon moved on in the direction of bakers' street. "He kept it short."

Elimelech laughed. "Yes, a man of few words."

After buying bread and milk, the men joined the congregation of workers. The men comprising the group were there for various reasons. Some, like Elimelech and Mahlon, were new arrivals to the area and had not found permanent jobs. Most though did not have the skills for the best jobs or if they did, were not reliable because of laziness.

"This city appears to be much larger than Bethlehem," said Mahlon to a man in the crowd.

"You are Israelites?"

"Yes, from Judah."

Several of the men laughed.

"You laugh at us?" Mahlon's face grew hard.

"No, not at you—at what you said. We know Bethlehem is in Judah."

"Oh." He grinned. "I would think more men should be here waiting for work."

Again the men laughed. "Fellow, it is raining." He tapped his head inferring Mahlon should think it through. "The lazy ones are still in bed."

"He is still learning," Elimelech said. "He—."

"Who wants to work?" A gruff man arrived and cut him off. "My vineyard needs tending. Soon the harvest is upon me. Need a man in the watchtower, too."

Many of the men moved away, making one excuse or another. "Never worked in a vineyard. I do field work," said one.

"I *said* vineyard," the man fired back, glaring at one and then another.

"We have a vineyard back home. We know all about grapes. My name is Elimelech, and yours?"

"Paebel. If you can do the job, good" He studied him coolly. "The last men did not have the stomach for hard ways and long hours. I need two men, men who will work and not whine."

Mahlon recognized the name from the previous night's conversation. He quickly began to study the man.

"My son," he touched Mahlon's shoulder, "is a good worker. He also knows grapes."

"Follow me. We shall know by the end of day if I can trust your word."

"We do not lie!" Mahlon snapped, not liking Paebel's attitude.

Instantly he regretted the words. This man was Ruth's father, and he so wanted to meet the girl. Did this kill his hopes?

Paebel wheeled about and stared hard.

Elimelech grabbed his son's arm. "He meant no disrespect."

"A high-strung fellow is he? Let us be going. We shall see at sunset if he has any vigor left to speak again in such a manner. You will work, or you will be gone from my property."

Mahlon eyed his father but remained quiet. Elimelech followed the man, but his son held back. "Hard man," Mahlon thumb-pointed over his shoulder toward Paebel. "Is that why none of you accepted his offer of work?"

No one answered, but the smirks covering several faces gave him the answer. He turned and fell in behind Elimelech as they passed the city gates.

Arriving at Paebel's vineyard the men strolled along toward the watchtower located in the middle of the grape rows. Several benches at the base of the tower offered a resting place for workers. Paebel motioned for them to sit.

"Tell me what you know about vineyard work. The harvest is near, and I need experienced hands."

Elimelech trained his eyes upon Paebel and never looked away. He intended to keep the man's attention and when done speaking this landowner would know the Israelite had an excellent knowledge of tending vineyards and producing quality grapes. "Vineyards require constant care. You must cultivate grapes properly, or the fruit will quickly deteriorate.

"I noticed as we walked beside the walls and terraces, several breaches have opened, made so by the abundant rains. Those need repairing immediately. The ground around the vines has been given proper care, but soon weeds will appear, again because of the rains. After a few days of sun, the ground must be plowed to root out the early development of thistles and nettles.

"Early next spring, the vines must be pruned of dead branches. Take them to an open place away from all other crops and burn them along with the weeds. It is—."

"Enough! Your knowledge is adequate. Now, how about this young man. What do you know about the watchtower and why it is here?"

Mahlon glanced at his father. Elimelech's look told him to stay with answering the question and not make any rude remarks.

"The watchman looks out over the entire vineyard unless it is too large, and then there are two or more watchtowers manned by watchmen. He is on guard for jackals, foxes or any other wild animal that could destroy the fruit.

"At Bethlehem, several vineyards are large enough that the owner's family and their laborers remain in the vineyard day and night during the harvest."

"We do the same," said Paebel.

Ruth's father ran an eye over Mahlon, considering the young man. "You appear weak—rather sickly. How is your strength?"

A rush of heat inflamed his face, Mahlon wanted to snap back at the man, yet held his tongue. Paebel had sized him up with quick perception. Both of Elimelech's sons were frequently ill, conditions they had endured from childhood. Both men tried to compensate by working hard for their parents.

"I am strong enough. There are men stronger and some weaker. I can do the job."

Paebel cracked a rare smile. "We shall see. Both of you appear to know vineyard work. Now, will you be up to the task? Son, you climb the tower and watch. A ram's horn is up there if you need to sound a warning.

"Come with me," he looked at Elimelech, "I will show you where we keep the tools. You can begin repairing the walls."

At midday, a gentle, feminine voice called out. "Hello! I have food."

Mahlon looked down, and his eyes grew wide at the fabulous sight afforded him. A pretty teenaged girl with a dazzling smile stared up at him.

"Climb down and eat," Ruth said in a cheerful tone. "My brother will relieve you while you take the midday meal."

On the ground, Mahlon tilted his head back so he might look eye to eye with a surly man, about his age, with granite eyes and a stone face. Her brother, big enough to snap Mahlon in two, said nothing and climbed the ladder.

Mahlon smiled at Ruth, and she returned it. "Sit there," she motioned toward a bench. Opening a bag, she pulled out bread, olives, and various pieces of dried fruit. "Let me fill your cup." She lifted the goatskin from the ground.

"No, that is too heavy for you," Mahlon replied. "I will lift it." He reached over and took it from her. "You hold the cup."

After setting the skin down, he took the cup. "What is your name?"

"Ruth."

"Ruth! I have heard about you. There could not be another. Your description—oh! No one lied."

She stood, eyes wide and mouth half open. *What is he going on about? Who has been talking about me—and why? This man is new to Father's land. How can he know anything about me?*

Mahlon waited for her to speak. Finally, he chuckled. "I am sorry. Sometimes I blurt out things before thinking. Please sit here and I will explain."

Ruth shook her head. "I must go. My father does not allow it. The workers are not permitted to converse with me nor me with them. If you are here tomorrow, I shall bring the meal at noon."

Picking up the waterskin, she rushed away.

"She never asked my name."

Hearing an evil laugh, he gazed up. Her brother stared with cold eyes, cold as winter ice. It sent a shiver through him.

"She never will! Your name is not necessary. Do your job and keep away from her."

Chapter 7

The next day Ruth delivered the midday meal to Mahlon. Watching from the tower, her brother gave them a hard-eyed stare. They exchanged few words, not only because of the brother, but Ruth feared her father. Nevertheless, yearning eyes do much speaking when unable to form words.

After two days, Elimelech and Mahlon had satisfied Paebel that they could do their jobs. So, Ruth's father permanently employed both and located the family at the place that had been occupied by Chasdiel. There, the lush pasture produced plentiful grazing for Elimelech's flock. In exchange for grazing rights, Elimelech agreed to provide wool for Paebel's use.

Paebel also gave Chilion a job alongside his father and soon Mahlon and his brother, with the approval of Paebel, began alternating between the watchtower and work on the ground. Naomi tended their sheep while the men labored in the vineyard.

Within days of Elimelech and Mahlon's employment, a major problem arose. The first day they worked was Yom Shlishi, the third day of the week. Four days later came Yom Shabbat, *day seven* of the week. Yahweh had commanded the seventh day as a day of rest.

"Tomorrow, finish the repair work on the walls and then began work on the terraces," Paebel said. "You have done an excellent job. No man could do better."

Elimelech's chest swelled with pride at the praise from his employer.

"Father?" Chilion cried out in a questioning voice.

He looked at his youngest and quickly glanced away. The man had no desire for this moment, yet it had arrived without warning.

"The repairs will be completed as you say." Elimelech turned to go.

"But father! It is—."

"We go now, son! We talk at our tent—not here."

Mahlon, not so easily cut off as his brother, blurted with hands on hips, "Tomorrow is Yom Shabbat. We rest."

Paebel peered through challenging eyes. Would the men refuse to work? He cared nothing for the Hebrew day of rest. Paebel worshiped Chemosh not some invisible God of the Hebrews. These people lived on his land, and they would work or find another place to loiter.

Elimelech found all eyes upon him. He hated it. Why must he have to choose between working for a hard man and resting for a demanding God? It was unreasonable. He considered the famine not fair and now this situation not equitable. Could there not be something in his life that would come easy?

"We will be here," he said with a steady, low-pitched voice. "There are times when we must set aside certain commands."

He walked away, and his sons reluctantly followed. Paebel, with arms crossed, watched them go. A smirk stretched wide across his face.

When out of earshot Mahlon spoke up, "Yahweh rested on the seventh day. Do we now refuse to do as our God did?"

Elimelech kept silent.

"Father," Chilion said, "We always rest and meditate on the Law given at Mount Sinai."

"Yes, and it is a command, not a custom," said Mahlon. "Remember the Sabbath day, to keep it holy. Six days you shall labor and do all your work, but the seventh day is the Sabbath of Yahweh your God. In it, you shall do no work: you, nor your son, nor your—."

"Silence!" Elimelech shouted. "Mahlon—I know the words, you do not need to recite them. I taught you." He stopped, turning toward his sons. "Can you not see that we must bend a bit when in another country? It is custom to respect another nation's gods when traveling through or sojourning in foreign lands.

"Moabites do not rest on the seventh day. We are expected to work, and that is what we will do. If we refuse, the man will find others who *will* work. Then what? I will tell you. We will be homeless and jobless. Do you want that? I must think of your mother, take care that she has security. Now, we will do what needs to be done, and you shall keep your words to yourself. I am the patriarch of this family, and you will do as I request."

The silence on the remaining walk home rang in Mahlon's ears. The only good about tomorrow would be speaking with the girl who had captured his heart. Secretly, his father's decision pleased him but, a twinge of guilt kept him wondering. Once a man sets aside a command, does it not become easier to neglect another?

❦

"Hello."

At the sound of the sweet voice, Naomi opened the tent flap. Ruth stood outside.

"My name is Ruth. May we speak for a few moments?"

"My son, Mahlon, has spoken of you." Naomi smiled. "He only has nice things to say. You have made such a delightful impression upon him, and my husband, also."

Ruth's bright eyes shone while embarrassment warmed her face. "Thank you, but I do not know why they should think such. My father is the one who has employed them." She shrugged her shoulders. "I bring the midday meal that is all."

"We can converse over there on the goatskin." Naomi indicated the black sackcloth lying near the smoldering campfire.

When seated, Naomi gazed at the lovely teenager, quite impressed by her meticulous clothing, including her sandals, which appeared to be new. Ruth's dark eyes sparkled, and her face radiated warmth. Mahlon had described Paebel and his harsh language and manners. Naomi would never have guessed this girl called him, father.

Butterflies flapped furiously in Ruth's stomach, yet she had an empty feeling in the pit, a paradox unexplainable. She rubbed sweaty palms on her clothing. "May I say something, and what I tell you, it must not be told beyond your family? It is essential my father does not know."

"I will tell no one."

"I know this is the seventh day," Ruth began, her voice barely above a whisper, "and it is special to the Hebrews. You call it a day of rest."

Naomi nodded and smiled.

"I want to tell you that I do not agree with my father's insistence upon your husband and sons toiling in the vineyard today. He should respect your beliefs." Ruth quickly looked away.

This young woman impressed Naomi. She had presumed all Moabites were abrasive and unsophisticated heathens, without the mental state of ordinary people. She defined Hebrews as normal. This brief introduction confirmed what her son had professed about this Moabitess.

Naomi hesitated before speaking. "Thank you." She lowered her head. "I apologize for hesitating," her chin trembled, "but I am very emotional today. It is as you say. Our God forbids us to work on the Sabbath day. I pleaded, asking my husband to remain in our tent. He would not listen." She let out a whimper. "I know Yahweh will withhold blessings because of this failure to keep the commandment."

Ruth reached out and took Naomi's hand. "I must hurry on. My mother has sent me on an errand to the city. I am buying at the market for our evening meal. May I ask a favor?"

Naomi placed a hand over Ruth's. "Ask."

"I go to market often. The next time, please accompany me." She peered at Naomi with imploring eyes. "We can talk. Oh, I realize we do not know each other. However, I have questions that only you can answer."

Naomi bunched her eyebrows. "Only me? It is a mysterious thing you say. I am intrigued. Yes, I had hoped someone would be so kind as to show me where to buy and whom to avoid. Surely not all the merchants are honest."

Ruth laughed. "Are there dishonest Hebrews?"

Naomi glanced away, momentarily ashamed to answer. She looked back and gave the girl a sly smile. Nodding her head, she burst out laughing.

Ruth got to her feet, and Naomi followed.

"I have learned an important lesson today," said Naomi. "All Moabites are not as I believed. Nor…" She did not finish.

"Nor?" Ruth questioned.

"We shall talk another day."

Ruth blew out a long breath. She smiled. "I look forward to our day at the market."

Bargain hunters crowded the narrow streets of Ar. Everyone haggled the price of everything, and would never consider paying the asking amount of any goods at the marketplace. The merchants priced their merchandise too high, and the customers refused to pay. However, with much back and forth, they would agree to a final price.

A scream and the sound of running feet, sandal upon stone, caught her attention. Men were in pursuit of a thief who had stolen from a merchant. Ruth clutched her leather scrip a bit tighter.

"Step over here," the eerie voice coaxed. "I have cloth that only royalty wears. Your garment is beautiful yet, this more so." He held it up as Ruth turned to look. Her insides turned cold. With evil eyes that appeared to look right through her robe, a man stood near a table of fine clothing and luxurious cloth.

Realizing this man, the same man as on previous occasions who had made suggestive remarks, wanted more from her than a sale, she jerked her head around and rushed on. Why must he keep bothering her?

While rapidly weaving in and out of the crowd, Ruth mulled over the problem. Suddenly the answer became apparent. The man would never stop, and it would be up to her to avoid him and his lecherous eyes. She must take another street to her destinations, even though it would be out of her way.

For most people, the solution to her problem would have been quite natural. However, a young woman so in fear of displeasing her parents, so bound by anxiety of enduring an episode of her father's wrath, and so beaten down with the belief that her views must align with Paebel's and Figat's in all things, this moment came as a breath of fresh air. No—much more, a fragrant cleansing rain after a dust storm.

Her parents excessively dominated Ruth over the years, and she had grown to resent it. Ruth had her opinions, and she would keep them—to herself for now. But, finally, she had come to acknowledge that she did not need to feel guilty for disagreeing with her parents.

She wanted to dance, shout her excitement with words yet unknown to her. But, gathering herself, she reluctantly kept her excitement contained.

After collecting all of her items, she left the gates and walked the same road as always, enjoying the time alone as it gave her time to think. A mile or so down the road she stopped to rest at a giant oak.

Ruth understood hate. Not that anyone would have reason to call her a hater of people.

She hated the senseless taking of life. Killing in battle certainly could be justified. Death for criminals who had killed—yes. But, the gods requiring human sacrifices, in her mind at least, crossed the line of acceptable worship.

Did the gods require it? They had never spoken to her nor any Moabite. The priests of Chemosh and Baal spoke for them. These holy men insisted propitiation for the people sometimes required a child sacrifice.

Ruth shook her head and moved on. Near the brook that ran close by her house, again she stopped to rest. The basket of goods carried on her head with great proficiency; she set at the foot of a tree, and there she reclined in the soft, luxurious grass which abundantly cuddled her body. She relaxed.

Each time she contemplated the Moabite gods, a silent warfare within her increased the inner pressure she endured to conform to her parents' religion. Not only did the human sacrifices disturb her, but also the temple fertility worship frightened her. Several young women, temple priestesses, served Chemosh by having sexual intercourse with the temple priests.

Figat had briefly explained the rituals after Ruth's brother told her of the practice. Her mother said, "Chemosh and the Baal gods continually bless Moab with fruitful land as a result of the fertility worship engaged in by the priests and priestesses. It is sacred worship, and the gods bless our country with plenty, which proves they keep promises."

Later that same day, her brother said, "One day you might be called for duty in the temple."

Ruth's hand flew to cover her mouth. "What! Me—a priestess?" She trembled.

Looking through stern eyes, her brother said, "Do you not understand, it would be an honor. Would you not want to keep our father's crops bountiful? It is a duty you must not refuse. Many beautiful, young women have fulfilled their turn in the temple."

Ruth, utterly speechless, walked away, disappearing into the vineyard. Since that day, she had contemplated her possible fate as a temple prostitute. And, from that day forward she had resolved to resist.

Requiring human sacrifices, and the use of temple harlots by Chemosh and Baal continually fueled her desire of learning about the Hebrew God. All of the gods of the Moabites, Ammonites, Edomites, and Canaanites had the practice of passing children through the fire. She understood this different God whom Israelites called, Yahweh, only required animal and grain sacrifices; and him being so dissimilar from the Moabite gods kept her curiosity high.

On the other hand, his apparent lack of care for his people confused her. Why allow that famine to linger on for years? Did he or not have the power to stop it? The Hebrews did not have fertility rites, so their land suffered. Chemosh required it, and the glaring contrast between the two countries was evident. Moab, lush with vegetation, clearly remained the superior land.

She longed for the day when all of this would be made clear? On the other hand, it might never be clear.

After dozing for a few minutes, a bird calling to its mate startled Ruth. Her eyes popped open, and she jumped to her feet—trembling. She spent too much time day-dreaming. The fear of her father's wrath gripped Ruth as though a coiled snake had wrapped her neck, slowly suffocating its victim. She swallowed hard. Lifting the basket to her head, the young woman hurriedly balanced it and walked toward home.

Late the same day Paebel approached Elimelech and his sons as they passed through the vineyard gate. "You men have done as I asked today. Next week on your seventh day do not come. Use it as a day of rest."

Elimelech smiled broadly. "Thank you."

"Why come today?" asked Mahlon, his voice cold. "Everything done today could have waited until tomorrow."

Paebel snorted. "I tested you."

"Tested?"

"If you believed it more important to remain in your tent today than keeping your commitment to me, then I wanted to know. Do you like resting or getting paid for working? You answered that question by showing up today. So, you have proven your loyalty to me. That is all I wanted. Take every seventh day off until harvest. At harvest time, we work seven days a week until the cutting is complete, and the grapes have been crushed."

Mahlon, unhappy at being tested said nothing and walked away.

"Thank you," Elimelech said. "We shall not disappoint you."

Arriving at the tents, Mahlon broke the silence. "Test! A test and we passed." His voice trembled with fury. "We did his bidding and pleased him."

"My son, what is this you go on about?" Naomi asked.

Mahlon sat next to his mother before the fire. A large pot hung over the flames containing the evening meal. The aroma of leek soup simmering reminded him of Bethlehem and that pleasant aroma summoned blissful memories of home. At that moment he yearned for familiar surroundings. His overbearing employer galled him, which intensified his longing for his hometown. Maybe they should have remained in Judah.

"Paebel required us to break the Sabbath to test us."

"Test?"

"Yes, he wanted to prove our loyalty. Father demonstrated his commitment—not mine. I only showed my loyalty to father."

Naomi eyed her oldest and then shifted her eyes to Chilion. "Do you feel the same?"

"I, I believe I do."

"A test?" Naomi said, her voice flat, eyes cold.

Elimelech frowned. "I lead this family, and we have kept our employment because I insisted we keep our commitment to Paebel. Now we will have silver to purchase the goods we need. As a Hebrew, it is vital to keep my word to others."

"Yes, all of you committed to laboring for Paebel," Naomi said tenderly, "but surely you realize your original and better commitment belongs to the Almighty."

"You will not speak to us with such words," Elimelech replied. He pulled back the tent flap. "I am tired."

After he went inside and lowered the flap, Naomi glanced from Mahlon to Chilion. "His voice is weak," she whispered. "Have you noticed a change?"

The boys nodded their agreement. "I shall ask Ruth tomorrow if there is a healer nearby," Mahlon spoke behind his hand. "Perhaps he has herbs that help."

"Herbs, they can be helpful," said Naomi, "but we want nothing to do with their godless incantations."

Mahlon's only day away from the vineyard would be the best of all days since he had arrived in Moab. The young man hurried toward the city gates. What possessed him to break the Sabbath he did not question—he knew, Ruth the Moabitess. She had told him the previous day that she would be at the market the next morning.

He whispered, "May I see you there?"

Her eyes flashed. She nodded her agreement.

He sighed, placing a hand over his heart. "At the gate."

She returned his look of admiration and hurried away. Her brother high atop the tower did not hear or see the exchange of words.

At the gates, he spotted Ruth and next to her stood another pretty young woman.

"Mahlon, this is Orpah, a close friend. She also shops at the market today."

Mahlon gave her a pleasant though reluctant greeting. He wanted Ruth to himself. Orpah would hear all he wanted to say, so now some things would have to keep until another time.

Entering through the gates, Ruth spoke first. "Is this not your day of rest?" she asked in a low voice that did not accuse.

Mahlon grinned.

"Stop here, sweet ones." The voice made both girls cringe.

Mahlon glanced over. A gruff, sour-smelling man with ugly eyes, which sunk into his skull, beckoned with his hand.

"I have bracelets, bejeweled bracelets. Come see."

"Keep walking," Ruth whispered. "He has propositioned me on other occasions. He is not alone, there are others, also."

They moved on without another word. Mahlon nudged Ruth's elbow. "He shall never touch you if I am along."

Ruth nodded, avoiding his eyes. "You did not answer me."

"You had a question?" He asked with a face that was child-like innocent.

"Your day of rest—day seven."

"I have worked on day seven and will again. Should I not give you as much time?"

Ruth glanced over, their eyes met for a moment. His face exhibited rebelliousness.

"Here," Orpah said, "let us buy fruit. I know this man."

They stopped and perused the fruit cart.

"Your father, did the healer treat him?"

"Thank you for recommending him. My mother purchased several herbs, but that is all."

"He did not pray to the gods for him?"

"No!" Mahlon's jaw clenched. "I am sorry that sounded harsh. My mother only wanted the herbs."

"I spoke to him each day when I brought the midday meal but hesitated to ask about it. Is he well?"

"He says he is," Mahlon said though his expression told of his doubt.

"I think he is not," Ruth said bluntly. "His eyes tell me so."

"His eyes?"

"A person's eyes say much," Ruth said with a serious look.

"That is so," Orpah agreed.

Mahlon's heartbeat quickened as he recognized an opportunity. He drew a bit closer and gazed into Ruth's eyes. She held his look, never glancing away. "What do my eyes tell you?"

A warm glow raced through Ruth's body. She understood at once his look, and the tender emotion that produced it.

Orpah giggled.

Ruth's eyes slanted over to her friend as she frantically searched her mind for the proper words. Then, looking back at Mahlon she began, "I—I…" A lump grew in her throat choking off her words. She looked away fumbling over the fruit. Finally, she eked out in a soft, tiny voice, "I should not interpret your eyes."

"Why?"

"You would, um, I think it might be, um. This peach is excellent." She held up the perfectly formed fruit and brought it to her nose. "Ripe, ready to eat. The aroma is wonderful."

"You cannot answer or do you refuse?" Mahlon laughed.

"I interpret eyes, too," Orpah interjected, saving her friend from an answer. "Your eyes tell of gentle kindness and sweet affection for Ruth."

"Orpah!" Ruth gently hit her friend on the arm. "You are mistaken."

"She is not mistaken, except— maybe a mite." He held up his hand with thumb and forefinger slightly apart. "It is more than sweet affection. I—."

"I must make my purchase and hurry on," Ruth talked over him, uneasy at what he would say.

Orpah glanced at Mahlon. He gave a knowing grin, and she understood this man had many sweet feelings for Ruth.

When Mahlon arrived home, he endured the wrath of not only Elimelech but Naomi, too.

"We labored on the Sabbath because I said it was essential," Elimelech shouted. "Meeting a girl is not necessary!"

"Ruth is a lovely person," Naomi said, "but she is a Moabitess. Do not become involved with her."

"You know her?" Elimelech asked with raised eyebrows.

"I have met her. She visited me here. We have shopped together in the marketplace of Ar."

Mahlon's eyes widened. "Why did she come here?"

Naomi eyed her husband. His expression told of disapproval because she had not told him. He regarded his position as the patriarch of the family seriously as did all fathers of Israelite clans. He wanted to know everything, and she had kept him in the dark.

"Ruth told me she did not agree with her father's decision to insist on you working the Sabbath."

"This is wonderful news," Mahlon said. "I had no doubt my influence upon her would have a positive result."

"You, brother?" Chilion laughed. "You have not been around her enough to affect anything."

"Maybe," he shrugged, "it makes no difference. She respects our beliefs."

Elimelech stared thoughtfully at Mahlon and when he spoke, the words came slow and icy. "Do not break the Sabbath again to see this girl."

Mahlon gave a little nod of the head and looked at his mother. "Ruth visited our tent with a message and you did not tell me. Why?"

"Did I need to pass along her words? She spoke to me. I promised to tell no one what she said. I believe she fears her father. "Mahlon, I implore you to avoid Ruth. Yes, she is a good person but, a Moabitess. She worships strange gods. What has she in common with you?"

"One day, she will worship our God." He turned and walked toward the tent. At the door, Mahlon turned. "It is three hours until sundown. I shall observe the rest of the Sabbath meditating upon the power of Yahweh to change Ruth's heart from her gods to our God." He gave a little half-wave and disappeared through the tent door.

Chapter 8

The weeks rapidly passed, and Naomi had accompanied Ruth to the market several times. Ruth's curiosity about the Hebrew God prompted questions, but Naomi added little to Ruth's knowledge of Yahweh. Naomi held back information. She recognized her son had become more than infatuated with Ruth. While Naomi liked Ruth, a Moabitess as a daughter-in-law was not acceptable.

Summer had brought the grape harvest. Seeing Ruth each day during that time, ignited Mahlon's love for her into a slow burn. His affection for this charming Moabitess had developed to the point that he neglected his duties while his mind wandered.

He leaned upon a hoe thinking or sat upon a bench focused on his desire for Ruth. After two days of watching him daydream, Paebel confronted the man

"Mahlon, I have noticed your lazy work habits the last few days. You stand idle, staring off. I pay you to work, not daydream. Many grapevines are yet unharvested."

Looking at him with sheepish eyes, Mahlon said, "I have fought it. It is—."

"Fought what?" Paebel cut him off. "Some enemy keeps you from working?"

"I have wanted to come and talk, but avoided you. Afraid you would not understand."

"What do you babble about? Make your words clear."

He stared at the ground. "It is—um, Ruth."

"Ruth!" His hands shot up in surprise. "What has my daughter to do with you neglecting your work? Has she been bothering you? I know her coming and going in the vineyard. I do not recall her loitering. She brings the midday meals and returns to her duties at my home."

Mahlon swallowed the lump in his throat. "Sir, she bothers me much." He bent his eyes upward, meeting Paebel's. "No, not by loitering, but by being the delightful person she is."

Paebel's eyebrows bunched. He eyed the Hebrew up and down.

"I love Ruth." He smiled at nothing. "She is in my night-dreams and my day-dreams. My desire is to marry her."

He gasped. "Marry? A Hebrew joined to a Moabite?" His voice rose in pitch with every word. "Your father would never give his blessing." He squeezed his eyes shut and sought to control his emotions. With a quiet voice, he asked, "Have you approached Ruth with your intentions?"

"No, I have never mentioned it. I am speaking to you first. As for my father, I do not know his reaction and have no intention of bringing it up at this time. What—."

"Why not? Why do you delay?"

"If you give your blessing then I will tell him." He shifted nervous feet. "If you refuse, then why bother him *and* upset my mother. She will not like it in the least." His feet shifted again. Mahlon's eyes locked strong on Paebel. "Will you give us your blessing?"

Paebel's eyes returned the stare. "What gives you the idea I want my daughter joined to a Hebrew?" He gave a nervous laugh. "You should know, we do not force marriage upon our children. In our clan, a woman has a right to refuse a proposal. Ruth also worships Chemosh. Would you?" His mouth spread into a wide grin.

Mahlon's insides seized as though frozen. *Worship that loathsome god? Does he demand I forsake Yahweh?* "Chemosh is not my God," he began in a cautious tone. "I worship Yahweh."

"I know that!" Paebel snapped. "*We* worship more than one god. *Will you?*" He tapped Mahlon's chest.

Mahlon's jawed clenched. Paebel had a knack of frustrating everything. *Why this? Is it so hard for the man to accept the fact that Hebrews have only one God? Does he test me? Yes, he must be testing me as he did with day seven work. Father considered it crucial to work the seventh day. He taught me it was necessary at times to set aside the letter of the Law for the benefit of others.*

"What is your answer?" He stood with folded arms. "Will you worship Moab's gods or not? Understand this Mahlon, we do not ask you to give up the Hebrew God. Is it not best to have several gods to shower blessings upon your family?" Finally, a smile spread across Paebel's face.

Mahlon deemed the smile very unusual for the man. It caught him off guard. It appeared forced, not natural on a face usually reserved for stern looks.

"I-I have not considered, uh, it has not occurred to me that I could worship Moab's gods. I must think this out. If I agree to worship Chemosh, will you give your blessing?" Mahlon stood very still in expectation.

Paebel, a hard man when it involved his land, animals, and ruling his family, had no problem with a marriage between him and Ruth under his conditions.

Mahlon worked hard, completed the assigned work, and did not cause trouble. If Ruth wanted it, then he would consent and give his blessing if Mahlon agreed to worship Moab's gods and remain on Paebel's property. He did not want Ruth leaving with Mahlon for Israel. He had turned plenty of suitors down because they would have taken her away, and he told them as much. He wanted her residing on his land.

However, Paebel had another reason, a secret reason, which was the most important motive. Figat wanted Ruth to remain unmarried even more than Paebel, although both had conspired to keep Ruth at home. Now, Ruth had turned sixteen, and Paebel saw no reason to keep his daughter from marriage. What Figat wanted was not going to materialize.

"My blessing is yours if Ruth agrees to your proposal, if you accept Ruth's gods, *and* if you remain on my property. Meet my demands and I shall give you a site to build a house."

Mahlon could not contain the joy in his heart. He danced and raised his hands to heaven, crying out, "Blessed be Yahweh, God of gods and Lord of lords."

Paebel's natural stern face returned. He eyed him, recognizing he would continue to worship Yahweh as his chief God. He had no problem with that as long as Mahlon accepted Ruth's gods and did not hinder her from worshiping them.

"We are spending too much time in idle conversation. I pay you to work," he cracked, "not day-dream or stand blessing your God. Do you want to be paid?"

"Yes, of course," he said in a high-pitched voice. "I will work past quitting time today to make up for my slothfulness."

Paebel gave him a pleased look, almost a smile. "It is well known that I am a good judge of character, and I am correct about you. I trust you will do as you say."

Later, Elimelech and Chilion paced back and forth at the front gate of the vineyard, impatiently waiting on Mahlon. Paebel met them instead.

"Go to your tent, Mahlon is remaining."

"Why?" asked Elimelech. "If work needs doing we shall stay and help."

Paebel shook his head. "It is *his* duties. He has been shirking and not working as he should. He promised to remain and finish his tasks."

"You should have told me." Elimelech's eyes shot fire. "I will not have it. I will severely reprimand him tonight."

Paebel quickly shook his head. "I have no use for idlers as you well know, but listen to his explanation before showing your anger. He is a man; do not treat him like a boy."

Elimelech's eyes narrowed. "Do you tell *me* how to discipline my son?"

"He is a man! His childhood is long past. How old is he?"

"Twenty-nine," Chilion spoke up. His father would not remember. "I am one year younger."

"As long as he is under my roof, he will do as I say."

"I believe the same," Paebel replied. "However, I want you to listen to him first!" Wishing to defend his future son-in-law, he hesitated, gathering the appropriate words. "I am not telling you how to discipline. I am telling you to listen. He has a satisfactory explanation. Will you do that?" Paebel grinned.

Suspicious of his grin, Elimelech did not reply. He waved a careless hand and walked on. The gesture told Paebel that Elimelech gave no weight to his advice.

Two hours passed, and Mahlon calculated that the time lost had been made up. At the washstand, he poured water into the clay basin and cleaned up. Then, removing his sandals he sat on a bench and washed his feet, a ritual normally done when home at his tent. Tonight though would be anything but normal.

Hurrying through the gate, Mahlon turned down a path that led to Ruth's house. He had never been there but was quite sure it would be easy to find. How could anyone miss a large home with a spacious courtyard?

His heart raced. His breath quickened. His words failed. Why could he not remember the speech he had been rehearsing all day?

"I love you," he spoke aloud with no one to hear. "I want to be your husband." He shook his head. "No, that sounds strange."

He started over.

"I want you as my husband. No! I mean wife. Oh! That's too formal." He tried to focus his thoughts, straining to bring the words to mind. He had time. Ruth's house was not in sight.

"Let me try again. I love you, Ruth. I want you as my bride. It is meant to be. No, she knows who she is, so do I. Leave her name off. I love you. I want you as my bride. I will—." He cut himself off.

The courtyard gate loomed up before him. Suddenly his heartbeat pounded within his neck and drummed in his ears. His mouth dried to cotton. He trembled. Even if he could remember the words, he would never get them out.

Mahlon feared entering the courtyard, so he sat on the grass outside the gate. Loving Ruth had become an obsession. He had known plenty of Hebrew girls in Bethlehem. Most were wonderful young women; any man would be happy to have any of them as a wife but, he desired Ruth. More than his desire to breathe, he longed to hold Ruth in his arms.

A slight moan escaped his lips. Pained that she believed in the Moabite gods—he considered it her only flaw. She would make a perfect wife except for her disgusting gods. Nevertheless, he convinced himself that it would be no problem to teach her the error of trusting in vain idol worship. After all, with Ruth's intelligence, she would understand that Chemosh and the Baals were worthless gods.

However, Mahlon failed to understand the polytheistic religions of all the nations surrounding Israel. The Moabites, along with the Edomites, Ammonites, Canaanites, Egyptians, and many others had no requirement to proselytize, and they did not. If a man journeyed through a country or sojourned there, he would as a courtesy worship that nation's gods. He would not seek to convert those in that area to his gods nor would he be expected to give up his gods. He would certainly have his household idols with him and worship in private.

So, converting Ruth to Yahweh worship, and convincing her to give up her gods would be a formidable task, one that Mahlon did not expect. She would consent to worship Mahlon's God, but only as an additional deity. Giving up the national gods of Moab would be unthinkable to her or any Moabite.

While walking to her home, he finally decided that attending the worship services of these pagan gods would not be a problem since he would always worship Yahweh the true God. Chemosh and the Baals could never replace the Almighty.

So, performing the rites of Moabite worship to please Ruth and win her hand in marriage, even though it would be a pretense, he could do. He rationalized it would be acceptable to make Ruth his bride in trade for his worship of her gods. He vowed never to forsake Yahweh and by that his conscience would remain clear.

The sun fell behind the horizon, and the western sky glowed brilliantly rust-red. He must steel himself soon and go to the door and ask for Ruth. He would sit with her alone in the courtyard, talk of his deep love for her, and finally ask her. It had seemed so simple, so easy when planning it, but now his nerves held him tight in the grip of anxiety. His stomach churned, his neck burned from the heat of apprehension, and sweat ran down that scorched neck, onto his back and soaked his tunic.

Mahlon had not spoken freely with Ruth since he met her at the gates of Ar, and that escapade had a miserable ending. Elimelech never showed concern over him seeing Ruth. His alarm involved Mahlon doing it on the Sabbath.

Naomi went further, telling him to avoid her. What she feared remained the same as before they departed Judah—her sons would marry Moabites.

After Mahlon had remembered that confrontation, he reclined on an elbow. Surely with Ruth's apparent concern for his family and her amiable attitude, she would have no problem agreeing to become his wife. He pulled a wildflower, plucked its petals, held them up, and dropped them into the evening breeze. They gently fluttered away. "So lithe, elegant, Ruth is like petals on a gentle breeze. I love—."

"Mahlon?"

He jumped to his feet. "Ruth! I, I...."

"Why are you here? You spoke my name."

"Ruth, you startled me. I have been sitting here for a short time waiting to speak with you."

"I have been at the brook. Lying in the grass is what I do, also." She laughed. "Were you talking to yourself—about me?"

He gazed into her dark, exquisite eyes. His desire for her inflamed him. He wanted her more than any man could ever want a woman, and she manifested womanhood in every way.

Having turned sixteen, Ruth's time for marriage had more than arrived. Many girls, Hebrew or Moabite, married at fourteen, and some younger.

"I had a brief speech but, I cannot recall it." He gave a nervous chuckle. "I must speak to you. I, you, uh, sometimes it is, my words do not come...." He glanced away.

Ruth reached out and touched his arm. A sensation words could not express shot through him. He sucked in a hot breath, holding it, afraid to breathe.

"Slow down," she said smiling. "Why have you come?"

A question to answer, yes he could do that. She had made it simple. Ruth had a way about her, knowing others' feelings and needs. She had taken the initiative to visit Naomi, realizing the hurt that she and her family must have suffered brought on by Paebel. Now she understood Mahlon and his anxiety.

He quietly exhaled. "Ruth, I love you." He placed his hand over hers as she continued to touch his arm. Without thinking, she pulled her hand back. He noticed. *I startled her.* "Forgive me, I did not mean to alarm you. I would never knowingly do anything to frighten you."

Ruth stared. She could not recall anyone ever saying they loved her. For a moment, she tried to think of a time when her parents might have said so, but she drew a blank. This man claimed to love her, and she had never entertained the idea of loving him—a Hebrew. How could she love a foreigner? They had nothing in common. Nevertheless, Mahlon was handsome, gentle in manner, and honest. His presence drew her to him.

"I love you. You are on my mind constantly. My night-dreams and daydreams are about you. I wish…." His words trailed off into silence. He looked away, afraid to see her reaction to such bold words.

A few moments before he could not speak; now *her* presence had such power over him that it unbridled his tongue. He wanted to chuckle, but she would misunderstand. He held back.

Now Ruth found the words difficult. "Why?" Her confused, naive, eyes peered up at him. Figat had so sheltered her that she was unaware of the men who had approached her parents with offers of marriage.

Paebel enjoyed the encounters with men who wanted to take his daughter as wife. It pleased him that they found Ruth desirable. But, he and Figat wanted something else, so they refused all marriage proposals.

Figat, who wanted her daughter to think and act like her, had driven a wedge between mother and daughter. Ruth sensed it and had for months. She recognized the growing separation that day when Donatiya died in the fire. Figat believed it a privilege. It repulsed Ruth. Their religion had begun to cause much tension.

"Why do you say this? I am confused."

"You are the most considerate, attentive and selfless girl I have ever known. Your gentle way draws me. You do not realize your nature, and that makes you attractive to others and especially me. It is who you are. I think it impossible for you to be anything less."

"Thank you, Mahlon. I am, uh, I do not know what to say. I am *me*." She chuckled. "That sounded silly."

"I want to marry you," he blurted.

Ruth's eyes grew to what seemed impossible, giant ovals. "Marry me?" Her voice elevated in tone. "I am a Moabite. You cannot marry a Moabite, and neither can I marry a Hebrew."

Mahlon's face dropped. His eyes fell. Her words pierced him like a sword through his heart. He stumbled back and then sat down hard. A hurt flooded through him like a swollen river filled with deadly debris. His insides were being battered, and his face told of a slow death consuming him.

"I hurt you!" Ruth fell to her knees. "I am sorry. The suggestion so surprised me that proper words failed me. I would never intentionally hurt you. I think marriage for us—well; I have never considered a marriage between a Hebrew and Moabite."

Mahlon's eyes reached out to hers. A glimmer of hope, so very faint, sparked in Ruth's compassionate eyes. She cared for him, and it was plain enough.

Nothing was impossible with his God's help. So, with his eyes still glued to Ruth's gentle face, he prayed. *My Lord Yahweh, I beg you to make it possible for me to marry Ruth. I call upon your power as God of heaven and earth.* He bowed his head for a moment. Then, raising his head, gave her a wide smile.

"Do you find what I said amusing?"

"A few moments ago I apologized because I did not want to frighten you. Now you apologize because you did not want to hurt me." He chuckled. "This is good, splendid." He clapped his hands. "Being from different countries will not keep us from loving each other, certainly not for me. Ruth, I-love-you!"

The attraction to her Israelite friend had developed slowly. She always enjoyed being close to him. In fact, she loved it. However, Ruth wanted to discuss the Hebrew God, but only seeing him briefly at the midday meal did not allow time for discussions. Now—if he took her as his wife—there would be plenty of time to learn of Yahweh.

This offer of marriage had hit her without warning. She considered their relationship to be as friends, although she, being quite perceptive, understood Mahlon wanted their friendly meetings each day to grow into something more. But, that always seemed impossible.

"You want me for a wife? I know nothing about being a wife."

Mahlon laughed loud. "Do you not have a mother? Have you not seen her each day as she carries out her duties in the home? Do you not see her respecting your father and loving her children? Imitate her."

Ruth's frown told him that his words did not encourage her. "Did I say something with which you do not agree? Your expression puzzles me."

She shook her head. Tears formed, teetering on the rims of her sad eyes.

"Ruth, you will never fail as a wife and mother. It is not in you to be less than the finest."

She rose from her knees and with head down walked away a few steps. Mahlon followed.

"Would you be my wife if your father consented with his blessing?"

She turned to face him, and her troubled eyes lifted to meet his. "Yes." Ruth's face brightened with the answer. Though her eyes glistened with the tears, she hastily brushed them away with a knuckle.

To describe his ecstasy at that moment, Mahlon did not have the proper words. A sudden rush of warm heat engulfed him. He lifted his eyes to heaven. "Thank you, my Lord."

Moving close to Ruth, he reached for her hand. She offered it. "Earlier today I spoke with your father. Told him I wanted to take you for my wife."

Ruth's eyes, bright and wondering, opened wide.

"He will give his blessing if I agree to worship your gods and not interfere with your religion."

"Oh, Mahlon. How did you answer? Did you agree? I know Hebrews worship only one God."

He stared into her eyes, trying to recall his words to Paebel. "I did not give him a direct answer. I thanked my God and danced."

"Danced!" she laughed.

"I wanted to hear your words first. If you said yes to my proposal, then I would certainly agree to worship your gods, and tomorrow will tell him so. However, Yahweh is my chief God as Chemosh is yours. Do you agree?"

"Yes."

Chapter 9

Evening crept through the trees bringing forth the night sounds. Mahlon emerged from the woods, crossed the meadow, and approached the fire. He took a place on the goatskin next to Chilion.

Mahlon had no memory of the walk home. Memories of his conversation with Ruth had consumed every moment. His mind remained in the clouds as he gazed into the fire.

Elimelech and Naomi sat crossed legged on a separate skin waiting patiently for an explanation of his late arrival. When the silence continued Naomi spoke first.

"Did you lose your way coming home?" Naomi chuckled. "It is well past mealtime. I have left the pot for you to dip your bread."

He never moved or acknowledged the question, but gazed into the flames while a wide grin slashed his face.

"Son!" Elimelech's nostrils flared.

Mahlon's head jerked about, and he found his father's intense eyes boring into his.

"Your mother spoke to you, and you ignored her. What is the trouble? Paebel reports that you have been shirking your duties. Now you ignore your mother's words. What has happened to our son that he now acts with such irresponsibility?"

"I am sorry, mother. Ruth has me distracted."

Naomi flashed a quick look at Elimelech. "Ruth? Is she ill?"

"No."

"Injured?"

"No." He looked away into the dark meadow.

Raising her eyebrows, Naomi let out a loud breath. She leaned forward to get his attention. "Mahlon—look at me!"

He turned his head.

"Tell us about Ruth. No more one-word answers. What is this distraction you speak about?"

He drew in a long breath. "She has agreed to marry me."

Naomi screamed as though hit by lightning. "Marry?" Her face tightened, and eyes narrowed. Clutching her heart, she asked through trembling lips, "What have you done?"

"Done? What do you ask? What do you mean?"

"She is a Moabitess."

"Yes, and I am an Israelite. I also love her."

"Son, it is more than marrying for the love of a woman," Elimelech said. "You have nothing in common. She worships heathen gods, filth gods."

"I forbid you to marry her," Naomi rushed the words out. "Israelites are forbidden to marry Moabites."

Chilion looked to his father. "Is *that* so?"

The old man did not answer. It did not matter. Mahlon knew the answer when Chilion asked the question.

"We are not forbidden to marry Moabites," Mahlon spoke up. "It is the Canaanites our God forbids us to marry."

Naomi looked from the corners of her eyes. She awaited her husband's answer.

"Father," Mahlon said softly, "You have never forbidden me to marry a Moabite. You know I am right."

After a few more silent moments, Elimelech spoke, and Naomi found his words detestable, enough to sicken her.

"It is as Mahlon said. In the Law, we are commanded to abstain from taking Canaanite wives."

"No!" cried Naomi. With clenched fists, she pounded her knees. "No!"

"It is so, woman. I know the words from the scroll of Deuteronomy and, it confirms what I say. There are seven peoples mentioned. The Moabites are not among them."

Chilion peeked over at Mahlon. They grinned at each other. Chilion also wanted a Moabite wife. He had met Orpah, and they were quite fond of each other.

Elimelech, quoting scripture in a solemn voice said, "When Yahweh your God brings you into the land, and delivers the Hittites, Girgashites, Amorites, Perizzites, Jebusites, Hivites, and the Canaanites to you, conquer them and utterly destroy them. Make no covenant with them nor marry them." He turned to Naomi. "No mention of the Moabites."

Her faced twitched. "The Moabites worship other gods like those nations do," she replied in a scorn-laced tone. "The command is to keep God's people from going after strange gods, and the Moabites worship strange, morally perverted gods. I will not have my sons joined to a family of idol worshipers."

Mahlon kept his eyes down. Seeing his mother's pain-racked face would break his heart. If she only understood Ruth as he did, she would grow to love her, also. It would be a process, a painful process, but she would come around. He did not doubt it.

"Silence! You do not have any part in this decision. I am the head of this family, and my judgment is that Mahlon is not breaking any commandment of our God."

She jumped to her feet and rushed away disappearing into her tent. The sobbing from his mother brought tears to Mahlon's eyes.

If it were not for his great love for Ruth, he would honor his mother's request, and not marry her. He understood his mother's anguish, and that she might turn her back on Ruth; however, over time Ruth's sweet nature would thaw his mother's heart.

Naomi deserved a happy, peaceful life. Regrettably, the situation could not be resolved without hurt for someone. Having Ruth, and the great happiness that would come with a marriage to her meant more to him than the passing pain that Naomi would endure until she accepted a Moabitess as a daughter-in-law. Once that happened, he concluded, his mother's pleasant disposition would return, and happiness would be assured.

"You have worried me," Figat pressed her lips together. "I was about to send your brother to look for you." With a wave of a hand, she dismissed her son.

Ruth pointed to a bench in the courtyard.

"I have news for you. Father knows and now you shall."

"You father has withheld something from me?" Figat frowned. "He knows to tell me everything!"

"Not this, not until it happened," Ruth said beaming her dazzling smile.

"What do you go on about? Say it!"

"Mahlon has asked me to be his wife. I said—."

"That Hebrew laborer?" Figat looked at her through mean, little eyes. "No!"

Ruth's face sagged. Telling her mother should be a happy occasion. Figat had no qualms about ruining it.

"Mahlon is a good man." Her chin trembled. "He loves me."

Figat rolled her eyes. The ever-present sour look that seemed always screwed onto her face tightened a bit. When young, her comeliness would have rivaled Ruth's, and still hinted at it. Regrettably, this older Moabitess' good looks had withered like grass with no roots, and she had brought it on herself.

"I will not hear of such foolishness."

Hatred burned deep within her mother's hard eyes. Pleasing her had always been a chore, and Ruth, though constantly seeking approval from her mother, rarely received it.

"I agreed to marry him. He—."

"Can you not understand?" she exploded. "He is a Hebrew! He worships one God; a pathetic, impotent God, which cannot even send rain on their land. His God is weak."

"Mahlon has agreed to—."

"I have hopes," Figat cut her off. Rushing on, she ignored Ruth. "When I turned sixteen the temple priest called for me. My parents recognized my beauty years before and held off all those men seeking to marry me. They held it as a high honor to serve as a priestess for the fertility rites."

Ruth drew a quick breath. "Mother! You have never told me this."

"I had in mind to tell you at the proper time, which I believed, and still do, would be when the priest calls for you."

A cold, no good feeling raced down Ruth's spine. As if a dense fog lifted it all became clear. She remained unmarried, not because of some flaw in her, but men had been turned away by her mother, and her father allowed it. Now, it appeared he had had enough. The priest had not called for her, and Paebel feared his daughter would be humiliated by remaining unmarried.

Ruth wet her lips and held up a hand—palm out. "Please, no more. I have no desire to be a priestess."

Figat reached out to grab her daughter's hand, but Ruth jerked it back to her chest. "How dare you speak in such a manner? It is a privilege. The fertility rites please Chemosh, and he sends rain to our fields. By giving of yourself, you bless all of Moab."

Ruth's eyes narrowed. She did not wish to fight with her mother, and continually sought to please the woman.

"You claim it is a privilege." She struggled to control her anger, pinching her lips together until they turned white. "I remember the same words about Donatiya. She had been privileged to pass through the fire."

"Yes! *And* a great honor it was. Look about, Chemosh continues to send rain and sunlight, sacred blessings to make our crops flourish."

Ruth's jaw clenched. She would never rebuke her mother. Chemosh obviously had the power to bless. However, child sacrifice and sex with the priest, she did not like. There must be a better way to please the gods.

Ruth steeled herself. Her mother would explode with fury at her next words. Nevertheless, she had it to do.

"I will not allow the priest to take my virginity. Mahlon wants me as his wife. I will go to his bed."

"No!" she pounded a fist into her palm. "This refusal to take your turn with the priest is blasphemous. I have wanted this. You were to be like your mother." Figat stared into the shadows. How had it come to this? She had raised a rebellious daughter.

Ruth smiled, relishing her next words. "Once the priest hears that I am betrothed, he will never call for me." She hesitated, awaiting a retort. Her mother refused to look at Ruth and kept quiet.

"Father has agreed to give his blessing *if* Mahlon agrees to worship our gods in addition to his God. Within this last hour, he agreed to that request."

Figat did not respond. Her dark, ugly eyes remained fixed on the shadows.

The sharp, high-pitched scream, was followed by a grating, nerve wracking death wail. Mahlon and Chilion sat straight up.

That pitiful, shrill, soul-tearing sound meant only one thing—the death angel had made an appearance and collected his intended.

Rushing from the tent, they witnessed their worst fear unfold: Naomi on her knees bent over Elimelech. Lying face-down, near the morning fire, he still clutched a chunk of firewood.

Rolling him over, the men observed a vacant, ashen face and sightless eyes. Mahlon dropped to his knees, and with an ear to his father's chest, he strained to hear a heartbeat. Nothing but silence confirmed his death.

Eyeing his mother and then his brother, he shook his head. Naomi collapsed across her husband, weeping uncontrollably. Chilion buried his face in his hands.

Mahlon, with tears streaking his cheeks and wetting his beard, remained at his mother's side. Placing a hand on her back so she would know he cared, he stared at the rising sun framed by streaks of brilliant yellow across the eastern sky.

A new day, dawning with the fresh hope that each day brings, drew a stunning contrast to his father's lifeless body. All appeared dark. He tried to think. *What now? I am in charge. I should be doing something.*

He caught movement from the corner of his eye, which quickly focused his mind on the moment. *Ruth!*

She held a rope and led a donkey. Her lovely smile, perpetu-ally affixed to that radiant face, had given way to a bleak frown of hopelessness.

She stopped several feet away. "I was on my way to the city for supplies when I heard a scream. Your father—is he?"

Mahlon nodded. He could not force the word out.

"Dead!" Chilion screamed the word.

Ruth looked over to see the younger brother's contorted face. Embarrassed at his outburst, he jumped to his feet and ran. Wishing to help, she took tentative steps toward Mahlon. He tenderly patted his mother's back as she wept. Ruth kneeled beside him placing a comforting hand on his back.

"What—do?" Mahlon wheezed the words. "What now— I?" His chronic condition had elevated to a full-blown attack of wheezing. In early spring, he wheezed, and when under stress the wheeze would plague him, also. Now it had come upon him with a vengeance.

He constantly struggled to inhale and never fully exhaled, which kept his rib cage partially expanded. This condition gave him chronically overinflated lungs and a barrel-shaped chest. Mahlon was short of breath almost constantly. Now his chest heaved, and drawing a breath had become a struggle.

Ruth's neck hair stood up, and sweat rolled down her back. Glancing blindly around, she searched for something, anything to help. With no idea of what to do for him, her mind raced for answers. Her hands shook, yet she slowly forced her hands to grasp his cold, clammy fists.

"What can I do to help?" she whispered.

"In the—tent. My scrip."

Ruth raced to the tent and found three bags. Grabbing all three, she rushed to his side. "I know not which is yours."

Reaching out, he grasped the one needed. "Inside—a pouch. Get…"

Ruth removed the smaller bag.

"Take—take a—handful of—of herbs."

Ruth reached inside grasping the concoction.

"Drop it in," he forced the final words, pointing at the fire.

Ruth stood, edged near the fire and sprinkled the green leaves onto the glowing coals.

"Help me." Mahlon reached out.

Ruth got him to his feet, and with unsteady steps moved close to the fire. Leaning over, hands on knees, he inhaled the vapors of the burning herbs.

As long as the smoke lifted from the campfire, Mahlon inhaled deeply. Naomi, weak from weeping had long since quieted but remained draped over Elimelech's body, unaware of Mahlon's distress.

Finally, the wheezing calmed. Straightening his shoulders, he bent backward to ease the tightness in his back.

"I feared for you," Ruth said. "Does that often happen?"

Mahlon shook his head. Speaking took too much effort. He motioned at Naomi. Ruth nodded. The sight of her prostrate over her dead husband caused a terrible hurt to pass through Ruth. Her gentle, loving nature took over, and she kneeled next to the grieving woman.

"Mother, please allow my family to be of service at this time." Stroking Naomi's cheek, she brushed away several remnants of tears. "Recently, we prepared one of our kinsmen. We understand the task and will relieve you of the duty."

Naomi could not bear to release her beloved husband from her embrace. With eyes closed, she said, "You called me 'Mother.' I do not have a daughter."

"I am Ruth. Soon I will be part of your family." She patted Naomi's shoulder. "May I call you Mother now?"

After a few moments, Naomi relaxed. She sat up and looked. Ruth's soft, compassionate eyes reached out to this new widow.

"Yes, call me Mother. Yahweh has never blessed me with a daughter." She offered a quivering hand, and Ruth quickly took it.

Naomi's tired eyes drifted over to glimpse Elimelech's face. "Oh! His eyes!" Leaning, weeping upon his chest, she had not noticed his eyes remained open in death.

Ruth got to her feet and searched the area. Finding two flat oval-shaped pebbles, she gently closed each eyelid and placed the weights on each.

In a whisper, she said, "This will help."

"Thank you," Naomi whispered back.

Preparing Elimelech for burial began within the hour. Ruth's brothers brought the body on an oxcart to Paebel's home and placed it on a table in the courtyard.

Figat, though opposed to Ruth marrying Mahlon, took the responsibility of organizing burial preparations. This act of kindness spared Naomi the agonizing burden. Figat also dismissed Ruth from the chore since she would soon be a member of their family and viewing the body would be awkward.

Soon, women, friends of Figat's family, gathered and completed the ritual of washing the body. After the cleansing, they covered the face with a white cloth and wrapped the body in a white shroud.

Not long after, the men returned from digging the grave. They placed the body on a bier that had a pole at each corner and professional mourners, hired by Paebel, began wailing.

Figat called for Ruth and instructed her to notify Naomi and family that the time had arrived for the funeral procession.

Before Ruth left to deliver the news, she spoke to her mother. "I know you do not want me to marry into this family." She touched the bier. "Thank you for putting that aside for now."

"What I have done today is because your father ordered me to do it. This event is of small concern to me. Now, go on and tell *your* family to come."

Ruth, well aware of how hard Figat could be, found the hurtful words too harsh, even for her stone-hearted mother. Silently Ruth turned and hurried down the path toward Naomi's tent.

Since Elimelech did not own property and had not resided in Moab long enough to prepare a tomb for the family, he would be taken to a public graveyard for burial.

When Naomi and her sons arrived, they joined in the loud wailing. The men raised the bier to their shoulders, and the procession began. Naomi, with Mahlon and Chilion on each side supporting her, followed close behind. Ruth took a place back of them. The professional mourners, with their shrill, ear-piercing shrieks, led the way. All the other mourners, which were few, brought up the end of the procession.

At the grave, the men slowly lowered the body into the ground. The loud wailing continued as Mahlon offered a prayer of blessing for the soul of his father. At the conclusion, Elimelech's sons took shovels and closed the grave.

Leaving the graveyard, Naomi held to Chilion and Ruth walked with Mahlon clutching his arm. They soon passed the hurrying brook not far from the secret spot where Ruth enjoyed sinking into the lush grass and fragrant wildflowers.

"I love this place," she whispered to Mahlon.

He smiled. "I love anyplace where you are. Thank you for the kindness shown to my mother."

Ruth touched her chest. "My heart is breaking. Your mother's grief wounds me like nothing I have ever experienced."

At Paebel's home food had been prepared for the mourners. It was customary to fast all day and eat after the burial. Naomi refused to eat, but took a cup of wine.

"Mother, you should eat, or you will become weak," Mahlon said. "Please, take this bread." He held it out.

Naomi lifted her vacant eyes to meet his. "Should I eat when my husband lies in the ground? Should I even drink this?" She held up the cup.

"Mother, father wishes you to eat and drink. You must go on with life," Chilion said. "It is good to mourn, but you must also eat and drink."

"Will I ever stop mourning?" she bitterly spat out the words. "Our God withholds rain from Judah and famine spreads. Now he punishes by taking my husband, and we suffer more."

Mahlon eyed Ruth. She gently shook her head, powerless to convey any meaningful words of comfort.

"Father died because he had grown old. It is not punishment," said Mahlon. "It is the natural course of things."

Naomi's face turned hard and bitter. She lifted a weary eyebrow. "Your father had not grown old! His health remained within him when we worked our land. Our land—in Judah. Oh! My sons, my sons! Why did he not listen? I begged him not to journey here. Moab is not our land or our people. The Almighty took him because of his disobedience.

"He forsook the Promised Land, forsook the seventh-day rest and worked, and then he gave his blessing…." Naomi's eyes went to Ruth. The unspoken words were unmistakable.

The suffering and intense grief of losing Elimelech had temporarily blotted from her memory the sweet exchange of words between her and Ruth only hours before. "Yes, call me Mother. Yahweh has never blessed me with a daughter."

Chapter 10

"Clear the drain hole."

Chilion, with a short rod in hand, leaned over the low wall of the upper wine press pit and inserted the instrument into the drain. As Mahlon watched from below, his brother pushed a clog of grape skins out of the short channel, thus allowing the juice to flow into the pit below.

Early autumn meant the end of the grape harvest and Paebel had his winepress in full operation. Mahlon's family sang and chanted as they stomped the grapes. This second harvest since they had arrived in Moab, had the family in good spirits, and wishing to forget the first harvest that came at the time of Elimelech's death.

One year had brought about several changes. Mahlon and Ruth had married before the harvest began. Chilion and Orpah would soon marry, also. Naomi out of her mourning clothes only recently treaded the grapes with the others.

Within a few days, after all of the juice had been bottled, and the press cleaned, Chilion and Naomi would learn a new trade—tent making. Orpah's father made tents and had agreed to expand his business by taking them on as workers.

Naomi longed for Judah and frequently asked Mahlon if he had heard any news from across the Salt Sea that the famine had ceased. The answer remained the same month after month.

Secretly, Mahlon rejoiced that the report continued the same for he had promised Paebel he would not take Ruth to Israel. As long as the famine continued, he would never have to tell Naomi he had no intention of leaving. Besides, he wanted to stay. Moab had become his home.

With the passing of his father, the mantle of family patriarch had passed to him. He made the major decisions for the family, and all looked to him as head of the clan and protector.

Naomi, being a woman, had no authority to make a decision to return home. While Elimelech lived, she belonged to her husband. Now, with Mahlon as head of the family, she belonged to her eldest son.

Belonging did not mean her son owned her as a slave. However, in Hebrew culture, women always belonged to a man, whether as a wife, daughter, mother or sister. Mahlon, as the family patriarch, provided for Naomi and kept her safe, which meant she belonged to Mahlon.

He understood that she longed for Judah, and at the first word of rains returning to their homeland, she would be packing for home. Mahlon wanted that moment delayed as long as possible. Telling her he had no intention of leaving Moab would not be easy. She would be heartbroken.

Watching his mother treading the grapes, Chilion noticed her slowing considerably. "Let us stop for a bit. We all grow weary."

His words caused a big smile to cross Orpah's face. She had seen Naomi's weariness, also. All of the workers took a seat on the wall of the upper pit with their feet still in the grapes. Mahlon, who worked the lower pit by filling skins with juice, joined them and took a spot next to Ruth. His feet and legs draped over the outside wall. A boy, ten years old, hurried up the incline with pitchers of water filled from a large water pot brought to the wine press on an oxcart.

Ruth lightly clasped Naomi's arm. "Which variety of grape do you prefer?"

Naomi glanced over with mischievous eyes. "I like—grapes the best."

Everyone laughed. The widow, after a year of mourning, had returned to her pleasant disposition. The relationship between Naomi and Ruth grew closer each day, also. Ruth constantly saw to her mother-in-law's needs, which served to tighten the bond between them. Since Elimelech's death, Figat had never visited Naomi or asked about her welfare. Ruth noticed the indifference but said nothing. Her mother was content to remain home, sulking over a lost daughter. Each day, Ruth grew closer to the pleasant mother-in-law and drifted farther from the sour mother.

Happy to see her mother-in-law in good spirits, Ruth continued the questioning. "Which do you like best: the fresh grapes to eat, the wine to drink, or the grape syrup?"

Naomi took a deep breath, and with closed eyes, she exhaled slowly. "Does that give a hint?" she asked, her eyes remained shut.

Mahlon looked at Chilion. He shrugged.

Ruth and Orpah laughed. "We know," said Orpah, cracking a sly grin. "The men are unthinking when it comes to these things."

"What things?" asked Chilion.

"Reading a woman's words and expressions."

Mahlon tugged on an ear considering her words.

Ruth rolled her eyes. "Mother likes the grape syrup."

Chilion's eyes darted to his mother.

"She is right—about both things." Naomi chuckled. "I love the grape syrup *and* at times my sons *are* unthinking."

Ruth and Orpah laughed loud and long.

"Tell us," Chilion demanded.

"Did you not see me breathe deep, and I am sure I had a pleasant expression on my face."

The men gave her blank stares.

"What is that aroma? Breathe! My sons."

They took deep breaths. The sweet perfume of boiling grape juice filled their senses.

A fire burned nearby, and a woman, one of Paebel's laborers, bent over a pot that hung above the hot coals. She stirred the contents of the container with a long-handled wooden paddle.

Mahlon peeked over at Ruth. "Grape syrup!"

Fresh grape juice, which Mahlon had poured into an enormous caldron hours before, now gently boiled, giving off a honeyed fragrance that permeated the vineyard. The intensely sweet syrup soon would take on the appearance and consistency of purple honey. By mealtime, it would be ready to enjoy, and Naomi looked forward to dipping her bread in the still warm sweetness.

After the midday meal, the women moved on to the area of the vineyard which produced the raisins. Mahlon and Chilion remained at the wine press. They finished the daily pressing.

The workers had extracted most of the juice from the grapes by trampling them in the pit, however not all. The brothers, along with others sacked up the grape remnants for further squeezing.

The men lifted a large stone and set it on top of several bags. Then, placing on top of the rock a wooden beam that had iron weights attached to it, they pressed the remaining juice from the grapes. This juice they collected for use as vinegar.

"Do you think we hurt their feelings," asked Ruth.

In a deadpan, mocking voice, Orpah said, "Men are different from women."

Ruth glanced over with curious eyes.

"If they have feelings," she chuckled, "they hide them."

"My sons do have emotions, feelings as you say, but Orpah is correct. They try to hide them so we will not know."

"Mother, you push the cart. Orpah and I will do the oiling."

The grapes had been laid out in straight rows at a far, sunny corner of the vineyard. Ample space between the rows expedited moving a handcart from one end to the other. The drying process, which had started many days before, slowly transformed the grapes into raisins.

Ruth and Orpah began sprinkling olive oil on the fruit, which kept the skins moist. Naomi followed close behind with a handcart loaded with jugs of oil. Without the oil, the hot sun would bake the raisins to the consistency of dry leather.

At sunset, the men came for them.

"The grapes are done?" Ruth asked in a questioning tone.

"All done," said Mahlon. "Now we can help with the raisins unless you prefer to keep them to yourself." He grinned. "We will understand if you do."

"My son, do not attempt to escape work by such devious means." Naomi shook a finger. "We are on to you."

"We are simply offering." He laughed. "At times women want to be left alone, so we are willing to stay out of the way."

"Tomorrow, we shall share the work. You men can work two rows and Orpah and I will work two others. Mother can move the cart. When the jars are empty, you may take the cart and have them refilled while your mother rests. That is fair."

"Who says it is fair?" Mahlon asked.

Ruth glanced about at each face and then said, "I do."

The women smirked. The men frowned but were wise enough to remain quiet. Ruth had worked the vineyard since before she could remember, and her father owned it. They did not argue.

"Mahlon!"

"Uhh."

"Mahlon! Mahlon, my son. We need you."

"Mother!" He sprung to his feet. "What is it? Come in."

Naomi pulled the tent flap back. Ruth sat up.

"Your brother writhes in pain! He is curled up, unable to sit. He has a raging fever and terrible pains in his stomach."

Mahlon's chest seized. He fought it. Anxiety and fear would bring on the wheeze. He breathed deep, frantically seeking to calm himself.

Chilion and Mahlon, 'always the sickly ones.' From their childhood, these words had been repeated countless times by many people. The men had long ago given up hope that God would make either of them healthy.

"Husband," Ruth cried out, grabbing his arm. "We must do something."

"Bring water and a cloth."

Ruth hurried to the water skin.

Mahlon and Naomi entered Chilion's tent. The sight wrenched them. Hollow-eyed, his eyes shiny with fever, Chilion suffered from a dull, pounding ache in his head. He shook from the chills, yet his forehead burned with heat. He had covered himself with several garments.

Ruth entered, dropped to her knees and began placing damp cloths on his forehead and face.

"I shall do that," Naomi said. "It is my duty."

"Mother, allow me to help," Ruth said.

"No, he is my son. I will care for him."

Ruth's eyes went to Mahlon. He shook his head and beckoned her to come with him.

Outside, Mahlon said, "Ever since a babe in arms, he has been sickly. This is not the first time he has shaken so violently. I fear for him. Each episode takes a longer time to recover than the previous one."

"I will pray to my gods for him," said Ruth. Her soft, warm eyes reaffirmed Mahlon's love for her meek and gentle spirit.

His eyes watered. He nodded. "I shall do the same," he said, his voice cracking. "My prayer will go up to Yahweh."

"There is a sorcerer across that meadow, and another man, a healer." She waved a calm hand toward the lush green field dotted with wildflowers. "I will go and ask them to come."

Mahlon's insides withered at the mention of a sorcerer. In the scrolls of the Law, God had condemned sorcery.

There shall not be found among you
anyone who makes his son or his daughter
pass through the fire, or one who practices
witchcraft, or a soothsayer, or one
who interprets omens, or a sorcerer....

"A sorcerer?" He finally spit out the word.

"Chilion must have this curse driven away."

Mahlon's forehead wrinkled. "This curse?"

"The sickly live under a curse. He must be cut for bleeding, have herbal treatments applied, and prayers offered. The sorcerer will diagnose Chilion's ailment, and the healer will concoct the potions to treat him. They will pray to the gods and offer certain incantations to bring about healing. While they do their work, we shall pray to our gods."

Mahlon's face grew hard. "I will pray to Yahweh, you pray to your gods."

Ruth placed her hands on her hips. "I go for the sorcerer and healer first," she insisted in a strong, yet not unpleasant, voice.

His new wife continually showed strength when needed. Always at times when he weakened, she stood strong. He could forbid her to go, and she would obey. However, she had stubbornly promoted these men as ones who could help, so why stand in the way.

Taking her hand, he kissed it. "Go, my wife, do as you believe best."

❧

Ruth had been gone less than an hour when she hurried up to the fire. "They prepare the herbs and will be here shortly."

Naomi, still at Chilion's side, and now in full control of her emotions, glanced up. "Who?" Her eyes searched Ruth's face.

"Two men, uh," Mahlon stuttered. "They—Ruth knows them. They bring healing herbs."

Naomi's eyes flashed suspicion. "Moabite healers?"

"Yes! Healers."

"We have *never* used a healer." She brought her arms tight to her body. "Yahweh is our healer. He will provide."

"Was it not Yahweh-Yireh who provided a ram for the sacrifice on Mount Moriah? Did not our God spare Isaac from death, and in that act of mercy, brought joy to Abraham instead of grief?"

"Mother," Ruth dropped to her knees and placed an arm around her mother-in-law. "Mahlon will pray to Yahweh, and I will pray to Chemosh and the Baals. While we do, the healer will apply his herbs and the sorcerer will recite his incantations over Chilion."

Naomi's eyes blazed with fury, and they landed on Mahlon. The heat from her scorn scorched his insides. "Do you *dare* bring a sorcerer into this camp? God forbids it! When illness or wounds come to Hebrews, we treat our own by praying to Yahweh for healing. Faithful Israelites never consult these healers, magicians, sorcerers or any other of like mind." She bowed her head sobbing. "Oh, Elimelech. My husband, my husband."

Naomi raised her head. "Your father would never welcome an evil enchanter, a necromancer among us." She buried her head in her hands. The tears flowed freely. "Oh, Elimelech, you left us much too soon. We need your wisdom."

Ruth, her arm still around Naomi, looked into Mahlon's hard eyes. He met her gaze with a blank look. He turned away.

For a few moments Mahlon stood with back to them, his hands clenched into fists. "Father is not here," he spoke softly. "I am head of this family now. I know it is difficult for you but, accept my decisions without complaint.

"Ruth has her gods, and her religion provides sorcerers and healers. They are holy men who work with herbs and other methods to bring about healing. She will also pray to her gods, and I will pray to Yahweh."

Naomi choked back a sob. "They are *not* holy! Only our Lord God can be called holy."

No one dared say another word and Mahlon walked away, never looking back. Ruth watched him go and before fading completely from sight, he dropped to his knees near a giant sycamore tree. Bending forward and placing his forehead on the ground, he began intercessions for his brother.

Two men approached, and Naomi got to her feet. She would not greet these men who were an abomination to her God nor remain to watch the vain oblations presented to their obscene pagan gods.

Inside her tent, she would not have to face them. No one would attempt entering the women's apartment of a tent without permission, including a holy man-sorcerer.

On her knees, she prayed fervently for Chilion. When the pleading stopped, she contemplated her situation and how her family had come to such a willful disregard for Yahweh's word.

Her boys, obedient as children, now ignored the direct commands of Yahweh. How had it happened? While in Judah, her husband and sons would never have entertained such ideas of working on the Sabbath, marrying foreign women, and asking help from a sorcerer.

"Lord God of heaven and earth, our Lord is one Lord. Hear my cry, Lord. Have mercy on me and my sons. We have sinned. We have forsaken our land for another. Forgive us.

"We dwell in a tent instead of our house. Plow another man's fields instead of our own. What is ours now, O God? A tiny flock, a tent, a few garments, and not much else. I want to return to my home. I never wanted this place. Please, Almighty God, grant me my petition. Allow me to go back to the Promised Land."

Naomi crumpled to the tent floor. A broken-hearted widow and mother, she clutched her heaving breast while endless sobs racked her body wetting the top of her tunic.

After the tears had milked her head dry, she fell to her side and lay catatonic, staring at a grain sack. The conversation from outside slowly seeped into her consciousness.

"Now that you have evaluated him have you a treatment?" Ruth asked the sorcerer.

"I do."

"Wonderful! He is so frail. Please, start now. We go to beseech our gods."

"Are you his brother?"

"I am Mahlon, and he is my younger brother. What do you give him? What is his problem? He has suffered for years. Can you help so he will not be plagued with this evil the rest of his life? His wedding feast is next week. He must be well."

The sorcerer's eyes strayed over to Ruth. It was not good. A lump grew in her throat. She tried to swallow, it caught, gagging her.

"The hand of the worm god is against him. We must appease Baal."

"Worm god?" Mahlon's eyes zeroed in on Ruth. "You have a *worm* god?"

Ruth froze. In a polytheistic religion, the gods were many. She did not know the answer. "I did not know. There are many gods."

Mahlon's eyes darted to the sorcerer. "Tell me plain. My brother has worms? Is that it?"

"Worms of the stomach, long worms that eat his food. Do you not see his emaciated condition? He is weak. Many Moabites called them stomach snakes."

Ruth looked at the healer. "What is the treatment?"

"I shall take a pomegranate root, soak it in water for a time, boil it for a time, and then strain the mixture. The patient will be given the extraction to drink. Within a short period, the magic contained in this concoction brings on palsy within the worms, which in turn causes them to surrender their grip on the patient's stomach. The paralyzed worms pass from the body by the end of the second day.

"On the third day we shall return and let a cup of blood from a leg. Bleeding will drain away any evil spirit that remains."

Mahlon rubbed his beard. "Why should I pray—or Ruth? You seem so sure of this treatment, is there a need for prayer?"

The healer glanced over to Ruth. "He is your husband?"

Ruth nodded.

"Not a Moabite, is he?"

Ruth shook her head. "An Israelite."

The healer slowly shook his head in disgust. "You need not pray. The prayers of Moabites will be sufficient. The prayers offered are not only for the bloodletting and herbal treatment to work on healing the body but also the deliverance from the curse."

"Curse!" Mahlon snorted. "What curse?"

"This man has sinned in some grievous way. The worm god has cursed him with these parasites. His god may have cursed him, too.

"Chilion is ill! It has *nothing* to do with a curse." Mahlon turned to walk away. "Work your magic." He flapped a dismissing hand at him. "I will pray to my God. He will give healing to my brother."

Chapter 11

Several days after Chilion's illness a golden shaft of light peeked over the city of Ar as he and Naomi passed through the gates. They hurried along the city streets weaving between the merchants' handcarts. Their jobs at the tentmaker shop would start today.

"You are prompt," said Keret, Orpah's father. His face quickly shadowed dark. "You must be if you want to remain employed in my shop."

"We wish to please," said Naomi. "So if you must be stern with the instruction, we are ready."

Keret had hard gray eyes, a gray beard with silver streaks, and temperament that had no give to it. He seldom smiled, and when he did a person could see right off it was a struggle.

"The instruction is exacting, and there will be no idle time. You are paid to work."

Chilion glanced about the shop. "Orpah? She is not here?"

"She works at home in the mornings. Only during the grape harvest does she help Ruth at the vineyard.

"Now that the vineyard work is done, Orpah usually arrives with the midday meal and remains the afternoon to help. From this day forward, she will not come."

Chilion frowned. *A day without seeing Orpah? What is this?*

Their eyes locked. "We have worked the grape harvest together. Why this?"

"I had no control over the grape harvest. Here, I own this shop and will say who works." He showed a tough face. "Our family's custom, and it is the custom of many Moabites, is to remain apart during your betrothal. During this time of betrothal, you are to be preparing for your wife a new tent or building a new room onto your house."

"It is done. I bought the tent from you, staked it out, furnished it, and now live in it awaiting my bride to share it. You know these things."

"I do."

"Next week we celebrate the wedding feast and consummate the marriage."

"That is next week. Today, you remain apart." He peered over at Naomi. Humor danced in his eyes. "Do you not have respect for customs?"

Chilion looked with eyes wide and a jaw that dropped almost to his chest. Naomi laughed, slapping her hands. "My son, you are outmatched. Now you must observe a custom, which is also a Hebrew custom." She turned to Keret, "Chilion ignores our customs, too."

Chilion wanted to argue but, backed down. He needed this employment, and so did his mother. He also did not want to be on strained terms with his future father-in-law.

"I shall wait," he said as though he had a choice.

"Follow me. We sell many things here, and you will recognize them all. When a customer enters, I will meet him and make a sale. After you have learned all there is to making tents and the other articles we sell, then you will be allowed to speak to the buyers.

"Since Orpah will not be here until after her marriage, I will be called away from you more than I would like. Of course, some of the things that we do I believe you are familiar. You have probably repaired your tent."

"We have a house in Bethlehem," Chilion said. "The only tent dwelling I have known has been sojourning in Moab."

"Sojourning? After two years do you still consider yourself a sojourner? Now that you marry my daughter, you will reside in Moab permanently."

Chilion glanced at his mother and a testy silence followed. Naomi, restless and irritable turned away, staring at the wall. An unexpected, sweeping loneliness came over her. The house in Bethlehem had begun to fade in her memory, and she struggled to recall it.

Chilion gave Keret a strained smile. "You are right. My father intended to sojourn, but now we have been here so long, it feels like home. I—."

"Not to me!" Naomi whirled around. "My home is Bethlehem. When the famine departs our land, we will go back as my husband intended when we left."

Keret shot Chilion a questioning glance.

"My brother, Mahlon, is now patriarch of the family. A young elder," he chuckled, "nonetheless, he is our leader." Chilion swallowed hard. He did not want to upset his mother by revealing Mahlon's resolve to remain in Moab. "Mahlon will make the decision if we are to return to Bethlehem."

Naomi flinched. "If?"

Chilion looked away unable to bear his mother's hurt. "The famine still ravages the land, so, for now, there is no plan to leave Ar."

Naomi managed a weak smile. "Any news of Judah and the drought? Surely travelers stop by this shop for supplies?"

Before he spoke, she noticed the hardness around his mouth. He had no time for this talk of Judah.

"It is infrequent but, wayfarers do stop for a needed item. Occasionally a man will speak of that area. It is always bad, though. The land remains brown!"

Naomi's eyes dropped. "Please, show us what to do today?"

His tone changed. Finally, these small matters would be put aside, and he could get back to business. "I shall tell you everything, although I am sure with many of our things in the shop you already know."

In the back room, he pointed out the workbenches and three-legged stools where they would sit to make the houses of hair. Suppliers wove on looms tufts of black goat hair and sold them to tentmakers. The tentmakers sewed together the strips of cloth into one large piece that formed the side or top of the tent.

Killing a goat to collect hair was not always necessary. When shedding their winter coats, tufts were attached to bushes or other objects where the animal had brushed up against it. The poor, who could not afford to part with a goat, collected the tufts and sold them to supplement their meager incomes.

Keret partially uncoiled a rope. "This line is made from goat's hair. We attach one end to the tent and the other to hardwood pegs that secure the tent in place."

Chilion examined it up close. "The rope we use is not this."

"If not goat hair," Keret said, "then probably hemp." He pulled a hemp rope from the top shelf. "Some people prefer this."

"Yes, that does look like what we have."

Keret ushered them from the back room into the area up front. "We have various items for sale up here. Mallets for driving the tent pegs," he picked one up, "and over here straw mats, goat hair mats and woolen rugs for the tent floor."

At another table he pointed. "These are goat hair bags, which as you know, can be used to store various items. We have an excellent supply of skins, too. They are to store different liquids: milk, water, oil, each to a separate skin."

Keret glanced over at Chilion. "I know that you and Naomi understand a person must always fill the skin with the same liquid. However, there are a few people not too smart. People fill a skin with milk that previously had oil in it." He rolled his eyes. "Yes, it *has* happened. You would think people would know better. Ha! We have some dumb Moabites living in this land."

Naomi laughed the loudest.

"How did the first day go?" Ruth asked.

Chilion finished chewing and drank from the water pitcher. "We learned a few things and started a tent."

He stuffed his mouth with bread.

"Short answer." Mahlon raised his eyebrows. "Did Orpah teach you or her father?"

Naomi eyed her son. He had grumbled about it all the way home. Now he had his older brother asking, and no way to escape the jesting that surely would come. Chilion shrugged his shoulders and tore a piece of bread.

Ruth looked at Mahlon with questioning eyes, and he would not let it go with a shrug from his brother. "What did that mean?

Chilion's lips flattened out, his jaw set. The men stared.

"What is it?" Ruth asked. "Did you argue with Orpah?"

"Keret taught us most of the time."

"So?" Mahlon's eyes bunched. "There is more to this." He glanced at Ruth and then his mother. "I know my brother quite well. Something has—."

"She taught me nothing! Now you know."

Mahlon, not one to let him off the hook so quickly, pressed him. "We now know she did not teach. So, who else was there? Keret taught most of the time, but who else. Orpah's mother? A brother? A near kinsman?"

"That is enough, brother!"

Mahlon looked over at Naomi. A tiny smile played on her lips giving him a hint. *This must not be anything serious, so it must be embarrassing for Chilion. Ha! He should have admitted it at first, now it will go hard with him.*

"Had an argument with your betrothed. You did not like her bossing you around. Maybe it will be what you will face after you consummate the marriage. Yes, she will probably be one of those quarrelsome women. It is said they are never satisfied. Now that may—."

"Son! You *have* said enough. It is nothing like that at all, and Chilion has only made this larger than it should be." She paused hoping Chilion would tell the story. He did not. "Keret commanded Orpah to remain at home. She is not to see or speak to him until the consummation and wedding feast."

Ruth stifled a laugh, but Mahlon had no intention of doing the same. After he had controlled his laughter, he said, "My brother, why have you made such a big event out of this? It must be their custom. So, abide by it without anger. If not, Keret will see the disdain in your face and actions. You will only place a strain on your relationship with the man."

Chilion lifted his eyes, meeting his brother's look. He nodded his agreement. "I know. I would not wish that nor putting Mother's job in jeopardy. Would he terminate our employment? He might. I do not know the man that well, so will not cause trouble."

"It is less than two weeks," Ruth said, "you can hold your anger and tongue for that short time. Then, you have a long life ahead with Orpah."

Mahlon remained at the fire long after the others had retired to the tents. He studied the dying coals as if to learn something from some unknown fire god. Although he goaded his brother earlier and laughed at his reaction of being kept away from Orpah,

Mahlon had a general depression settling over him, and he recognized it.

Keeping the pretense of a happy mood had grown onerous. A twinge of anger at being unable to control his circumstances went through him. The position of family patriarch meant responsibilities, including the happiness and well-being of all the family.

Chilion's health continued to deteriorate. His mother wanted to go home. Mahlon's chronic breathing problems remained. Now, the worst of all: Ruth had not given him a son.

Taking a long stick, he stirred the gray coals, and a small flame flickered to life. The sudden light should have brightened his outlook. It did not. Was not everything better in the light? He had been told that but trying to recall where only frustrated him. Moreover, it was a lie. Day or night, all remained the same—illness, unhappy mother, and no son.

He had first taken Ruth to his tent over a year ago. By this time, he should be holding his child. Since that first time, he had held Ruth in his arms countless times, kissing her, caressing her, planting his seed within her. He had done his part, yet God had shut up her womb.

A memory came to him. Paebel had promised to build him a house if he stayed in Moab. *Where is my house? I will go to my father-in-law tomorrow and demand he keep his promise. If he will not, then I shall threaten to leave and return home. I have no son, no house, nothing of value.*

Again the fire flickered low, giving scant light. He watched it die and had no desire to poke and blow life back into it. He kicked dirt on the coals. They smoked.

"My Lord, why me. Why do you withhold a son from me?" He whispered into the night. "Will my family name die out? You have blessed me with a gentle and caring wife. She is a blessing not only to me but my mother, also.

"Is it because she is a Moabitess? We have not broken any commandment with this marriage."

Mahlon regretted the words immediately. Did he presume to tell God anything concerning the commandments?

"Lord, forgive me. I do not want to instruct you regarding your commands. Oh, that I could say the right words, words that would move you to bless us. Give me those words and I will use them. I will repeat them until I have no strength remaining.

"Please Lord, open my dear Ruth's womb."

Getting to his feet, he kicked more dirt on the fire, turned and walked toward his tent.

"Mahlon." Her soft sweet voice stopped him.

"Ruth?" He peered into the moonless night toward the direction of her voice. "I cannot see you. Do you hide in the dark? Why are you not within the tent?"

Without a sound, she moved on cat feet and was at his side. He jumped.

"Ruth!" He exclaimed in a loud whisper. Pulling her close, he held her. "Do you wish my heart to stop?" He chuckled. "Where did you learn to move about like a spirit?"

"I practiced as a child. My brothers tormented me, and I had to fight back. I watched the house cats and the bigger ones—the panthers. They sometimes appear in the meadow." She laughed. "Did I frighten you?"

"I am thirty years old, but feel fifty. You scared twenty years onto me." He stroked her cinnamon face. "I forgive you and to prove it…."

Slowly, precisely, as though it would be the last time, Mahlon brought his lips to hers. Kissing Ruth was like placing his lips on the perfumed, pink satin petals of a rose. He wanted that warm thrill that engulfed his body to linger—and linger more, all night if possible.

She had become his life-giving water in a dry and thirsty land. He drank and drank again. Ruth gave as much as he wanted and then more. The love she possessed and gave to her husband, only a few ever experience. She manifested a love far beyond the erotic and sexual. She had bound herself to an Israelite for life. She had willingly taken on an often sick man who lived in a tent and appeared to have a scrimpy future in obtaining much of this world's goods.

Ruth, a strong young woman, proved that strength by entering into a marriage with a Hebrew, a foreigner, a man whose people were much-despised by many Moabites. Hers was not a marriage arranged between families from when she and Mahlon were babies. She willingly took on the additional trials of a mixed marriage, a yoking together of Moabite and Hebrew.

Finally, their lips parted. "I love you, Ruth."

She laid her head on his shoulder. "I love you," she whispered in a throaty inflamed tone.

Mahlon burned with desire for his wife. Kissing the top of her head sent a blazing heat coursing through every inch of his body. Ruth did this to him, and not only this night but each time he held her in his arms. He greedily lusted for *this* heat.

That other one, the heat of the day—he hated. The sun scorched him, which created within him a hunger for the night breezes. At that moment, one of those quiet breezes swayed the treetops. It did nothing to cool the fevered passion in Mahlon's body.

He smiled, thinking about the cover of darkness and coziness of their tent. He longed for Ruth's warmth, and the heat it produced in him—the same inner fire he enjoyed at this moment. His beautiful, loving wife provided succor to his troubled soul.

The blessed relief Ruth offered each night when receiving him into her gentle, loving arms, constantly kept his thoughts on her and a prayer of thanksgiving in his heart.

"You have not told me why you are out here in the dark."

"You are the one in the dark," she breathed out the words, warm on his neck. "I waited for you and you did not come to our bed."

"No need to wait for our bed. I wish to have those rose petals now." He kissed her again.

"Your prayer for me was sweet."

Mahlon tightened his arms around her. "I pray that my God will open your womb. I weep for you."

"I cannot see your face nor your eyes," Ruth whispered. "Your words, your tone, they tell of your love for me. If I would become blind and never see your face again, I would know your care and love for me by your words and tone.

"I too have beseeched my fertility gods to begin copulating at the exact moment we join our bodies. If the gods have destined to give me fertility, then it will happen."

Mahlon kissed her neck. "Let us go to the tent and offer more prayers. Trust your husband's judgment. These prayers are best offered lying down."

"*Mahlon!*"

Chapter 12

Spike-toothed edges of enormous black clouds raced across the sky pushed along by an unusually cool breeze, which built into a stout wind, angry enough to separate blossoms from their branches. Springtime in Moab had arrived giving Mahlon fits of coughing, producing painful spasms in his chest. The wicked wind would only worsen his symptoms.

"Six years my brother and no son."

Mahlon stopped pruning long enough to glance up. "It has been seven for me." He trimmed another grapevine and tossed it to the middle of the row.

"It is time to stop the praying. It is useless." He sighed heavily. His shoulders slumped. "I have discussed it with Orpah, and we are calling in the sorcerer and healer. Moabites have had many good results from their herbs and potions."

"Ruth has pushed me to do the same. Now is the time, in fact, long past time when we should have tried." A dark scowl clouded his face. "Mother still believes Yahweh will open my wife's womb. She wants us to refrain from any Moabite sorcery, and we have deferred to her demands. No more shall we bend to her. I have begun to doubt that—."

"Doubt? You do not believe in our God?"

"I believe." Mahlon's eyes darted back and forth, concerned that they were not alone.

"She is not here." Chilion laughed. "Mother does not look over your shoulder every moment." He grinned. "I believe you fear her."

"I am the head of this family, I fear no one," Mahlon barked. "It is that I care for her feelings."

"As I do. Now, what do you doubt?"

Mahlon stopped pruning and relaxed in the shade of the grape vines. "I doubt that Ruth will ever give birth. God will not bless me, a Hebrew, with a son. A Hebrew baby born of a Moabitess? No—God will not allow it."

Chilion vacantly stared at the next row of vines. "If that is so, then I have no hope, either."

"Hold your words, my brother." He held up a hand. "Since Yahweh refuses to open the wombs of our women, let us turn to the gods of Moab. They shall be more willing to listen to our pleadings because our wives are from Moab and worship Chemosh."

Chilion scratched his beard. "Have we not worshiped the Moabite gods as we promised? Should they not have blessed us already?"

Mahlon shook his head. "The Moabite gods know we divide our allegiance and continue to worship Yahweh. Do you believe Chemosh and the other gods are stronger than Yahweh? I do not.

"Ruth and Orpah *do* believe. Do they not continually point out the lush green of Moab and compare it to the dust of Judah? Yes, the gods of Moab will surely bless our wives for their loyalty to the Moab religion."

Squinting through questioning eyes, Chilion looked at his brother. "So, actually the gods will bless our wives' pleadings, not ours? We will benefit because of them?"

Mahlon peeked over. "Now you understand." He grinned. "The gods care nothing for us. We are Hebrews, and though we give lip service in their worship, we have not fully committed to them. However, they *will* bless obedient daughters of Chemosh."

"What will change? Our wives beseech their gods daily. Is it that we will now call in the healers?"

"Yes, the healers *and* we shall deceive the Moabite gods when they no longer see us worshipping Yahweh. We remain believers but, the outward sign of our belief we will relinquish."

Chilion gave him a round-eyed look. The plan hit him full-force. *No longer worship Yahweh.* His insides bunched as though seized by giant hands.

A long silence followed. Both men went back to work, and they would have no further discussion of the subject that day.

The crimson dawn came early streaking the eastern sky. For three weeks, Ruth had eagerly anticipated this day. The temple priest, along with a sorcerer, and a third man, a healer, would receive her and Mahlon at the temple for prayers and treatments. If the gods looked favorably upon them, then the curses that kept them childless would be removed. Only the day before they did the same for Chilion and Orpah.

At the temple, in the presence of the idol Chemosh, Ruth fell to her knees bowing low until her head touched the brick pavement. Mahlon followed her actions. Though he frequently worshiped with Ruth at the temple, he still did not know all of the rites. After a short time of complete silence, she rose to her feet, and Mahlon followed.

Entering a room reserved for the priests, sorcerers, and healers to confer with people who came for help, the couple met the temple lords.

"Ruth," the priest began, "you and your husband are here because you have remained barren. Our understanding is you are childless. Do you agree?"

"Yes, holy one."

"Do you know the cause?"

"No." Her chin dropped. "A demon I assume," she said in a voice barely above a whisper.

"Yes, a demon has been sent to afflict you because the gods are angry. You have done deeds to anger them."

Ruth nervously shifted her feet. A massive brick with sharp edges rolled in her stomach. "I, I cannot imagine what it might be. I worship our gods, Chemosh, and the Baals. Great is Chemosh of the Moabites."

"We soon shall know if they have shut up your womb for-ever." He looked her up and down through dark, solemn eyes. "Pray the gods will show mercy."

She hated his gaze, and the lump in her throat, which his critical look produced. It gagged her. "I have prayed—many times each day."

The sorcerer stepped forward. "There are tests that will tell of our gods' decision."

Mahlon eyed the men. "What decision? You men frighten my wife."

"The gods decide who can conceive and whom they curse permanently," he said with a cold voice. "If permanent, she will never bring forth a child."

Ruth glanced at Mahlon. Tears welled in her agitated eyes.

"Come forward, Ruth," the priest commanded. He made no effort to change his icy tone.

She stepped forward and stood directly in front of the man.

"You shall remain perfectly still." He reached out and flicked her lips with the tip of his finger. She twitched. "You are to remain perfectly still," he commanded in a stern tone.

"I am sorry," she said with a quiver in her voice. "I did not wish to move. I shall be still."

The priest raised his hand and flicked her shoulder with the tip of his finger. She twitched.

Ruth peeked at Mahlon through wide, startled eyes. "I tried," she whispered. "It is useless."

"It is not!" The healer barked. "You will conceive! Though you tried to remain still, the gods would not allow it. You twitched, which means you can conceive. Great is Chemosh god of the Moabites!"

"Oh, Mahlon! The gods have not shut my womb forever." She fell into his arms. "Praise be to our gods."

Mahlon stroked her cheek, gently brushing the tears away. "The gods have spoken."

"Ruth." The healer touched her arm. "The gods will reveal the number of babes you shall deliver. Come with me."

He led them to the inner courtyard of the temple. Pointing to a spot on the brick pavement, he said, "You will sit there after it is prepared."

Beckoning with a hand at two temple priestesses, he indicated the place where Ruth would sit. "Prepare the ground."

The two young women carefully brushed the ground clean with freshly cut branches from a leafy bush that Ruth did not recognize. Then, the women dropped dates and other small pieces of fruit over the spot. When they completed the task, the healer motioned to Ruth. "Sit here."

Once seated, he handed her a goblet filled with a concoction of herbs and wine. "Drink all of it."

Taking it to her lips, she drank, expecting bitterness. To her surprise, it was quite pleasant. Mahlon watched from a bench a short distance away as the priest, sorcerer, and healer conferred in hushed tones with one another.

After several minutes, Mahlon walked over to confront the men. "What is this?" He gestured toward Ruth. "Why does my wife sit on the hard pavement? What does this tell us?"

The priest's eyebrows shot up; he stared with glassy eyes. "We wait," he snapped, a tinge of irritation in his voice. "It shall not be long, and the gods will reveal their will for Ruth. Then you will know the number of children she will bring forth."

Ruth vomited. Mahlon turned to the sound. "Ruth!" He started for her, but the healer caught his arm.

"Let her alone."

She vomited again and then again.

"She is ill!" Mahlon shouted. "I must be with her."

"She is not ill," the healer said quietly. He patted Mahlon's arm. "The gods are speaking."

One of the priestesses hurried over with a wet cloth. Ruth wiped her face and smiled at her husband. "I am not ill."

The healer released Mahlon. "Vomit spewed from her mouth three times," he said in a high-pitched, excited tone. "She will produce three babes. Great is Chemosh!"

Mahlon helped Ruth to her feet, held her close while stroking her back. Peering at the healer with doubtful eyes, he asked, "When? You have not told us when she will conceive. It has been seven years, and the gods have shut up her womb. When will they open her womb for conception?"

"We do not know," said the healer. "There *are* ways to speed it along. If you heed our words and do these things, it will please the gods, and they will give conception quickly."

"What are we to do?" asked Ruth.

"First, we must determine if you are ready to conceive. The gods have spoken, and you will, however, is the time now? Follow this instruction for the answer. Tonight," he looked at Mahlon, "rub olive oil on your wife's breasts, covering them completely. In the morning, if her veins are distinct then she is ready. If the veins are not evident, you will inform us immediately, and we shall offer more prayers and incantations to the gods. We will implore for mercy from them to remove the demon that blocks your seed from being planted in her womb."

Mahlon nodded his understanding.

"Also," the healer continued, "you shall eat lettuce each evening before you lie with your wife. Lettuce is an aphrodisiac, and the milky sap within shall make the seed you plant within Ruth more potent."

"I shall do as you say." He eyed Ruth.

"I agree," she said.

Then the sorcerer gave more instructions. "Today, when you leave the temple, go to the silversmiths' street. Enter one of the shops and tell the craftsman that you want to purchase two monkey amulets, male and female. Wear them on a necklace, Ruth the female, Mahlon the male. Never take them off.

"You shall also purchase two fertility statues of Astarte for your home. Pray to Astarte each evening and place the icons near your bed before you come together in sexual union."

After Ruth and Mahlon had agreed to follow the instructions, the priest chanted words that the couple could not understand. Once all of the prayers and incantations had been invoked, he said, "May the gods soon bless you with a child."

Ruth bowed. "Thank you, my lords. Great is Chemosh, god of the Moabites."

Ruth and Mahlon wound their way through the crooked streets and alleys of Ar, heading toward the street lined with silversmiths. In Ar, like other cities of Moab, streets did not have formal names. A particular street was known for the trades that congregated along it. The bakers had a street, the potters, the carpenters, and all other trades.

"After we make our purchases at the silversmith, we can go to our garden for lettuce." Ruth glanced over at Mahlon. "We want the milky sap to increase that potency of yours." She laughed.

He clasped her hand, gazing at her with heated eyes. "Yes, and tonight I must precisely follow the healer's instructions. I will not neglect my duty and that is a promise."

"The healer's instructions?" Ruth said with a questioning tone.

Mahlon gave her a crooked grin. "My love, *the olive oil.* Surely you have not forgotten the olive oil test. I will be very conscientious in…" He bent down and whispered into her ear.

"Mahlon!" She slapped him playfully on the arm. "I believe you take your duty much too seriously."

Both laughed. At that moment, having an indescribable lightheartedness from the new hope that the men of the temple instilled within them, they walked briskly to the silversmith. The cloud of despair had been lifted. The day drew near when Ruth would be with child. Her faith in the gods had never been stronger.

Entering the first shop, they went straight to the proprietor. "We have come from the temple with instructions to purchase monkey amulets and fertility idols," said Mahlon. "Do you have these items?"

The silversmith chuckled. "It is my business to have all types of amulets and idols. If you can name it, I have it. Frog amulets, locust amulets, monkey amulets, the list is endless. Chemosh idols, Baal idols, any Baal god you want, I have."

"May we see the monkey amulets?" asked Ruth. "We need one female and one male."

The silversmith took them to an area of the shop with shelf after shelf of charms, jewelry, and amulets. "You wish to have a child."

"Yes," Mahlon said, "how do you know?"

"You asked for fertility gods along with these amulets."

"Oh!"

"I have various monkey amulets; not all are for fertility." He selected the ones that increased fertility and handed the female to Ruth and the male to Mahlon.

"This is definitely the male." Mahlon held it up for Ruth to see. Ruth glanced over, and embarrassing heat flamed her face.

"May I see the female?" He asked with a wry grin.

"No!"

The silversmith smirked. "Come this way and I will show you the fertility god Astarte."

Ruth spotted her before Mahlon. Naomi sat before her tent mending a garment.

"Do we tell her where we have been?" asked Ruth.

"She knows."

"You told her?"

"Chilion told her this morning. While you and Orpah were at the brook filling the water skins, my brother with a large and chatty mouth informed her. I warned him to keep it a secret, but like so many other times over the years, he ignored me."

"What did she say? Did she weep?"

"She did not weep and said nothing. However, her cold, stony expression told me she was angry."

Mahlon grasped her arm and stopped. "My mother would never hate her sons, yet the look on her face; it chilled me, all the way to the core of my being. I think my bones rattled."

She looked up at him with grave eyes. "Oh, my dear husband. Naomi has been so good to me—so pleasant. I ache for her. Her disappointment in us must be overwhelming."

"Mahlon nodded and looked away. "She did not want to come here. My father believed it best, but Mother spoke against it. She believed…." His voice trailed off.

"What?" Ruth placed a hand on his chest. "Tell me. I should like to know her beliefs."

"No, it would hurt you too much."

"Mahlon, please—."

"No! Do not ask again."

"As you wish, my husband. Let us go, she stares at us."

Naomi kept her eyes on Mahlon as he approached the tent. He looked at the ground, the trees, over at Ruth, every direction except toward his mother. She had great contempt for what he had done.

"Do you carry the idols in your scrip?"

Mahlon ignored the question and walked on. He would hide the scrip, which indeed held the amulets and idols. Inside his tent far from her prying eyes, he would secure it.

"Mahlon! Do you disrespect your mother? I know you disregard my words."

"You need not ask the question for you know the answer." He dismissed her with a wave of the hand.

Naomi cocked her head toward Ruth. "My daughter, the fifth commandment is: 'You shall honor your father and mother.' My son no longer honors me." Naomi slowly shook her head.

"Mother, he loves you. He—."

"Ruth, a man who loves his mother, honors her wishes. A man who loves his God honors his God's commands. Mahlon has lost his way. He ignores many of our God's commands."

"He is a good man," Ruth said. "He loves you."

"I grow bitter, my daughter. My husband is dead, and my sons rebel against Yahweh. They no longer listen to my words. Do they? Tell me, do they?"

Ruth's eyes looked past her focusing on their tent door. "How have they hurt you? They still worship Yahweh. What commands of your God do they ignore?"

"On the mountain, Yahweh delivered ten commandments to Moses. The first: 'You shall have no other gods before me.' Nevertheless, my sons worship other gods, gods of the Moabites.

"Yahweh said, 'You shall not make for yourself a carved image.' My sons buy idol gods from the silversmith and now trust them to open their wives' wombs.

"Our God said, 'You shall not take the name of Yahweh your God in vain.' When my sons cry out to Yahweh, it *is* vain, worthless speaking. Why? Because, they trust in Chemosh.

"Yahweh commanded us to 'Remember the Sabbath day, to keep it holy.' My sons frequently profane the Sabbath by working or going to the city.

"Yes, my daughter Ruth, our God commanded these words, also. 'Honor your father and your mother that your days may be long upon the land that Yahweh your God is giving you.'

"I fear! Mahlon and Chilion have brought disgrace upon their mother. They dishonor not only me but also their God in heaven. Will their days be long upon the land? It frightens me. We do not even walk upon the land that Yahweh gave us.

"They have rebelled against me and Yahweh. Mahlon refuses to take me home."

Naomi's head dropped. She wept.

Ruth watched the woman she had come to love and respect crumble into a heap. Naomi lay on her side, and Ruth tried in vain to console her with words and hugs.

"Leave me Ruth—please!"

"I wish to hear about your God. Mahlon tells me little. I have always wanted to know more."

"Ruth, I hurt too much today. Another time we can talk of Yahweh. I will say this. It is not your fault that you have not carried babes in your womb. I fully believe you are barren because of Mahlon's disobedience. Our God is punishing him."

Ruth stared at her mother-in-law. Naomi's words, so unexpected, had struck a nerve. This thought had crossed her mind, and now Naomi had said it. Ruth felt a calming relief flow through her body and mind.

Placing a hand upon Naomi's shoulder, Ruth said, "I have considered many times what you have said. Perhaps his God has cursed him with worthless seed. My mother has told me the same, but she is hateful when she says it.

"You have disappointment in your words, yet not hate. You love Mahlon and me. Is it not so, Mother?"

Naomi nodded her answer.

Ruth patted Naomi's back. "I prefer your loving ways to my own mother's spite-filled attitude. Thank you."

Naomi sat up and held Ruth for several moments.

Finally, Ruth stood up and rushed away to her tent. "Mahlon, we need to talk. Mahlon?" She peeked inside.

Mahlon had fled.

Chapter 13

The yellow morning sun hung bright and unmercifully hot on the newly cut fields of grain. Heat waves rippled up from the ground as reapers stacked their bundles high on an ox cart driven by one of Paebel's sons.

Four thousand cubits away, high atop the nearest hill, lush with greenery, Mahlon struggled to supervise the winnowing process at the threshing floor. Each day had grown increasingly warmer than the previous, slowly leeching away Mahlon's strength in each drop of sweat.

Although his body had weakened, his anger had grown stronger. He had an intense longing for a son, an heir, to secure the family from dying out. That yearning for posterity had kept his emotions raw. Any perceived slight brought forth an angry outburst. Ruth bore the brunt of his wrath, yet never complained for she understood the genesis of his anger.

His emaciated body broke her heart. Mahlon was desperately ill. Anyone could see it by looking at his bony, underweight frame.

Naomi and Ruth, along with Chilion had warned him repeatedly to rest. Time after time he refused their advice. Claiming the winnowing could not be done without his supervision, he ignored them with a wave of the hand.

Ruth did not accept his claims and had told him he was not indispensable. The same threshing floor, filled with wheat from her father's fields had been operating for years, long before Mahlon had married her.

"My great grandfather winnowed barley and wheat on that floor," Ruth said that morning. "Today, my family can continue the work without you."

"No! It is my responsibility. Your father demands I be there."

Ruth eyed his haggard face. She cringed at the deteriorated flesh. He believed he was indispensable.

"Mahlon, you are weak. We have endured many days of heat, and it has sapped your strength and your judgment. Take a day off. I shall go to my father and tell him your condition."

"You will not!" He squared his shoulders and spoke through angry lips. "Shall I have a woman speak for me as though I am a child?"

He brushed past her and started for the threshing floor. Ruth followed begging him to remain with her. Still within sight of their house, he turned. "Go back! Grind the wheat I brought home last night. Make bread for our evening meal. Do your chores and I shall do mine.

"Eight years! It has been eight years Ruth and no son. My seed is too weak to open your womb. I accept that truth, but I am not too weak to provide for you. Do not take that away from me."

He gazed at her through dull eyes. His stooped posture broke Ruth's heart. Her proud husband, crushed in spirit, had resigned to his circumstances.

"My God has cursed me and your gods are too weak to break that curse. So, you shall remain barren because of me. I live with that every day and can do nothing about it. I have tried—we have tried.

"But, I refuse to give up my obligation to provide for you and my mother. Now, go back. Leave me."

Mahlon turned away and never looked back. Slowly he climbed the hill to the threshing floor.

The days were heat, dust and sweat, sunup to sundown. At midday, Naomi, Ruth, and Orpah sat in the shade of an ancient oak enjoying their meal of bread, cheese, melons and pomegranates. Mahlon remained at the threshing floor, eating with the workers. Chilion took his food with him each morning to the tent maker's shop.

"This melon is refreshing," Ruth said.

"I love it!" Orpah agreed.

"My people ate melons in Egypt when they were in bondage," Naomi said. "They missed the fruit and vegetables while wandering in the wilderness and they complained to Moses."

Ruth's eyes lit up. "Tell us. We wish to hear about your people and your God."

Naomi had come to love and respect her daughter-in-law. Ruth never spoke unkind words to her or anyone. She was a great example of tender-hearted love that Naomi found so endearing.

"You have asked me to speak about him on other occasions, and I have not said much." A slight smile parted her lips. "No longer, I shall speak of Yahweh and answer your questions."

"Since our marriage, I have asked many questions of Mahlon about your God and the Hebrew religion. He does not want to discuss the subject."

The sweetness and innocence of Ruth's dark brown eyes gave proof of her words.

Leaning toward Ruth, she placed a hand upon her daughter-in-law's arm. "Ask, what is it you want to know."

"You worship an invisible God. Why? How can you believe in a God you cannot see?"

"The Israelites see his powerful works and believe. Our leaders have talked to him, and he has given them instructions to obey. Even now, he speaks to our judges."

Orpah frowned. "Why does he not reveal himself? Let his followers see him."

"He has revealed himself by his deeds. Moses, the leader of our people when they came out of Egyptian bondage, asked to see the glory of our God. Yahweh said no."

"Why deny such a request?" Ruth shrugged. "The Moabites know of Moses and the forty years of wandering in the wilderness. It is well-known Moses was a great leader. Yahweh should have granted his request. Do you agree?"

"No, Ruth. Yahweh, though he denied Moses his request, answered him with a good reason. Our God said, 'You cannot see my face; for no man shall see me, and live.'

Ruth peered through confused eyes.

"A god who refuses to allow his people to see him makes no sense," Ruth said. "The people want to see their god—and bow before him."

"The brilliant light which surrounds Yahweh cannot be looked upon by mortal men. We know not for sure what this light is. It may be that he is that light; if not, then he is shrouded in that light."

"That is strange," Orpah said. "A god brighter than the sun?"

"Yes, much brighter. Yahweh told Moses these words. 'Here is a place by me, and you shall stand on the rock. So it shall be while my glory passes by that I will put you in the cleft of the rock, and will cover you with my hand while I pass by. Then I will take away my hand, and you shall see my back, but my face shall not be seen.'"

"So, your God has revealed himself partially, yet keeps his face hidden."

"Yes, to Moses. When Yahweh gave the Ten Commandments to him a second time, Moses returned to the people but they were afraid to come near him."

"Mother, you tell us strange things," said Orpah. "What happened to Moses that they were afraid?"

"His face shone with brilliance so intense that it frightened all of them. He had been on the mountain with God for forty days and being near to our God, and his brightness caused the face of Moses to shine."

"When the flames of Chemosh burn, he cannot be approached either. Anyone would die from the heat."

"My dear Ruth. Those flames and the light produced is man-made. Your god is also invisible. Men toss wood into the idol that keeps the fires burning. Your god does not do anything without men to start and fan the flames."

Orpah's mouth tightened at the apparent affront to her god. "At least we can see our god!"

Naomi smiled. "I do not wish to insult you my daughter, but when did Chemosh reveal himself. Who carved out the image after looking at your god?"

Orpah and Ruth eyed one another. They had no answer. "We do not know," said Ruth. "Surely at some point he revealed himself to a silversmith who carved his image."

"So, you also worship an invisible god," Naomi said with a gentle smile crossing her face. "What you see is a graven image, but never the god. You trust that the first person to carve the image of Chemosh was accurate.

"Chemosh remains invisible. Why? My daughters, you have never seen him as I have never seen Yahweh."

Ruth looked at her with eyes of respect. "You have made me think about things I have never considered. I will—."

"Ruth! Ruth!"

She immediately recognized the voice of her older brother. The urgent tone sent through her a feeling of revulsion that bordered on panic. She sprang to her feet.

"Here I am!"

"Mahlon," the brother gasped for air, "Mahlon, he, he has collapsed. He lies on the threshing floor."

Ruth screamed and like an echo Naomi did the same.

"I must go to my husband."

"Ruth, he is being brought down to his tent. Remain here."

"No," she called over her shoulder. "I will meet them. I cannot wait. I must go."

The men had gently placed Mahlon on the ground in the shade of a giant sycamore tree. Naomi held a cloth freshly dipped in water to her son's forehead while Ruth patted his face, neck and arms with another wet cloth. His skin radiated heat like red coals in a campfire.

Ruth's brother brought another pot of water and set it under the tree. Orpah dipped and squeezed out several more cloths.

"We told him to rest and then go on home. He would not listen. Kept mumbling he had to be good for something."

"What happened up there?" Ruth asked.

Her brother stooped down and quietly told her. "About mid-morning, Mahlon complained of a throbbing headache. He kept rubbing his forehead and temples. I asked him to rest for a while. Of course, he refused.

"Then, before the midday meal he began staggering around speaking words that made no sense. His confusion worsened, and I took him by the arm to lead him into the shade. He jerked away, said he was going to his house.

"That is when he cried out, mumbling that he was sick; within moments he vomited and collapsed. I rushed to his side. When I touched his head, he began shaking violently. I placed my hand under his head to protect him from injury. After the shaking had stopped, I noticed his dry skin, he did not sweat.

"I ran to inform you and asked the men to bring him here. I am sorry Ruth. He never spoke a word after he fell to the ground."

Ruth could only stare at Mahlon while a dark fear gripped her heart. He looked dead, and soon would be if she did not do something. "Bring the healer! Now!" She leaned over, stroked her husband's cheek, and then kissed him.

Getting to her feet, she entered the house and quickly returned with the household gods. Placing them on a small table, she set the gods near Mahlon.

Naomi watched as Ruth prostrated herself before the small shrine. "Oh, Chemosh, my god Chemosh. Save my husband! Great is Chemosh, god of the Moabites. You have the power, holy one; please give Mahlon strength to live. Take away the curse of Yahweh. Oh Chemosh, my god Chemosh, you have the authority to break the curse."

Ruth stood and grasped the idol, kissing it. Returning it to the table, she went to Mahlon. Naomi said nothing although she believed none of it. She certainly did not believe in any of the Moabite gods.

The idea of a curse from Yahweh upon her son had raised her suspicion previously. It must be true. Mahlon had followed in his father's footsteps by straying from the commandments and refusing to return to the Promised Land. Also, her son had not fathered a grandchild. No one but God understood how much she grieved over those things.

Within the hour, Ruth's brother returned with the healer. Mahlon remained unconscious. Naomi continued the cool compresses to his head, and her lips never stopped moving. Silently and fervently she prayed for her firstborn.

"The hand of the sun god has struck this man," the healer said. He gazed at Ruth. "What is his sin?"

Ruth slowly shook her head. "I do not know. He told me this morning his God, Yahweh, has cursed him. We are without children, and he believes it is his fault."

The healer, grim-faced, caught Naomi's eye. "He is your son?"

"Yes, my firstborn." Naomi, frantic and wishing to hold onto any tiny hope that even the Moab healer could help, cried out in a strained, sob-choked voice, "Give him something! Do not let him die!"

The healer slowly shook his head. "It is in the gods' hands but, I believe it is hopeless."

Naomi gasped. Ruth whimpered as tears washed from her eyes. The man's blunt words caught them off guard.

"He understood his condition. You must also. His God has cursed him and removing the curse is not likely. Nevertheless, I shall offer incantations to Chemosh and the sun god to break the spell of Yahweh."

The healer brought forth from his scrip an amulet shaped in the form of a serpent. Holding it up toward the sky, he mumbled words to the sun god. When finished, the healer placed the serpent on the chest of Mahlon.

"Remove that serpent!" Naomi cried out. "The serpent is evil. He caused Adam and Eve to sin."

Suddenly, as though hit with one of those spells the gods doled out, the healer became a tight-faced, hard-mouthed man with dark, mean eyes. "The serpent is no such thing! It is a means of regeneration and transformation. Do you not know it sheds its skin? In the same way, the serpent assists the ill to shed their ailments.

"If a god has set his hand full upon the afflicted, so heavy that it cannot be lifted, then the serpent assists the cursed one to shed his mortal body and pass over to the next life.

"I am unable to do anything. A healer intercedes between the gods and the cursed. It is the deities that give me the power to heal. What I hope for this man or what you wish will have no influence on the gods' decision."

"You speak of your gods—not mine," Naomi spat out the words. Getting to her feet, she cried, "Yahweh is my God, and I will entreat him day and night! He will listen to me, and if gracious, change his mind if he has cursed him. He can and will give my son healing."

"He is your God." The man shrugged his shoulders. "I only speak for my gods."

Orpah drew her mother-in-law into her arms and held her close as Naomi wept for her son. Only a few more moments elapsed when the ear-splitting wail rang out.

Ruth's death cry brought Naomi to her knees. Mahlon, her firstborn son, had died.

"My husband! Oh, my husband!" Ruth collapsed on his chest, the serpent between them. "No!" she screamed. "Oh, please no! Mahlon! I am childless. Shall I now be a widow, too?" She wailed. It grew louder, much louder.

Naomi began to weep, beating her breast. "My son is dead! First my husband, now my firstborn. Where is the heir? Shall Mahlon's name be lost forever? I, I cannot bear it."

The wailing went on endlessly. Neither Ruth nor Naomi could be comforted.

Orpah, with tears streaming her cheeks, tried desperately to offer words of comfort, awkwardly switching from one woman to the other. Finally, rising to her feet, Orpah left them alone. She entered the house.

The healer followed close behind. At the door, he said, "I shall leave the serpent, Orpah. It lies between Ruth and Mahlon. At this moment, with the serpent's assistance, Mahlon is being ushered over to the other side."

Orpah nodded her understanding. "Thank you for coming. I know Ruth appreciates your being here at this time. We will return the serpent to you soon."

The healer bowed low and walked away.

Chapter 14

"Ruth, it has been over a year. Come back to our home," said Figat. "We are your family. Naomi is not your mother, and she is poor. To live, she relies on her son. Can you not see by staying you are a burden?"

"She is my family. When I married Mahlon, I became part of his family. You know that."

A hard-eyed look flashed from Figat's cold face. "You have no children! Stay there and you will never have children. Can you not see you have not provided me a grandchild? My sons have given me many. It is the gods, Ruth; they have cursed your womb for marrying that Israelite.

"Come home! Get away from that family. The gods curse them. The father died. The son died. A curse weighs heavy upon the son and wife, too. Have they produced a son? No! Open your eyes Ruth."

"My eyes are open, and I see clearly. Naomi is a gentle, pleasant woman. She has endured much grief. How can I forsake her when she depends on the comfort and support I give her daily? She is my husband's mother. I love her."

"You do not have a husband. Stop speaking as though he is still alive."

Ruth sighed heavily. "Mahlon *was* my husband, but Naomi is still my mother-in-law. Do those words meet your approval?"

"You will not speak to me in such a manner. For that kind of talk, when you were still under our roof, your father would have laid the rod on your back. It appears you no longer respect your parents. Oh, how far you have wandered from us."

Ruth's pain-filled eyes dropped. "I love you and father and always will. My love for you has nothing to do with loving Naomi and caring for her. Can you not understand there is enough love in my heart for all?"

Figat moved over to a water pot. Dipping a cup, she sipped the cool refreshment. "It is time you make it known that you are no longer a grieving widow, and you can offer yourself to another man. Take off the mourning clothes and go to the market. Make it known to your friends and relatives that you are now available for marriage.

"I know there are several men who are aware of your situation and would be willing to take you as a wife. You are still young and can produce a child."

Ruth struggled to keep her radiant face from turning ugly at her mother's remark. Though reserved and polite about most things, she did not shy away from speaking her mind. She had no problem expressing her views on things that she considered important.

Ruth got to her feet and walked outside. Figat followed along behind. At the courtyard gate, Ruth turned and peered into her mother's eyes. "These men, the ones so eager to take me to the marriage bed, are they the same men who sought me when I was a young virgin? The ones you and father turned away when they came to you offering a marriage contract?

"Did it not occur to you that I might wonder why no men wanted me, yet my friends had husbands?"

Figat's eyes had grown larger with each question. She would not or could not understand her daughter, and wanted to scream an answer at her. However, the words would not come. She stood slack-jawed as Ruth, with tears of deep hurt welling up and blinding her, turned and rushed away.

On her way to the public cemetery, Ruth reconsidered her confrontation with Figat.

Her mother had never been a pleasant person, and like most mothers and daughters they did not agree at times. Making it even more difficult, Figat made a habit of speaking harshly to Ruth and being hypercritical of her daughter when they had a difference of opinion.

Figat was one of those who believed her way was always best, and no one should disagree. So, when Ruth lived at home, she tried to avoid conflict with her if at all possible. After she married Mahlon, she had not been so obliging. She did not go out of her way to irritate her mother, yet she no longer backed down like she did when younger.

Entering the burial ground, Ruth walked briskly toward the graves. Although Naomi did not want another family member under Moabite soil, she could do nothing but watch as Chilion and others buried Mahlon next to Elimelech.

"Hello, Ruth."

Naomi's gentle voice brought her daughter-in-law from deep contemplation. Ruth cringed, realizing she could not be alone with Mahlon. Carrying on a one-sided conversation had become a weekly event for her.

"Naomi!" Her hand flew to her chest. "I did not remember that you would be here today. You told me, but I forgot."

"Daughter, your contorted face tells me you had other things on your mind. The look was not one of mourning your husband. What troubles you?"

"I apologize, mother. I do not wish to interfere with your visit."

"Ruth, I have been coming here every week for years. You have never interfered and are not now.

"One day, and I hope it is soon," she clasped her folded hands under her chin, "I will no longer be able to come out here because I will be home in Judah. My heart still aches for Elimelech, but I long to see my homeland, too."

Ruth hugged her. "You are so pleasant and graceful. I so hope you can return to your country."

"Thank you for understanding. I wish Chilion did. He knows I want to go, but tells me the famine is still devastating the land. I tell him that it matters not to me. My people are there—I should be there.

"He is so much like Mahlon. Mahlon refused to go back, so Chilion follows in his brother's footsteps. My sons are very much like Elimelech, so their mother's wish is not fulfilled."

"What is it like?"

Naomi's brow furrowed into a questioning look.

"Judah and your hometown, Bethlehem—tell me about them. Can you still remember, after all, it has been years since you left?"

Naomi burst out laughing.

"Why do you laugh?" Ruth's eyes darted about for any onlookers. She considered it inappropriate to laugh in a cemetery. "What did I say?"

"I have lived in Moab for ten years! All of my years, except the last ten, were spent in Judah." Naomi chuckled. "So, yes, I can remember the other years of my life. My mind has not turned feeble, yet."

Ruth gave her a sheepish grin. "My question was rather foolish, I guess."

"No, no, not foolish. Let us walk toward home and I will tell you about the Promised Land."

"Why do you call it that?"

"I shall tell you words from our Scriptures. Israelite children, at least the children of faithful Israelites, are taught daily from Scrolls of the Law. They contain the commands we call the Law of Moses.

"Hebrews commit much of the Law to memory. From the Scroll of Deuteronomy are these words about the Promised Land.

"'Now this is the commandment, and these are the statutes and judgments which Yahweh your God has commanded to teach you, that you may observe them in the land which you are crossing over to possess that you may fear Yahweh your God, to keep all His statutes and His commandments which I command you, you and your son and your grandson, all the days of your life, and that your days may be prolonged.

"Therefore hear, O Israel, and be careful to observe it that it may be well with you and that you may multiply greatly as Yahweh, God of your fathers has promised you—'a land flowing with milk and honey.

"Hear, O Israel: Yahweh our God, Yahweh is one! You shall love Yahweh your God with all your heart, with all your soul, and with all your strength.'"

Naomi's voice quivered as she said the last few words. With a quick swipe of her hand, she flicked away tears.

"Mother, you are weeping. Those words were beautiful. Why the tears?"

Naomi kept her head down watching her feet as she stirred the dust along the well-worn path. She gently shook her head.

"I have never heard such sweet words about a god. I have been taught all my life to respect Chemosh, fear him, and do not anger him or surely he will curse you.

"But, love Chemosh? No, never. Many times each year, we express our thanksgiving for his blessings upon the land and boast of his power to provide, but never speak of loving him."

Ruth paused and clutched Naomi's arm stopping her. She looked over into the soft dark eyes and sweet, kind face of her daughter-in-law.

"Your God intrigues me. He gives a command to love him—with your whole being. Now I see why Mahlon refused to give him up altogether. Even when I tried to discourage him by making light of Yahweh, he continued to defend him as the high God.

"Moabites always like to compare your parched land to our good earth which flourishes. We like to say Yahweh is unable to bless like Chemosh, and other times we attribute the famine of your land to Yahweh's evil eye. We always believe he gives Israel the evil eye and curses his people.

"Oh! My lovely Naomi! I am so ashamed of my words. What have I done," she muttered in a quiet voice. "What? You love your God. I, I cannot grasp that idea. It is foreign to my thinking."

Naomi gently took Ruth's hand and kissed it. "You truly are a blessing to me. I should have told you of Yahweh many years ago, but I assumed Mahlon…." She shook her head, realizing Mahlon had not told Ruth much, if anything, about Yahweh.

"Let us take another way home," Ruth said. "I want to show you a private place, a place where I go when I wish to be alone. Mahlon accompanied me there many times."

Naomi raised her eyebrows. "Your family?"

"Especially my family does not know this place. I went there as a child to get away."

Ruth pointed to an obscure opening, and they plunged into the woods taking a scarcely traveled trail.

"I remember a boy," Ruth said, "actually a young man, maybe twenty years old. He and his father worked for my father. Our conversation about Yahweh has brought the memory of him to me. He went home to Judah not long after I met him. His name was Zaylin. In those days, I sought to know of his God. He promised to tell me about him."

"Did he?"

"Zaylin told me it was a commandment of Yahweh, *not* a custom of the Hebrews to rest on the seventh day. That is all I learned. I am sure we would have had more talks, but, unfortunately, his family returned home."

Ruth walked ahead, turning off on what appeared to be a faint, rather narrow game trail. Within a few moments, they stood at the edge of a babbling brook.

"This is so beautiful, so peaceful. Now I see why you like it. I see no signs of anyone coming here, only animals." She pointed at a pile of animal dung.

"Let us sit over here." Ruth chuckled. "No signs of animals." She searched a small grassy area and beat it with a stick. "No, droppings—no snakes. It is clean and safe."

After getting comfortable in the lush grass, Naomi asked, "Is that all he told you of Yahweh?"

"Yes, but—."

"Ruth! That is almost nothing."

"He would have told me much more, but as I mentioned, his father and mother wanted to go home to Judah. They left Moab, and I never got to ask the questions that I so wanted answered."

Naomi frowned. Her lined face grew much older when her mouth turned down. "My son did not answer your questions." She shook her head in disbelief.

Naomi's statement told it all. Mahlon, a man, torn between his God and his wife's god, could not bring himself to speak of Yahweh and his commands. Doing so would convict him of ignoring the Word of God. Then, Ruth would ask more questions as to why he did not follow the precepts of his God. He did not have any desire to discuss the Hebrew God or his religion with her.

Ruth ignored Naomi's comment about Mahlon. "Tell me more of your God."

"I will quote from the Genesis scroll. The first words are: In the beginning God created the heavens and the earth. The earth was without form, and void; and darkness was on the face of the deep. And the Spirit of God was hovering over the face of the waters. Then God said, 'Let there be light'; and there was light. And God saw the light that it was good; and God divided the light from the darkness. God called the light Day, and the darkness He called Night. So the evening and the morning were the first day."

"This is written in a scroll?"

"Yes, and Hebrew children learn this early in their training."

Ruth gazed at the sky, considering Naomi's words. "I believe Baal took his sister as wife, and she is the goddess, Anat. They are co-creators of the world, and they continue to renew nature when it rains his seed."

Naomi twisted her neck a mite and slanted her eyes to meet Ruth's. "'Rains his seed?' Does that mean?"

Ruth nodded. "Fertility rites are part of our temple worship. A landowner with crops in the ground can worship at the temple in Ar and have sexual union with a temple priestess. While coupled together the landowner cries out to Baal, the lord of rain and dew. He asks for Baal and Anat to have sexual intercourse, which will bring about Baal giving up his seed, and it falls upon the landowner's field in the form of rain."

Naomi stared into Ruth's solemn face. "Do you believe all of that?"

"It is my religion's teaching. I know nothing else."

"You also said, 'took his sister as wife.' This goddess, Anat, she married her brother—Baal?"

Ruth went back to gazing at the sky. "Yes, they are brother and sister. Does that seem strange to you?"

"Yahweh forbids sexual relations between a brother and sister—in fact, any close relative. Hebrews are to be holy."

Ruth sat up, her eyes sharpened. "Holy? The gods are holy, not people. Do you wish to be a god?"

Naomi chuckled and quickly looked into Ruth's offended eyes. "Forgive me, I do not mean to laugh at you. Trust me, I have no intentions of trying to become a god. My people have Yahweh, and he is enough."

"Do not holy things, the sacred, belong to the gods?"

"It is recorded in one of our scrolls that God said, For I am Yahweh who brings you up out of the land of Egypt, to be your God. You shall, therefore, be holy for I am holy.'"

"Mother, this is strange to my ears. I must not understand what holy means."

"Yahweh's people are to be like him. No, not gods or all powerful beings, but we are to be like him in that he is different. He is not like the gods of the Canaanites, Amorites, or the Moabites. So, as he is different, we as his people are to be different from all the peoples around us. Sadly, many of my people have not kept the commandment of God. They have gone after the gods of the nations around them."

A muffled thunder rumbled in the distance. The air hung heavy with nearby rain. So engrossed in conversation, both women had neglected to notice the looming storm.

Ruth glanced up at the first thunderheads forming. "We should go. We are far enough from home that we will probably get wet if we do not start now. It may already be too late."

Naomi chuckled. "I will not melt. It has been a hot, lazy afternoon." She stood and brushed a twig from her garment. "I need a good washing."

The sky ominously clouded, an eerie gloom settled about them. Ruth glanced up. "Yes, I rather think we both could use the rain."

Another clap of thunder got them moving and within moments the scent of rain freshened the air.

"Should we run?" Ruth called over her shoulder.

"You can if you like. I am old and my running days are behind me."

They retraced their steps up the tiny game trail and made their way to the spot where they had turned off the main pathway. A light mist had begun to tickle Ruth's face.

"We *are* going to get wet."

"See, my daughter, running would have been in vain. Let us enjoy the shower."

The sky lowered, and the clouds darkened. Although it was late afternoon, the sun's rays had been so entirely hidden by the thick overcast that it appeared well past sundown.

"I can barely see you," said Naomi. "Do not get too far ahead of me. Can you see the pathway?"

"Yes, I have been this way many times and at night, too."

The rain, like a dark, enormous, non-penetrable wall, moved ever closer. The gentle mist upon Ruth's face was about to end. Lightning flashed, followed by a crack of thunder. The wind picked up, and then came the lashing rain.

The torrent soaked Ruth and Naomi to the skin. Their garments clung to them, making it even more difficult to move toward home.

Thunder rolled, the wind threatened to blow them off the path, and the rain became a deluge. They splashed through freshly formed pools.

"I am clean now," Naomi shouted above the storm's fury.

"I am the same," Ruth chuckled, "except for the mud caked to my feet and sandals."

Suddenly the storm turned dangerous. The sky split wide open with lightning. It jumped from tree to tree, and they had not made it out of the woods. With each lightning bolt, Ruth could see the meadow ahead and not far beyond it, their house.

Near the edge of the trees, close to where the meadow swept away toward their house, lightning streaked straight down striking an old tree. It exploded in flames. Both women screamed in fear.

They ran through the trees and rushed out into the broad meadow. Holding hands, the women reassured one another they were going to make it. Now, out in the open, the rain came at them sideways, slapping their faces. It stung.

"I was wrong," said Naomi. "I can run."

Lightning continued its mighty display from cloud to cloud and cloud to ground. Green, blue and white streaks shot across the night sky burrowing into the ground. Ruth's hair danced.

Exhausted, and with the ordeal nearly over, they drew near to the house. The thunder still rolled, the wind savagely whipped them, and the rain pounded their backs. All of the noise combined almost to deafen them.

Ruth cocked an ear to the side. "Do you hear that?"

"What?" Naomi shouted. "The wind, the thunder, the rain?"

"I-I am not sure. Listen!"

Close by the house, Ruth heard it again.

"Someone weeps. Oh, Mother, it is Orpah."

"Chilion!" Naomi cried. "It is Chilion. I know it is."

Ruth placed her hand upon the door latch. Orpah wailed louder. Ruth hesitated. She did not want to enter.

"Open the door!" Naomi demanded.

Upon entering, they saw Orpah holding Chilion to her breast. She looked up. Her eyes became like marbles; she stared at nothing and never blinked. "Chilion, oh my precious Chilion."

Lethargically she turned her head, settling her vacant eyes upon Naomi. In a harsh, bitter voice, she said, "He is dead."

Chapter 15

"My daughters, it has been almost a year since we buried Chilion next to his father and brother, a long year without my youngest son. My grief is more than I can bear." Naomi hunched over choking back a sob. "Ten years without my husband, two without Mahlon and one without Chilion."

"We love you, mother," said Orpah, her sad eyes glistening with tears. "We have all grieved over the dead—you the most. We shall go on together. Somehow we must put it behind us."

Ruth placed an arm around Naomi. "We are still a family."

Naomi walked outside the small house and stood next to a large rose bush planted by Mahlon several years before. A bee buzzed and settled on a flower.

She watched the bee for a moment. Not liking the rose, the insect flew away. Naomi liked roses and buried her nose in a flower. She inhaled deeply of the sweet fragrance. Looking toward heaven, she cried out, "Why? My God—why? You have taken all I have."

She dropped to her knees and pitched forward, her face to the ground. Bitter tears gushed from her eyes and disappeared into the grassy earth. Orpah and Ruth stood outside the doorway and helplessly watched their mother-in-law writhing in deep agony. Could she ever know contentment?

They had seen this same scene many times, discussed it frequently, and concluded her life was over unless something momentous happened—and soon. Naomi would die of a broken heart and the time for that event rapidly approached.

The women went to Naomi and sat down—one on each side. Each daughter-in-law placed a hand on her back signaling to the grief-stricken woman they cared and would always be there to support her.

The sister-in-laws had their own heart-wrenching grief of losing a husband, yet this woman had lost a husband plus two sons, her whole family.

Ruth and Orpah had assured her on many occasions they were her family always, but it was not the same.

Finally, after a long period, Naomi rose up to her knees and then Ruth and Orpah supported her as she got to her feet.

"I am a terrible burden to you," Naomi whispered.

"You are not," Ruth said. "We know the grief you suffer. Orpah and I have lost our husbands, and it has devastated us. *You* have lost so much more. We cannot imagine your pain. Each time, though you grieved for your loved one, you also supported us through your gentle but firm encouragement."

Orpah placed a hand on her arm. "Yes, Mother, you have been a great blessing to us. Thank-you!"

"What shall we do?" Naomi asked. "Our funds will not last the year out. My family came to Moab over ten years ago with silver in our bags and a sizable flock of sheep. Over the years the flock grew, we sold the wool, had lambs for our sacrifices, and for our table.

"Now look." She pointed to the meadow. "The flock has dwindled to almost nothing. Paebel has bought sheep from me as a favor." She gave Ruth a cautious look. "I am sorry to say this, but he has never given a fair price. He knows our situation. The Moabites believe I am cursed because I have lost my family, and I believe you two inherited the curse because you married my sons.

"Now those who bought, no longer buy from me when I wish to sell, so Paebel takes advantage and gives me his price, not mine."

Ruth nodded. "I know, mother. My father always considers how he can help himself first. If it means taking advantage of his daughter—he will.

"He will continue to do this as it is his and my mother's way of forcing me to come home where I will have all I want and never want again."

"You may go home anytime Ruth and you also, Orpah. Your families will welcome you. I want to return to Bethlehem. I relied on my sons for information about the drought in my land. Now, I am on my own. So, I will visit the campsite we stayed at the first night when arriving in Moab. I shall inquire of travelers from the west. They may know of conditions in Israel."

Ruth shook her head. With a wave of her hand, she indicated the house and meadow. "No, this is our home."

Naomi's lips pressed together until they turned white. "All of this belongs to Paebel. My sons built the house from materials your father provided, and the house sits on his land. No, my daughters, this is not my home. My home is in Judah.

"Why should I wait any longer? Whether the rains have come or not, I should go home. I have lost everything here. At least in Judah I can starve and die on the soil of the Promised Land."

Orpah clasped Naomi's arm and pulled her close. "Come with me now into the city. We shall go to my father's shop and ask for work. I know tent making, and you learned it many years ago. We shall beg if we must."

Naomi stroked her sweet daughter-in-law's cheek. "Have I not asked before? He listens to others and believes their words that I am cursed. He wants me to go home and take the curse with me. Is he not like Paebel? He will provide for you, but not as long as you live with me."

"I shall go and try. He is not an unreasonable man—like…." She stopped, blushing. Ruth realized that she was speaking of Paebel, but Orpah needn't have cut herself off.

"My daughters, can you not see and understand? Keret and Paebel believe I am under the judgment of my God. They are right—I am. I should leave and go to my people."

"No! You are not under Yahweh's judgment, and we wish you to remain with us." Ruth exclaimed.

"It is so. Yahweh judges the entire nation of Israel by bringing famine on the land and judges me for leaving the Promised Land."

"No, Mother, he would not curse you. You have done nothing wrong and could do nothing to persuade your husband and sons to go home. You tried."

Naomi shook her head. She did not argue. "I will think more about going home, but for now let us go into Ar. If I must beg let it happen today, not when we are starving."

Naomi sat on a stone bench across the street from Keret's shop. Orpah and Ruth stood in the open doorway pleading with the man to employ Naomi and Orpah.

Too far away for Naomi to hear the conversation, yet his answer was quite evident from his shaking head and her daughters-in-law's long faces.

Getting to her feet, she weaved her way through the noisy crowd. Naomi did not want Orpah and Ruth to take the brunt of Keret's words of rejection. She would confront him.

Neither the women nor Keret noticed as she approached. She stopped close by and listened. Being a Moabite, he remained faithful to Chemosh and the Baals. Nevertheless, his condemnation of her and Yahweh surprised the women. He had no use for the Hebrew God, believing Yahweh a God of condemnation. His god, Chemosh, blessed the Moabites. Naomi's God, Yahweh, cursed the Israelites.

"Keret, I have listened to you blaspheme my God, a God you do not understand. Yahweh is the High God, the God of gods, and Lord of lords. I will—."

"Silence! You and your family have brought the curses of Yahweh upon your heads, and it has kept Orpah barren. I will not employ any of you. To hire you would invite my gods' curse upon me."

"You taught me tent-making," said Naomi. "Now I am not worthy to enter your shop?"

"Much time has passed since those days. It was foolish to have invited you into my shop. Do you not understand that it is now obvious you live under a curse, a curse that has extended to my daughter?

"When Orpah finally comes to her senses and returns home, she will be received back into our family, and things will be as before you Israelites, and your God brought curses on her."

"I do not hold your daughter. She is free to return to your home." Naomi pinched her lips together.

He glared but kept quiet.

Throwing her hands up, she wheeled about and stalked away, disappearing into the crowded market. Ruth followed.

"Father, you know I am part of Chilion's family. I—."

"What family my daughter?" He spoke through clenched teeth. "One old woman—cursed by her God. Come home to your flesh and blood family."

"I—I cannot. Yes, it is as you say. She is old but cursed by her God? I do not know. What I *am* sure of is she needs me more than you do, Father."

Passing through the city gates, Naomi found a bench within a few paces of the entrance to Ar. She took a seat.

Ruth stood a few feet away allowing Naomi to be alone.

The situation looked bleak. The women belonged to no one. A female, whether Hebrew or Moabite, belonged to a husband, father or near kinsman. The men in Naomi's life were dead. Ruth and Orpah's husbands were also dead, and these widows refused to leave Naomi and return to their fathers.

Being a female without a man was almost a scandal. Without a steady income, they must rely on charity or prostitute their bodies. Either option was a bitter herb to swallow.

Orpah emerged from the crowded city gates, eyes straight ahead, apparently heading for home.

"Orpah!"

Ruth's sister-in-law turned her head.

"Over here." She beckoned with a hand.

"Where is Naomi?"

Ruth motioned, and Orpah's eyes followed. Naomi remained almost catatonic.

"Is she in a trance?"

Ruth shrugged. "I know not. I believe she grieves."

"Her husband? It has been ten years."

Ruth's face tightened into a hard grimace. She held her answer. Both women gazed at their long-faced mother-in-law.

After a short time, Ruth said, "Yes, her husband." She clasped Orpah's arm. "But—it is so much more. Her sons, no family in Moab, cursed by her God, shunned by those who once associated with her, and other heartaches. She longs to return home to Judah. In fact, she never wanted to journey here."

Orpah took a slight step back. "Surely she does not hate us."

Ruth shook her head. "No, my sister, she loves us, so much that she is willing to give us up to our parents. She would be alone, and that is unacceptable. Naomi would die from a broken heart and may anyway regardless of what we do."

Orpah looked away, staring at the crowded gateway to the city. "Her God has indeed cursed her for leaving Judah."

"I think it might be so, yet how can we know? Should such a good woman be cursed? She has told me of her God, how he has blessed her people over the years. She says he blesses the just and unjust. He supplies blessings to all.

"Maybe she is right in going home, even if the rains have not come to Israel. She will die here."

"What I do not understand is Yahweh's curse upon their land. Good people like Naomi are caught up in the evil." Orpah shrugged. "Surely she *has* done evil of which we are not aware."

"Naomi? Orpah, you know better. She would not know how to do evil. Her nature is good, a pleasant person, within whom there is no guile.

"No, no, her God's ways are a mystery. He blesses those who do not deserve it and removes blessing from those that do. I do not comprehend his ways."

Ruth's eyes suddenly caught sight of a man leading a donkey, his wife sitting on the beast. They passed in front of her, and she could hear the conversation.

"How long my husband? I wish to see the banks of the Jordan River."

The man looked back. "Two days at the most and another day to Jebus."

Ruth flung a look at Orpah. "They go to Naomi's country! A three-day journey. I must speak with them. Stay here. Keep an eye on Naomi."

Ruth hurried away and caught up with the man.

"Sir!"

The man glanced back.

"May I speak with you?"

He tugged the rope stopping the donkey. The man had soft, kind eyes and a welcoming smile.

"I am Hebrew." He chuckled. "Do you still wish to speak?"

"Yes, I do." Ruth returned his smile. "I know your nationality. Your Israelite accent is quite discernable. My husband was Hebrew, an Ephrathite of Bethlehem."

"Ah, yes. Bethlehem is high country, a short distance south of Jebus." He reached for his wife's hand. "We have kinsmen at Bethlehem."

"I noticed you when you passed me back there." Ruth thumb-pointed over her shoulder. "You journey to Jebus?"

"We do." He grinned. "Our land is outside the city wall to the north."

Ruth's heart quickened. "My mother-in-law wishes to return to her home. She and her family journeyed here many years ago because of the famine in Israel."

"The Almighty has visited his people with mercy. No longer does he withhold rain from our land."

Ruth's lips trembled. "Oh sir, please, wait here. I must tell Naomi. She is my mother-in-law. She rests back there on a bench.

Please give her a few minutes of your time. Surely you wish to hurry along, but I beg you—wait here. I want her to hear from you that the famine is no longer."

He smiled. "We will wait."

Ruth bowed low. "Thank-you!"

She ran to the bench. "Mother! Mother! Come now!" Ruth grasped her hand. "A man! You must talk to him. Come."

Naomi looked up. "What, my daughter? Is there trouble?"

"Is it the man leading a donkey?" Orpah asked. "Is he a Hebrew?"

"Yes! Mother, a man, and his wife," she motioned with her hand, "they wait to speak to you. Guess where they live."

"They are Hebrew." Naomi smiled. "My guess is Israel."

"Jebus!"

Naomi sprang to her feet. "Jebus! Jebusites—people from home?" Her melancholy mood had disappeared. "Oh, how I long for news from my country."

"The man said he lives north of the city wall. It is near your town of Bethlehem."

"Not far at all, my daughter. This news is wonderful. To speak with Hebrews from Judah, Jebus no less. I, I can barely believe it. Are you sure?"

"They wait." Ruth grasped her hand and tugged. "Let us go and you will see and hear them."

The three hurried to the spot where the man and his wife waited. "Sir, this is Naomi, my mother-in-law and Orpah, my sister-in-law."

The man bowed. "I am Eliezer, and this is my wife, Deborah. We are traveling to our home at Jebus."

Naomi's eyes glistened with tears.

"You weep," said Eliezer.

"Your voice, it has been so long. My husband, oh I have not heard his voice in ten years. You sound like him. I had forgotten the sound. His face, I still see. His touch, I still feel. But his voice, I could not remember. You have brought it back to me."

"I am pleased. Is it the Hebrew accent?"

"Yes, but more. It is your tone and how you deliver your words.

"Please tell me of Judah. I so wish to be home. I do not fear the famine. My family and friends remained when we departed, and I am sure the Almighty has blessed them. It has not been so with me."

"My Israelite sister, not fearing the famine is good, but even if you did fear, it would be in vain. Our God has visited his people with rain—much rain. The fields of barley and wheat will yield much this year."

Naomi's eyes had widened to such an extent as to appear the size of two very dark pools of water. "The famine is no more?"

He bounced on his toes and rocked back on his heels. "The rains began about one year ago and the land again thrives."

Naomi dropped to her knees and bowed her head to the ground. "Praise Yahweh, My God, the Almighty." She remained quiet for a short time, then lifting her head; she rose up but remained on her knees. "Thank you for this good news of my land—the Promised Land."

Glancing from Orpah to Ruth and back several times, she finally blurted, "I will go home!" A surge of energy shot through her, and she sprung to her feet as though a child of seven. Naomi had forgotten how good it was to have the liveliness of a young one. "Tomorrow! I will leave tomorrow."

Orpah and Ruth exchanged looks of fear. They understood this woman could not be allowed to leave Moab to journey home. Perils are fierce along the road to Judah.

"Mother, tomorrow is too soon," said Ruth.

"It has been ten years," Naomi said with a bite to her tone. "I will wait no longer."

"A few days," said Orpah, "to gather our supplies. Then we go."

"I will not allow you—."

"These young women are right," Eliezer said. "See our two donkeys. We have come from Kir-hareseth. It has been two long days, and we have three more ahead of us. We will gather more supplies here in Ar for the remaining journey.

"You must choose sensibly." He hesitated a moment, glancing from one woman to the next. "You must not overload your animals. Take only food for three or four days, and other items you feel you cannot leave behind."

"Yes, you speak wisely," said Naomi. "We will plan carefully. We have one donkey and a cart. We can take supplies to last several days."

Eliezer looked through solemn eyes. "Inspect your cart carefully. A three-day journey to Bethlehem is not on a smooth stone pavement. The roads will test your cart severely."

"My sons kept the cart in good condition, but I will do as you suggest. I do know the roads as we traveled the same coming here ten years ago."

The man smiled. "They are no better today. We have kinsmen who reported such a few weeks ago when they came to give us the good news that the rains had come to Israel.

"Now, we must hurry along. Yahweh bless you and keep you; Yahweh make His face shine upon you and be gracious to you; Yahweh lift up His countenance upon you and give you peace."

Naomi's bright smile grew broad across her face. "Thank you again, Eliezer. You have truly blessed my home today. We offer Yahweh's blessing upon you and Deborah, also. Yahweh bless you and keep you; Yahweh make His face shine upon you and be gracious to you; Yahweh lift up His countenance upon you and give you peace."

Naomi bowed low to Eliezer, and he bowed to her.

After several days of preparation, Naomi was ready to depart Moab. The elation of that first day had begun to wane. With each passing day, she grew more melancholy.

Naomi had to face the reality of leaving the graves of her husband and sons, never to visit again. Each day the burden of guilt for abandoning Judah and journeying to Moab weighed upon her mind. She sincerely believed the punishment for leaving the Promised Land was the loss of those dearest to her. It nagged at her daily. Many questions would come when she again lived among her family and friends. How would she answer?

What happened to Elimelech, Mahlon, and Chilion? Where are your grandchildren? Surely after ten years your sons and their wives produced children.

The humiliation of going home empty, with hardly more than the clothes on her back, would be almost unbearable. Now, after a few days of contemplation her desire of being home barely tipped the scale in favor of leaving Moab. It would not be easy facing all of Bethlehem, yet it was hers to do. It would take backbone to do it, and if nothing else, she did have a backbone.

To the land of Judah

She went out from the place where she was,
and her two daughters-in-law with her;
and they went on the way to return to
the land of Judah.

–Ruth 1:7

Chapter 16

A wet, silent, morning, graying towards light greeted the women as they arose from their beds. Scurrying about, they finished packing and started out as the sun peeked over the horizon.

Stubborn, the donkey Mahlon named for his persistent trait of not obeying, moved out fast pulling the cart loaded with supplies. The animal had earned his name when young and difficult to handle. He could be hair-pulling obstinate and proved it on many occasions. Today, he obeyed orders. Perhaps he sensed the excitement of the journey and what it held.

In Moab and many other countries of that region, accompanying a person to the border was a custom. Although Naomi had determined to return home to Judah alone, Ruth and Orpah would not hear of it. They had packed several personal items and loaded them into the cart. They were going.

Naomi protested, but her daughters-in-law would not accept any of her arguments for staying behind.

"This land has been death to me. A land that has buried my husband and my sons." She dabbed her eyes. "Yahweh has dealt with me according to the sins of my family. We should never have stayed." She bit her lower lip and swallowed hard. "We only came to sojourn. It was to be brief. Oh, my soul longs for home. The green pastures of Judah are always before my eyes, so also the cattle upon a thousand hills, those hills of the Promised Land."

Finally, Naomi regained her composure. "Now, when we reach the Arnon, I shall go on alone." She glanced over at Ruth and Orpah. "You *must* return to your mothers."

Silence—the women gave their answers. Ruth and Orpah had determined to continue with Naomi all the way to Bethlehem. It had become a test of wills and for the daughters-in-law it meant keeping commitments made.

When within sight of the river, Naomi stopped, and again broached the subject. "The Arnon is the border. Your service to me will end at the river's edge. Will you return to your homes when we reach the river?"

The intense regard that Ruth and Orpah had for their mother-in-law manifested in their actions and silence. They had packed their garments, a few items of cosmetics and jewelry, and the marriage coins given to them by their husbands, expecting to journey all the way to Judah.

By marriage to her sons, Ruth and Orpah had transferred their identities from their fathers, Paebel, and Keret, to their husbands, Mahlon, and Chilion. Each woman was considered a member of her husband's clan, and in that act of marriage they had become servants of Naomi, also.

However, by insisting they should return home, she had released them from service. Nevertheless, they intended to remain faithful to their clan and commitment.

Naomi's anxiety for them ran deep, affected by several factors. Regardless of how much they loved her, they would not be accepted by many in Judah. As she had experienced in Moab, so also in Bethlehem, they would find it almost impossible to find employment.

Because the Moabites worshiped Chemosh, most Israelites loathed them, and it had gnawed at the Hebrews for centuries.

In addition, the Israelites were very aware all Moabites came from the incestuous union of Lot and daughter, and, for this reason, the Israelites looked upon the whole race as illegitimate.

Another reason Israel held a grudge against Moab was because the Moabites did not meet the Israelites with bread and water on the road when they came out of Egypt. And, to add more insult, Balak, the king of Moab hired the prophet Balaam to curse the Israelites.

So, Naomi had plenty of reasons to concern herself with her daughters-in-law journeying to Judah.

"Mother, you need us and we need you," said Ruth. "We will cross the river with you and journey on to your land."

Naomi checked the supplies on the cart. All appeared stable. "Each step takes you further from your mothers' homes. Shall you go to a land of which you know nothing? My people will shun you at the least. There are evil men there who will try to take advantage of you. No, my daughters, turn back."

Naomi understood the pull that the Moabite gods had on the women. Those gods were still their gods. They had not relinquished them. Consequently, two idol worshiping women would not be welcome by her family and friends. Oh, some Israelites still clung to their household idols, but she believed most did not. At the Arnon, if Ruth and Orpah still insisted on remaining with her, Naomi would try one last time to discourage them.

"We shall go on," Ruth said.

Orpah glanced back. The tug of her family begging her to come home had begun to draw her. Although she did not like her father refusing to employ Naomi, she understood. Her father was a good man, so also her mother. She had better relationships with them than did Ruth with her parents. However, she had agreed to go with Naomi. "Yes, we shall go with you," Orpah said.

At the ferry crossing, the women watched the man shove off with a full load of people, animals, and goods. On the other side of the river was Reuben in the land of Israel. During the interval it took the ferry to cross the river, unloaded and returned, Naomi must convince Ruth and Orpah to turn back.

Naomi believed her life was over. She was too old to have another husband, her God had all but forsaken her, and her life no longer had significance or purpose. What did she have left?

A family of three women—in Moab or Israel, was no family. Without a husband, father, or son to be head and protector, Ruth, Orpah and Naomi had nothing.

Although she dearly loved Ruth and Orpah, she must insist they remain in Moab. Their best opportunity for a reasonably normal life meant to give them up to their flesh and blood families. She would manifest loving-kindness to them in the sacrifice of leaving Moab without them and ask Yahweh to bless them with that same loving-kindness.

Naomi spoke softly, yet with a voice that demanded. It was a command to Ruth and Orpah, and they recognized it. "Go!" She pointed toward Ar. "Each of you must return to your mother's house. May Yahweh deal kindly with you, as you have dealt with the dead and with me. Yahweh grant that you may find security, each in the house of a new husband."

The women remained silent, not budging. They made no move to leave. So Naomi kissed them and gave them a gentle push in the direction of home.

An emptiness within left Ruth and Orpah weak. Both gazed at Naomi with bleak, almost lonely eyes. Then the tears came, and they wailed.

"Surely we will return with you to your people," Ruth cried.

"Yes, Mother," Orpah said. "We will remain with you."

Naomi's face tightened, deepening the age lines. "Turn back, my daughters; why will you go with me? Are there still sons in my womb that may become your husbands?"

The wailing subsided. They looked at Naomi through red, bleary eyes. She tried again.

"Turn back, my daughters, go—for I am too old to have a husband. If I should say I have hope, if I should have a husband tonight and should also bear sons, would you wait for them till they were grown? Would you restrain yourselves from having husbands? No, my daughters; for it grieves me very much for your sakes that the hand of Yahweh has gone out against me!"

Then the weeping started again. Nevertheless, Naomi's arguments for them to go home had finally gotten through to Orpah. It appeared logical that if she wanted a life it would be in Moab. Though leaving her mother-in-law truly broke her heart, she wanted that life. Her desire for another marriage, which undoubtedly would produce the grandchildren her parents longed to hold and love, was greater than her love for Naomi. She would accept Naomi's offer to release her from her commitment to Chilion's family.

Orpah kissed her mother-in-law, gathered her things from the cart, and walked toward home. Ruth watched her go.

"See, Orpah has gone back to her people and her gods; return after your sister-in-law."

Hurt showed in Ruth's face. She shook her head and clung to Naomi.

"Please Mother, stop imploring me to leave you, and turning back from following after you. For wherever you go, I will go, and wherever you lodge, I will lodge. Your people shall be my people, and your God, my God. Where you die, I will die, and there will I be buried. May Yahweh deal with me, be it ever so severely, if even death separates you and me."

Naomi smiled and gave Ruth an intense look, deep into her eyes, a look of respect. This daughter-in-law was not a woman you could shake loose.

Of all the emotions Naomi felt at that moment, she could not distinguish between relief and guilt – guilt because of the relief she felt that she would not be alone.

As one they turned their eyes toward Ar watching as Orpah disappeared into the horizon.

The river crossing went without incident. It consumed half a day to reach the Arnon, wait to board the ferry, and then unloaded on the other side.

Naomi held the rope attached to Stubborn and walked several hundred cubits along the road that led away from the river landing. Ruth followed the cart.

Away from the activity of the ferryboat, Naomi fell to her knees and offered a prayer of thanksgiving to Yahweh.

Ruth smiled and watched through eyes of reverence. Gentle tears wet her face as she considered this anguished woman on her knees. Naomi loved Ruth and Orpah so much that she had been willing to send them home, which would have further deepened her heartbreak.

Her mother-in-law deserved great honor, and Ruth was determined to give it to her. Only Naomi had survived the stay in Moab. Ruth had been considering Naomi's words. She had commented more than once in Ruth's hearing that Yahweh *had* punished Elimelech and his sons for leaving their Promised Land, and also for worshiping another god.

Ruth could not understand why Yahweh worked in such a way, but she believed he might. Now he would be her God, yet giving up Chemosh would not be easy. She did not like the sex worship and the human sacrifices her god demanded, but she always believed he was a god and a superior god to Yahweh.

However, she had promised Naomi that Yahweh would now be her God. She meant every word but, Chemosh and the Baals had been her gods for all her life. She knew them, prayed to them, and worshiped them. The idols she bowed before remained in her bag on the cart. It is not always easy to give up one way of life and take on another.

With words and intentions, she had rejected her gods, but she was human and humans have strong emotions. Emotionally she remained attached to her gods. Purging herself of a lifetime of feelings would not be easy.

Naomi got to her feet, smiled at Ruth and waved her on. Ruth hurried to her side, and they walked the road together. The two-day journey across Reuben to the Jordan River crossing had begun.

The morning had been cool and pleasant, no wind. After the midday meal, which they ate at a small rest stop not far from the crossing, the women took to the road. Stubborn had no mind to hurry, and Naomi being ten years older than the first time she traveled the road, found the old donkey's pace comfortable.

The three-day journey now shaped up more like a four-day. The sudden realization that she had aged ten years hit her. She had not considered her age when planning the trip. However, she brought four days of food supplies and could make it stretch further if needed.

From the Arnon to Jordan's banks would be two long days through the country of Reuben. Then uphill another long day, and probably a day and a half to reach Bethlehem. The road through Reuben she had traveled on her first trip. Safety was always a concern, but not like the road from Jericho to Jebus. It had a reputation for being dangerous, and not one to travel alone. The Egyptian caravan came to mind. Elimelech attached the family to those men when coming from Jebus to Moab. She and Ruth would need to do the same. Finding a group of travelers would be a must. On a well-traveled road like the one from the Jordan to Jebus, she believed would not be too difficult.

The mid-afternoon sun burned hot upon their backs. Although it was spring, the month of Nisan, the plains of Reuben proved to be warmer than they had anticipated.

"It will be much cooler at Bethlehem," Naomi said. "The town is in the highlands and this time of year is pleasant."

"I look forward to seeing your land," said Ruth. "By what you have told me over the years, I am sure I will love it."

Naomi smiled. "Yes, the hope of returning to my country has saved me from total despair. My troubles have weighed heavy at times, but the hope of returning to the Promised Land has always given me the courage to face each day."

As they traveled, Ruth studied the countryside. The rain had been plenty, evidenced by the lush grass growing in the meadows and on the low hills. However, it had not rained for a few days, and the road showed it. The well-traveled, dry road, created dust, which choked their throats and caked their faces. Scorching heat added to the miserable conditions. Sweat ran, leaving mud streaks on the faces of both women.

When the afternoon was full upon them, they stopped to rest. Stubborn stood still, twisted his neck and rolled his eyes toward the cart that held the goatskins full of water.

"Time for water."

"Allow me, mother. Sit down and rest."

"Water the animal first," said Naomi with a weary sigh.

"I have cared for animals all my life." Ruth chuckled. "I know the rule—always care for the donkey first. We need him more than he needs us."

Naomi nodded her agreement, found a grassy spot, and dropped. She sat staring at the hot earth. After a short time, a lizard scooted in front of her, stopped, sides panting, and looked straight at her. Then, as suddenly as it came, it was gone. She closed her eyes and bowed her head attempting to screen the bright light from the afternoon sun.

Ruth filled a bowl with water, and Stubborn drank it all. Taking a water pitcher from the cart, she filled it and offered Naomi the first drink. She drank and drank again.

Three hours later, although bone tired, their feet dragging, both women forced themselves to keep walking. The more road they put behind them this first day would mean less on the second and third. Shadows crept slowly across the land as the sun slid toward the western horizon.

Ruth caught the muted sound of rushing water, a sound that held promise of a cool drink. As the women topped the next rise, she spotted a group of travelers at the bottom of the hill. Several men and women stood at the edge of a stream, watching it rush over stones, all worn smooth from ancient times by the never-ending erosion from the current.

"Mother, they have stopped for the night. We should do the same. I see a fire going, perhaps we can ask for a few coals to start a fire for us."

"I am ready."

The small group, Reubenites all, were on their way to Gad, the country that lies due north of Reuben. They invited Ruth and Naomi to the fire. When Ruth asked for a few coals, promising not to bother them for anything else, the Hebrews would not hear of turning them away from their fire only to make another.

The women thanked them profusely. After leading Stubborn to the nearby stream and allowing him to drink his fill, Ruth staked him out on a lush stand of grass and joined the group.

The man who appeared to be the patriarch of this band of Reubenites eyed Ruth much longer than she believed necessary. "We journey to the country of Gad, which is home to one of the twelve tribes of Israel. Naomi has been telling us about you."

Ruth smiled. "Is it permissible to sit at your fire?"

"Of course, do not be concerned. Your mother-in-law has delightful things to say about you. Please, sit."

Ruth's face warmed from his remarks. "My mother is very kind to say nice things."

"I apologize," the man said. "I must have misunderstood. She is your mother?"

"I call her mother though my mother by flesh and blood lives outside the city of Ar."

Ruth told her story and kept the Hebrews' attention until the end. Naomi remained quiet and let her speak. It gave Ruth an opportunity to tell the Israelites what she would have to repeat many times after entering Bethlehem.

Soon, the dim light of evening faded into night, and the stars came out. Storytelling time had ended. The travelers, weary from their journey, craved a good night's rest.

Ruth had hoped the conversation would last a while longer. She loved associating with the people, and the acceptance she received. It filled her with hope that she would receive the same in Bethlehem.

One of the men stirred the dying fire; it blazed up, giving enough light for all to move to their sleeping mats.

Ruth continued to gaze into the feeble flame as the firelight danced on her soft cheek. "There is something comforting about a fire." She turned her head and looked at her mother-in-law. Naomi nodded.

Much later, Ruth lay staring at the sky. The early spring night had cooled, and the stars twinkled clear and bright. A slight wind was enough to chill her, so she pulled her mantle tight about her neck.

On this first night, she found it difficult to sleep. Sleeping under the stars was new to her and the night sounds of scurrying, unknown animals kept her alert. She feared snakes and they slithered quietly, which worried her even more.

On no occasion had she ventured this far from home, and certainly never from Moab. It also meant she had never been this far away from her husband. When she needed to talk or think, she could always go to his grave. Ruth had considered this before leaving Moab, but now the realization of it had begun to sink in. She would never see his grave again.

Ruth tried in vain to stop the tears. They ran from the corners of both eyes, down the sides of her face and into her ears. Never moving her head, keeping her eyes upon the stars, she brushed the wetness away with her fingers.

The long, lonely howl of a wolf pierced the night, and suddenly a cold, empty, loneliness ran through her. She had seen numerous times what a wolf could do to her father's sheep. Her heart quaked. Wolves will kill and eat their fill, but kill the rest, not for hunger, but because they are wolves.

Then, from the corner of her eye, Ruth caught a glimpse of movement and turned her head. One of the men had gone to the fire, stirred it, and tossed several sticks in the flames. It blazed up. She smiled, knowing what he was doing. Wild animals are afraid of fire. The wolves would not come close tonight.

Again she stared at the sky. The stars hung like torches in the blackness. After several minutes, Ruth's eyelids grew heavy as a gentle breeze whispered into her ear. She finally relaxed and fell asleep.

Chapter 17

The first red streaks had already ignited the eastern sky when Ruth awoke to the ear-grating sound of a squawking bird. She could not see him nor identify the species. He refused to be silent, which was a sure indication a snake had riled him. A new day of trudging the remaining miles across Reuben to the Jordan River crossing had begun.

Bone tired when she laid her head to sleep, a night's rest had refreshed, but she wanted more time on her mat.

Finally, Ruth strapped on her sandals, reluctantly she got to her feet and rolled up the mat storing it on the cart. Naomi slowly pushed herself up to one elbow.

"Mother, I will water Stubborn and gather a few sticks for the fire." Naomi looked through bleary eyes and nodded. Ruth smiled. "You rest a bit more."

Leading the donkey to the stream, she let him drink his fill. While Stubborn dipped his head in the water and drank, Ruth mulled over the words of Naomi. When pressing Ruth and Orpah to return home, she said, "...the hand of Yahweh has gone out against me." Ruth regarded it as a strange thing to say.

Naomi, an Israelite, loved her God, yet Yahweh did not love her. Could that be so? Naomi gave the impression she believed it. On the other hand, it *had* confirmed what she believed about

Naomi. Her mother-in-law trusted that Yahweh God is in control at all times.

Nevertheless, Yahweh had cursed her with terrible hardships. It was quite evident that God had turned against her. Ruth found it difficult to reconcile Naomi's belief in a loving God who bestowed gifts on his people, with a God, who would destroy her family leaving an old woman without hope.

Ruth picketed the donkey and let him graze. Slowly walking back to camp gave her time to think and consider how she could best help her mother-in-law with such bitterness.

What would it take to change such an unhappy person? Ruth hoped Bethlehem would do it. However, she had reflected on some of the challenges both would face and understood it would take more than showing up in Bethlehem to turn Naomi's bitterness into sweetness and contentment.

Ruth had a desire to ask Yahweh for help, but he was not her God—not yet. He would be, she promised, but how? She could ask Chemosh for help, but that would be foolish as he had no power outside Moab. He would not help an Israelite anyway.

Ruth walked up to the cart and found that Naomi had spread a goatskin on the ground and was waiting with bread, dates, and raisin cakes for breakfast. On this short journey, the variety of food was limited. Before leaving Moab, they had laughed about it, agreeing they could do without fresh items for a few days.

"Mother, I have been thinking about how different it will be in Bethlehem. I have lived my entire life in Moab and only know my parents' home and land. Now," she stared at her empty hands, "I go to a country of which I am not familiar. I have promised you I will remain with you always regardless of the circumstances, and

I *will* remain faithful to that pledge. Yet, I am leaving my parents, brothers, and my near kinsmen in Ar."

Naomi tapped the skin motioning for her to sit. Dropping down beside her, Ruth searched the western horizon. Judah lay somewhere beyond.

"I am forsaking my gods for a God, your God, and I do not know all his ways nor understand what I do know about him. My friends begged me to remain in Moab, so actually I have forsaken them, too."

She held up the raisin cake and dates. "Will my food be different there? My clothes, surely the Hebrews will scorn my Moabite clothes.

Naomi chuckled. "My dear—."

"I know the Hebrew language, Mahlon taught me, although it is not much different than what the Moabites speak. Will it be so different in Bethlehem? I am not afraid of all those things, but it will take time to adjust. You must help me—I know you will."

Ruth took a breath, interrupting her rare outburst.

"Ruth, your sweetness is always evident to everyone. These people, she motioned toward the Reubenites, they have mentioned it to me. Certainly, I will help you. Bethlehem is not much different from living in Moab. You shall see for yourself in two days." Naomi chuckled. "And, Yahweh my God, I will tell you of him and his law. Soon you will come to believe and trust that he rules heaven and earth."

The women trailed behind the Reubenites for most of the day. On their right, to the east, Mount Nebo towered above them, and to the left the Salt Sea lay in plain view.

Toward evening, their new friends bid Naomi and Ruth goodbye continuing north toward a small village south of the Jabbok River in the country of Gad. The women turned toward the west and followed the road that would bring them to the bottom of the Jordan River valley and a spot where they could ford without a ferry.

The road would take them from the highlands of Reuben downhill all the way to the winding river, which flowed below sea level and emptied into the Salt Sea. The narrow and challenging trail, which some called a road, but hardly qualified, took much longer to negotiate than Ruth or Naomi had considered when gazing down upon the Jordan.

The sky had become an unbroken gray, and when they neared the river, a gentle sprinkle of rain began to fall. Naomi glanced over with questioning eyes. Ruth noticed a stand of trees near the river, and soon Stubborn pulled up under a giant oak. It would provide good cover unless a heavy downpour started. The heavily leafed tree caught most of the moisture, and if it let up soon, the women would be damp but not soaked.

Ruth picketed the donkey nearby on a good stand of grass and hurried to where Naomi sat on a goatskin at the base of the tree. Within moments, the sprinkles stopped, and the sky began to clear.

"Not enough to settle the dust," said Naomi.

"No, but we are dry, and our fire starter is the same." Ruth stood and began pulling items from the cart they would need for the evening. "I will get a fire going."

She carried a clay pot that contained the fire-starters to a spot previously used by some traveler. In a circle of stones, a few coals remained—none active. Setting the jar next to one of the stones, she began a search for kindling.

Stepping carefully through the brush and fallen logs, Ruth found several dry branches broken loose from trees. On the return walk to the fire pit, she stumbled across a packrat's nest that produced additional sticks good for sparking a fire.

Removing the lid from the pot, she pulled out a flint, one large reddish Jasper stone, a char cloth made from linen, and an old bird's nest. Placing the stone on top of the fabric, Ruth began striking the Jasper with the flint. After several strikes, the hard-edged flint sparked off a tiny piece of iron from the Jasper stone that landed on the cloth and ignited.

The char cloth smoldered a thin tendril of smoke and Ruth bent over and blew very lightly. Red showed, and she blew a bit stronger. Finally, it burst into flames. Carefully, she placed a piece of the nest on top of the cloth, and the fire took hold. Then came the small sticks and soon the fire blazed up.

Although the day was not cold, the heat would knock the chill off produced from the damp clothes the women wore.

While Ruth built the fire brighter, Naomi moved the goat-skin near and then unpacked the bread, raisin cakes, and dates. "I have a surprise."

Ruth looked over, and her mouth fell open. Naomi held up two large oranges.

"I could not leave Moab without bringing fresh fruit. Oranges were the perfect choice."

Ruth chuckled. "Mother, you brought them out at the perfect time, also.

Naomi's eyes twinkled. "Do we eat them now or later?"

"Life is unpredictable," Ruth said. "Eat them now!" She laughed. "Why wait?"

For a fleeting moment, the bitter memory of Elimelech's sudden death crossed Naomi's mind. "Yes, now." She handed the largest orange to Ruth.

Ruth noticed, said nothing, knowing Naomi would refuse to take the larger one. "Thank you."

As they peeled the fruit, a few stray raindrops dripped from the trees and the flames guttered and hissed.

Naomi gazed toward the east where low hanging clouds shrouded the middle of Mount Nebo. "I want to tell you about that mountain." Early evening shadows had begun to cover the canyons, but the lofty heights of the mountain remained in full sunshine.

"Mount Nebo?" Ruth asked in a questioning tone.

"Yes. Moses' grave is up there. No one knows where."

"I am aware of Moses and his law though I do not know what his law prescribes. It is common knowledge he was a great leader of the Hebrews. Many great leaders have monuments built at their graves, yet the Hebrews made nothing for Moses. It is strange."

Ruth took a seat on a rock which lay near the fire, and Naomi took a place on the goatskin, reclined on one elbow, and began her story.

"Alone, Moses climbed Mount Nebo from these plains, all the way to the summit. At the mountain top, he had a grand view of Jericho and all of the land west of the Jordan.

"Yahweh showed him the whole land—from Gilead to Dan in the north, all of Naphtali, the territory of Ephraim and Manasseh, all the land of Judah as far as the Great Western Sea, the Negev in the south, and the whole region from the Valley of Jericho, the City of Palms, as far as Zoar."

The fire flickered in the breeze, and Naomi reached out and dropped another branch into the flame.

"From the hills of my father's land, on clear days, I have gazed at the lands west of the Salt Sea. From up there," Ruth motioned to the top of Nebo, "it must be an incredible sight to see all the way to the Great Sea. I understand that sea goes to the end of the earth."

"It does," Naomi said, smiling. "All of the land Moses beheld that day Yahweh had promised on an oath to Abraham, Isaac and Jacob. We call it the land promise. He said, 'I will give it to your descendants.'

"Then our God said, 'I have let you see it with your eyes, but you will not cross over into it.' After those words, Moses died."

Ruth gave her an uncertain look. "Is it not strange that Moses led the people to this land, but your God refused to allow him to enter, and then took his life?" She slowly shook her head. "Yahweh's ways are so mysterious."

"Yes, it was my God who buried him in the valley opposite Beth Peor, and no one knows the location of the gravesite." Naomi shrugged her shoulders. "My God's ways are higher than our ways.

"It *is* true. He required the life of Moses. The great prophet was a hundred and twenty years old when he died, yet his eyes were not weak nor his strength gone. He had many years of good health ahead of him, yet God determines when it is our time to die, and it was his time. I shall tell you why it was his time, but not now. That is another story." She gave a quick smile.

"Another great man of God, Job, after he had suffered many losses in his life said, 'Yahweh gave, and Yahweh has taken away, blessed be the name of Yahweh.'" The skin around Naomi's eyes twitched and bunched, her face hardened. "I shall tell you of Job and his troubles, but on another day."

Ruth caught Naomi's anguished look and would not push her for more information. "You have given me enough to ponder, yet I *would* like to know why your God refused to allow Moses entrance into the land. And—this man Job, his story sounds very interesting, too. I have much to learn."

As twilight drew on, Ruth and Naomi, weary after two days of walking, sat quietly staring into the fire. An hour slipped by unnoticed while the women reminisced. Soon the sun dipped below the western peaks and night arrived early. "I will get the mats," Ruth said. "I am tired."

"Not as tired as your mother-in-law." Naomi chuckled.

The long, lonely howl of a wolf split the night air. Ruth trembled. Fear tightened her throat, but she fought down the panic. The nearby woods were dark and thick, and inside the wolves slinked through the trees. Ruth could not decide which she hated and feared most—wild animals or evil men. Some animals could do much harm, but men were known to sneak into a camp, rob everyone, kill the men, and carry the women away to make them slaves.

Ruth's contemplations were interrupted by a giant owl searching the night air, swooping down not far from the fire. She crowded the fire pit and fed more sticks into the flames. The wild animals would stay away she reasoned. Wild men were another matter.

"Will your God protect us?"

Naomi lifted her eyes to meet Ruth's. Firelight danced on the weary faces of the women as they stared across the fire. "He knows his own. He will protect us from evil."

Ruth, her face etched with fear, slowly shook her head. "I do not know him," she said with a quivering voice. "I am not his."

"You have committed to being one of his. You promised that my God would be your God." Naomi gave her a warm, comforting smile. "He will protect you."

Ruth relaxed a bit and returned the smile.

Red-eyed from exhaustion, Ruth and Naomi unrolled the mats and stretched out for the night. The overcast sky hid the stars and moon. It was very dark. An eerie spirit wind moved among the trees and Ruth caught her breath. Out in the dark the owl hooted. 'He knows his own. He will protect us from evil.'

She mulled over Naomi's words, and it brought her comfort. Twenty-seven years old and never away from home, Ruth had always been protected by father, brother or husband. Suddenly alone, and she must rely on God, whom she could not see or hear. It was alien to her way of thinking. Everything must be experienced by touching, seeing, hearing, tasting or smelling. Yahweh provided none of those things.

'Your God will be my God,' she remembered the promise. Ruth meant it, every word. Yet, the words were much easier said than done. *Can I make Yahweh my God? I must not doubt, yet—can I?*

Ruth watched the fire burn down to a lonely flicker in the Jordan River valley. Her eyelids fluttered shut.

The first gray light of dawn broke cool with a lowering sky and an uncomfortable mist. It would deteriorate from there.

Ruth peeked out from under her covering and the gray, dreary morning welcomed her. The heavy, sullen sky gave good reason to remain covered and warm.

The pungent smoke of the dying night fire drifted up from the white coals that lingered. Ruth watched it for a few moments. Finally, it prodded her from the sleeping mat.

She took a long stick and stirred the remains until it revealed the buried red embers. Then, with additional fuel laid upon the gasping cinders, she gently blew them back to life. Within a few moments, a flame had been restored, and Ruth gently added more sticks.

"Mother, the fire is going, come warm yourself."

Not hearing an answer, she turned around. Naomi's mat was empty. Immediately a lump swelled in her throat that she could not swallow, and fear made her heart pound.

"Mother!" Ruth scurried to the mat. She frantically looked around the campsite, her eyes darting back and forth for any sign of Naomi. "Mother!"

"Is there trouble?"

Ruth whirled about looking toward the sound of her mother-in-law's voice. She spotted her emerging from the woods where she had gone to take care of her needs.

"You sound frantic, is there trouble?" she repeated.

"You did not answer when I called. You were not on your mat. I—I…"

"Ruth, it is morning, and I needed to go to the bushes." She laughed. "I know I have lived many more years than you, and you wish to be with me and help me, but daughter, I can still go and take care of my needs without assistance."

Ruth's face darkened with embarrassment. "I am sorry. I have never been on a long journey, and I was…." Her voice trailed off, she turned away and stoked the fire.

Naomi came alongside and put an arm around her shoulders. "I understand. It is lonely out here, but we shall see the fields and vineyards of Bethlehem by evening. Remember, Yahweh's eyes are upon us, and his hand will keep us in his care."

Ruth turned and hugged Naomi's neck. "Thank you. I have left all for you. I am not sorry."

The women took seats on two large stones and stretched their hands toward the fire. Ruth opened her scrip.

"Mother, I cannot go on until I dispose of these. I promised to make Yahweh my God, yet I brought my household idols with me. I packed them because they have always been part of my life. I prayed to them the morning we departed Moab.

"Yet, when we reached the Arnon, I promised to make your God, my God. I do not fully understand what that means. I must learn, but I do know, I cannot keep these. You have taught me Yahweh forbids any graven images."

One by one, she tossed the carved idols of Astarte, Baal, Anat, and Chemosh, along with the fertility monkey amulets into the fire.

Naomi's eyes widened, looking on in amazed silence. Finally, Ruth turned her head.

"I could have had them melted down and sold the silver, but I have no desire to increase my silver bag from those symbols of my former religion."

Naomi got to her feet and helped Ruth to stand. They held each other, Ruth shedding joyful tears and Naomi weeping for this moment which meant much to her daughter-in-law, yet the same joy, Naomi lacked. God had taken so much from her that rising above her bitterness, even at this moment, was too much.

After loading the packs into the cart, Stubborn moved out from the cover of the brush and walked the gentle slope to the Jordan River. The donkey had a mind of its own, and he minded very much getting into the water with a loaded cart. Stubborn began to live up to his name, and it took all the coaxing, pulling, and pushing of Naomi and Ruth to get him across the river. The crossing was shallow, but the donkey had no idea how deep the Jordan ran at that spot and had no mind to find out.

Finally, in Judah and worn out from the river crossing, Naomi found a large rock and sat. The morning air rushed cool and fresh off Mount Nebo, and she breathed deep. After a few moments, her eyes began to glisten.

"Those are tears of happiness," Ruth said, giving Naomi her best smile. "You have finally entered your country."

Naomi only nodded, too choked with emotion for words. She closed her eyes and recollections from her life in Moab, good and bad, marched through her head.

Ruth sat silently watching a caravan of traders from Egypt cross the river heading toward Moab. From the river to the foothills was about five miles and from there it would be all uphill to Bethlehem. The crooked, eighteen-mile road began outside Jericho and ascended 3800 feet to Jebus. From that town, their journey would take them another five miles ending at Bethlehem.

Although the latter rains usually tapered off by springtime in Jericho and the surrounding area down to the river, some years the rainy days came unexpectedly.

Several minutes had passed when a muffled, low rumble of thunder popped Naomi's eyes open. She glanced toward the sound. The clouds had swallowed up the hilltops to the west.

Ruth scanned the clouds and hills with careful eyes. "We may get wet."

"Yes, and if it rains too much, we will not see Bethlehem today." She pressed her lips together in a flash of anger. "That road to Jebus will become a rushing stream. We need to be going and when in the hills keep a sharp eye for places we can get in out of the weather. There will not be many."

Crossing the five miles from the river to the foothills was uneventful. The scent of rain grew stronger as they approached the spot where the road began the steep ascent to Jebus.

Within an hour, the clouded sky had lowered somewhat and began to spit rain. It was but a few minutes, and it slowly turned to a drizzle. As they began their ascent to the low clouds and drizzling rain, the road up to Jebus looked gray, treacherous, and menacing. A cool wind blew through the hills. The women wrapped their mantles closer.

The day had barely begun and now the prospect of reaching Bethlehem before dark was in doubt. Both women understood the dangers and possible delays on the journey from Moab to Bethlehem, so this day did not come as a surprise.

Because of the dangers encountered by travelers, rarely did anyone travel more than two days without first setting his affairs in order. A man or in this instance women would settle all debts, and all final goodbyes were said as they understood they might not return. So, for two women to venture out alone to cross the eighty miles from the Arnon River to Bethlehem was quite remarkable.

By midday, Ruth and Naomi had made good time considering the uphill climb. Their clothes were wet as the rain continued to spit, although nothing substantial yet. They plodded on, not stopping for a midday meal. Instead, they munched on the last of the raisin cakes as they walked. Reaching Bethlehem that day was possible as long as the pouring rains did not come.

Moving slowly along, both kept eyeing the hills, gullies, outcroppings of rock, any spot along the road that would make a shelter from the weather.

They rounded a bend, and the land dropped off from the roadside into a deep ravine partially hidden by tall bushes. A quick movement caught Ruth's eye, and she glanced up. Several circling buzzards began to swoop down, disappearing behind the rocks.

Ruth stopped. Naomi glanced over. Nothing else stirred.

"I will go and see," said Ruth.

"No!" Naomi blurted, giving her a round-eyed look. Then, a sudden, faint memory of Elimelech climbing down into another ravine came to her. She tried to dissuade him from lending a hand to a fellow traveler. He did not agree and Ruth would not, either.

"I must. Someone may be hurt."

Without further protests from Naomi, Ruth edged her way down five feet and moved about the same to the side. She looked into the ravine, and her face paled. Robbers had jumped a traveler, beat him, stole everything including the clothes on his back, and left him for dead. He was. The first buzzards had begun to pick the bones clean.

"It is a man," Ruth said when she got back to the road. "He is dead. Mother, would you pray to your God for our safety?"

"I have. He is the Almighty. I have no fear, and neither should you. He will protect us."

"I believe you." She remembered her vow to make Yahweh her God. The memory swept through her mind in an instant. "Mother, for twenty-seven years all I have known are the gods of Moab. Changing from many gods to one will be a process. Yes, I have given up the Moabite gods, now I must learn to trust in my new God. It is a process, a big change, a new way of life for me."

The skin at the corners of Naomi's eyes crinkled from her gentle smile. "I love you, Ruth. I understand, no need to explain. My God, though harsh at times with wrongdoers, is patient with a woman of virtue. You shall make a wonderful follower of God."

Naomi embraced her daughter-in-law, and they moved on.

The wind picked up, and soon Ruth could hear it howling through the canyons. She peeked over, and Naomi's lined and haggard face startled her. Her mother-in-law's eyes appeared glazed as if in a trance.

Naomi wanted to rest, but reaching home had become an all-encompassing goal, and she would never stop unless forced. Bethlehem drew her like a flower draws a bee. She had looked forward to this journey home for years, and now it was close to completion. She would refuse to stop unless it became almost impossible to continue. She would put up with the burning pain in her legs and the shortness of breath to make it home this day.

Looking over the countryside, Ruth gazed upon a wild and impressive land, an area that appeared to have nothing more than wind and echoes, a lonely country. This high ground, half-way to Jebus, was littered with rocks large and small, thick bushes, and stumps left behind by tree cutters.

They passed among rugged hills of white rock occasionally punctuated with scarlet-colored stratum. Flocks of sheep were spotted here and there on green terraces high up the valley walls. Somewhere in the crags and crevices a quail called.

The long, uphill climb to Bethlehem had begun to take its toll on Naomi. Ruth watched as her mother-in-law, steadfast but slowly put one foot in front of the other. In the distance, thunder rolled, resounding through the hills. Naomi would not make it home this day.

Neither woman had said a word. However, both had been keeping an eye out for shelter. All of a sudden the road dipped down and Ruth spied it first. She pointed. A wide-mouthed cave, not far above the road, invited them to stop for the night. If only the rain held off, they could make it home without spending another night on the road.

This time the thunder boomed, and the rain came with a rush. Ruth looked over, said nothing and hurried up the narrow, well-used pathway to the cave. The path, barely wide enough for donkey and cart, led to overhanging rock. Stubborn quickly came along, and Naomi followed close behind.

The overhanging rock, to the right of the cave entrance, offered enough coverage for Stubborn to stand and remain out of the storm. This small shelter had a manger, and some kind soul had left it full of hay.

Ruth tied the animal to a post attached to the manger, unhitched the cart, and pulled it inside. The cave allowed the women to stand without stooping. How far it went into the hill, they could not determine. Within a few feet of the entrance, signs of use by travelers appeared everywhere. On the floor Ruth found a broken knife blade, an old water skin split from much use and broken pieces of pottery. Charred wood lay scattered about the entrance, which told of many fires.

Naomi found firewood stacked against the cave wall, more than enough for the night. "We can use this for our fire and leave what we gathered along the way for the next person. Ours is wet, but we can set it near the flames, and it should be dried out by morning."

"Your God has blessed you with this shelter." Ruth clasped Naomi's hand. "Leaving our firewood is what he wants you to do. He will bless you abundantly for your kindness."

Naomi pulled her hand away. Her heart had been numbed by what life had dished out to her. "My God has taken everything from me!" she said irritably. "Blessed me with this?" She waved her hand. "If there is a blessing here, it is for you. He wants you to serve him, you said you would, and so he will bless you. Me—no, he has dealt with me severely."

Ruth started to speak, reconsidered and turned away. Taking several pieces of wood and the fire starters, she soon had smoke that finally burst into flames.

"Mother, come sit by the fire and warm up. Your clothing is wet."

Naomi's lips tightened. She had a sudden burst of anger go through her. She wanted to be home, not holed up in some cave on the Jericho road. All of a sudden, she had become as short-tempered as a snake backed into a corner. Her situation ate away at her. No family, a tiny bag of silver, and humiliation facing her when she did make it home. The Almighty blessing her? Ruth certainly was naive.

Naomi sat on the goatskin Ruth had spread on the cave floor. She quietly stared glassy-eyed at the steady rainfall. Soon it would be dark, and she could go to sleep and blank out memories of the past and trepidations of the future.

Later, after sundown, with the only light coming from the fire, Naomi continued to remain silent, staring into the flames. Ruth had made several attempts at starting a conversation, yet Naomi's mood remained gloomy.

Ten years before, she had rejected going to Moab but had no choice. Now, upon her return, she feared the reaction of any friends remaining in Bethlehem.

Ruth perceived what was affecting her mother-in-law. "I wish to speak plainly to you. It hurts me that you are so unhappy. It *is* difficult—I well know. Should I live with hurtful memories in the past, live in anticipation of what lies ahead in an unknown country, or live now in the present, and be thankful for today and its beauty?

"It is a choice I must make each day and some days I do choose poorly. Nevertheless, most days I forget the past.

"The future? I certainly can do little about that. I will be a foreign woman, a Moabitess in Judah, which is only one step above the lowest rank of being a slave.

"So, I choose to live in the present and make the most of it. I have given up the gods of my country and have committed to making Yahweh, my God. However, I must have your help, your guidance. At Bethlehem, we will face the challenges together."

Naomi slowly lifted her chin and without expression, nodded her agreement. Her eyes slanted over to Ruth. "You know the right things to say, my daughter-in-law. Each day will be most difficult as I bear the heartache within me. My God has dealt harshly with me. There will be some days I too shall make poor choices."

Her eyes went back to the fire that had burned down. Picking up a stick, Naomi tossed it into the flickering flames. She pitched a couple more and within moments the fire blazed cheerfully.

Ruth got to her feet and peeked out the cave entrance. In an occasional lightning flash, she could see Stubborn, head up, ears back. He was uneasy. The stormy conditions he knew, but the familiar surroundings of home in Moab were far away.

Glancing back, Ruth watched the firelight flickering against the cave walls. She smiled at the pleasant sight. When closing her eyes, a satisfying speculation that she would choose to keep secret came to mind. *One day Mother shall blaze to life like this fire.*

Chapter 18

Dawn broke over Mount Nebo throwing daggers of sunlight onto the road below the cave entrance. The eastern sky pinked up, and the last stars slowly winked out. Ruth got to her feet and began the process of coaxing the dying embers into flames. She had found a mound of leaves several feet back into the cave. After crumpling and sprinkling them on the lingering coals, she took a stick and softly stirred the dying fire into life.

Looking out from the warm and dry cave, Ruth beheld a rain-soaked countryside. Thinking about life, her life—and how it was about to change, kept her in a somber mood.

She walked to the rock shelter where Stubborn had spent the night, untied him and led the old donkey to a pool of water created by the storm. While he drank, Ruth breathed deeply of the fresh, rain cleansed air.

Bethlehem, a half-day journey away, disturbed her. Getting there would be the easy part of this day. The anticipated reception by the Hebrews kept her anxious. Known for their superior attitude toward the Moabites, she wondered if they would accept her as Naomi's daughter or shun her as a foreign idolater.

The history of relations between the Moabites and Israelites had been rocky at best. She would certainly be rejected by some—maybe most. Nevertheless, she knowingly chose to risk security by clinging to Naomi.

Spying a broken piece of pottery, she looked it over, and then flung it onto the road. *I have no more future in Judah than that shard,* Ruth mused. What people had said of her suddenly came to mind. It caused her to chuckle.

"You are crazy."

"You will never have a home."

"Poverty is your future."

"Who will you marry? No Hebrew will have you."

"Stay home. That old lady has family. They will care for her."

All of those things and more had been said, and still she had no reservations about leaving Moab. She understood the sacrifice. Her future would be to remain a poor widow and serve Naomi. The astonishing thing in the eyes of family and friends, including Naomi, was that Ruth had no doubts about her decision.

After several hours of plodding uphill, Naomi lifted her eyes. There in the distance, outlined against the sky, the jagged ridge on which set her beloved Bethlehem came into view. "Ruth!" She choked that out and nothing more. A giant lump seized her throat.

Looking beyond Naomi's finger, Ruth's eyes swept the distance hillsides. She spotted an object—and then another. Houses, mostly small, here and there outside the city walls. Naomi had described it many times, so at first sight Ruth recognized it.

Drawing closer on the uphill road to the city gates, Ruth let her eyes roam the countryside. She stared close-up and wide-eyed at a country she had known only from gazing across the Salt Sea.

In the valley, the grains grew lush and by the look of the fields, the barley harvest had scarcely begun. The wheat fields, gently waving in a pleasant breeze would be ready for the sickle within a few weeks. The women slowly strolled the road that cut through the teeming fields of grain. The ugly famine no longer plagued the land.

Naomi glanced over catching Ruth's eye. "Ten years ago the crops were anemic. Now look at them. Yahweh has truly visited his people. What was said in Ar is true. The Almighty blesses his people again. Those who stayed, God has blessed. Those who forsook the Promised Land..."

Giving out a long, low sigh, she did not finish. The words would have condemned her, and she could not bear to say them. What she could not understand at that moment was how God's overruling providence in the affairs of his people had brought her home.

Ruth considered Naomi's words and did not let them go unanswered. "Mother, this is a new day, the old is behind us." Silence met her comment. *Encouraging her to eliminate the bitterness is going to take time, no need to push it.*

Ruth understood her faith in Yahweh would grow, and believed Naomi's bitterness would soon die.

Bethlehem sat on a ridge with terraces on three sides, north, south, and east. Loaded with olive and fig trees, grape vines, and gardens of various vegetables, these terraces were a welcoming sight to both women. The wheat and barley grew in the valleys and flocks of sheep grazed on nearby hillsides. Everything they looked upon gave evidence that the stream of Yahweh's blessings flowed freely upon the land.

Naomi's homecoming became a rush of familiarities. Memories, sweet memories of former times flooded her senses. Ten years had come and gone and her last memory of Bethlehem, Judah, was a parched land of weak crops and trickling streams.

Now, this day, the city, her birthplace, and home, surrounded by green hills and abundant vegetation, beckoned her with invisible hands. As her eyes roamed the countryside, God's abundance was exhibited everywhere on the hillsides and in the valleys. Reapers in the barley fields sang the old familiar songs, and the women, gleaning behind them, mingled their sweet voices with the deep voices of the men.

Two women, separated from the others, gleaned near the edge of a field. "They are not part of the harvesters," Naomi said. "Our law allows the poor and stranger to reap the corners of the field and glean any grain that falls to the ground."

The fragrance of fresh cut barley wafted the air, and Naomi breathed deeply, remembering her childhood days in the fields. Approaching a ripening field of wheat, she motioned to Ruth. They left the road and stood next to the ripening crop. Naomi touched the heads. It had been years since she had done that in the fields of Judah.

The sights and sounds and smells and feels of the countryside had the old woman weeping in delight. All that remained was tasting the bread, fruits and vegetables of the land. She did that in her mind, and soon would do it for real.

"Ruth, my heart is pounding. I feel it in my throat. How can I face people? Look at us. Two women, no protectors, and an old donkey loaded with a few items of little value."

"It must be done." She smiled prettily. "We will go together through the gates." Ruth's face shone with hope, and her eyes glowed with eagerness. "I am sure your friends will welcome you. I believe your God has brought you home. You have taught me that he is your protector. Now, shall we greet your people together?"

Ruth held out her hand. However, Naomi was nauseated, and her stomach churned. She ignored the hand and quickly clasped her daughter-in-law's upper arm. Then, grim-faced and bitter, she climbed the final slope and passed through the city gates into Bethlehem.

They had arrived at the eighth hour, which in Hebrew reckoning of time is two hours past noon. The city marketplace had begun to crowd with shoppers, many wishing to bargain for goods, and others buying for the evening meal.

Ruth noticed heads turning, eyes centering on them. She mistakenly assumed that the people stared at her. She had not anticipated this reaction to her arrival.

"Naomi?"

A whispering ran through the crowd. Several women seemed to appear from nowhere, drawn like moths to a flame. Within moments, Naomi was surrounded by women—older women. No one was Ruth's age.

One elderly woman with a wrinkled brow and curious look, asked, "Is this Naomi?"

"Naomi! It is," someone cried out. "I am sure of it."

"Are you?" another asked.

"Do not call me Naomi!" She looked away. "Call me Mara, for—."

"Mara! No, you *are*, Naomi. Look at me." The statuesque woman had large, brown eyes set in a chiseled face, with deep laugh lines about her mouth and eyes. The look of sympathy she gave Naomi and the gray hair about her temples bespoke the years of life experience she had garnered. "It has been many years. Do you not recognize me? I am your friend, Aleeza."

Naomi gave her old friend a cold, stern, measured look. "Call me Mara, for the Almighty, has dealt very bitterly with me. I went out full, and Yahweh has brought me home again empty. Why do you call me Naomi, since the Lord has testified against me, and the Almighty has afflicted me?"

"You are Naomi! How long has it been? Why do you speak in riddles?"

The crowd grew, and word spread that Naomi had returned to Bethlehem. Questions were being asked. People talked over each other as they clamored for information. The excitement increased by the second as did the noise of the crowd. Soon the whole town would be afire with the news of Naomi's return.

Elimelech and Naomi had been prominent citizens of the community, a wealthier family than most. The crowd quickly grew as old friends pushed forward straining to get her attention. They shouted questions.

"Naomi, where is Elimelech? Your sons—where are they?"

"Gone!" she cried out. "They sleep in the earth—Moabite earth."

"Your husband—sons, all dead?"

Naomi's eyes brimmed with tears. She nodded. Aleeza wrapped her arms around her old friend and held her close. She softly wept on Aleeza's shoulder.

Some the women, not many, had begun to drift away. They had no words of comfort for a Hebrew who had forsaken her land for Moab. They had stayed in Bethlehem, remained faithful, and now refused to sympathize with this woman, who wept over her losses.

A grave, old, unsmiling woman with boney fingers pointed and shook her head. "Yahweh has cursed her because of her sins."

Others went about their business, not because they were hard-nosed like the old woman, but they could not form the words to comfort this prodigal.

Ruth's eyes darted about searching for more friends of Naomi's. Where were they? Why not step up and greet her? Then, it hit her. Those women had appraised the foreigner up and down, many with curious, hard eyes. They did not ask about Ruth or why she entered the city with Naomi.

Finally, Naomi stepped back from Aleeza and brushed the tears from her cheeks. She forced a smile. "This is my daughter-in-law, Ruth. She is Mahlon's widow."

"Hello!"

Ruth gave the lady her best smile. "Hello."

"Chilion's widow, Orpah, remains in Moab," Naomi said without any hint of emotion.

Aleeza stared, her brow furrowed in wonder. "Why are you here? Do you not belong to someone or are you without family, also?"

"I have family in Moab. My father and mother live a few miles outside the city of Ar. My—."

"You have left your father, choosing your mother-in-law instead? It is unheard of," she said, her voice rising. "Do you not honor your father and worship the gods of Moab?"

"My father has much in this life, and he did plead with me to come and abide in his house. However, my mother-in-law needs me far more than my father needs me, and unquestionably I am closer to Naomi. She is my family, and I have made it clear to her that I shall always honor my commitment to my husband by remaining within his family, not my father's."

Aleeza stared wide-eyed at this young woman so full of love for Naomi. Never had she come across such love, even among the Hebrews. She believed it marvelous, but unthinkable. This Moabitess without doubt worshiped that heathen god Chemosh, yet she preferred a Hebrew mother-in-law over her parents. It absolutely did not make sense.

"At the River Arnon, I pleaded with her to go back. She is a woman with much love in her heart, but a stubborn one, too." A wry smile came to Naomi's face. "I could not ask for a more loving daughter-in-law.

"We must go to the inn and settle for the night. Is it still here?"

"You shall do no such thing, my dear Naomi. Come with me and stay the night at my home. Bethlehem has an inn, but Hebrew hospitality is still the custom in our home."

"Will the inn allow a woman of Moab to lodge the night? I can also keep Stubborn with me." She placed a hand on the donkey's back.

"Ruth, please forgive me. I did not make myself clear. You are welcome in my home, also. Your donkey—uh, did you call him Stubborn?"

Ruth chuckled. "Yes, he earned his name many years ago."

Aleeza touched the animal's neck. He shied a bit. "He is welcome, too. We have more than enough room for him."

Ruth bowed to Aleeza. "Thank you. It is most kind of you to show hospitality to a stranger."

"My dear, is that not what hospitality is? Kindness, not only for our people but for others, too."

"Does your God require it?" Ruth asked.

Aleeza took Ruth's hand. "He does. Our law reads: the stranger that dwells with you shall be unto you as one born among you, and you shalt love him as yourself for you were strangers in the land of Egypt. I am Yahweh your God.

"Yes, from the scroll of Leviticus, which is one of the scrolls of the Law of Moses, our God's command is found."

Ruth's face beamed. "I wish to know more about Yahweh and his commands. I have promised Naomi that your God will be my God."

"Follow me," Aleeza said. "We shall have much time to talk of the Almighty."

Ruth looked about and spied a baker's oven across the square. "We must purchase bread. Our food supplies have dwindled to almost nothing. The journey took one more day than we planned."

Aleeza glanced at Naomi. "She has much to learn about our ways."

Naomi draped an arm around Ruth's shoulders. "Aleeza will provide our meal tonight. Shall we insult her by offering to buy bread? No, my daughter."

Ruth nodded. "I beg your forgiveness. I do have much to learn about your customs."

Aleeza led the way through the gates, down a winding path to her home, which sat less than one mile away. As Naomi and her old friend talked of by-gone days, Ruth gazed at the countryside. This land rivaled her own for bountiful crops. The man from Jebus told the truth. The years of famine in Israel were gone. The God of Israel had sent the rains and the hills and valleys of Judah teemed with life.

Terracing of the hillsides was most impressive. The terraces had been designed to preserve the soil from eroding with the rains. Rocks and larger stones plucked from the fields built the walls that were so prominent downhill. Landowners also used the stones to mark boundary lines, and neighbors would not dare touch them lest they fall into the condemnation of Yahweh. Ingrained in the minds of the Israelites was Yahweh's command not to remove landmarks.

You shall not remove

your neighbor's landmark,

which the men of old have set…

cursed is the one who moves

his neighbor's landmark.

Ruth looked with wonder at the abundance of fruits and vegetables blanketing the terraces. Wheat and barley fields in the valleys, as far as the eye could see, gave abundant proof that the famine no longer gripped the land. In addition, thousands of grapevines, along with fig, olive and almond trees, were so thick, it appeared to her as one giant forest. Later in the growing season, the land would produce onions, cucumbers, melons, various spices, and many other crops. Flax would provide fibers for rope and linen.

Sheep grazed along the tops of the hills and after many days when the grass would become scarce, the shepherds would move their flocks down the hillsides to new pastures in the Judean plain toward the Salt Sea.

Entering the courtyard of Aleeza, Ruth noticed the grape vines clinging to the low walls and climbing into the trees surrounding the house.

"We have a bench, basins, and water to cleanse your feet. Eden my servant-girl shall assist you. Excuse me while I announce your arrival to my husband.

After Aleeza had disappeared into the house, Ruth turned to Naomi. "Her servant-girl? She does not appear to be a woman of wealth. She has servants?"

"The girl may be an orphan, or possibly a daughter of a poorer family. She may work for wages to help support her family in Bethlehem. Elimelech and I had such a servant at one time. They are not bondservants, but free and receive pay for their work."

Eden arrived almost immediately and set a clay water-basin at Naomi's feet. She placed her feet into the basin and Eden poured water and washed the guest's feet. After completing the task, she turned to Ruth. "I shall empty the basin on the flowers and return to wash your feet."

"I am a Moabite." Ruth's eyes widened. "Do you wash a foreigner's feet?"

"You are a guest in the house of Hadar. Your race or nationality is of no concern." She bowed and rushed away.

At that moment, Aleeza returned and with a strikingly handsome man accompanying her. "This is my husband, Hadar."

The man bowed to Naomi and then Ruth.

"I remember your husband," said Naomi.

Hadar was a strapping, powerfully built man, with kind eyes and a face creased by many years in the sun. He stood tall and straight.

"I am pleased to welcome you to our home. I overheard your question to Eden. We welcome all people, Israelite and stranger alike. As long as you remain here you are under my protection, and I shall defend you from any enemy regardless of cost."

Naomi and Ruth bowed to him. "Sir, thank you for your generosity to a stranger," said Ruth. "You are most kind."

"Naomi, please follow us into the house," Hadar said. "It is good that you have come home. Ruth, Eden will show you the way after she washes your feet."

Again he bowed to Ruth and she did the same. While Eden performed the foot washing duties, Ruth mulled over what she had experienced in one day.

The bitterness that her mother-in-law carried inside would soon destroy her. Ruth understood, without any doubt, that her mother-in-law must rid herself of this terrible burden, and soon. *Naomi is too good a woman for her God to punish her forever. I must make her see that. I am sure it will take considerable time, but it needs doing. I will beg Aleeza's help.*

"Ruth." The servant girl paused. "Ruth!"

"I am sorry, Eden. Many things have happened, and I had those on my mind."

The servant girl smiled. "Your face is full of pain. May I ask what would trouble you so much? Can I help in some way?"

"When my mother-in-law and I entered the city, it caused a great commotion. Women appeared from everywhere, crowding about us, asking questions. I rather think Naomi was well-known and highly respected when she lived here. Even several men were there. It caused quite a stir. Am I correct?"

Eden nodded. "Aleeza has spoken on several occasions about her friend Naomi, wondering what happened to her and if she still lived. Her husband was an Ephrathite of high reputation according to Aleeza and Hadar. Elimelech and Naomi had many possessions, even more than my master and his wife."

Ruth gave her a knowing look and an understanding smile. Naomi's former situation was as her daughter-in-law believed. Pleasant Naomi, always concerned to keep her God's commands, at one time had much in this world's goods. Tragically, she lost almost all, and Naomi believed it was due to disobedience. Yahweh had punished her because Elimelech forsook their Promised Land for a foreign country.

The task of supporting her mother-in-law with uplifting words and encouraging her to rekindle the hope and trust she once had would not be easy.

Ruth touched Eden's shoulder. Thank you for your service and answering my question. "Please take me inside."

Chapter 19

Boaz stood on the roof of his house in Bethlehem watching the dawn paint the eastern sky assorted shades of amethyst and ruby. Surveying the spectacular scene before him, he not only gazed upon the awe-inspiring sunrise but also took in the lush, green rolling hills. From Bethlehem, the landscape dramatically plunged toward the Judean wilderness ending at the Salt Sea, a mere fifteen miles as the crow flies. Then, it was only seven miles across that body of water to the eastern shore where the hazy, purple hills of Reuben began to rise.

Boaz turned toward the southeast. His eyes followed the coastline of the sea and spied the country of Moab sitting high above the Salt Sea gorge.

This warrior and mighty man of God dropped to his knees and offered the morning prayers of thanksgiving for all of the bountiful blessings given by the hand of the Almighty.

All of the houses had flat roofs with a slight tilt for rain run-off, and many had upper rooms that accommodated guests. Boaz stood on the roof of the upper room. It provided him a remarkable view of the Judean countryside.

Although Boaz resided within the town walls, his fortune consisted of the fields and crops on the hillsides and valleys outside of Bethlehem. He employed many Hebrews to work in his vineyards and fields, some were righteous, and others had forsaken the precepts and commands of Yahweh.

This man of God lived during a time when judges ruled in Israel. It was a period when much evil would reign for years, followed by a general repentance of the people, and then followed by years of wickedness and idol worship. This cycle of good and evil lasted for hundreds of years.

Everyone did what was right in his own eyes regardless of what the Law of Moses said. That was a generalized statement of the conditions in Israel, and Boaz, along with a few other faithful Hebrews, was an exception.

He would have preferred hiring all honest men and women, people he could implicitly trust, but there were not enough of those with the high standards he held dear to go around. So, although many of his workers were conscientious laborers who worked diligently, those same people had lascivious ways and worshiped the Canaanite gods.

Several times when walking through the corn rows or grape vineyard, he had come upon a man and woman having sexual relations. Of course, he did not approve but kept walking as it almost always happened during meal time or after the day's work was over. The few times he discovered people lying together or at times loafing when they should have been working, he gave them a warning—the next time he would banish them from his fields.

Boaz worshiped Yahweh as his parents did. His ancestors were men and women who wandered in the wilderness for forty years, had seen Moses and were at Mount Sinai when God wrote the Law on tables of stone. With such tradition in his family tree,

Boaz would do nothing other than worship the God of Israel and keep his commands.

It was not so with many of the inhabitants of Judah. The Hebrews lived among Canaanites. God's people had failed to drive out all of the idol worshipping people, so now their ways and religion had influenced many in the tribe of Judah.

The Canaanites worshiped the Baal gods and participated in the depraved custom of foundation worship. It was the practice of sacrificing a newborn to the gods and then taking the body and having it placed into the foundation of a man's new home for good luck. Without access to a newborn, a family would take their youngest child, sacrifice him or her, and use that body in the foundation. It was an abhorrent practice that Boaz or any other righteous Hebrew could not abide. The Law expressly said:

> Do not put an innocent
> or honest person to death,
> for I will not acquit the guilty.

These things and many others passed through his mind as he meditated on the many blessings he enjoyed each day. He gave thanks for the privilege of serving a loving and merciful God.

His meditation time included thoughts of his family. Boaz was often perplexed about his uncle, Elimelech, and was this day as he looked toward Moab. Why had he not returned to Judah? Ten years in Moab was not a sojourn.

The last words from Elimelech before he departed Bethlehem, still stuck in Boaz's memory ten years later.

"If God is good, which you claim, then I will be home soon."

"Boaz."

He turned to the sound of his mother's voice. "I have finished my morning prayers and am enjoying the view."

"Food is on the table. Will you join us?"

Mother and son descended the outside staircase to the courtyard below. There a table had been spread with bread, cheese, dates, walnuts, and honey to dip the bread. Salmon sat at the table awaiting his son.

"Sit beside me, my son. Your mother and I have news, sad news."

Boaz gave him a guarded look and reclined at the low table next to his father. "What has happened? Is there a problem in the grain fields?"

Salmon tore a piece of bread and began to eat. He shook his head. "No, it is nothing of the sort." He hesitated, thinking of what to say. His brother, Elimelech, had died, and it brought a lump to his throat.

"Naomi has returned from Moab," Rahab broke in.

Boaz touched his father's arm. His mother would never omit Elimelech's name unless he were dead. His uncle was the patriarch of that family. Naomi would always mention Elimelech's name first.

"Mahlon and Chilion—they remain in Moab?"

Rahab looked deep into his questioning eyes. "They lay in the earth beside their father."

Boaz's jaw dropped. "All—dead! How? My father, how is it possible that all three are gone. Was it an accident? A plague?"

Salmon shrugged his shoulders, too choked to speak.

"Mother, do you know?"

"Keziah informed us last evening. You were still in the fields. Naomi, and one of her daughters-in-law arrived yesterday in the afternoon. They began the journey from Moab four days before. We know nothing more. Keziah said Naomi wept on Aleeza's shoulder. She said the Almighty had testified against her, and that her husband and sons were buried in Moab."

Boaz leaned back on an elbow staring at nothing. His eyes appeared to glaze over. The last meeting with Elimelech came to mind, and he regretted the harsh words said by both men.

"Where is Naomi? At the inn? She must stay here—with family. I will—."

"She is not at the inn," Rahab said. "Aleeza took her in. I am sure she will give her shelter until Naomi can make other arrangements."

"Elimelech sold their property. They have no place to go."

"We remember. The man who owns it has done very well with the crops he has planted."

"I would like to visit with Naomi," Boaz said.

Salmon looked over. He swallowed hard and got his emotions under control. "It appears that Naomi has lost everything. Keziah reports that she has an old donkey and a cart falling apart from much use. The cart had a few items and some no doubt belonged to her daughter-in-law.

"Son, she may not wish to see you, at least not yet. My brother and Naomi had much in this world's goods when they lived here. Now she appears to be destitute. Do not rush over there. Give her time."

Boaz sat silent for a short time considering his father's words. "Your suggestion is wise. I will not go today, maybe tomorrow."

"Tomorrow?" Rahab asked.

Boaz grinned. "I shall not force myself into her life. I do wish to learn of her needs, and there are ways." His eyes twinkled with mischief.

Rahab nodded. Boaz had not become a successful man by being foolish. Skilled in the ways of business and dealings with men, he would find a way to assist her.

After they had finished the meal, Keziah, their servant girl, came to clear the table of food and dishes. Boaz motioned for her to sit across from him.

"I have an important duty for you today. Go to the home of Hadar and inform their servant that Boaz has sent you, and you want to speak with Aleeza. When she comes out, take her aside out of the hearing of others. Tell her I wish to pay a visit, but not when Naomi is there. Ask her to inform me when Naomi leaves the house for a few hours? Make sure she understands I want to be there when Naomi is not. Also, Naomi is not to know I have asked about her or will be visiting Aleeza."

"I will do as you say."

On the third day after arriving in Bethlehem, Ruth awoke to gray light filtering through the latticed window. Rising to her feet, she passed through the doorway of the small room off the courtyard. The odor of wood smoke filled the air, and she walked toward the source. Eden pushed a loaf of bread into the oven and stoked the fire.

"May I stand near the oven?" Ruth called out. "The morning chill has me shivering."

"Please do. Did you sleep well?"

"Yes, thank you."

"Naomi appeared in good spirits last evening. Is she stronger now?"

Ruth nodded. "She is, and today we go to the city seeking a small place to live. Our burden upon you shall end soon."

"Burden? You are no burden upon me. I enjoy our conversations, and I am sure the mistress does, also. Come to me when you are ready to leave and I shall send along food for your midday meal."

After breakfast, Aleeza sent Eden to inform Boaz that Naomi had entered Bethlehem for the day. Eden found him sitting with Salmon and Rahab in their courtyard.

"My mistress has sent me. Naomi and Ruth have entered the village to look for a place to live. Please come now if you still wish to speak with Aleeza."

"Tell her I shall be there within the hour. Thank you."

After Eden had departed, Boaz turned to his father and mother. "Do you have any questions for Aleeza?"

Salmon shook his head. "We shall leave it to you my son. Only advise her we wish to know if we can be of help to my brother's wife. I do remember her temperament, and she is very self-reliant. She has shown such in journeying from Moab by herself."

Rahab's eyebrows raised a mite. "She *has* a daughter-in-law with her."

"Yes, that is so, but I am sure she would have come without her." A broad grin crossed his face. "She is that independent."

Boaz chuckled. "I shall gather as much information as Aleeza will see fit to give. She has no reason to withhold anything."

"Give her our blessing," said Salmon.

Not wanting to meet Naomi on the way, Boaz walked toward the city gates keeping an eye out, although she might have changed so much he would not recognize her.

It was early spring, and the barley harvest was under way. In the hill country of Bethlehem, the early mornings were cool, and Boaz wore a mantle that he would soon shed when the day warmed.

Taking the same pathway as Naomi and Ruth had walked three days before, he soon arrived at the home of Hadar and Aleeza. Entering the courtyard through the front gate, Boaz met Eden as she worked stoking the fire of the bread oven. She bowed, and he bowed also.

He was a prominent citizen of good reputation and certainly had no need to show such courtesy to a servant girl. However, Boaz did not always feel the need to keep aloof from the lowly in position. At times, he did not comply with customs that would have kept him from associating with those who worked in the fields and vineyards.

"I am here to visit with Aleeza, and Hadar if he is available."

"Welcome, sir. I shall tell the mistress you are here. The master of the house has gone to the vineyard."

Eden rushed away, and Boaz strolled about the courtyard. By all indications, the grapevines that grew all along the walls and into the trees would soon produce a bountiful crop.

Hadar's house was much like others in Judah. The walls consisted of stone from the Judean hills, while woven branches and clay, smoothed with a stone roller, covered the roof.

Several rooms surrounded the central courtyard, all with entrances facing the courtyard. The rooms were not large, and all had a window for ventilation. Lattice covered the windows, and shutters framed the windows on the outside.

The inside walls had been plastered and smoothed. The more wealthy citizens like Hadar and Aleeza typically hired Hebrew artists to paint murals on the walls.

A woman's voice called out from the stairs leading up to the roof. Boaz turned and waved at Aleeza.

The Israelites had been tent-dwellers for hundreds of years and only recently many began to live in houses. There were still a significant number who continued the tent life mainly because they did not wish to live in towns and villages. City dwellers spent most of their time on rooftops and courtyards. Rooms were mainly for sleeping and getting inside out of inclement weather.

Boaz bowed to Aleeza. "I thank you for seeing me today."

She smiled and motioned toward a bench. "I have been on the roof threshing flax."

"You do this yourself, no servant to help?" Boaz chuckled. He knew when Aleeza said she was "threshing flax," that she was pressing the seed for oil and removing the fibers for linen. He was impressed to hear that she did such menial tasks.

"Everyone works in this household. What would I do with myself without work? Surely you understand—a man who works the harvest with his laborers."

"I do. The flax I leave for my mother. She still does the same as you. She is not as quick as in days gone by, but she keeps busy.

"Now, may I ask of Naomi's welfare? I wanted to ask you first before I paid a visit to her. It has been so very long and now I have been made privy to her condition. Keziah has told us it is not good. Is that true? I have no reason to doubt but desire to hear it from you."

After they had taken a seat on the bench, she began. "All the city was aroused when Naomi entered. She brought an old donkey, a dilapidated cart with meager supplies, and her daughter-in-law. It is a complete change from ten years ago. When she departed Bethlehem her appearance was so attractive, now she is pale, almost sickly in face and form. She stoops, where once she walked tall. She departed with feet shod with the finest sandals, now she walks on the thinnest of leather. Her robe, made of fine wool, is gone. Now, even her linen garment is in tatters."

Aleeza turned her head hiding her teary eyes. Boaz sat quietly pondering the fact that one of his family, his uncle's wife, had come to ruin. It seemed impossible.

"I tried to give her a new robe; she refused it. She offered to work for it. Naomi is a proud woman, Boaz. She did have a change of clothing on the cart. It was very simple, nothing like she wore at one time."

Boaz shook his head in bewilderment. "How did the men die?"

Aleeza gave him a running account of the last ten years since the family had left Judah. She told him what Naomi had passed along, which did not amount to much.

"You did not say how and when the men died."

"I have told you what Naomi passed along to me. I know nothing more. I assume it is too painful for her to speak of it now."

Boaz scratched his beard. "Tell me about her daughter-in-law. She is a Moabitess?"

"Ruth! Oh, she is so pretty and has a lovely temperament, too. She left her parents and family to remain with Naomi. This young woman refused to forsake her mother-in-law. Naomi tried to get her to turn back. It was useless. She clung to her, promising to be with her unto death. And—the most thrilling thing is Ruth promised to make Yahweh her God and give up the gods of the Moabites."

"Unusual, very unusual. A Moabite does not give up his gods; at least I am unaware of anyone doing it." He gave Aleeza a look she could not read. "I must pay a visit another day when Naomi is here—and her daughter-in-law. You have told me amazing things today. I must carefully consider them.

Chapter 20

At the city gates, Ruth and Naomi approached the elders who sat daily listening to grievances of the people. These men would render judgments that carried enough weight to keep law and order in the city.

Naomi had been a life-long Bethlehemite and was well-acquainted with the men. If a small apartment, an upper room, or anything of the like were available for rent, they might know.

She bowed. "Ruth, my daughter-in-law, and I have come from Moab and now look for a small abode in the village. Can you help?"

The number of elders at the gate varied each day depending on if a man had the opportunity to come and sit. Most were there daily. However, illness or business would keep a man away. The village required a quorum of ten men to render a judgment. Ruth and Naomi had come for information only, so a minimum number of men need not be present.

After a pleasant exchange of greetings, the women were told of several places that were known to be available. Not all of the elders had arrived so there might be more information forthcoming from the others. The women had a start. Thanking the men, they hurried away to make their first inquiry.

Leaving the area of the city gates, one of the many scavengers that roamed the streets, a one-eyed dog—black as midnight, confronted them. Almost always meek and gentle creatures, dogs kept the city cleared of much of its garbage. Most citizens hated the animals because of their incessant barking at night yet tolerated them because of their propensity to clean up the messes of humans.

Dogs almost always ran in packs and protected their area of town. Any dog that happened to stray would meet with brutal resistance from a pack protecting its home territory. Ruth, being a gentle soul, spoke to the dog. However, she did not give it part of her food that Eden had sent along. Doing that would cause the animal to follow them begging for more.

After several stops, the women finally secured an upper room of a house that sat in the center of Bethlehem. Naomi paid the rent out of funds she had saved from selling the few remaining sheep of her flock in Moab. The upper room would be temporary until they could afford a more suitable abode.

Naomi had understood, when still in Moab, she must have a means of income. Having a good knowledge of spinning and making tents produced a plan in her mind. She kept it to herself.

Finding the room had taken several inquiries and hours to accomplish. It was mid-afternoon when Naomi and Ruth made their agreement with the homeowner.

"Let us return to Aleeza and inform her that we will no longer be a burden to her," said Naomi. "It is good to have a dwelling."

Ruth nodded her assent. Walking through the marketplace on the way to the city gates, Ruth gazed at the buyers and sellers. "This looks much like Ar."

"Yes it does," Naomi said. "Buying and selling is much the same in all lands."

"I see the usual loafers. They wait for employment," she said chuckling. "Yet, they rather hope no one hires them because they do not care to work."

"My husband found it so at harvest time," said Naomi. "Some men would hire out, expect wages at the end of day, yet did little work to earn the silver."

"When we walked at the edge of the fields the other day, you mentioned the landowners who allowed the poor to glean. Please tell me more."

The city well sat outside the walls near the gates. Naomi motioned to sit on the curbing, and the old lady sat down beside her.

"We shall rest a moment, and I will tell you our law. The Law of Moses has strict protections for the poor. Three come to mind at this moment.

"The first is a landowner is forbidden to reap his crop to the borders of the field. Another is if a bundle of grain is overlooked it must be left, he cannot retrieve it later. A third law is there can be no second reaping of the same field nor picking up grapes that have fallen to the ground in the vineyards. Once reaped, the landowner is done. Whatever is left can be taken by the poor and foreigner.

"All of these laws apply to the orchards and vineyards. Also, after beating olives from the trees an owner cannot go back a second time over the same branches. The law applies to grapevines too."

Naomi motioned toward a narrow pathway. "Let us take this way. It cuts through the grain fields and over a low rise to where our property lies. I wish to see it again."

"I have not seen you before," the voice came from the side.

Ruth turned to face a tall, quite handsome man of about thirty years of age. He had a lean, rawboned body. She noticed a scar on his left cheek made by a man with a quick blade.

"We have recently arrived from Moab," Ruth said, wishing to be polite.

He looked her up and down with eyes that made Ruth's skin crawl. Her strong, yet delicate face and sweet temperament would draw any man's attention.

"I want to see more of you—much more," he said with an undisguised suggestiveness in his voice.

Ruth's eyes turned cold, and he recognized it plain enough.

Is this what I will have to endure each time I come to market? He thinks me a harlot or an easy woman he can seduce? Buying and selling are the same everywhere and so are some men at the city gates.

"Mother, we are going now, there is nothing here to keep us."

"I will escort you. With me, you shall have no concerns. With me at your side, no man will bother you."

He was a powerfully built fellow who cast a long shadow. A man long on smooth words, but short on common sense—dumb as a week old donkey.

"I have an escort," she clasped Naomi's arm, "and with or without you I have no concerns." Ruth had ice in her voice. "Please move away as we are leaving."

The man's eyes grew large. He faced a young, attractive woman, yet she stared through old eyes. She had seen plenty and had experienced much. She was no wisp of a girl he could fool. She was quality, a lady with class. Ruth was all he was not.

He quickly recognized she had fire, with iron woven into her backbone—no pushover. He stepped aside.

Once they had gone down the narrow path a short way, Ruth spoke up, her voice strong without a hint of being upset. "You referred to this property as ours. I do not understand. I have always believed that you do not have any land. I certainly do not."

Naomi glanced over. She smiled. "Ah, my daughter, there you are wrong. We have property that can be redeemed. Good land that produces wheat, barley, and grapes, along with pastures for flocks."

Ruth's forehead furrowed. "Redeemed? Explain what you mean. I know the word, but how do you redeem property in Judah? Is it land you owned before moving to Moab?"

"Yes, it is, and being Mahlon's widow, you have the right to redeem it."

"How can that be? I am a Moabite."

"True, but your mother-in-law is an Israelite, and I have rights to the land because my husband and sons are dead. You have rights to the land because your husband though dead, is my son."

"Mahlon never told me this," Ruth sputtered. "I, I never...."

Naomi frowned. "Now you know. I certainly cannot redeem it, at least not now—probably never. I shall tell you more at another time. At this moment, look there."

She pointed, and Ruth's eyes followed. Settled in a valley between two low hills were fields of grain; barley ripe for harvest and wheat almost so.

Ruth's hand went to her mouth. "This," she spoke through her fingers, "all of this was your family's land?"

After a few moments, when Naomi did not respond, Ruth looked over. Her mother-in-law stood speechless, big tears rolling down her cheeks. Slowly Naomi's eyes slanted over; she nodded her head. "Years, many years ago," she whispered.

"You left all this and journeyed to Moab. Giving up your land for a tent on my father's property, can it be so?"

"Understand this; your father-in-law wanted an easier way. He had things of this world and wanted to keep them. Famine covered the land in those days, and he had no desire to fight it. "Look!" She waved a hand around. "Ten years ago these hillsides were brown with drought. The streams trickled. However, a man could make it regardless of famine. Many did. It was not easy—but certainly possible. You have seen the land surrounding Bethlehem. I tried to talk Elimelech out of going. Many others did, also.

"Please do not misunderstand. Elimelech sincerely believed he was doing what was best for his family. However, a man should consider his motives. You can live with drought if you know the rules. Those who stayed have proven that. No, living through a drought is not easy, but it can be done. I believed it, many others did, too. We accepted the fact of doing without and adjusting our lives to what the Almighty would give us. Elimelech refused to accept the punishment of Yahweh on the Promised Land.

"Our Lord God took my husband from me because he forsook his inheritance. My sons put their faith in and believed their father, so they refused to return when they had the opportunity. Yahweh took them, also. I believe it!

"It has made me Mara. At one time, Naomi lived in this body and walked these hills. Now, it is Mara who looks from these eyes and sees what had been ours, but will never be again."

The last rays of the dark pink sun faded below the horizon bringing in the cool, spring evening. At meal time, Naomi and Ruth told of the day's events.

"Both of you are welcome here," said Hadar.

"Thank you, but no. We wish to have a place of our own."

Ruth nodded. "Yes, we have imposed upon you, and now it is past time we should leave."

"Naomi, do not feel you have to go," said Aleeza. "I—."

"No! This ... forgive me. I did not mean to be abrupt. Thank you for your hospitality, but we must go. This awakens memories of what my family had at one time." She motioned toward the fields and vineyards that belonged to Hadar. "I cannot bear to see it every day. It reminds me that Elimelech's land can be redeemed, and I cannot do a thing about it.

"Ruth and I visited it today. For a moment, a fleeting moment, I dreamed of walking those fields again and preparing meals for my family. It was pleasant, but my situation is not. I am not! I am Mara—all I will ever be."

"Mother, please do not speak such words. Someday you will go home. It will happen, surely it will."

"Do you blame God?" Hadar's words were harsh.

"The Almighty has judged me unworthy. It is plain. I shall live in my poverty, but not here. Not where I can see what was and will never be again. My life is near the end, and I shall return to the dust of the earth, brokenhearted and shamed."

"Remember Job?" Aleeza asked, gently. "His scroll tells us he was the greatest man in the East. He had seven sons and three daughters. All were killed. He had many possessions: sheep, camels, oxen and donkeys. All were killed. If any person had reason to charge God, Job did.

"My dear friend, Naomi. What was written about this great man of God? Did he accuse Yahweh?"

Naomi glanced at Ruth. Her daughter-in-law, not knowing the Hebrew Scriptures, gave her a blank look.

Naomi had the answer. However, she did not want to form the words, words that would condemn her as one who had fewer problems than Job. She fidgeted, staring at her hands.

Ruth broke the silence. "I would like to know the answer. I have promised to make Yahweh my God. Did your God curse this man, Job?"

Aleeza shook her head. "He did not. It is written in the scroll what Job said. 'Naked I came from my mother's womb, and naked shall I return there. Yahweh gave, and Yahweh has taken away; blessed be the name of Yahweh.' That is amazing, is it not? And then, it is written in the scroll: 'In all this Job did not sin nor charge God with wrong.'

"My friend," Aleeza looked over at Naomi whose head remained down, "all of God's people have suffered at one time or another. Your pain is extreme, no one would deny that. However, Job is our example of how to react to such misfortune in our lives."

Naomi remained quiet.

Again Ruth spoke. "Job did not charge God with wrong, but do you know if God did it? With all of the evil that befell him, surely Job was a terrible sinner."

"Satan caused it," Hadar said. "Job was a righteous man. Our adversary, Satan, asked to test the man as he was sure Job would curse God if given enough adversity in his life. He was wrong."

"So, Yahweh allowed this test?"

"Yes. Our God trusted his servant Job. He refused to curse God and die as his wife told him to do. Job did question God as to why all of the bad things had come his way."

"What did Yahweh answer?"

"He did not answer him. He *never* gave him an answer. Job had to trust Yahweh even though he would never know why."

Ruth's education of Yahweh's ways had taken a giant leap. She had much to think over.

Aleeza reached out and took Naomi's hand. "You are bitter because you have lost almost everything—are you not?"

"Yes! You know I am. Yahweh *has* sent heartache upon me?"

"Why would he?"

"Does not God afflict the sinner? My husband and sons chose Moab; I certainly did not. I am punished with three deaths and poverty. I have done nothing wrong. I did not want to forsake this land."

Aleeza smiled. "Naomi, can you not see, Job did nothing wrong, either. He was righteous, yet the Almighty allowed terrible things to happen to a good man. So, it is with you. Bad things have happened to a good person. Nevertheless, you should not let it make you bitter. Did not Job say: 'Though he slays me, yet will I trust in him?'"

Naomi nodded. "I remember."

"I know you do. I only want to bring it to your mind anew. What were Job's latter days like?"

Naomi gave a startled look. Her face remained grim.

"Yahweh gave him twice as much as he had lost," Aleeza answered her own question. "I know you recall that."

Naomi's face pinched tightly. "I am not Job! His scroll also says: 'man is born to trouble as the sparks fly upward.' I should do as Job did, curse the day I was born.

"Do you believe Yahweh favors me—one old woman out of all Israel?"

"You believe he cursed you—one old woman out of all Israel." Aleeza chuckled. "He knows who you are. If he can curse, he can also bless the same old woman. Oh, my dear Naomi, we are his chosen people. He cares for us."

Ruth and Naomi entered Bethlehem the next day shortly after sunrise. Winding their way through the narrow streets, they came to the house that would serve as home. Unloading the cart they soon had all of their things inside.

The house surrounded the courtyard on three sides like many in the city. Ruth led Stubborn to a stable in the corner, filled the manger with grain, and unhitched the cart from the old donkey.

The upper room had the barest of furnishings. A table, two lamps, a wash basin, and two shelves along one wall with various sized pottery to hold foodstuffs. A jar of oil, a bag of grain, and a few pieces of fruit sat on the table. The women dropped their sleeping mats on the floor along with various bundles that contained cooking utensils, plates, cups, a hand mill, extra clothes, a few pieces of jewelry, and other miscellaneous items. In a leather pouch, Ruth kept several ointments and a small bottle of perfume that Mahlon had given her.

"Let us rest for a while before we arrange everything," said Naomi. "This is a good time to finish our conversation from yesterday when we walked in the field."

Ruth plopped down in a corner with her back against the wall. "I am ready." She smiled. "Tell me about redeeming your land."

Naomi placed a large bundle on the floor and opened the top. Spreading a goat skin, she made herself comfortable.

"Mother, I noticed that bundle on the cart this morning and assumed Eden had placed it there. Did Aleeza send a gift with you?"

Naomi, sitting straight, her eyes alert, smiled. Ruth believed it not a forced smile, but one that expressed an inner happiness. She had not seen this upturned face and bright eyes from her mother-in-law since long before they departed Moab.

"Aleeza sent it, but it is *not* a gift. I would never have accepted it. The bundle contains goat hair. I am going to spin the hair and then weave it into cloth. Then I shall sell the cloth to the tent makers.

"Wonderful! Since it is not a gift, I take it you are going to pay Aleeza for the hair out of the first sale."

"Yes, and then I shall buy more hair and wool also. We shall have a small income and not starve."

Taking a large amount of hair, Naomi stuffed it under her arm and then drew out a tuft tying it to a stone. Holding the tuft with one hand, she began spinning the stone and gradually added more hair. This process produced a relatively uniform thread, which along with many other threads produced in such a manner were woven into cloth. Then, she would sell the cloth to merchants who make nose bags for donkeys and camels, and goat hair sacks that hold grain.

Naomi glanced up from her spinning and began her explanation. "Yahweh gave the land of Canaan to the Hebrews. Since Yahweh is God, and he created all, therefore, he owns all. As the owner, he had the authority to give land to the Israelites.

"His command was to drive out the Canaanites. Some were defeated, but many remain and continue to worship the Baals. Most of the Hebrews took up Baal worship, and that brought judgments upon us. We have suffered famine, defeats in battles, and other nations destroying our crops—all because the Hebrews did evil in the sight of Yahweh.

"Sometimes a few good people must endure hardships because the majority has sinned. Elimelech kicked against it. He believed our God was unfair to him. So, he sold our land and forsook his inheritance knowing that he could redeem the property when he returned to Judah.

"The Law of Moses states that the land shall not be sold permanently, for the land belongs to Yahweh. We are strangers and sojourners with our God.

"However, Hebrews can sell a possession with the understanding that it can be redeemed by a relative or by the seller if he is able at a time in the future. This is why my husband believed it would be wise to sell and redeem later. What he did not consider was the possibility he would not return to carry out his plan. He calculated and weighed the good and bad of leaving. It was not a quick decision, but months of thinking and planning."

Naomi closed her eyes. She allowed all of those memories to flow through her mind. It depressed her even more.

"Yesterday you said 'we have property that can be redeemed.' I assume there is more to your law since Elimelech is no longer with us to reclaim the land."

Naomi looked over. "Yes. A man's son can redeem the land."

Ruth stared, thinking of Mahlon and Chilion. "And—if no son?"

"A daughter may redeem, but it must not leave the possession of the tribe, and in our case, the tribe of Judah."

Ruth's faced screwed up in thought. "A wife cannot redeem the property?"

"No."

"A daughter, but not a wife?"

"A wife could marry a relative that redeems, but the land belongs to the redeemer, not the wife. A daughter who inherits must marry a man in her tribe, and their sons would then inherit the property. The property must always remain with the tribe.

"I shall tell you more at another time."

Ruth laughed. "There is more?"

Chapter 21

Ruth had been awake for an hour when a rooster crowed from some unknown location, signaling the day had begun. She rolled her sleeping mat and hurried down the steps and across the courtyard to the manger. Dawn broke clear and bright yellow as Stubborn eagerly began his breakfast. She checked the water level in the trough, judging the old donkey had plenty, she patted his side and rushed away.

Climbing the steps, Ruth entered the upper room and found Naomi preparing bread for the midday and evening meals. She had placed yesterday's bread on the table for their breakfast.

"Mother, I wish to discuss something with you."

"I am listening." She glanced over and then returned to her task.

"I have been considering our circumstances. You have taken on spinning to produce income, but what of me? I do not wish to live an idle life. I am ready to do almost anything to help us. Of course, there are some things I will not do, such as prostitute my body."

"Never!"

"When in the fields you mentioned the gleaners. I have worked the fields of my father and know how to glean. My duty is to you, and I want to help. So, I respectfully ask, let me go to the fields and pick up the leftover grain behind anyone in whose eyes I find favor."

Naomi stopped her work, pulled up a stool, and sat. "Bless you, Ruth. Let us eat our food and discuss this.

"Working in the fields can be dangerous for a young woman. Beware of the men, not all are righteous. If fact, most are not. To Israel's shame, she is a land full of wicked people."

"I understand. I have dealt with wicked men in the marketplace of Ar. I—."

"My daughter," she shook her head, "it is not the same. The fields are places of lust and wanton sex. Many of the field workers, both men, and women, do what is right in their own eyes instead of what is right before the Lord. They pervert the commands of our God. Men have been known to force themselves on innocent females between the rows of crops."

Ruth nodded knowingly. She was not shocked; this was not news to her. "Is it any different than Moab?"

"No, but I did not want you to think it does not happen here. It happens all the time. It is shameful that Israelites are guilty of such vile behavior."

"I am fully aware of the risk. However," she gave a half-shrug, "this is harvest time, and there are many laborers in the field, both men, and women. No man will molest me with so many around. I shall work close by a group."

Naomi looked away mulling over her daughter-in-law's words. Fear prickled the hair on the nape of her neck. *She did confront that man at the city well and stood her ground. She is strong.*

"Have you not taught me that Yahweh will protect me?"

Naomi turned her head. "You know the right words to say at the right time." Naomi chuckled.

"I have learned from you."

Naomi's eyes brightened. "Meet the women, ask them to point out the owner of the field or his overseer. Then, go to him and ask to glean. Do this first. Ask permission. Now, go to the fields, my daughter. Yahweh be with you."

"I serve Baal," Kefir, the overseer said. "My father and his father worshiped Yahweh, but I think for myself. They grew old and died still worshiping a God they could not see. I am not like them. I have a wooden image of my god in the courtyard of my dwelling."

The young man, Matan, slowly shook his head. "My father is dead, also. He died like your father, worshiping Yahweh. My mother continues to live and would never allow me to set up a deity to worship."

"Your mother!" Kefir laughed. "Does your mother rule? She belongs to you. Have you no spine?"

"I leave her to her ways. She is sickly and has not many days left." Matan shuffled from one foot to another. "I go to the altar in the hills and offer to Baal." He went back to reaping.

Kefir, the biggest man in the field, had weasel eyes and a hard-edged voice. He was a man of evil intent, no good from start to finish, and mercilessly goaded all of the young men.

"Look at the women who glean."

Matan straightened up from the cutting.

Giving a knowing laugh, Kefir said, "Some of them are beauties. Who do you lay with tonight?"

Matan grinned. "Zemira, she is special. I had her last week, very fine. She knows men."

"Since your mother is a devout Israelite, a worshipper of Yahweh, what does she say when you bring her home?"

Realizing that he was being goaded, Matan gave him a cold look. "I do not bring her home! You think me stupid. We lay in the field after the day's reaping is done."

"Ah, deceiving the old lady!"

Wishing for help, he looked around at the other reapers. They kept quiet. Matan wanted to hit Kefir in the face, but it would cost him his job. He needed work to support his family, so he took the abuse and went back to cutting.

"When the harvest is over and no more barley and wheat stalks to hide you—what then?"

Matan, resigned to the fact that Kefir would not let up, made the best of the situation. He pointed up the hill toward the vineyards. "The grapes are on the way home." He chuckled. "*Very* convenient."

"Look there," the overseer nodded toward the women. "I have not seen that beauty before. *Who* is she?"

Ruth turned aside from the pathway and weaved her way through the barley bundles toward the women who gleaned behind the men.

"She sees me," Kefir said. "It is good. I attract the women." He snickered. "She does not reside in Bethlehem or anywhere close. I know all of the gorgeous women in this area, actually all the way to Jebus."

Matan gave him a wary eye, debating within himself whether he should call him out on his boasting.

"I see your look of doubt. Trust me, I have lain with most of the young women around here and would remember her without a doubt. She is *something* special."

Ruth had natural femininity, beauty beyond most, and a mystique hard to define. She flaunted none of it. She quietly moved along, and all of the reapers' eyes moved with her.

Several of the men had overhead the overseer's boast, yet none had the courage to speak up.

Finally, Matan could not let Kefir's boasting go unchallenged. "No doubt you *have* taken every woman under twenty years old from here to Jebus—in your imagination!"

That brought a big laugh from all of the reapers.

"You laugh at me? I should dismiss all of you. Go find another field to work, if you can."

"You will not do it. The owner would not allow it," a reaper said. "We are the best, and he does not want to lose us. We jest, and you should take it in jest."

The men continued to stare at Ruth as she spoke with the women. They were too far away for the men to make out the words. After a moment, one of the gleaners pointed to the overseer and Ruth walked on.

"She comes to me. See, I told you. It will not be long, and I will have her. The women cannot resist."

Again the men laughed.

"She wants to glean," said Matan, "that is all. It has nothing to do with you."

"Look at all of those women you allow to glean," said a reaper. "You have more than enough. Get too many and no one can gather sufficient grain to eat for one day."

"You men keep quiet. Believe me. I would let that woman work here even after the gleaning was completed. She could bring me water, and I would watch her walk. Yes, that could be her job," he gave an evil laugh. "Walking around looking good."

"The owner of this field would never allow it," said another reaper. "He would have your job if you paid her for doing nothing."

"I will give her part of my wages."

"To do what? Pay her to lie with you? Look at her, she is no prostitute," said Matan. "You could not pay her enough. I know something about women, too, and you cannot buy her."

Nothing more was said and within a few moments Ruth arrived in front of the men. No one greeted her.

Her large eyes were an amazing deep brown, caressed about with long lashes. Ruth's natural smile, her face, everything about her demeanor, drew men like honey draws flies.

She glanced from man to man. All of them appeared to be surly, dangerous men, with ugly as sin looks. Sweat broke out on her forehead, but she did not allow her face to show fear.

Ruth's gaze fell on Matan. "You are the overseer?"

All of the men laughed long and hard, remembering the overseer's boast.

Matan thumb pointed. "He is."

The overseer ran lust-filled eyes over her, taking in her beauty. "My name is Kefir. How can I help you?"

His tone of voice and roving eyes told Ruth all she needed to know about this man. She was not surprised. Accepting crude, lascivious talk and innuendos from the men would be necessary to glean in this field.

"May I glean after the reapers?"

"You may do anything you like." He gave her another indecent look. "I have the authority to help you in many different ways."

Suspicion ran hot in Ruth's dark eyes, and her heart skipped a beat. An uneasiness swept over her, and the skin on her back was crawling like a caterpillar. She backed up a step.

Although she was a young woman, her eyes told of maturity.

Kefir observed those eyes, and they worried him a bit, yet a slight smirk played on his lips. "You are not from here. I know all of the women *very* well."

"I arrived two days ago with Naomi, my mother-in-law. We come from Moab. Naomi is Hebrew. I am a Moabite."

Kefir stared at her through small, cruel eyes. He had the look of a mean, dangerous man. "Ha! I have known several Moabite women." He snorted. "They are quite helpful to have around."

For a long moment, nobody spoke as Ruth glanced from man to man. Being smart and accustomed to the men of Ar, she was alert to her surroundings. Each man had a look that told her she did not belong here and must move on—quickly.

"You are welcome to glean with the others. If any of them complain, you let me know. I will set them straight."

Ruth needed the grain, yet the situation was not good for her to remain. The words slipped out, and she regretted them immediately. "I will glean with the others. Thank you." She hastily turned away.

"What is your name?"

"Ruth," she called over her shoulder.

"You are welcome, Ruth the Moabitess, and you can thank me properly—later." He had a sly look from his evil eye, and the right eye appeared no better. "I will see you after today's work."

When she reached the corner of the field where the women were gleaning, Ruth told them she had permission. Some gave her hard looks but said nothing.

I shall gather for now, she told herself, *but not all day. He may try to assault me at the midday meal. I will not have that, so I will be gone.*

Landowners had set large stones at the borders of their fields that kept the reapers and gleaners from straying. Occasionally there were stone walls to separate properties, but usually it was a large stone or pile of smaller stones that served as landmarks. Ruth had seen them when she walked the road to Bethlehem that first day. Today, she kept close to the landmarks with her head down, awaiting an opportunity to slip away.

Periodically she looked up to see if the overseer still had his eyes on her. He did, and she watched him like a big cat watches a snake. After several times of peeking and ducking her head, she looked up, and he and the reapers were walking to the hut in the middle of the field.

It is but an hour after sunrise, and the reapers must take a break? The landowner is not around, so they loaf and probably tell stories.

Ruth placed the grain basket with its meager amount of gleanings on her head and quietly walked away from the reapers in that section of the field. Once on the narrow road, she looked for other sections out of sight of the overseer.

Passing a stone landmark, she happened to turn aside stopping at the edge of another division of the field. She took in the ground with quick, observant eyes.

Ruth must have grain for Naomi, at least until her mother-in-law could sell her goat-hair cloth. This time she would ask more questions before gleaning in this sector.

Ruth wore a mask, an invisible mask, which hid her sorrow, hurt, and loneliness. Integrating herself into life at Bethlehem did not erase her memory. She longed to be in Mahlon's arms. He had given her his love when she needed it most. He treated her better than her parents did. He was a loving and tender man, frail in health, but strong in masculine ways. Always supportive, she never doubted his love, even at her lowest point when the full realization came that she could never conceive.

Could Ruth ever love a man as deeply as she loved him? She had believed it was not possible.

"Do you wish to glean?"

The pleasant, feminine voice brought Ruth back from her daydreaming.

"Hello, yes I would. I need grain for my mother-in-law and me. Can you help?"

The young woman smiled, and Ruth relaxed. After the rough men from the other field, this smile was like a refreshing rain.

"I cannot, but go to the overseer and ask." She turned and looked at a man standing on the far side of the field.

Ruth grasped her hand. "Thank you for your kindness. Do you glean here too?"

"Yes, I arrived after the others. The overseer allows it. I must fulfill duties at my home before I come to glean. My father is gravely ill. He cannot work."

"I am sorry," Ruth said. "I shall pray to my g… I shall pray for him. Thank you again." She rushed away before the young lady could ask any questions.

How can I pray to my gods? I have given them up. Shall I pray to Yahweh? Is he my God now?

She pushed the doubts aside and approached the overseer. Bowing, she said, "Sir, a young woman," she motioned toward the women, "told me to ask you if I may glean here. My mother-in-law and I desperately need the grain. Please let me glean and gather after the reapers among the sheaves."

"What is your name and your mother-in-law's name?"

"I am Ruth, a Moabitess from Ar, and Naomi is my mother-in-law. We have recently arrived from Moab."

The man nodded. "Yes, I am aware of you. I understand that you left everything to keep your commitment to Naomi." The man smiled warmly. "You may. Go and gather with the others."

Ruth's forehead wrinkled. *He is aware of me? How strange. Gossip travels like lightning. I wonder what else he knows or believes about me. Does he think he can treat me like those other men?*

"Thank you for allowing me to glean." She swallowed hard and continued. "I gleaned for a short time in another portion of the field this morning but hurried away."

The overseer gave her a puzzled look.

She took a deep breath and fixed her eyes on the man. "I am here to glean and nothing more. I still mourn my husband. He lies buried with his father and brother in Moab.

"The overseer at that other field made it plain he would have me accommodate his cravings. I have no desire or intention of doing such a thing, with him, or with anyone else." She looked away, expecting the worse.

"Ruth, do not fear me or the owner of this field. We follow the laws of Yahweh and would never ask you to compromise yourself. You are safe here. Now go and glean."

Ruth bowed low. "Thank you for your kindness."

Chapter 22

"Are the barley heads full?" Salmon asked.

Boaz's eyes brightened. "The harvest is bountiful this year."

Salmon laid a hand on his son's shoulder. "The Almighty has been gracious to you and all of Judah. Do you go to the field today?"

"Today and every day until the harvest is completed, barley and wheat. Then we shall celebrate with a feast."

Rahab entered the courtyard and motioned to the men. "Come to the table." The morning meal consisted of bread, olives, figs, and raisins. After they had settled on cushions, she gazed up. "The sky is clouded this morning. The latter rains are not done."

Boaz tore a piece of bread and grasped a handful of olives. "Yes, it could rain, but it should not slow the harvest much. Most of the storms have passed."

"Tell us about your visit with Aleeza," Rahab said in an eager tone. "Naomi, what is the report of her condition?"

"She is in good health."

"Wonderful news."

"Yet, I *am* concerned." Boaz raised an eyebrow. "According to Aleeza, Naomi is bitter toward our God. She did not wish to leave Judah and now believes Yahweh punishes her. She told the women who surrounded her in the market the day she arrived that she went out full and has come home empty."

"You and Salmon tried to convince Elimelech to remain. It is not her fault."

"I am sure she understands that. But, she suffers because of the decisions made by another. To her, it is not fair."

Rahab frowned. "Many things we endure in life are not fair. Thieves steal our goods. Evil men rape women in the fields. Naomi's husband and sons die. Yes, bad things happen to people who are innocent."

Boaz popped a handful of raisins in his mouth. Chewing slowly, he considered the situation. "I must visit with Naomi. Perhaps I can help her understand these things."

"She knows," said Salmon. "It is very hard to accept that life is not always fair. In fact, a good share of the time that is so."

"Did Aleeza mention her daughter-in-law?"

"She did, mother. Her name is Ruth, and she gave up everything to come here with Naomi. She is a devoted daughter. According to Aleeza, Ruth is much closer to Naomi than her own mother whom she left behind in Moab."

"How long has Ruth been a widow?" asked Rahab.

"Less than two years is my understanding."

"Son, I am the family redeemer for Naomi." Salmon ran his fingers through his hair. No one spoke, awaiting some unknown pronouncement from him. Then, he repeated the finger combing, appearing to pull the words from his head. "She needs her land returned to her. I have the means to buy it."

"Is not Dov a redeemer?" Boaz asked.

"Yes, but I am the oldest brother."

"Naomi is too old to bear children," said Boaz. "What happens when she dies? Who will inherit?"

Salmon scratched his beard thinking it over. "It should go to her sons, and if no sons, to the daughters. She has neither." He closed his eyes for a few moments. "This daughter-in-law, Ruth, is she young? Can she bear children?"

Boaz looked at his mother, his forehead scrunched. "She is a young woman; Aleeza believes less than 30-years-old. Bearing children may not be possible, though. I understand she was the wife of Mahlon for many years and remained childless."

No one said a word for several minutes. Finally, Boaz spoke. "We are the kinsmen redeemers. It is our responsibility to solve this problem."

Salmon nodded his agreement. "Let us think on this situation and pray Yahweh will guide us.

"But for now, let us talk about the harvest. Do the reapers work or stand idle?"

Boaz chuckled. "Carmiel, my overseer, keeps a careful eye on the workers. The reapers will not stand idle for long for if they do, Carmiel will send them down the road. We do not abide slackers.

"We must keep the harvesting ahead of schedule if possible so if the rain does come we shall still finish before the wheat harvest begins. If we do get behind, I will go to the marketplace and hire more men from the day laborers."

"It is good. You are well ordered in mind and habits." Rahab placed a hand on her son's arm. "You take after your father."

Salmon looked through wise old eyes at Rahab. "He is more like *my* father, Nahshon. Yahweh, our God, spoke to Moses and commanded him to appoint Nahshon, a captain over the people of Judah. My father's army numbered over 74,000 men. A great responsibility indeed. Boaz has the mind and will of his grandfather."

Boaz, uncomfortable with listening to such praise, rose to leave. "Thank you, father. What I am, I owe to you and mother first."

He grabbed a large handful of raisins and dropped them into his scrip. "I am not waiting for rain. I am going now to the marketplace and hire additional men for today. I want to move the harvest ahead of schedule. I believe the sky tells me it will rain and soon.

"Do not expect me back until evening. I shall go to my field and break bread with my workers at midday."

A gentle breeze moved over the barley, and the heads of grain waved across the field. Each reaper stooped and with one hand grabbed the stalks and with the other sliced it with a sickle. They let the fresh cut barley lay where it fell. The women came behind them, gathered the stalks, bound them into sheaves, and then moved on.

Ruth took a place far behind the women and began to glean the few stalks that remained untouched. Several of the women glanced back at her, whispered, but none walked back and spoke.

Alone in a foreign country, Ruth remembered her father's fields in Moab and a feeling went through her, a feeling she could not identify. She had made her choice of Naomi over her parents and did not regret it. However, a bit of homesickness affected her.

It must be because I am lonely and do not know anyone in this field. In fact, besides Aleeza and Hadar, I have no one to call a friend in Bethlehem.

Ruth shook her head, desperately trying to shake the negative thinking from her mind. She understood it would take time to make friends, maybe much time since she was a Moabite.

Ruth's hands were large for a woman and her back strong. Her experience in Paebel's fields qualified her be a reaper. She could handle a scythe. However, her lot in life at this moment was of a lowly gleaner picking up the few stray heads of grain left by the women.

Time seemed to creep. Finally, after three tedious hours of back-breaking work, the sun broke through and the morning grew warm. In the valleys below Bethlehem, the afternoon sun would sizzle, even in the spring. She did not look forward to it.

Although gleaning was a hot, grimy task, Ruth had no regrets. It seemed so long ago that she had bound herself to Naomi and watched Orpah walk away.

Twice, Ruth had stopped her gleaning to quench her thirst. Water bags, brought to the field on carts, were readily available when needed. Now, she needed to rest from the back-breaking work and get into the shade.

A small house sat in the middle of the field for this purpose, and leaving her basket; she walked toward the only shade available. Two of the servant girls who had been bundling the stalks were there resting on a bench. They nodded, recognizing her presence. Ruth took a seat across from them and closed her eyes.

After a short time, one of the servants said, "My name is Bina."

Ruth opened her eyes. Bina smiled, the other girl did not.

"I am Ruth."

"You were not here at dawn," Bina said in a tone that Ruth took as critical. "We always begin our day when the sun rises."

Ruth forced a smile. Seeing Bina's smile had given her hope this girl would be friendly. She desperately wanted a friend. One at this moment would be wonderful. "I began the day at another field." She motioned toward the west and Bethlehem. "I—."

"The field of Bela?"

"I do not know the owner. A man named, Kefir, is the overseer. He allowed me to glean."

The girls eyed one another. "Why did you leave the field?"

It was the other girl who asked. Ruth hesitated.

She does not tell me her name, yet she asks me questions.

"You are not an Israelite," the second girl continued. "You have an accent. What is your country?"

"May I ask your name?"

"I am Bat-Yam," she said in a deadpan voice.

"Hello, Bat-Yam. I have journeyed here from Moab with my mother-in-law, Naomi. I am a Moabite and Naomi is Hebrew."

"A foreigner gleans our grain?"

"It is allowed," Bina said.

"I must go," said Ruth.

The two maidservants watched as she walked back to her spot in the field. Bat-Yam spoke up. "She takes our grain. Why is that allowed? Will our master agree?

"He will," said Bina. "He will follow the law."

A warrior and mighty man of God like his grandfather, Boaz led the militia at Bethlehem. Although a prominent man, he found time to inquire of others and their welfare. Everyone held him in high regard as a wise and righteous man who cared about his workers.

After hiring more men from the group of dayworkers who stood in the marketplace, he rode out of Bethlehem on a chestnut colored horse. Ownership of a horse was a sign of wealth and power, and Boaz sat that animal as one deserving the prestige that he had acquired.

Reaching the valley floor, he rode quickly to his field to see the progress of his reapers. He wanted to encourage them with his presence and inquire about any needs. Supplying the workers with food and water was a priority with Boaz.

Dismounting at the edge of the field, he picketed the horse and walked to where the reapers were busy cutting. "Yahweh be with you!"

The men stood straight and answered, "Yahweh bless you!"

"Carmiel, let us walk and survey the field," Boaz said.

The men left the reapers to their work and walked to where the horse stood cropping a patch of grass which grew along the boundary line of the field.

"I have hired more men for today's work. The sky tells me rain is coming, and I wish to not fall behind on the harvest. They should be here shortly."

"I will put them to work," said Carmiel. "Do they bring their sickles?"

"Some, not all. Supply them with what they need. Pay them a full day's wage."

"Full day?" His eyebrows raised. "A fourth is gone and soon a half."

"I want to give them no reason to complain. When we hire them again, they should be eager to work."

"I shall do as you say."

Boaz scanned his field from side to side satisfied that the work, thus far, had been completed to his satisfaction. Next, he watched the women bundling and stacking the sheaves.

Then, looking beyond his maidservants, his eyes landed on Ruth. His breath caught. Unknowingly he held it for a few seconds and then exhaled. Her loveliness excited him.

Watching silently for several minutes, he came to the conclusion that this eye-catching woman was also a conscientious worker. After gathering the few stalks within reach, she would straighten up, sometimes stretch, walk a few feet and bend her back for the gleanings. He found he could not take his eyes from her. She did not rest. This young woman was impressive, in looks and her diligence.

She is not one of mine. In fact, I have never seen her before. How is it that Bethlehem has hidden her?

"Whose young woman is this?"

"She is the young Moabitess, who came back with Naomi from the land of Moab."

Boaz turned his head, his jaw dropped.

"Your face tells me you are surprised. The gossip is all over Bethlehem and now this field. Do you not know that Naomi has returned?"

He smiled, and it went ear to ear. "Yes, I received the news of her arrival from my parents. In fact, I have inquired about her. She is my uncle's wife. Well, she was. Elimelech died in Moab."

"Did you know about her daughter-in-law, Ruth?"

Boaz's eyes went back to the field and his newest gleaner. "Only that she arrived here with Naomi and that she left her family to live permanently in Judah."

He silently watched her. Sweat popped out on Ruth's forehead and cheeks. She glowed.

This young lady is striking—radiant. "The fact that she is attractive of face was not mentioned."

Carmiel chuckled. "Oh, you noticed, did you?"

Boaz gave a boyish grin. "How is it possible to miss it? Does she know who I am? Did she come here to glean because I am a near kinsman of Naomi?"

Carmiel shook his head. "I think not. She was gleaning in the field after the reapers, but after an awful experience, she hurried on and happened upon your section. Whether by luck or the guidance of Yahweh, I do not know."

Boaz glanced over. "I do not believe in luck, and neither do most Israelites. The Almighty has a hand in all things. You know that. At least you *should*."

"You are right. I see Yahweh's providence in this. Now, to further explain what happened, Ruth spoke first to the maidservants. They pointed me out and then she came to me. After bowing, she said, 'Please let me glean and gather after the reapers among the sheaves.' I agreed to allow it, and she has remained in the field from morning until now though she rested for a short time in the house."

"What is this awful experience of which you speak?"

Carmiel's face grew hard. "She asked to glean in another field, and the overseer made it plain he would lay her down in exchange for allowing her to glean."

Boaz's lips thinned out, his teeth showed, and fire shot from his eyes. "Who? Who would dare demand such a thing?"

"She did not tell me his name, but I asked two of your maidservants. They had talked with her in the house. It was Kefir."

Hands on hips, Boaz slowly shook his head. "I have known him for many years, and this does not surprise me. His parents were faithful servants of Yahweh. It is appalling that he shames them by being a Godless man." His mouth tightened, and he gazed toward the horizon. "What causes a man to refuse his parents' guidance and instruction? They taught him God's law, and he rejected it."

Carmiel had no answer. He kept quiet.

"Did you comfort the young woman, tell her no harm will come to her here?"

Carmiel gave him a look, not one Boaz expected. "I told her she would not be bothered by you or me. But—."

"What? There is more?"

"Yes. I have overheard some of the young men. They want to touch her, and some have made remarks about her being from Moab. They lust after her, would take her to their beds, yet make terrible remarks about her being a daughter of incest."

Boaz's face hardened, his lips became white and drawn, and he spoke fast. "Gather the men—now! Meet me in the house."

Carmiel asked no questions. He rushed away.

Boaz strode away and met three of his maidservants entering the house about to take a break from the hot sun. He greeted them as he did the men. "Yahweh be with you. Please rest for a moment. When the men come, I wish to meet with them alone. You may return when the men have departed."

The women glanced at each other but did not ask. Refreshing themselves with water from the goatskin, they rested for a few moments and departed when the men arrived.

Boaz greeted them and then wasted no time setting them straight on his expectations.

"Ruth, a young Moabitess, has come to glean in my field, and be under my protection. She is alone and does not belong to a man. Her husband is dead less than two years.

"Only this morning she asked to glean in a neighboring field. She needs enough grain to feed her mother-in-law and herself. The overseer treated her like a harlot, and she feared for her safety because of things said. At the first opportunity, she removed herself from there. Now she is in my field and wishes only to glean.

"Can we not all understand she is a woman of character? She gleans to provide for her mother-in-law. You have seen she is lovely of face, one who could sell herself and provide quite adequately—and more if she would choose such a life. She does not. The woman sweats in the sun and remains pure. No one in my field will seek to take that from her.

"So, my command to you is—leave her alone. You are not to touch her. She is a widow who has no desire to be touched by any man. Although a widow of more than one year, I believe she continues to grieve over a husband taken in his prime.

"Also, I am told you know she is from Moab. Do not taunt her about being a foreigner. Speak kindly to her, and if you find that too difficult, then do not talk to her. Keep comments about her to yourselves.

"Finally, when she is thirsty, allow her to go to the vessels and drink. Do not forbid her. She is welcome in my field and shall receive the same treatment as any other worker.

"Are there questions? Ask now. I will not abide any deviation from my orders."

The men remained silent.

"Does each man understand?"

Every man nodded and said, "Yes."

Chapter 23

She had her head down, and her face half-averted as he stood watching from across the field. Ruth's seemingly never-ceasing hands continued to pick up barley heads and drop them into her basket, unaware curious eyes observed.

A few minutes passed, and she straightened up, taking a load off her back and knees. She watched slow-moving cloud shadows dotting the hills. Lowering her eyes, she noticed Boaz gazing at her. *He watches me.* An uneasiness stirred within her chest. She continued her gleaning.

Why does this foreigner provoke such warm feelings within me? Boaz started toward her, then stopped and stared again, mesmerized by the lovely woman from Moab. *I am in my forties, she, her twenties. She could be my daughter.*

He gnawed at his lower lip thinking about lost opportunities. He could have married any number of young women yet had not found the right one. Boaz had standards far above many of his fellow Israelites, men, and women. Hebrews by birth, yet they did not conduct their lives according to the Law of Moses.

Most of the women worshiped the Canaanite gods and neglected Yahweh. Others wanted, like Mahlon, to worship the heathen gods and Yahweh. Boaz would never enter into a marriage with any of those women. So, of the few available who were still faithful to his God, he never found his mate.

Salmon had on various occasions reminded him that he did not have an heir, and he must marry soon and produce a son.

Ruth would draw any man. Boaz was one. However, he wanted more than a pretty face. Bethlehem had many pretty faces.

Being attracted to a woman from Moab did not concern him. A woman's character and the God she worshiped were the important things to Boaz. He had grown to manhood knowing his mother was a Canaanite from Jericho.

Treating Ruth kindly like he did all of the men and women in his employ, never was in question. Suddenly a remark he had made came to him. '*A Moabite does not give up his gods….*'

He understood that she *would* abandon her gods to worship Yahweh. Had she? If not, when? Boaz *would* find out, maybe even today. He would look for the right moment.

A kind man, Boaz would not treat Ruth as trash nor be condescending. Neither would she work alone in his field. He fully intended to include her in the group of women. A few might not like it, but he was the owner, and his word would be respected.

Weaving his way around the sheaves, which the women had left for gathering later, he walked to a spot a short distance from Ruth. He wanted to welcome her and reassure her that she was safe in his field.

Boaz was a man of character, but some of the workers were not. Although he had warned the young men, he was not naive. A few would try to seduce her, if not in the field, certainly at someplace outside of town.

Ruth caught a glimpse of movement and glanced up. Had one of the women or possibly the overseer come with a message? She *had* noticed a man ride up earlier and dismount. Looking closer, Ruth recognized this man as the rider. He dressed as one of wealth, and the horse confirmed it.

He must be the owner. Quick notions came and vanished. *A very distinguished man—powerful. He carries a short sword on his hip—a warrior.*

"I am Boaz, owner of this field."

His warm smile relaxed Ruth.

"My name is Ruth." She smiled suddenly, prettily.

"I have been told your name by my overseer. You are welcome to glean here."

"Thank you."

Ruth's voice came to him soft, sweet, almost melodious. He fought the urge to grin like a boy.

"Listen, my daughter. Do not go to glean in another field, nor go from this area. I want you to stay close by my young women. Keep your eyes on this field and follow them.

"I have commanded the young men, not to touch you. And when you are thirsty, go to the vessels and drink freely from what the young men have drawn. I have given my permission, and you do not need to ask."

An outsider and Moabite, she had endured scornful looks and watched many Hebrews turn their backs to her. The small village attitude, which looked with suspicion upon strangers, was alive in Bethlehem.

Finally, a warm acceptance swept over her, a feeling she had not known outside the home of Hadar and Aleeza. This kindness brought tears to Ruth's eyes. She knew that he did not have to offer her this protection and care. She had been unaware of how much she missed the security of Mahlon until this moment. This man had put her at ease. He did not ask her—he told her to stay, even commanded her. 'Do not go…stay close…keep your eyes on this field.' Boaz spoke with authority, and she was more than willing to obey.

The man not only had powerful shoulders and arms, but another power, one which radiated from him and Ruth could not put a name to it. It was there nonetheless and gave her a sense of security. This lonely woman, in an unfamiliar town, among immoral men with designs on her, needed the comfort that he gave her at that moment.

In the fields, her status ranked below the lowest handmaids, yet she had no shame for she did it to provide for Naomi. A woman from Moab, known immediately because of her accent, and vulnerable with no protector, she would be easy prey for any man seeking to take advantage of her.

Amazed that this apparently important man would take notice of her, Ruth gracefully went to her knees, bowing low until her forehead touched the ground. "Why have I found favor in your eyes, that you should take notice of me since I am a foreigner?"

Boaz reached down and touched her shoulder. She raised up. Offering her his hand, she took it, and he helped her to stand. In that instant, feeling the warmth of her hand, he recognized Ruth stirred emotions within him that could quickly race out of control. He was a righteous man, one who feared Yahweh and followed the Law of Moses. Nevertheless, even this honest man recognized the draw of a fascinating woman. His pulse quickened. Ruth the Moabitess captivated him like no woman ever.

He struggled to gain control and give his speech, which he had rehearsed in his mind while he had walked the field. He had determined to take care of Naomi, his relative, and would do it through Ruth.

Boaz cleared his throat to gain time to collect himself. "It has been fully reported to me, all that you have done for your mother-in-law since the death of your husband. I am aware of how you have left your father and your mother and the land of your birth and have come to people whom you did not know before. May Yahweh repay your work, and a full reward be given you by Yahweh, God of Israel, under whose wings you have come for refuge."

He asks Yahweh to bless me? Does he not know that I have worshiped Chemosh all of my life? Now, he would have his God gather me as a hen gathers her chicks under her wings.

Ruth was unaware of Naomi being his relative. All she could figure was gossip had flown around town about that woman from Moab and that she had promised to worship Yahweh and make him her God. So, bewildered by his knowledge of her, she stared at him with quizzical eyes.

He called me daughter. She stifled a chuckle. *Maybe he is old enough, although I think him only in his forties. Most men do not marry until they are thirty. No, I am not young enough to be his daughter.*

Ruth gazed deep into his eyes and gave him her best smile. "I ask to continue to find favor in your sight, my lord. You have comforted me with sweet words and have spoken to my heart, although I am lower than all of your maidservants."

Her tender spirit left Boaz speechless. He smiled and walked on. *I have spoken to her heart.*

He shook his head in disbelief. The warmth of this woman had moved him. No woman had ever affected him like this one. He could lose himself in those dark brown eyes of hers.

Boaz, the warrior, a prominent citizen of Bethlehem, and a man of great wealth had allowed this young woman of Moab to distract him. In fact, she had disturbed him so much that he could not keep his mind on anything but her.

At midday, Boaz watched as his tired workers slowly trudged toward the house. I was time to eat and rest. Ruth continued her gleaning alone.

She has brought nothing for a midday meal. Not one of my men or women has asked her to eat with the group. Common courtesy calls for it, and my people have failed.

The prejudice against this young woman from Moab ran deep. He could order them to treat her right, but an order would not change their hearts.

"Ruth."

She looked around, and her heart skipped a beat. He stood behind her, not far. Attraction to this man had begun to grow, and Ruth's emotions troubled her.

"Come with me." He stepped forward holding out his hand. "Eat of the bread and dip your piece of bread in the sauce."

She took his hand, and he helped her rise.

"Please overlook my workers' rudeness. You are always welcome at my table."

Ruth's eyes slanted over, too uncomfortable to make eye contact. "Thank you."

They silently walked side by side toward the house. Neither found the words for more conversation.

Ruth's mind raced. *Why am I embarrassed? Oh, Mahlon, I love you so much. You gave me many years of happiness.*

Boaz was nothing like Mahlon. Her husband had been slight of build and sickly. He often wheezed and frequently inhaled the smoke from the herbs.

The man who walked beside her now stood head and shoulders above her. He was strong, almost princely of poise and stature, and by his stride—very healthy. Magnetism—he had it in abundance.

Her imagination had begun to work. *Boaz has been giving me extra attention. Why? Surely he has eyes for me.* She chuckled quietly. *Of course, it is only my imagination. This man of wealth and renown would have no romantic feelings toward a poor and common Moabitess.*

Boaz pointed to a spot beside the reapers and she took a seat at the low table. A plate of bread sat before her, and bowls of wine vinegar and olive oil sat at intervals along the middle of the table. Platters of cheese and bowls of fruit were also there to enjoy.

Boaz took a place beside Ruth. He placed a huge bowl of parched grain before her, which he had heaped up to over-flowing. "Eat until you are filled. We have plenty."

"Thank you, sir."

The workers eyed each other; some smirked. They all had various unspoken assessments of her. Ruth felt their strong contempt and kept her eyes lowered.

Many at the table had unspoken words about her.

It is obvious the master is smitten with this Moabitess. She sits between the reapers and him. She should be with the women. She is a Moabite and an impoverished gleaner. She should be outside, not at the table of the owner.

Boaz not only has her sit with the men, but he also goes beyond all accepted customs by serving her. Does he not have any dignity when it comes to this woman? He should be ashamed by his actions, yet he appears not in the least concerned.

What his workers failed to understand was Boaz cared for all of his workers, which all good leaders do. He led by being there and overseeing the operation and the needs, instead of remaining up the hill, at the cooler elevation and the comfort of his home.

Several of the men would have liked to seduce Ruth. However, it appeared to them, because of their evil minds; Boaz was doing the seducing.

Boaz wanted to elevate Ruth in the eyes of his workers. He wanted her treated with respect. She was a woman who had given up her gods and the others should know it.

"I have been told you have given up your gods." Boaz turned his head and caught her eye as she glanced over. Their eyes held for a few moments. He wanted her to speak, yet what could she say. Yahweh continued to be a mystery to her.

Ruth ducked her head. "It is true. I have not worshiped the gods of Moab since leaving my country."

"Do you worship, Yahweh now?" Boaz glanced around the table. All eyes had turned to Ruth.

"I promised my mother-in-law, Naomi, that I would make Yahweh my God. However, I have not worshiped him, yet. I do not know how. It has been but a few days since we have arrived in Judah."

"Do you wish to place your trust in him?" Boaz asked.

"I do trust him. He conducted us safely to Bethlehem.

"Naomi has told me much about Yahweh, and I wish to know more. You have feast days, sacrifices, and a written law. I know these things, but of the meanings of the feasts, sacrifices, and law, I know nothing."

"You shall learn, and soon," Boaz said.

Ruth, uncomfortable because of the stares, placed her remaining bread and parched grain into her scrip and stood to leave. "I must return to my gleaning while there is still daylight."

After she was out the door, Boaz spoke to his men. "She kept some of her food back and took it with her. I have inquired and know her situation. Without a doubt, she is taking that food home to her mother-in-law. Both are poor and lack necessities. I learned this only yesterday.

"Now, so that you will understand, Naomi is my dead uncle's wife. Ruth does not know this, but I am sure she will hear of it soon. Say nothing to her about it. I want her supplied with extra grain so she can take it home for her mother-in-law.

"You are to let her glean even among the sheaves and do not reproach her. Also, let grain from the bundles fall purposely for her; leave it that she may glean and do not rebuke her."

The men smiled, and when they did, they were all teeth.

Boaz shot a cold, careful look around the table. "Do you find what I said amusing?"

Carmiel, the overseer, said, "My master, we understand your concern for your relative. She *is* your responsibility." He chuckled. "Yet, the young woman, we rather think you have eyes for her and wish to help her equally. Am I wrong?"

Boaz pretended to be offended. "Do you question my charity for others? Carmiel, have you not witnessed me give of my means to many who are in need?"

"Yes, I have."

No one else spoke, yet Boaz had not answered the overseer's question directly. Then, after a few moments, the slight smile of Boaz, almost imperceptible, played on his lips. Their master, the bachelor, had an eye for the young woman. He fooled no one.

Chapter 24

Ruth moved the basket and dropped in her gleanings. Straightening up, she twisted about trying to take the pressure off her back. It ached from bending over.

Why have I been so blessed by this man?

She gazed into the distance and considered all his kind words and good deeds toward her. Overwhelmed, she wept.

Finally, drying her cheeks with the sleeve of her garment, she went back to gleaning. She determined to discuss all of this with Naomi at the end of the day.

The day had been long, and there remained several hours until evening. She continued to glean, and soon noticed the amount of stalks left on the ground had increased. First, it did not draw her attention but then after a short time it had become apparent. The workers were purposely leaving more for her. Ruth soon reasoned this could only happen on orders from Boaz. Again her eyes welled with tears.

With the day far from being over and her basket full to overflowing, she removed the stalks and piled them in a heap. She would have to come back and beat them at the end of day.

Her basket was sufficient for a day's work if it had been an ordinary day. This day was far from ordinary.

Working alone gives plenty of time for thinking and Ruth had many memories of the day run through her mind. Recollections of the other field made her shiver. Doubts about Boaz's intentions crowded in, and she fought to rid her mind of them.

'Ruth, do not fear me or the owner of this field. We follow the laws of Yahweh and would never ask you to compromise yourself. You are safe here.' The overseer's words came to her, and she believed them. *Until proven different, I accept Boaz as the man he appears to be.*

Along the boundary of the field, a lone tree stood. The men had hung from a branch a goatskin filled with water. Ruth went to drink and met Carmiel draining the water cup.

"Stand in the shade and drink." He handed her the cup.

"Thank you, sir."

"Boaz returned to the city."

Ruth gave him a puzzled look.

Camiel grinned. "You were looking around the field. Maybe watching for him?"

Ruth quickly turned away, opened the skin and filled the cup. "I only look for the stalks to glean."

She told the truth but quickly confessed to herself, maybe she did look around for another reason, also.

"You have gleaned much today. It may be too much for you to bear into town."

"I plan to beat out the grain."

"You have at least half an ephah. It will still be heavy. One of the workers could help."

"I have carried heavy loads for many years. My father's house is four miles from the city and many times I have carried on my head heavy loads, some which weighed more than a half ephah of barley grain."

Carmiel looked her up and down, sizing up her strength. "I believe you. Working in the field, almost non-stop from morning tells me you are quite strong.

"I offered the help because I know my master, and he would want me to. If you change your mind, let me know. Also, do not wait until all of the workers have departed to beat out the grain. Stop gleaning early and have your basket filled so that you may walk into town with the others. You should not walk alone from this field."

He had no laughter in those dark, cool eyes. The chill of his words sunk deep inside her and it was like a slap in the face. Ruth awoke to the realities of the time in which she lived. That man from the first field might be lying in wait or even a man from the field of Boaz. He had warned them, but some men ignore warnings.

"Thank you, I shall do as you say."

Late in the afternoon, Ruth carried her basket back to the heap of gleanings she had stacked earlier in the day. Grasping a handful of barley stalks and a stick that the overseer had given her, she began beating the heads of grain causing them to fall into her basket. Since the heap of barley was much more than expected, this process would take her until quitting time, and even then she might not have it all beat out. Ruth hurried.

This part of the harvesting was done on the threshing floor by the workers, except for a gleaner like Ruth. She must beat the grain in the field and take it home. There, Naomi could finish the process the next day while Ruth went back to the field for more.

Two more steps must be completed before the kernel would be ready for grinding. At home, Naomi would first thresh the kernel from the husk by placing a small amount between two stones. Then, she would move the stones back and forth which would result in breaking the husk away.

Then, taking the heap of kernels and husks to a place where a breeze could catch and blow away the husks, she would toss a handful or cupful into the air. The husks would be taken away by the wind, and the kernels would fall to the ground that had been swept clean of any debris. If there were no breeze, a second person would help by using a large hand-fan. While Naomi tossed the grain, this second person would blow the husks away by fanning.

After scooping the grain from the ground, it would be stored in a sack awaiting the grinding process with a hand mill.

"Would you like to walk with us into town?"

Ruth looked over. Bina smiled. Bat-Yam stood next to her with the same dour look of earlier in the day.

"I would, thank you. I have a few more stalks to beat."

"We shall wait."

"I must go," Bat-Yam said.

"Please wait." Bina held to the girl's arm.

"No, I must go now." She turned and joined the others leaving the field.

"We can all leave now. The rest of my gleanings will wait for tomorrow. No one will take them."

Bina shook her head. "No, let her go. She prefers not to walk with us."

Ruth raised her eyebrows. "You mean me."

"I am with you, so she prefers not to walk with both of us."

Ruth touched Bina's arm. "Thank you. I hope I have not caused you problems."

"I do not believe you have." She shrugged. "What problem could there be?"

"I do not know."

Ruth finished the beating process, which produced about an ephah of barley. Lifting the basket, which weighed close to forty pounds, she balanced it on her head and asked, "Shall we go?"

On the road, Bina did most of the talking while Ruth concentrated on walking carefully, avoiding holes and ruts made by the spring rains. Balancing the basket was no problem, a twisted ankle would be. This day began many weeks of gleaning and she must be in the field each day, not laid up with a sprained or broken ankle.

"Ruth, I heard your comments about our God that you want to learn more. I can teach you some things while in the field. Would you care to hear?"

"Yes! I do want to hear."

"We shall talk tomorrow."

At the city gates, the women parted ways. Ruth wound her way through the streets arriving home as Naomi crossed the court-yard after filling the manger for Stubborn.

"Ruth!"

With the basket atop her head, she cried out, "Mother, see what I have brought home."

"Your gleanings! Is it enough for tomorrow's bread?"

"Come see."

Ruth had unusual strength, not only in her neck and shoulders but legs. A country girl, well acquainted with toiling in the fields and vineyards, she ascended the stairs with ease.

In the room, she placed the basket on the floor and removed the covering. Naomi's eyes grew large, and her jaw dropped.

"All of this is yours?"

"Ours."

"How is it possible in one day? It is a miracle."

"I—."

"Where did you glean? Whose field? May the Almighty bless the man who took notice of you."

Ruth removed from around her neck the leather strap that held her scrip and placed the bag on the table. Inside were the bread and parched grain that she had held back at mealtime.

"This is for you. Please eat while I give an account of all that has happened to me. Your God—my God, has blessed us abundantly."

"I do not understand any of this." Naomi gazed at the basket and then the table. "How? Why? I—."

"Sit and eat. I shall tell you everything."

Naomi bowed her head. "Thank you, Almighty God, the one who is from everlasting to everlasting. The blessings from your hand are more than we could ever ask."

Ruth placed the bread and grain on a plate and gave it to her. "I requested to glean in a field. The men there frightened me, so I moved on. Then—."

"Ruth! I feared it might happen. Were you harmed?"

"No, I am fine. It *could* be dangerous, so I found another field. Yahweh must have selected it for me and sent me to glean there. I know not another answer.

"I came to the field, asked to glean, the man said yes, and I began my day. Later that morning, a man, a valiant man with a short sword upon his hip visited the field. He is strong, robust, a righteousness man!"

"His name, Ruth? What is he called?"

"Boaz."

Naomi choked a bit and dropped her bread. "The man's name is Boaz?"

"Yes. Do you know him?"

"Oh, my dear, Ruth. Blessed be this man of Yahweh. Boaz has not forsaken His kindness to the living and the dead!" Naomi shook her head in disbelief.

Ruth's voice rose in tone. "You do know him!"

Naomi's eyes sparkled. "Yes, my daughter. This man is a relation of ours, one of our close relatives."

"Yahweh truly does work wonders. He *is* powerful. My whole life I was taught the Hebrews served a weak God. That Chemosh had the strength of ten gods like Yahweh.

"My eyes are opening. I was deceived. I must know more about your God. I do want to make him my God and serve him. Boaz serves Yahweh. I shall, too."

Naomi gave her a quizzical look. She studied Ruth's words. *I believe Ruth is smitten by Boaz.*

Naomi said nothing to Ruth about it, but in the days ahead would mull over the relationship between Boaz and Ruth as each evening Ruth described her day in the field.

"Tell me more of today's happenings." Naomi chuckled.

"Boaz insisted that I should stay close to his young men until they have finished all his harvest. That includes the wheat crop, also. Is it not wonderful?"

"Yes, quite delightful. It is good, my daughter, that you remain near his young women and that you do not meet anyone in another field. His women will know where to go."

"I rather think Yahweh is using this man, Boaz, to bless us. How else can we account for this happening? I happened upon his section of the fields and I not only got to glean but, suddenly the gleanings increased with handfuls of grain being dropped on purpose. I am sure the man told his workers to do it."

Naomi's lip quivered. Her eyes welled with tears. "Ruth, oh my wonderful daughter. I have been wrong. My bitterness has given you heartache and so to my God has grieved over me.

"I am sorry for my bitterness toward Yahweh. He is blessing us, although *I* certainly do not deserve it. I have sinned and pray my God will forgive my unfaithful attitude. You are right to seek Yahweh in all good things and what has happened today is the hand of God working in our lives."

Ruth drew Naomi close, and they held in a sweet embrace. "Mother, I have not forgotten my vow to you. For wherever you go, I will go. Wherever you lodge, I will lodge. Your people shall be my people, and your God, my God."

"Thank you, Ruth. You are truly a great blessing to me."

Ruth pulled back and held Naomi by the shoulders. "I asked him to favor me," Ruth said with a chuckle in her voice.

Naomi's eyebrows raised. "Boaz blessed you, *and* you asked for more favor? You *are* a bold one."

Ruth's eyes twinkled. She smiled sweetly and said no more.

Mid-morning the next day Bina sat with Ruth in the house. While resting from the early morning work, they talked about many things. Several of the other women listened, and though some did not care for the Moabitess, no one mocked or said anything against her.

"My people will soon celebrate Passover," said Bina. "Do you know the day?"

"Slightly, I know nothing of its significance. My husband was an Israelite and observed only the Passover meal. Of the other Hebrew feast days, he did not participate."

Bina's eyes brightened. "I shall tell you more. Passover is a feast day celebrated each year on the 14th day of Abib. Then, the next day a seven-day festival known as the Feast of Unleavened Bread gets underway.

"As you may know, the Hebrew day starts at sundown. So, what we call preparation day is at sunset the evening before Passover. The morning of preparation day, we will only work until the midday meal. At that time, Boaz will allow the workers to go home and make preparations for the Passover meal.

"Will your mother-in-law observe Passover?"

Ruth's forehead wrinkled. "I do not know. She has said nothing. Maybe she has forgotten."

Bina leaned close to Ruth's ear. "Possibly she cannot afford the animal and other things to celebrate," she said in a whisper.

Ruth turned her head and gazed into Bina's knowing eyes. "Perhaps you are right. Tell me of your celebration?"

"Our practice is to slay a male lamb or kid that is without blemish and in its first year. This takes place three hours before sunset. The animal is then roasted whole. After sundown, the meal is served. All of the meat must be consumed, and no bone is broken. If there is any meat not consumed, it must be burnt before morning.

"If a family is too small to eat it all, they will join with a larger group. Usually the groups number between ten and twenty people. Your mother-in-law should seek out her clan and ask to join them for the Passover meal."

"What you have told me is how my husband ate the meal. Passover meal consists of meat, bread, and herbs, does it not?"

"A lamb, unleavened bread and bitter herbs."

"I have always considered it a strange combination of food," Ruth said smiling.

"It is not strange to the Hebrews. Each has meaning."

"I should like to hear of the significance of each before I eat. I am sure Naomi knows. She can tell me. My husband told me almost nothing about his religion. Now, I must get back to my gleaning."

Before Ruth got to her feet, Bat-Yam broke the silence of the other women. "You cannot eat," Bina's friend interjected in a flat, hard-edged voice.

Ruth looked over. The young woman's eyes were cold, and Ruth sensed those chilly orbs had no love in them.

"You are not an Israelite," she continued. "It is not allowed."

"I have agreed to worship Yahweh," Ruth countered. "It is true. I did not eat with my husband in Moab since Yahweh was not my God. Now, I have promised to make him my God and worship him only."

"That does not matter. You are a Moabitess, and the law requires that any who eats must be Hebrew. Do not profane the Passover by seeking to insert yourself into an Israelite feast."

Ruth could have been slapped in the face and not hurt as much as she did at that moment.

"Do not take her word," Bina said. "Rahab the Canaanite eats the Passover—I am almost sure of it. She is the heroine of the siege of Jericho when the walls fell. She did not betray our spies but hid them under the flax drying on her rooftop."

The young woman's face changed to one of doubt. She paused thinking it over. "Bina, you do not know that. I think you are wrong."

"We shall ask Boaz. Rahab is his mother."

Ruth stared at the girl with careful, searching eyes. "Boaz is not an Israelite?"

The girl smirked.

"His father is," said Bina. "He married Rahab after Israel destroyed Jericho. Ask Boaz about it," she smiled, "if it interests you."

Ruth smiled, and dimples creased her pretty cheeks. "It *does* interest me. I shall ask."

Chapter 25

Ruth awoke to a cool, damp, foggy morning. After tying her sandal straps, she rose up, washed her face, and while patting herself dry, the sky opened up. She had hoped to feed the donkey before the rain started. Cracking the door open, she watched as rain hammered the city drawing a curtain across the courtyard. The stairs filled with water, which gave the appearance of rushing rapids gushing through the middle of a mountain stream.

"No gleaning today," she glanced back, "the crop will be soaked and the field too muddy to walk."

Naomi got to her feet, walked barefoot to the door and gazed out on the storm. She pinched her lips, stifling a laugh.

"Is it humorous?" Ruth asked with a stern look. "If I do not work the field, we shall not eat."

Naomi gave her a playful shove. "Ruth, Ruth, can you not ease up for one day? Boaz has provided us with enough for many days. Missing one day will not cause us to starve. I sold a roll of goat hair cloth yesterday. So, we now have funds to buy at the market. Yahweh keeps us under his wing."

Ruth nodded; a sheepish grin crossed her face. "Thank you, I must remember to trust our God more."

Naomi peeked at her through shrewd eyes. "Maybe it is not so much the grain which concerns you." She smiled.

Ruth closed the door. "What do you mean?" Turning around, she stared into the old woman's eyes. "What else is there?"

Naomi held her daughter-in-law's stare until Ruth glanced down.

Naomi drew her shoulders back and said with twitching lips and a cocky tone, "A man." She bounced lightly on her toes.

Ruth gave her a sharp look. Then a wry smile parted Naomi's lips.

"Am I wrong?"

"The gleaning concerns me," Ruth said weakly.

"Gleaning *only*?" She casually anchored a hand on her hip. "Only? That is a word like always." A flickering smile suddenly crossed Ruth's face and then vanished. "*Rarely* is anything *always.*"

Naomi, wise from years of living, and not to be put off replied, "So too—rarely is *anything* only. The gleaning indeed involves both of us, yet I rather believe a man also concerns you. Do you miss going to the field today because you shall miss seeing a particular landowner?"

"Mother! Do you—do you—accuse me of, of…"

"Accuse?" She chuckled. "That is a strong word. Accuse you of what?"

"Suggest. Yes, do you suggest I am deceiving you?" Ruth fought to keep the smile from her face.

Naomi gently shook her head. "My dear Ruth, I do not accuse nor do I suggest. I know you. Knowing you for over ten years has accustomed me to your eyes, your words, and your voice. I even know much of what you think.

"So, no I do not accuse or suggest—*I know*. You have feelings, tender feelings for Boaz. It cannot be hidden."

Ruth's face warmed with the sudden realization that Naomi could read not only her actions but her inner feelings. She told the truth. Each time Boaz came near, she sensed a stirring within for a man, this man. Such excitement, lightness in her chest, thudding heartbeat, and dry mouth had not affected her since those first days when speaking with Mahlon and bringing him the midday meals.

Boaz appeared huge on that horse when he first appeared at the edge of the field. Riding tall and with an air of confidence, oh—Ruth noticed him all right, but quickly ducked her head and kept working. She, a poor gleaner from Moab, had no right to expect anything from him, and surely he would not give her a second glance—yet, he did.

Now, after several days, she had become more relaxed in his presence, and he drew feelings from her that she could not understand nor identify. Watching him arrive each morning sent a quick excitement through her.

His robust manliness contrasted sharply with her soft femininity. Ruth, a strong, resilient woman with rough, calloused hands from arduous field work, considered herself soft as the down of a young bird when near him. When in his company, she found herself breathless and her heart beat a little faster.

"We have an invitation."

"Hmmm?"

"Do you daydream?"

"I—yes, I was thinking over your words about Boaz. It brought about memories of Mahlon. Yes, sweet memories."

"What are those thoug—?"

"You mentioned something, an invitation." Ruth cut her off, not wanting to answer her obvious question.

Although Ruth loved her mother-in-law, she believed her to act somewhat pushy at times, and Ruth was not ready to discuss any feelings she might have for Boaz.

"Yesterday, Rahab shopped at the market. We talked about many things, and one was the weather. We both know the sky and the weather patterns of the Judean hills.

"She invited us to visit her home for midday meal if it rained today. With a day off from the fields, she believed it a perfect time to talk about the old days, and for her and Salmon to meet you. So, we go today."

A quick glance confirmed the suspicion in Ruth's eyes. "What are you thinking, daughter?"

"Do you only want to talk about *old times*?" She smiled prettily. "Or, maybe you have other motives?"

"Rahab invited us." A glint of humor flickered from shrewd eyes. "I know not of her thinking."

"Mother, it is your thinking I ask about."

Ignoring Ruth's question, Naomi opened the shutters of the one window. The rain had let up. "Stubborn needs to be fed when the rain stops. Should I go?"

Ruth chuckled quietly. "I will go."

The sun peeked through the clouds, the day brightened, and the refreshing air, cleansed by the rain, was glorious indeed. Ruth took a deep breath, again and again as she made her way to the home of Boaz. Naomi chattered almost continuously. The dark cloud of gloom which had hung over her arrival in Bethlehem had begun to rise.

"Here!" Naomi pointed to an entryway that opened into a beautiful courtyard. "This is the house of Boaz."

They walked under a vine-covered archway, and Ruth stopped, stunned at the magnificent house before her. Boaz was a wealthy man, but she had no idea of the extent of his riches.

Ruth stood wide-eyed, taking in the courtyard and home. Grapevines covered the walls surrounding the flat stones of the court. It was common to find beaten clay for a yard, but this was stone slabs carefully placed together like a jigsaw puzzle.

To one side was a round cistern. On the other side, a water course or gutter ran from outside the courtyard, under the wall and into a larger more spacious cistern. This tank emptied out the other side into another gutter that carried the overflow away. Ruth walked over and eyed it carefully, taking note of steps that led down into the water. She gave Naomi a questioning look.

"A cistern with steps? Why?"

"This is a mikveh," said Naomi.

"Mikveh?"

"Mikveh means a collection of water. This is a special pool of water which flows from nearby springs. Women, to restore their ritual purity, immerse in the water. A flowing river is a usual place, as long as it is deep enough to immerse fully. Men of wealth can afford to build a Mikveh such as you see here."

"Is it part of the Israelite religion?"

"Yes."

"I want to know more. What do you mean by ritual purity? Do you consider me impure? Should I dip in the waters?"

"Do you want to worship the Hebrews' God?"

Ruth turned to the sound of a familiar voice. "Boaz!" She bowed. "Thank you for allowing your maidservant and her mother-in-law to break bread with you."

He smiled, and Ruth's heart quickened. Chills raced down her backbone like a snow-fed mountain stream. She shivered.

"You and Naomi shall always be welcome at my table. I have thanked my mother for her kindness in inviting you today."

Ruth noticed a flicker of a grin as he continued. "I also thanked Yahweh in my morning prayers."

Naomi chuckled. "It was not for me you thanked the Almighty." Her eyes slanted over to Ruth. "I *do* understand your words."

Naomi's comment mortified Ruth. Her face grew hot.

Boaz noted Ruth's expression. The moment was awkward. "I apologize. I asked a question and did not allow you to answer."

Ruth squinted through questioning eyes.

"Yahweh, our God, do you wish to worship him?"

She nodded. "Yes. I have come to realize he is a God like none other. He is powerful *and* loving. The gods of Moab are not like Yahweh.

"I pledged to Naomi before we departed my country that I would make her God, my God. What must I do?"

"Come, let us sit on the benches and we can talk. Keziah mopped away the rain so your garments will remain dry."

"I shall go and visit Rahab," Naomi said. "Is she inside?"

Boaz started to answer, but Naomi was well on her way. Ruth watched her go with mixed emotions.

"Please sit here." He motioned toward a wooden bench beneath a sycamore tree. "The carpenter made it quite comfortable. Much more so than these other stone benches."

"Thank you."

Ruth sat down on one end of the bench, and Boaz took the other end. Now it was his turn to have a rapid heartbeat and dry mouth.

Ruth looked deep into his quiet face. He returned the stare by searching her bronzed face. The sun had done a marvelous work on this graceful and elegant woman. She was dazzling.

Both searched for words and finally Boaz pulled his gaze and nodded toward the mikveh. "I overheard your conversation with Naomi. Please believe me. I was not trying to eavesdrop. Would you care to know about the mikveh?"

"She told me it is for restoring ritual purity. I would like to know what that means. Am I impure?"

He caught the full gaze of her eyes and something stirred deeply within his body.

"Ruth." A giant lump in his throat gagged him. "I think…" He did not finish. Naomi had referred to the Law of Moses and its teaching about ceremonial impurity. He surmised Ruth meant something entirely different.

"Sir, are you not feeling well? You seem choked up. Horseradish will cure congested sinuses and a stuffy nose. I can make a poultice for you."

Boaz smiled from ear to ear. "I feel fine, very fine. Thank you for the offer, but no, it is not a sickness that affects me. I was thinking of how to answer your question.

"Ruth, I should have allowed your mother-in-law to explain, and not have interjected myself into your conversation."

She stared at him, confused.

Boaz took a deep breath. "Our law requires women to immerse fully in the mikveh after completing their monthly cycle." His face grew warm.

Ruth looked away, staring at nothing. She had no idea how to respond.

"It is for women who have become ceremonially unclean according to the Law. Men use it also when they are ceremonially unclean. It is for bathing, completely immersing in water," Boaz said, his voice barely above a whisper. "Speak to Naomi and she will explain that portion of Yahweh's Law."

"I shall."

"Remain here. I will return momentarily."

Ruth watched him rush away. An uneasiness ran through her. What was he doing? Her agitation did not last long. He reappeared quickly carrying a scroll.

"I want to read a portion from the scroll of Deuteronomy. This is one of several Hebrew scrolls that teach us about our God, his Law, and the account of his creation of the world. The scrolls also tell the story of our people from Abraham to Moses.

"This is a copy of the original written by Moses."

Ruth could not remove her eyes from the impressive scroll. It was enormous, compared with the small scrolls she had seen being read at the city gate of Ar. Those scrolls were usually one or two pages that contained some edict from the king of Moab.

Boaz sat down, this time much closer to Ruth. She noticed and a tingle went up her spine, lingered and slowly subsided.

He placed a finger on the parchment. "These are the words of the covenant which Yahweh commanded Moses to make with the people of Israel in the land of Moab—."

"Moab!"

Boaz smiled. "Yes, our people went through your country and the Almighty spoke to them there."

He placed a finger further down the page and began to read again. Ruth closed her eyes and listened intently.

" Therefore keep the words of this covenant and do them that you may prosper in all that you do. All of you stand today before Yahweh your God: your leaders and your tribes and your elders and your officers, all the men of Israel, your little ones and your wives—*also the stranger who is in your camp*, from the one who cuts your wood to the one who draws your water that you may enter into covenant with Yahweh your God, and into His oath, which Yahweh your God makes with you today, that He may establish you today as a people for Himself, and that He may be

God to you, just as He has spoken to you and just as He has sworn to your fathers, to Abraham, Isaac, and Jacob.

"I make this covenant and this oath, not with you alone, but with him who stands here with us today before Yahweh our God, as well as with him who is not here with us today (for you know that we dwelt in the land of Egypt and that we came through the nations which you passed by, and you saw their abominations and their idols which were among them—wood and stone and silver and gold); so that there may not be among you man or woman or family or tribe, whose heart turns away today from Yahweh our God, to go and serve the gods of these nations.

"That is enough for now," said Boaz. "Did you catch what Yahweh proclaims for those who are not Israelites?"

"I did," Ruth said smiling. "The covenant is with the stranger, also."

"Yes, even a Moabitess if she is willing to keep the words of Yahweh's covenant."

After the midday meal, Ruth, Naomi, and Rahab gathered under the sycamore tree and discussed the Israelite religion. Ruth had many questions, too many for one day, but Naomi and Rahab answered several.

"You have explained how Yahweh created the world. Also, you have told me of Joseph in Egypt, and how the Almighty brought his people out of that country by the hand of Moses.

"Now I know of the promises to Abraham and that he is the father of your people. Mother, I want to be recognized as a convert and new citizen of Israel. Everyone should know that Ruth no longer worships the gods of Moab, but accepts only Yahweh as her God. I want all doubt removed from the minds of any who know me as the Moabitess that I now pledge my faithfulness to Yahweh and will only serve him."

"Ruth, may the Almighty bless you for your decision. It was one thing to promise before we departed Moab that you would make 'my God your God.' However, we have been in Judah for many days now, and you still wish to remain and not return to your home and your gods.

"So, we shall do as you say and proclaim it far and wide."

"My son is known in the gates," said Rahab. "I shall ask him to advise all of the elders of your decision."

"One more thing," said Ruth. "You have explained what it means to be ceremonially unclean. I *am* unclean at this time, but I finished my monthly cycle more than seven days ago. So, it is time for me to dip in the waters of the mikveh, and begin my new life as a worshipper of Yahweh."

Naomi wrapped an arm about Ruth and pulled her close. "You have chosen wisely, my daughter."

Rahab smiled and reached for Ruth's hand. Holding it firmly, Rahab said, "Naomi is blessed because of your faithful love. You have journeyed to a land foreign to you, promising to remain with your mother-in-law until death. It is quite remarkable."

"Ruth has always been different," said Naomi. "Her ability to love exceeds the capacities of everyone around her. It is one thing to have a feeling type of love, but quite another to have a love which transcends feelings and does for others when others cannot or choose not to acknowledge such love."

Rahab looked at Ruth. "We Hebrews call it *hesed* love. It is a love which does not demand to be reciprocal. My dear Ruth, you have it in abundance."

Ruth opened her mouth to speak but said nothing. Her eyebrows bunched in thought. She remained quiet.

"Ruth, you shall enter the water at once," said Rahab. "We have a mikveh, and you can immerse yourself before you return home. Salmon and Boaz should be returning any moment from the fields. They will stand at the courtyard entrance and stop anyone from entering while you carry out the cleansing ritual."

"They will not witness the beginning of my new life?"

Naomi looked through kind eyes. "Ruth, a woman disrobes completely before entering so that the waters can touch every part of her body."

"Oh!" She smiled. "Yes, it is good that they will stand at the gate."

At that moment, Boaz and Salmon entered through that same gate and approached the women.

"We have surveyed our field, and the crop is too wet and the ground too muddy for work today or tomorrow," Boaz said. "With a day of sunshine we can start anew the next day."

"We assumed that would be the situation," said Rahab. "Please allow me to tell you our *good* news. Boaz, my son, Ruth has reaffirmed to us that she will worship Yahweh and him only. She wants it published far and wide. I have told her you will gladly do that and start by informing the elders at the gate."

Boaz cried out as he looked toward the heavens. "May Yahweh bless you and keep you safe under his wings!"

Ruth remembered his workers greeting in the field. She bowed and repeated it to him. "Yahweh bless you."

"She has another request," said Naomi.

"If I can fulfill it, then it shall be done."

"Ruth has asked to enter the waters and receive her ritual cleansing. Rahab, Keziah, and I shall witness. We ask you and Salmon to stand at the courtyard gates."

"It will be our honor," Salmon said. "Let us go, son."

Boaz bowed to Ruth. "You are truly a blessing to Naomi and everyone with whom you associate." He turned and walked toward the courtyard entrance.

Stunned, Ruth could not speak. Her master, the man who allowed her the humble task of gleaning had bowed to her.

"He is truly righteous," Naomi said.

Ruth stood on the top step of the mikveh awaiting Rahab to return with Keziah. She lifted her eyes gazing intently at the courtyard entrance, searching the shadows for any sign the men would betray her privacy.

Boaz and his father Salmon filled the opening with their frames. Both were big men, Boaz having the broader shoulders. She sighed quietly. Both stood silently with their backs to her and the witnesses. Her pretty smile came quickly. They were men of righteousness. She need not worry.

Rahab reappeared with Keziah at her side. "We are ready to witness your immersion and proclamation of faith in Yahweh."

Ruth removed her head covering and outer garment, stepped out of her sandals and then pulled her inner garment free. Stepping down into the water, which rose slightly above her waist, she moved to the center of the pool.

Looking up at her mother-in-law, she asked, "Are there any words I am required say before I dip in the water?"

Naomi shook her head. "No, Ruth."

"Then I shall say what I told you in Moab. Your people shall become my people, and your God my God."

Immediately Ruth bent her knees, plunging straight down, thus covering her whole body with water. Then rising, she ascended the steps where Naomi covered her with a large wrap of lamb's wool to dry herself.

Naomi embraced her and said, "The Lord God of Salvation and Deliverance now numbers you as one of his own."

"May I ask a favor?" Ruth directed the question to Rahab.

"Of course you may."

"I have been told your Passover meal is near. May we eat the meal with you? We do not have a lamb for sacrifice. If Moabites are not allowed, I will remain home, but please allow Naomi."

Rahab wrapped her arms around Ruth. "You have embraced Yahweh as your God as I did many years ago. You are Moabite, and I am Canaanite. However, we have made Yahweh our God. We *can* partake of the Passover meal. You and Naomi are welcome to celebrate here."

Chapter 26

Day dawned with a bright late spring sun. By mid-morning, white cotton ball clouds had spotted the clear blue sky.

"Naomi, over here." Rahab waved her over. "It has been weeks since I have seen you. Was it not the day Salmon died?"

"I believe so. How have you been?"

"I miss my husband, but my son is a constant help. Have you been well?"

Naomi nodded. "Yes, my health is fine. I have been busy with my spinning and today I come to sell. There are several merchants who are regular customers."

She eyed the cart pulled by Stubborn. "That is wonderful."

"With the gleanings that Ruth brings home and silver I earn from my sales, we survive. Yahweh is gracious to us."

"You appear happy."

"I arrived home a bitter woman. It is true. Now, that root of bitterness is gone. It has been—how long?" She rubbed her forehead as if trying to extract the information. "Why, almost two months now since we entered the gates of Bethlehem. Enough time to ask the Almighty to forgive me for my harsh conclusions concerning my God."

"You said you have enough to survive." Rahab raised her eyebrows. "That does not sound hopeful."

"I do want more for Ruth." She smiled, yet her eyes were somber. "I am old and do not need much. She is young and needs more than I can give her. I want security for her.

"Since she has been here, and word has spread that she worships Yahweh, it seems all of Bethlehem has taken notice of her. People call her a worthy woman, a woman of valor. Surely," Naomi breathed deeply and her eyes drifted toward the heavens, "there will be a husband for her one day."

Rahab grasped her arm. "I am sure there will be," she said with meaning. Her eyes filled with tears, and Naomi patted her shoulder. -

"I am so very sorry that Salmon has been laid to rest. I know you miss him terribly."

"It is true, yet I had him much longer than you had Elimelech. The Almighty blessed me with many wonderful years with my husband."

"And I had Elimelech much longer than Ruth had Mahlon. I pray to Yahweh for a husband and children for my dear daughter."

"Is she not barren? No children after years of marriage."

Naomi looked away, staring with unseeing eyes. Finally, she raised her chin and declared in a soft, but clear voice, "It breaks my heart, but I will say it. I have come to believe Ruth was barren because Mahlon refused to worship only Yahweh and leave Moab after his father died. He should have returned to Judah.

"I do not know that for sure. God has not revealed that to me, but I feel it."

"We cannot always depend on feelings," said Rahab. "Feelings can deceive, too."

"You speak the truth, but I do believe this to be so. Now, I must hurry on and sell my cloth."

"Boaz works at the threshing floor tonight and every night until the grain is winnowed and stored. The threshing will take several more days, but after it is completed, we shall have you in our home for a feast."

"Thank you for your kindness. We will look forward to it."

Ruth sat cross-legged on the floor weaving goat hair thread into cloth for sale to a tent maker. Naomi had taken the order a few days before when delivering cloth to a merchant.

The barley harvest had wrapped up, and the wheat harvest was a few days away. Ruth no longer had a field to glean, so she had begun helping Naomi with her business. With Naomi away from the house making deliveries, Ruth had plenty of time to think about an assortment of things.

Today she centered on loneliness. Mahlon died two years before, and she missed him terribly. She tried to put reminiscences of him behind her, but she had failed. Her first and only love, how could she ever blot him and the years they had together from her memory? It was not possible. She understood that fact very well. So, what was possible? Could she live with another man someday and not think of Mahlon? Would she not continually compare a new husband to her first? No, that would not be fair to either man.

"Why do I even consider such things," she suddenly said aloud. "I am a Moabitess. I now worship Yahweh, yet how will I ever get past my heritage. What self-respecting Hebrew would take me on and have the gossips of Bethlehem whispering."

She laughed out loud, and it *was* loud. Her agitation had brought on a sudden heat. She began cooling herself with a hand fan.

"Now, I talk to myself. What is next? A vexing curse upon me for my foolishness? Will Chemosh curse me?"

Ruth sat in silence. She continued to fan while speculations of insanity, possibly brought about by some god, filled her mind.

"No!" she cried out. "I do not worship the gods. Yahweh is my God now; he will not allow any foreign god to place a curse upon me."

The door opened, and Naomi stepped in. She looked around the room. "To whom do you speak?"

"It was my voice." She frowned. "Do you not recognize it?"

Naomi smiled easily. "Yes, I recognized your voice. I always assumed only old men and women talked to themselves."

Ruth chuckled softly. "Sometimes young women."

"We must talk," said Naomi, her eyes alert and on Ruth. "No weaving. I want you to listen and not be distracted."

Ruth stared at her, square in the face. "It is serious?"

"Yes, but not bad. It will be very good, I hope."

"You sound mysterious. Tell me."

Naomi gave a long look at her daughter-in-law, taking the measure of her. She had rehearsed the words several times on the way home from the marketplace. It was a bold, maybe foolhardy plan she had devised, one she had mulled over for days, and now the appropriate time had presented itself.

"You hesitate, should I fear?"

"No Ruth, trust me. I want only the very best for you. Now my dear, listen closely. Your mourning days for Mahlon are over. I know you loved him, but it is time to move on with your life.

"It is appropriate that I try to find a husband for you. I want you to be happy."

Ruth's dark brown eyes peered from her elegant, bronzed face, a face lovely as the morning dawn. Then quickly, an amused look brightened her eyes.

"I want security for you," Naomi rushed on. "You need not live hand to mouth, hoping each day brings enough income to buy food to eat. You deserve a home, husband, and children. Our kinsman-redeemer will buy our land from the man Elimelech sold it to, and then he will marry you. So, you will have a husband, and the land will go to your heirs. That is our offer. The land and you. Who could ever reject that deal?" Naomi gave Ruth her sweetest, most innocent looking smile.

Ruth's jaw dropped at Naomi's suggestion. "How can I abandon you? I have promised to be with you until death. I shall be buried next to you. Besides—."

"I wish to find you a home, a home where a man will love you as much as you love me. I have considered in my mind a list of eligible men. As I deliberated this weighty matter, the name Boaz came to mind. Why, yes! Boaz!" Naomi said with a voice inflection that sounded as if she had just thought of him that very day. "Is he not a kinsman-redeemer?"

"Well, I—."

"He is," she cut Ruth off again. Naomi walked to the window and gazed at the courtyard. She watched Stubborn munching from the manger. "Boaz is Elimelech's nephew. He has never married and surely he is quite lonely. At times, do you not think that he appears miserable and lonely?"

Ruth rolled her eyes. "Mother, I am—."

"What do you think?" She turned around. "Is he not lonely?"

Anticipating she would be cut off again, Ruth hesitated.

"Why do you not say something?"

A smirk played on Ruth's lips. "I am…." She waited a moment for another interruption. "I am a Moabitess. Do you actually believe Boaz or any other Israelite would take me for a wife?"

"You worship Yahweh, not some pagan god."

"True enough, nevertheless, I am still from Moab. What Israelite would want to defend his decision to marry me?"

Naomi did not reply. Ruth's remark pried from her memory a long forgotten conversation with Mahlon. His words came to her as though they were said yesterday. *'Israelites hate Moabites because of Lot and his daughters. Is it not time to lay aside such feelings? Do you condemn these people, for something they did not do?'* A stab of pain shot through her remembering that long ago day and her answer. *'We should have nothing to do with them.'*

"You live in Judah now and have embraced our God. No one has to defend you or anything about you."

"Mother, I am barren. Look out that window again. Do see any grandchildren running around the courtyard? A man wants heirs. I cannot provide even one child."

"Ruth," Naomi's eyes dropped. "I have come to believe you were barren because of Mahlon. I remember a time when Chilion was gravely ill. You asked the Moabite healer to come, and Mahlon allowed it. I went to my tent and grieved over that situation, asking myself how my family had come to such a willful disregard for Yahweh's commands. I know now. It was little by little, first with forsaking the Sabbath. Over time, a person makes excuses for many things which were done that are against our God's commands.

"Shall I speak against my son? I must. He worshiped pagan gods and refused to journey home when his father died." She raised her eyes and the glint of hurt and disappointment in those sad eyes was quite evident. "Yahweh shut up your womb because of those sins. I honestly believe it."

Ruth remained silent. What could she say? It had crossed her mind many times, and she partly believed Naomi's words.

"It is hard to accept my words," Naomi said. "I know that."

"You have not been around Boaz for many years, and we only arrived here two months ago," Ruth timidly argued but without a convincing tone.

"I have known him all of his life. He has not changed. Boaz remains the same righteous man I have always known."

"Mother, he is fifteen or twenty years older than me. And, consider my relationship with him—a lowly maidservant gleaning in his field. He is a man of renown, a mighty man of God. Should he lower himself to take me as a wife? He can have his pick of Hebrew women."

"I am old, but my eyesight has not failed me. I have seen his actions when near you. He has eyes only for you—and you for him. It is—."

"Mother! It is plain now. Boaz is not some afterthought you suddenly have." She took a deep, satisfied breath. "Seeking to match us in marriage has been in your mind for some time now. Tell me, is it not so?"

"I happen to know that Boaz will be with his men tonight winnowing barley at the threshing floor." She smiled, her eyes filled with female mischief. "Listen carefully and I will tell you what to do."

"It is plain. You have a plan. Well, Boaz must ask me to be his wife, and he has not."

"Ruth, listen to me. I shall tell you Israelite customs."

She shrugged her shoulders. "I am listening."

"You must bathe, anoint yourself with perfume, and dress in your best garments. Then tonight, go down to the threshing floor, but do not—."

Ruth sucked air. "The threshing floor! At night? During threshing days? Mother, it is not done. Surely you know the prostitutes frequent the threshing floors at this time of year offering their unholy services. They know the men will be there guarding the grain."

"Do not make yourself known to the man until he has finished eating and drinking," said Naomi ignoring Ruth's concern.

"Then, when he lies down, you shall take notice of the place. When the time is right, go in, uncover his feet, and lie down.

"This is our way of proposing marriage when asking help of a kinsman redeemer. It is perfectly acceptable, and Boaz will understand. He will tell you what to do concerning redeeming our land and a marriage for you two."

Ruth's eyes narrowed, and she lifted a skeptical eyebrow. *So, I am to go secretly to a place known for sexual activity, hike up my master's garment exposing his bare feet, and then lie down and await his words. Can he not help but believe I am there to engage in fornication?*

"What if he does not speak of marriage? Maybe he will be appalled at my forwardness and ask me what I am doing."

"It is Hebrew custom. He will know."

"Should I not say *something*?"

Naomi's eyebrows bunched. "He has never known a woman, so, he may become tongue-tied. If he only looks at you and does not say anything, then by all means you will need to speak. Tell him to take you under his wing and spread the corner of his garment over you. Remind him that he is our kinsman redeemer. Tell him to make you his wife."

"Tell him? Do I demand?"

"My dear Ruth." She gently shook her head. "I know you are a strong woman, a bold woman, in fact. However, it is in the voice," she touched her throat, "and look." She fluttered her eyelids. "No, never demand, but do not beg, either."

Ruth gave a nervous shift to her feet and wiped her sweaty palms down the front of her robe. Her face had drawn tight. "I will do all that you have said to me."

Boaz and his men silently watched the sun grow crimson, sink in the west, and then hide its face below the horizon.

"It has been a long harvest, my friend," said Boaz. "The Almighty has richly blessed the land of Judah. We have more than enough for sale *and* to feed our families."

"It is so," Carmiel said. He lifted a cup of wine in a toast to the bountiful harvest. "We celebrate a bit tonight and more so at the end of threshing."

Boaz raised his cup, and all the other workers raised theirs.

"Let us eat and drink." Boaz looked at each man sitting by the small fire that burned far from the threshing floor. "There is plenty. God has been good, and we will enjoy and eat to the full. A warning, though, no one is to drink in excess and become drunk. I need men alert at the sound of thieves. We shall sleep and rise to work another day."

After a few moments, Carmiel leaned over and whispered, "As you said, we do have enough for our families, yet you remain without a wife. Am I too bold to ask why?"

Boaz gave him a pained look. "You are bold, my friend." He went back to eating.

"You have no heir. It is not good to wait so long. May I say there are young women aplenty who await your invitation for marriage?"

"No, you may not say it." He grinned.

"My lord, I have already said it. Do I take it back?"

"No, it is true. I have been told many times by my mother and so also my father, even up until the day he died."

"I am sorry for your loss. He would have liked to have seen the grain piled high over there." He pointed to giant mounds of recently threshed barley.

"He did see the many sheaves stacked higher than he could reach. That made for a great visit to the field."

A worker tossed a small log on the fire. It blazed up sideways under the stiff breeze. Boaz had built the fire downwind from the threshing floor so that the sparks flew away from the grain. He always made it a priority to keep the grain and chaff safely away from any chance of fire burning up weeks of work.

The stars glittered at each other, and the half-moon lit the night. Ruth passed through the gates taking a path that led up to the threshing floor. A few moments later, she came up over a low rise and the blaze in the distance caught her eye. Her heart began to race, and she dried her hands on her garment. She took a deep breath and tried to compose herself.

Many people had described Ruth, and most of the assessments were similar. No one who had known her long would say she was naive. She had seen many things and had been a participant in some.

She walked on, and memories began flooding her mind. Ruth remembered the days when she and Mahlon were desperately trying all sorts of methods for her to conceive. She had agreed to try the fertility rites to Chemosh. Everything else had failed. So, why not try.

"We go to the threshing floor tonight," said Mahlon. "Your father has suggested it."

Remembering that night, she shook her head. The fertility gods failed that night as did everything else they had tried. She remained barren. *Is Naomi right? Was it Mahlon's fault?* Her stomach did a flip-flop. A wave of nausea went over her. *What am I doing? She has talked me into approaching a man on the threshing floor. Did she not think he might molest me? He has never married and has waited many years to touch a woman.*

Ruth swallowed hard. Her mouth had dried up as though she had eaten sand. The giant lump in her throat grew.

He is righteous, but he is also all man. This is a dangerous situation lying near a man who has never known a woman carnally. Maybe that is so, who knows for sure but Boaz.

The fire grew brighter as she drew nearer, and new doubts stole into her mind. Ruth slowed, walking on cat feet, she carefully placed one foot in front of another. Then, another memory seemed to come from nowhere.

"*Please Lord, open my dear Ruth's womb.*"

"*Mahlon.*"

"*Ruth, I cannot see you. Do you hide in the dark? Why are you not within the tent?*

"*Ruth! Do you wish my heart to stop? Where did you learn to move about like a spirit?*"

"*I practiced as a child. My brothers tormented me, and I had to fight back. I watched the house cats and the bigger ones—the* panthers. They sometimes appear in the meadow. Did I frighten you?"

"I am thirty years old, but feel fifty. You scared twenty years onto me. I forgive you and to prove it...."

Ruth stopped dead in her tracks. She remembered what happened when they returned to the tent. They placed their fertility idols on a bench and then Mahlon laid her down.

Afterward, Ruth clung to him until she fell asleep. No memory remained of the next morning. Only that night, a night that she had relived in her mind many times. There were other nights, many, yet it was that night which she could never blot from her memory.

Ruth trembled. Her emotions ran wild. *How can I have such beautiful remembrances of my husband while on a mission to ask another to marry me? Oh, Yahweh, my God, how can this be right? My husband lies in the grave, and I go to another man's arms. Naomi has put me up to this, and I cannot cope. It is too much for me to handle. A Moabitess will soon ask a righteous Israelite to marry. Give me the wisdom to understand. Open my eyes to this custom.*

Ruth stood watching the fire flicker down to red coals. She would obey her mother-in-law. Though terribly conflicted, she trusted Naomi's judgment.

Quietly creeping closer, Ruth riveted her eyes upon Boaz. Shortly, the laughter and merriment died away, and he got to his feet. She moved deeper into the shadows her eyes following his every move.

He motioned toward the grain. "You men sleep around the grain toward that end. I will sleep at the other end. Yahweh be with you."

Boaz walked away from the fire and Ruth followed at a safe distance. Finally, he removed his mantle and lay next to the heap. Pulling his legs up at an angle, he covered himself with the garment and soon fell into a deep slumber.

Chapter 27

Ruth hesitated. Her eyes slanted over to the spot where the men had sat eating and drinking. The fire, burning down to coals, still had fiery red spots, which she watched intently for a few moments. Finally, the glow of red embers faded to black.

One more time Naomi's words and plan ran through her mind, and Ruth rehearsed her response as to why she had come. Would Boaz believe her or think she had lost her senses and become a Bethlehem whore?

Slinking forward, she glanced around for any sign of watching eyes. The sounds of men snoring rumbled about the grain heap. They had put in a hard day's work, and the wine had quickly laded their eyelids in sleep.

The moon gave scarcely enough light to see the place where Boaz lay. She stopped and gazed into the shadows, barely making out the form of the one she was to approach.

I know he has feelings for me. He cannot hide them. His eyes have told me of intense emotions. He is attracted to me, and I am to him. I do not deny it. Could I be so forward with a man tonight if it were not that I believe he would take me as his wife?

Ruth stood alone in the night—heart pounding. She glanced toward the end of the grain heap. Another man lay with his back to her, but not far. It would not take much of a noise to wake him and the others.

Tiptoeing the last few steps, she stopped within a foot of Boaz. She trembled. Her knees had grown weak from fear of being noticed. The moment had come. She wavered.

What if he rejects me? Shall I be heartbroken? Yes—no. Why should I? This is so bold, so daring. So—impossible.

What if one of the men awakens, and goes to relieve himself. He may notice me lying here. I will be humiliated beyond words.

Boaz! Oh, his reputation could be ruined. It would be an enormous scandal. A prominent man of Bethlehem caught with a Moabite whore. Surely that would be the story.

She dithered a few more moments. Then, bending over, she raised his garment, hiked it up, exposing his feet. Then, without a sound quietly slipped down to the ground.

Ruth lay within inches of him. She shivered. *Coming here is the most provocative thing I have ever done. Naomi, what are you doing right now? Sleeping soundly? You have encouraged this, but I am the one out here in the dark with a man not my husband. I will get no sleep tonight.*

Ruth lay on her back, her body taut with anxiety. She gazed at the stars. The moon, half-way up the eastern sky kept the dimmer lights in the night sky invisible.

Do I awaken him? Tell him why I am here. Ruth! You cannot do any such thing. You would have to touch him, and that would startle the man, and he might cry out. Or, turn over and attack you, thinking you are a thief.

Oh, my God, Yahweh. Help your new servant. I know not what to do.

Whisper, yes, I could whisper. A loud whisper would wake him. No, that does not make sense. Is there such a thing? A whisper is quiet, not loud.

I need clear thoughts, O God. Naomi, my mother-in-law, has cast me into this situation. Now, what?

Ruth fought back tears. She covered her eyes with a forearm. *Yahweh, I know you hear my pleas. Naomi has taught me that you are all-powerful, all-seeing, and all-knowing. Forgive me for trying to inform you of Naomi's identity. My thinking is clouded. She loves me, wants the best for me, yet she has placed Boaz and me in a compromising situation.*

Ruth raised her head, her eyes darting back and forth. Boaz and the men continued to sleep. Lowering her head to the ground, she stared wide-eyed at the moon.

What is there to do but watch the sky and wait? Let Boaz do or say something. Why do I need to initiate the conversation? Naomi said he would tell me what to do. Thank you, my God, for reminding me.

An hour passed, then two, and then another, she was not sure how many. Ruth had turned on her side, her back toward Boaz. She peered into the dark, searching for any dying embers of the fire. Nothing, the fire had burned down to gray ash. Her anxiety grew. She worried about what to say like a dog worries over a bone. The animal keeps nipping and chewing and slowly, but surely the bone gets smaller. Ruth nipped and chewed on her words until she had reduced them down to a short, concise speech.

A memory came to her. Naomi's words, those she spoke earlier in the day.

"Do not make yourself known to the man until he has finished eating and drinking. Then, when he lies down, you shall take notice of the place. When the time is right, go in, uncover his feet, and lie down."

I waited too long! I should have gone immediately. He is asleep now. Awake, he would have known what I was doing and told me what to do. Yet...the other men were still awake and would have seen me. What if he refused? We both would be fodder for jests; derision would rain down upon us throughout Bethlehem.

Ruth jerked. Boaz stirred. Something touched her backside—his bare feet. He had begun to turn in his sleep, and a muffled sound came from behind her.

A chill filtered through her as fear started to mount. Her heart throbbed with quick, heavy beats.

She rolled onto her back as he turned over to face her.

Too dark to recognize her face, yet Boaz understood it was a female who lay beside him. Fear struck at his heart. His cool, uncovered feet had touch something soft and warm. Intruder! But, not a thief or he would be dead with a dagger in his back.

That soft flesh he had touched with his feet told him a woman had sneaked into the threshing floor. The sweet aroma of perfume piqued his senses. His first thought was a harlot. She had come to bargain sexual pleasure in exchange for silver or maybe grain.

Boaz raised up to an elbow. Looking down at the female form at his bare feet, he demanded, "Who are you?"

Ruth sat up, and with a bitter, awful fear clutching at her throat, she fought to gather her wits. Her racing thoughts sent her blood leaping. Finally, burying her fears, she said, "I am Ruth, your maidservant. Spread the wing of your cloak over me, for you, are my kinsman-redeemer."

His shoulders had bunched at the sound of her sweet voice. He stared, mouth gaping. Ruth turned her head, and the moonlight illuminated her face entirely. Boaz's heart beat wildly; he stared while inhaling the scent of her. For an instant, he could neither believe his eyes nor his ears. Then, it hit him full force—her words and the closeness of her body.

He had never loved a woman, never married and never been sexually intimate. Now, this young woman had come, lain at his feet and offered herself in marriage. He, the well-known, mighty man of God, the righteous Boaz, at that moment wanted to encircle her with his arms, hold her, and never let her go. The temptation to touch her was overwhelming. To take her carnally, he did not consider, for he *was* that righteous man, and he would not betray his God.

However, he was lonely and so needed this woman. He wanted to envelop her with his arms—love her, although he had suppressed such cravings. She would never want an old bachelor when so many young men were available.

Then, scarcely thinking, his words flowed. "I thank Yahweh for a young woman like you!" He kept his voice low. "For your kindness and loyalty to Naomi is greater now than when you first agreed to journey here with your mother-in-law.

"I believe it is only natural you would prefer younger men, whether rich or poor. However, you have cast aside your personal desires so that you may buy back Naomi's land by marrying a redeemer. Now put aside any fears about your security.

"Your deeds are known in the city gates. All the people of Bethlehem know you are a virtuous woman, a woman of valor. I will do what you have requested and handle all details."

Ruth smiled, and Boaz's heart fluttered. The man wanted her more than words could express. He leaned toward her ever so slightly so that he might breathe in her freshness while he figured the options of what could be done.

"Ruth, it is true that I am a kinsman-redeemer. However, there is a redeemer closer than me. Remain here this night, and in the morning if he will act as kinsman-redeemer—good; let him do it. But if he is not willing to buy back the property, then I will perform the duty. As Yahweh lives, I will do it!"

Ruth inhaled sharply, her face stiffened upon hearing there was another, closer kinsman-redeemer.

"My words have troubled you?" Boaz asked in a voice strained with emotion.

Ruth's soft brown eyes burned with tears. "I am not so worthy as you think me," she whispered. "I do love Naomi, and for her I would wed this other man. But it is *you* I want."

Ruth's words, spoken with her soft, warm voice, caught his breath away. The pounding of his heart roared in his ears. Of all the words Ruth could have uttered, she said the perfect ones.

Boaz leaned closer, so close that the moonlight highlighted large tears slipping down her cheeks. The scent of her perfume sent a wave of manly desire through him. He was a gentleman, but even a righteous man has an almost uncontrollable desire when this close to the woman he loves.

Boaz brought his hands to Ruth's face, and with a tender touch he gently brushed away her tears with his thumbs. Their eyes met. "Ruth, it is you *I* want, too. I promise I will do everything in my power to make you mine." He drew back.

"Lie here at my feet until the morning."

Ruth's eyes reached out to him begging for resolution to this unexpected problem. His eyes bespoke determination, and she felt a wave of peace flood over her. In the power of Yahweh, he would make it happen.

All night, the two of them lay there silently, minds racing. They both prayed and thought, and prayed and thought some more. Their bodies never touched, but their souls became intertwined in the silent solidarity of this experience.

With the first gray light of dawn, Ruth rose to her feet. Boaz followed. The morning birds had yet to chirp their morning messages to each other, and the men around the grain heap slept. Nothing stirred. Boaz put a finger to his lips, and Ruth kept silent.

"We must avoid any appearance of wrongdoing. So, do not let it be known that a woman visited the threshing floor."

Ruth, wide-eyed, nodded her understanding.

He motioned for her to follow him to the far end of the grain heap away from the workers. "You shall not go empty unto your mother-in-law. Now, remove your shawl and hold it."

She took the covering from her head and shoulders, holding it out. Her black tresses fell loosely down her back, and Boaz saw Ruth as the most gorgeous woman he had ever beheld. Her raven colored hair framed a perfectly formed face. How utterly fortunate he would be to make her his wife. No longer would anyone ask, 'Whose woman is this.' Everyone would know that Ruth belonged to Boaz.

He tore his eyes away and scooped measures of barley into her shawl. Then, tying the corners snug, he placed the bundle on her head. She adjusted it, so it balanced perfectly.

Looking deep into her eyes, he kept his desires in check with great difficulty. Boaz, well versed in Hebrew history, kept Joseph, son of Jacob, in his memory. He resisted the advances of Potiphar's wife when most men would have succumbed to her wiles. Joseph was the righteous man whom Boaz sought to emulate each day.

Ruth, of course, was nothing like that profane woman. Ruth had made herself attractive but, had not tried any type of seduction. She only stood next to Boaz, and that was enough to send shivers down his spine.

"Tell Naomi that the grain is a gift. It will assure her and you that I will have this matter settled today. Naomi must rest in the knowledge that I intend to see that she and you are secure."

He took her hand and placed his other over hers. "May Yahweh bless you and keep you and make his face to shine upon you."

"Thank you for this gift and your blessing."

"The eastern sky grows lighter. You must go before anyone can make out who you are. I will follow at a distance and see to your safety. I have my sword and will bring it with me. Now go."

Ruth squared her shoulders, turned, and vanished into the gray dawn. Boaz quickly awakened his overseer to advise that he had urgent business that must be settled today. Then, strapping on his short sword, he hurried off to secretly follow Ruth into the city.

The gates had swung open a few minutes before, and she entered the city. Within moments, she reached the courtyard of their house. The nearby rooster had done his duty by awakening the neighborhood and Naomi was already at the manger with Stubborn when Ruth arrived.

The sun peeked over the horizon, but shadows still filled the courtyard from the many trees that surrounded the house.

"Is that you, my daughter," cried Naomi.

Ruth stepped from the shadows and dumped her burden onto the ground with a thud. "I am home."

Naomi pointed at the shawl filled with grain. "Tell me what happened, and what is this?"

"It almost went as you said." Ruth gave a sly grin. "Boaz sent six measures of barley grain to you as a gift."

"A gift? Why? He has done enough for us. Now daughter, do you marry the man or not. Does he redeem?"

Ruth motioned toward a nearby bench. Carrying the grain from the threshing floor had shortened her breath. She wanted to rest.

Once settled, Naomi asked again. "What of last night?"

"I did as you told me to do. Except…."

"Except?"

"After he lay down to sleep, I went to him. However, too much time had passed. When I uncovered his feet, he had already gone to sleep."

"Did you awaken him?"

"No! I believed it too dangerous. I did not want anyone to hear."

"Tell me all of it."

Ruth proceeded to give Naomi an exact accounting of the previous night and the early morning hours when Boaz sent her home.

"Now what do I do?" Ruth's worry lines grew deep into her face, and she could not sit still. "He said he would settle this today."

"Daughter, stop fidgeting. Sit still until you know how the matter will fall. Look, I know the man. Trust me; he will not rest until it is settled this day."

Chapter 28

Boaz met his mother in the courtyard. "You surprised me," said Rahab. "I did not expect you until the evening meal."

His soft, brown eyes stared from a sun-darkened, leathery face. The gleam of humor in those eyes told her he had good news.

"Do not keep me in suspense, my son. You have good news; your face cannot hide it."

"Ruth came to the threshing floor last night."

All expression left Rahab's face; only her eyes were wide with alarm.

"You are speechless." Boaz chuckled.

"You find humor in her act?"

"She is innocent of any wrongdoing. She came asking me to be her kinsman-redeemer."

Rahab turned and started across the courtyard for the wooden bench. "I must sit down, and then you tell, me what this means."

Boaz walked to the water jars. Lifting the gourd dipper to his lips, he drank and then dipped for a second time. "Thirsty! I walked in from the field. I did not want my horse out there last night tempting some thief." He took a seat next to his mother.

"The threshing floor is not a fit place for a proper woman."

"Naomi told her to come. You know she can be quite bold, and it appears Ruth is cut from the same piece of cloth. It must be a family trait." He laughed. "Do you not think it so?"

"Does she not consider your reputation? It could be ruined."

"It is done. No one knows and nothing untoward happened out there.

"Now, do you wish to know what happened? I do want to tell you my plan, see if you agree."

"Plan?"

"Ruth wants me to redeem the land that Elimelech sold and that includes marrying her."

"Dov is closer."

"I know, and I am sure Naomi does, also."

Rahab smiled. "Yes, I am sure she does. However, does she not know that Dov would love to have that land? To get his hands on the property, he would provide for his brother's wife. He is a greedy man, yet would feel a sense of duty to Elimelech."

Boaz grinned. "I had that notion, and you are right. He is greedy. And also, I am sure he has a sense of duty to his brother—but, not to his brother's daughter-in-law.

"That land went to Mahlon when his father died, and if Chilion had lived, he would be obligated to take Ruth and have an heir by her. That is our law."

"I know the law."

"So, without living sons, the property belongs to Ruth." He smiled. "Do you recall the matter of Zelophehad's daughters? They pleaded their case to Moses that they should have an inheritance in the land?"

"Yes, I do recall Salmon told me of that incident."

"Yahweh instructed Moses to allow them an inheritance so that their father's name would not disappear from the clan because he had no sons.

"Then Yahweh gave further instruction that applies to Ruth. I cannot quote the law precisely, but this is how I would say it.

"If Mahlon dies and leaves no son, give his inheritance to his daughter. Of course, he did not have a daughter. So, without a daughter, the inheritance goes to his brothers. He had one brother who was Chilion. So, Chilion inherited the land, but he died. Then, with no other brothers to inherit, the property is to go to Chilion's father's brothers. Now that would be Elimelech's brothers, and there is only one still living, Dov.

"So, Mother, this is where I come into this situation. The law states if there is not a brother, then the inheritance goes to the nearest relative in his clan. I am the closest relative after Dov."

Rahab gave him a blank look. "I shall not ask you to repeat that." A wry smile forced its way onto her face. "Tell me if I am wrong, but the outcome of all your explanation is what we already know, Dov is a closer redeemer than you."

"Yes, but I am next."

"And you have a plan to step in front of Dov and redeem."

"I would never step in front of the first redeemer without him asking me to take his place."

"So, my greedy brother-in-law will step aside and allow you to take the land. Please tell me this plan."

"I weighed the possibilities most of the night and here is my conclusion to the matter. The land must remain within the clan and be redeemed by the closest family member willing and able to buy it back from the man who bought it from Elimelech. Of course, that is Dov if he is willing to buy. We know he is able.

"Now, why did Zelophehad's daughters want land? To raise up heirs so that their father's name would not disappear from the clan. Naomi wants heirs for Elimelech and Mahlon that is why she wants the land redeemed so that an heir can inherit.

"Naomi is too old to have a son. If she could still bear a child, Ruth might wait until a son would be old enough, and then marry him. Not likely. So, it is Ruth who needs the husband and land for a son to inherit. Dov must be willing not only to buy the land but also marry Ruth. Of course, he is not required to marry her, only Chilion was obligated to take her and raise up heirs.

"However, I do not believe he would take the land and not take Ruth, also. He would not betray his brother Elimelech and block any hope of Elimelech's name being carried on. Dov is a greedy man, but not to the point of denying an heir, plus the terrible condemnation he would invoke from our people."

Rahab's face broke into a big smile. "You do believe he will pass, do you not?"

"As you said, he would love to have the land, but why would he want to give it up to Ruth's son, plus give part of his own property to him, also. No, Dov is too greedy for that.

"I also have an advantage that Dov does not. I love Ruth. I am willing to share my inheritance with children who would be born to us. Dov does not love her."

"I know you love her. I have read that message in your eyes for many days. Still, a tiny chance remains that he will redeem."

"I have considered that and have concluded he must know everything. So, when I mention Ruth the Moabitess comes with the land, he will back out of redeeming." Boaz chuckled.

Rahab gave a wry grin to her son. "You are a sly negotiator. He does not like the Moabites. No doubt that *will* put him off."

"After our breakfast, I will go to the gates. Dov will be passing by going to supervise the workers in his vineyard. I shall confront him then and settle the matter.

"Before going to the gates, I will call for two of my men to accompany me. We will need a donkey and cart, too."

Rahab stared with questioning eyes. "A donkey and cart?"

Boaz chuckled. "I need help moving all of Ruth and Naomi's household goods to my house."

"You *are* confident, my son, are you not?"

His mischievous eyes flashed. He grinned but said nothing.

"I shall send Keziah to Naomi's home with a message that you are meeting the elders at the gates."

He nodded, turned, and hurried away.

Boaz entered the gateway to the city and informed the elders that he had a matter to discuss with Dov and wanted witnesses.

"Please be available," said Boaz. "Dov should be passing this way at any moment."

"We will have ten men ready," replied the spokesman.

The gateway to a city in Israel usually had four rooms, two on each side. All of them were open on the street side so citizens of Bethlehem could hear the proceedings, whether legal or public announcements. Legal proceedings required ten men, so Boaz had made sure the elders were present and then sat down to await Dov's arrival at the gate.

Within the hour, Dov passed by. "Ho there, Dov! Turn aside and have a seat."

The man glanced over, gave a quick wave of the hand, and walked into the room.

"I have an important matter to discuss."

"Tell me."

The ten elders, who were in various rooms and on the street, quickly gathered around the men.

"I have asked for the elders since this is a legal matter that I wish to have settled today. As you may know, Naomi has returned to us from Moab without her husband and sons. They sleep in the earth."

"The news of her arrival has come to me, but I have been much too busy with the harvests and grapes to visit her."

"I thought I should inform you that she wants Elimelech's land redeemed. You have the opportunity to buy the land now in front of these witnesses. If you wish to redeem it, then do so. If you choose to pass on the redemption, tell us now.

"You are the kinsman-redeemer with the first right of redemption. I am next."

Dov, a deliberate man, gazed about the room. He knew all of the elders and most of the people looking on from the street.

Redeeming the land will increase my wealth, he said to himself. *I can plant more crops, have greater harvests, and count more silver into my coffers. Naomi is old, and she will not require much for her care. Soon she shall go back to the dust, too. Yes, this will benefit me greatly.*

"I will buy it."

A low murmur went through the crowd. Heads nodded with smiles all around at his decision to redeem.

Boaz spoke up, and the crowd quieted. "You should fully understand this transaction. On the day you buy the field from the hand of Naomi, you must also buy it from Ruth the Moabitess, the wife of the dead, so she can have children to carry on her husband's name and to inherit the land."

Dov threw a quick, angry look at Boaz. His eyes darted from one man to another. *So, my nephew seeks to trick me! A Moabite woman? Me, marry a Moabite? I am not required to marry anyone, whether Naomi or some Moabitess. Yet, if I take the land and not the woman I shall be small in the eyes of my Hebrew brothers. They will accuse me of denying Elimelech a name in Israel. He has me cornered, and he knows it.*

"I cannot redeem it for myself. The burden on my finances would ruin my own inheritance. The cost would be too high for me, so I pass my right of redemption to you." Dov gazed about the room with sorrowful eyes as though it broke his heart that he could not afford to help Naomi. "I cannot redeem it, you may buy it for yourself."

Dov removed a sandal as was the custom in those days and handed it to Boaz. This act confirmed the transaction and the right of purchase passed to Boaz.

"You are witnesses this day that I have bought all that was Elimelech's, and all that was Chilion's and Mahlon's, from the hand of Naomi. Furthermore, Ruth the Moabitess, the widow of Mahlon, I have acquired as my wife, to perpetuate the name of the dead through his inheritance that the name of the dead may not be cut off from among his brethren and from his position at the gate. You are witnesses this day."

All the people who were at the gate, along with the elders, cried out, "We are witnesses."

Then, the spokesman for the elders stood. "May Yahweh make the woman who is coming to your house like Rachel and Leah, the two who built the house of Israel. May you prosper in Ephrathah and be famous in Bethlehem. May your house be like the house of Perez, whom Tamar bore to Judah, because of the offspring that the Lord will give you from this young woman."

The elder gestured toward the crowd. Boaz turned, and his eyes found Ruth. Upon hearing Keziah's message, she and Naomi had rushed to see the outcome.

The new bride of Boaz smiled and when she did her entire expression brightened and her eyes beamed with delight. He held out his hand, and she came to him. Placing an arm around her shoulders, he drew her to his side, and the people of the gate cheered.

The priest of Bethlehem stepped forward and spoke the priestly blessing that Yahweh had commanded Aaron the High Priest and priests after him to use when blessing the people.

"The Lord bless you and keep you. The Lord make His face shine upon you, and be gracious to you. The Lord lift up His countenance upon you and give you peace."

Boaz took Ruth's hand and guided her into the empty room next door. Naomi stood outside.

"Take me to your dwelling," said Boaz. "I wish to know its location."

"It is a humble place, my lord."

Boaz put the back of his hand under her chin and gently pushed upward. Ruth's face tilted up, and their eyes met. "You are a humble and gracious woman. Your dwelling matters not to me. However, the person you are is all important."

He cupped her face in his giant hands, bent his head, and placed his lips so very lightly upon Ruth's sweet mouth. She thought she would faint. His touch thrilled her, her heart beat heavily, and she kissed him as though it would be the last time.

"I love you, Ruth."

Naomi turned away, smiling. She walked toward home.

"I have not heard those words in such a long time, longer than I can remember."

"Ruth, no young woman has ever said those words to me?"

"Oh, Boaz," she clasped his hands, "I do love you, too. Happiness and great joy have returned to my life. The shadow of death has vanished."

"It shall take time," his voice trembled, "a short period I hope, to become accustomed to calling you, my wife. Each time I do, it will be like music upon the harp."

Realizing the gravity of the moment for Boaz, Ruth with a feather light touch, kissed his hands. Then, glancing to where Naomi had been standing, she said, "Naomi is gone! I should find her."

Boaz chuckled. "Naomi knows her way. She was born here."

"I am entrusted with her care. I—."

"Ruth, now I am responsible for Naomi."

"I think I will like that." She smiled and relaxed softly against him. His arms encircled her, and she rested in his embrace.

Finally, Boaz said, "Let us go. My men are with me and will load your household goods on a cart and bring them to my home." He stepped into the street. "Men, follow us."

"We do not have to pack our cart?"

"Ruth, you shall be making plans for the wedding feast tomorrow. We go to our marriage bed tonight and celebrate tomorrow."

"Thank you, my husband. Let us go and tell Naomi—and Stubborn."

"Stubborn? What?"

"Come, let us see if he will go willingly."

With the agreements made, and the customs fulfilled, the people of Bethlehem recognized the marriage of Boaz and Ruth. At that time and place, official ceremonies were unknown. When the wedding day arrived, a man took his wife to his tent or house and consummated their marriage. Generally a wedding feast followed. Later that day, Boaz and Ruth followed the accepted custom.

"Forty-five years and never with a woman," he whispered, bringing a trembling hand to her cheek.

Ruth gave him a gentle look, deep into his eyes. She lightly touched his face, skimming her fingers along his jaw, over his ear, and then to the back of his neck. Her eyes flashed, her lips parted, and the words came softly—"I love you."

Boaz held her gently, fearing his massive arms would crush her. Each day since he first gazed at her in the field, she had touched his heart and moved his emotions like none other. Now he held her in his arms, his body longing for what God had placed within him to desire.

Tenderly he kissed her cheek and then her mouth. Her eyes, aflame with passion for her righteous, mighty man of God, fluttered shut. Ruth trembled in her man's arms, and he drew her closer. She cherished the moment.

He had waited a lifetime for the woman of his dreams. No longer was she a vision in the night and a thought in the day. Ruth had become his wife by grace of the Almighty.

Boaz whispered close to her ear things only said between husband and wife. She smiled, her breath quickened, and he swept Ruth off her feet. Carrying her to his bed, he laid her down and made love to her with all the passion of a new husband; one who had never known a woman carnally, and she responded to his gentle touch. Each gave to the other as Yahweh intended for husbands and wives.

God instituted marriage in the beginning with the first couple. Adam made love to Eve, and she bore a son. Boaz made love to Ruth and Yahweh enabled her to conceive, and she bore a son.

Moses wrote in the Genesis scroll:

A man shall leave his father and mother and be joined to his wife, and they shall become one flesh. And, they were both naked, the man and his wife, and were not ashamed.

Epilogue

Ruth, with the help of the over-ruling providence of God, transformed herself from a lowly foreigner to the wife of a wealthy and prominent citizen of Bethlehem. Placing her faith in Yahweh, gave her the courage to lay aside the pagan gods of Moab and pledge her faithfulness to the one true God of Israel.

She manifested the highest form of love, hesed love, by sacrificing her needs and placing Naomi first, expecting nothing in return. God took the Moabitess under his wing and rewarded Ruth beyond what she or Naomi could have imagined.

Yahweh blessed her as he did the man Job. She received more material and spiritual blessings than when she began her journey.

The scripture reads: So Boaz took Ruth, and she became his wife. When he made love to her, the Lord enabled her to conceive, and she gave birth to a son. --Ruth 4:13 (NIV)

Yahweh blessed Ruth and Boaz with Obed. He was the father of Jesse and grandfather of King David.

The prophet, Samuel, referred to David as a man after God's own heart. The King undeniably followed in the footsteps of Ruth.

'Salmon was the father of Boaz (Rahab was his mother); Boaz was the father of Obed (Ruth was his mother); Obed was the father of Jesse; Jesse was the father of King David.'

–Matthew 1:5, 6 (TLB)

The Messiah was to come from the tribe of Judah. However, within that ancestry were two gentile mothers: Ruth and Rahab. The story of Ruth is much more than a love story. Within its pages, we see God loves not only the Israelites but also Gentiles. The Book of Jonah expresses the same theme. The prophet refused to preach to the Ninevites. Yet, the book plainly teaches that God wanted Jonah to understand, he cares about all people.

The Old Testament books of Ruth and Jonah agree. Yahweh loves all people, wants all to come to him, and stands with arms wide open to receive everyone into his family who will be obedient to his will. Whosoever will may come.

Thank you for taking time to read:

Ruth-Woman of Valor
A Virtuous Woman in an Immoral Land.

If you enjoyed it, please consider telling your friends or posting a short review. Word of mouth is an author's best friend and much appreciated.

Scripture References by Chapter

Chapter 2

Exodus 16:4

Genesis 46:1-7

Joshua 2:1-6

Chapter 4

Joshua 18:28

Genesis 19

Judges 11:18

Chapter 5

Numbers 21:28

Exodus 20:1-17

Judges 16:23

Judges 10:6

Numbers 25:1-9

Chapter 7

Exodus 20:8-10

Deuteronomy 12:29-31

Chapter 9

Deuteronomy 7:1-3

Chapter 10

Deuteronomy 18:9-11

Genesis 22:13-14

Chapter 12

Exodus 20:12

Chapter 13

Numbers 11:5

Exodus 33:18-23; 34:29-35

Genesis 3:1-14

Chapter 14

Deuteronomy 6:1-5

Genesis 1:1-5

Leviticus 18:9

Leviticus 11:45

Chapter 15

Numbers 6:24-26

Chapter 16

Numbers 23

Deuteronomy 23:3-6

Chapter 17

Deuteronomy 34:1-7

Job 1:21

Chapter 18

Leviticus 19:34.

Deuteronomy 19:14; 27:17

Chapter 19
Exodus 23:7
Judges 5:28
Joshua 2:6

Chapter 20
Leviticus 23:22; 19:9-10
Deuteronomy 24:19
Job 1:1-22; 13:15
Judges 1:28-33
Leviticus 25:23-34

Chapter 22
Numbers 2:3-4

Chapter 24
Exodus 12:1-20

Chapter 25
Leviticus 15
Deuteronomy 29:9-18

Chapter 28
Numbers 26:33; 27:1-11; 36:1-13
Genesis 2:21-25; 4:1-2

Works Consulted

A Loving Life: Paul E. Miller

A Walk Thru the Book of Ruth: Baker Books, Publisher

All Of The Women Of The Bible: Edith Deen

Ancient Gods, The: E.O. James

Atlas of the Bible: The Reader's Digest Association

Bible As History, The: Werner Keller

Bible Commentary, The: Exodus—Ruth, F.C. Cook, Editor, Abridged and Edited by J.M. Fuller

Bible Manners and Customs: G.M. Mackie

Commentary Critical and Explanatory on the Whole Bible: Robert Jamieson, Andrew Robert Faussett, and David Brown

Commentary on Ruth: James Burton Coffman

Complete Commentary on the Bible: Matthew Henry

Daughters of Eve: Lottie Beth Hobbs

Exposition of the Bible: John Gill

Fausset's Bible Dictionary at www.StudyLight.org

Geneva Study Bible: 1599 A.D. edition, **www.StudyLight.org**

Halley's Bible Handbook: Henry H. Halley

Holman Bible Dictionary at www.StudyLight.org

Holy Bible, American Standard Version: 1901

Holy Bible, King James Version 1611 A.D.

Holy Bible, New King James Version

Holy Bible, New International Version

Holy Bible, Orthodox Jewish Bible

Insights Into Bible Times and Customs: G. Christian Weiss

International Standard Bible Encyclopedia: Edited by James Orr, John Nuelsen, Edgar Mullins, Morris Evans, and Melvin Grove Kyle, 1939

Jewish Encyclopedia: 1906 Version, www.jewishencyclopedia.com

Judges & Ruth: James Burton Coffman

Manners & Customs of Bible Lands: Fred H. Wight

The Cyclopedia of Biblical, Theological, and Ecclesiastical Literature. James Strong and John McClintock, 1880

Nelson's Complete Book of Bible Maps and Charts: Thomas Nelson

Nelson's Illustrated Encyclopedia of Bible Facts: J.I. Packer, Merrill C. Tenney, William White, Jr.

New Bible Dictionary: J.D. Douglas, Editor

New Manners and Customs of the Bible: James M. Freeman

Pulpit Commentary Volume 4, Ruth
Edited by H.D.M. Spence & Joseph S. Exell

Rose Then and Now Bible Map Atlas: Paul H. Wright, Ph.D.

Ruth: A Story of God's Grace: Cyril Barber

Ruth – loss, love & legacy: Kelly Minter

Ruth – Sermon Series: Kent Holcomb, Calvary Baptist Church

Sketches of Jewish Social Life: Alfred Edersheim

Wesley's Explanatory Notes: John Wesley

Women in the Bible.net, www.womeninthebible.net

About the Author

Born in Wichita, Kansas, Jim Baumgardner grew up in a Christian home. The author's mother gave her life to the Lord in her late teens, and she brought his dad to Christ after they were married in 1939. April 30, 2015, marked Jim's 58th year as a Christian.

The author continues to reside in Wichita with his wife, Linda. They have three children and nine grandchildren. All of Jim's books are primarily written for his grandchildren's benefit. He also makes them available to all others who wish to read and enjoy the stories.